*Coming soon from DAW Books

MISS AMELIA'S LIST

The Elemental Masters:

The Regency

MERCEDES LACKEY

DAW BOOKS
New York

Jacket illustration by Jody A. Lee

Jacket design by Adam Auerbach

Edited by Betsy Wollheim

DAW Book Collectors No. 1972

DAW Books
An imprint of Astra Publishing House
dawbooks.com
DAW Books and its logo are registered trademarks of Astra Publishing House

Printed in the United States of America

Publisher's Cataloging-in-Publication data

Names: Lackey, Mercedes, author.
Title: Miss Amelia's list / Mercedes Lackey.
Description: First edition. | New York, NY: DAW Books, 2024.
Series: Elemental Masters ; book 17
Identifiers: LCCN: 2024947873 | ISBN: 9780756419097 (hardcover) | 9780756419103 (ebook)
Subjects: LCSH England--Social life and customs--19th century--Fiction. | Magic--Fiction. | Fantasy fiction. | Romance fiction. | Historical fiction. | BISAC FICTION / Fantasy / Romance | FICTION / Fantasy / Gaslamp | FICTION / Fantasy / Action & Adventure
Classification: LCC PS3562.A246 M57 2024 | DDC 813.6--dc23

First edition: December 2024
10 9 8 7 6 5 4 3 2 1

1

AMELIA Stonecroft seized the shoulder of her cousin Serena Meleva's woolen cloak forcibly, just before her cousin made a spectacle
of herself, and hissed at her. Hissing was the best way to get Serena's
attention. "Do you want to scandalize everyone on the dock?" she
said just loud enough for her cousin to hear—and Serena had very,
very good ears. "A lady does not fling herself down a gangplank un-
assisted and throw herself at a gentleman, even if that gentleman is
her cousin!" Her insides tightened; she did not want to draw unwanted attention.

Gulls flew overhead, crying. Cold wind cut through her cloak.
Her nose wrinkled at odors very alien to someone who had spent all
her life on a farm in North Carolina; tar, salt-air, rotting fish,
and mud.

Serena pouted a little, and contented herself with waving at
James Stonecroft from the rail of the ship they were on—supposedly
something called a "Baltimore clipper," a sort of ship that was known
for making fast passage across the Atlantic. She certainly carried
enough sail to do so, though "fast" was relative. James waved back,
as the cold, damp wind sent more seagulls skating across the sky,

casting back and forth above the docks, sounding as if they were crying out their desire for tea. Serena relaxed a little when James waved back, and stopped looking as if she was about to try to win a footrace. "I hate this ship, I hate the sea, and I want to get *off* and—" She subsided. "We mustn't scandalize the English, I suppose. They already think we are barbarians."

"Or worse," Amelia replied darkly, and let go of Serena's indigo cloak, which was a match for her own. "It was only a year ago they tried to burn Washington to the ground, and very nearly succeeded! Just because we signed a treaty with them, it doesn't follow that there are no bad feelings!"

And if I weren't an Elemental Master, I would still be very angry with them. But no magician can afford to hold a grudge. Grudges tend to take on a life of their own when one can wield magic.

Then again, the burning of Washington was very far away for most of the English, who likely only thought of America as a vague place in the west and were uninterested in it. Privately, she was quite sure that the longshoremen offloading this ship, and most of the people who had come to meet it, didn't give a toss about wars and city-burnings far away, but if this would rein in Serena's impulses, then she'd play that song and pretend to believe it.

Serena sighed, her tawny hair escaping a little to mingle with the lace and flounces inside her cherry-trimmed bonnet, with a few curls forming over her forehead. "I should think they should be more concerned with the French. I still don't understand why Uncle Charles wants to expand the business here if they hate us Americans so."

"Because business has very little to do with politics, and it will be good business to return some of our family interests here," Amelia replied, with an authority she didn't really feel. "Besides, *our* main interactions will be with other Elemental mages, and the White Lodges have almost nothing to do with politics." That last probably wasn't entirely true, but it was near enough. Even during the American Revolution, the Stonecrofts and their kin and kind had kept their business and magical interests going overseas, in England in particular. For that matter, even through the French Revolution and the wars with Napoleon that followed, they were still selling to France, through various secondary parties on the continent.

Fortunately, indigo dye was not considered to be a military resource. The British soldiers were not called "Bluecoats," after all, and those American forces that wore blue uniform coats were already sufficiently supplied with indigo.

More gulls called overhead, their plaintive cries exactly the same as the ones that had bid their ship farewell in Wilmington. Amelia steeled herself against another wave of anxiety. She was so used to anxiety that she rarely took note of it—and no one, even in her family, even realized how anxiety always lay beneath her carefully cultivated veneer of calm and competence. She often thought of herself as being not unlike a swan—an image of serenity above, frantic paddling beneath the surface. But right now that "paddling" felt particularly frantic. Did their hosts *really* want them here? Would they receive a civil but cold "welcome"? Were James's plans far too ambitious? What if everything fell apart and she and Serena would be forced to return home, the expenses of their travel all for nothing? What if Napoleon escaped and resumed his war with the British? What if, despite all of her father's assurances, the British Elemental mages regarded them with contempt?

The London docks, where their ship had just berthed, churned with activity, which only heightened her anxiety, but she reminded herself sternly that she had a job to do—an entire list of jobs to do— and she should not allow her own weakness to get in the way of doing them. *No time for vapors,* she told herself, a phrase that over the course of her adult life had become a litany.

Serena looked around with unalloyed interest, and Amelia envied her the ability to look at everything as a new adventure and not a new nest of hazardous obstacles to be navigated. Serena was always positive and astonishingly cheerful, and the only time Amelia ever found that irritating was when Serena's impulses ran away with her, which didn't happen very often anymore now that she was old enough to take other people's opinions into consideration.

The ship was tied up, her sails furled, but until she was securely fastened to the pier, the captain did not permit the gangplank to be deployed. And even then, when he did, he waved to his two passengers that they must wait until the cargo that had been stowed on the open deck had been moved. This ship was a cargo ship and rarely carried passengers, a fact they had been made aware of when Amelia's father booked passage. But James had been very specific in his letter that he wanted them to come over on *this* ship and this ship only, one which the family often used to bring their dyes to England. Once Amelia and Serena had met the captain, the reason became obvious. He was an Elemental magician, of Water, of course. Such a man would be able to bring every voyage across the Atlantic home successfully, even in February and March, so there was no doubt why the family shipped with him. His command of the Elementals of Water allowed him to evade pirates, privateers, blockades, and storms with ease. In fact, James himself had made this voyage with this captain two years ago; Captain Smith had welcomed them as valued passengers rather than an inconvenience, and had joked that it was too bad they were not Air Masters as James had been, to bring the ship into port faster. But Serena's Fire magic had been very useful in the galley, as well as supplying hot ballast stones to put into beds and hammocks every night. Sadly, Amelia's Earth Mastery had been absolutely useless.

Once all the cargo had been cleared from the decks, the captain waved them off, and they hurried down the gangplank to where James was waiting, wearing a smart hat and enveloped in a cloak of the same blue as theirs, but with at least five shoulder-capes. Perhaps six. Possibly seven. *That seems excessive . . .* Amelia thought. Surely one would do.

She stumbled a bit; it was going to take some time to get used to walking on something that was not moving again. Serena managed to get down the gangplank decorously enough, but she then completely ignored Amelia's instructions once on the dock and flung herself into James's arms. He caught her up and spun her around before setting her down on the dock, while Amelia sighed and approached at an unsteady walk. "How now, my wenches?" he said as Amelia reached his side with more composure. "And how was the trip?"

"Dull, uncomfortable, and far too long," Amelia said, trying not to sound disagreeable. "We weren't prepared for the tedium, to be honest; we had but one book between us and no fancywork, the captain is not a reader and had nothing for us, the cabin was the size of a cupboard, and we were unable to make a change of clothing the entire trip."

"But we did while away some of the time by mending the sailors' things," Serena offered. "I think they were surprised we wanted to, and even more surprised that our work stood their scrutiny!"

"Well," James said, "your timing was good. There was some nasty work about the Corn Laws—riots right here in London, actually—but you've missed all that. Things have settled, and we're glad to see you."

People swirled around them like the gulls swirled above; mostly longshoremen carrying enormous bales and boxes on their shoulders, but a few with empty hands who seemed to have other business, or who were proceeding to other ships. The dull gray sky and the dull-colored clothing of the sailors and workers was a stark contrast to the overall cheerfulness of the folks thronging about them. *I suppose they are just as happy to be off that ship and out of quarters that were even more unpleasant than ours,* Amelia thought. *And, of course, looking forward to being paid and spending that pay ashore!*

"Then the two of you pop into the carriage while I wait for the consignment, and I shall whisk you away to our representative's home where a hot bath awaits," James replied agreeably. He was very much a Stonecroft: like Amelia, brown of hair and eye, with a pleasant countenance, and with a sturdy, reliable quality about him that Amelia felt must make him very desirable in female eyes. He gave off an aura of quiet strength and competence that she felt would make a lady certain that he would be a good protector. This, despite his Element, which was Air, which in Amelia's experience tended to make its possessors more introspective and dreamy (not to say flighty) than clever and practical. It was very like him to have thought of arranging for a bath directly on their arrival, and she stood on her tiptoes and kissed his cheek as a thank-you.

Serena clapped her hands and would have run for the carriage, had Amelia not firmly taken her arm, and required her to proceed at a walk. *I am so jealous that she is so sure-footed immediately. I feel like I did when I first got on the ship and tried to move.*

It was an unexpectedly large carriage of pleasant reddish-brown, pulled by four chestnut horses—perhaps the conveyance had been chosen because James had been expecting to transport a number of trunks and boxes as well as the precious chests of indigo and cochineal powder. The cochineal was a relatively new product to come from the Stonecroft farms, but with so many Earth Masters and magicians among the inhabitants of the plantation, it had proven to be trivial to get the prickly pear cacti that the cochineal insects fed upon to thrive in North Carolina, and the insects themselves responded well to a little magical prodding. Initially, the Stonecroft business had sold all their product within the United States and Canada, but production had increased to the point where it was profitable to export it further afield and compete with Mexico and South America now. *Hmm. Some revenge, I suspect, if the redcoats end up paying us for the dye for their uniforms.*

The young ladies were handed into the carriage by the footman, and settled themselves on the beautifully upholstered forward-facing seats. In fact, the entire interior was upholstered in a dark green plush, and Amelia was very impressed. And, after the discomfort of the journey, very relieved. There were beaver lap-robes waiting, as well as a cast-iron foot-warmer, and she tucked a robe around herself without hesitation and put both feet near the heat. She felt her entire body relax into the softness and warmth, and had to fight off the sudden urge to nap. The last few miles of the journey had tested even her patience—first having to wait for the pilot boat carrying the special London pilot required to get them up the river, then the river journey itself, then finally, slowly, warping into the docks.

A faint, but much more pleasant scent countering the dock miasma lingered inside the coach; lavender, mint, and rosemary, from metal potpourri balls tucked into the four corners of the roof.

They waited patiently while their trunks and boxes were unloaded from the ship and stowed on the roof of the carriage above them, then waited a while longer as brother James got the very precious containers of indigo and cochineal and secured them to the coach as well. This probably occupied less than a quarter-hour, certainly not more than a half, but to Amelia, and probably to her more fidgety cousin, it felt like forever. But at last James joined them in the coach, taking the rearward-facing seat.

With a lurch, the coach moved off, wheels rumbling over the planks of the dock, then rattling over the cobblestones, and Serena burst into speech before James could say a single word. "Cousin! We have missed you very, very much! You did not tell us nearly enough in your letters! Have you got a house of your own yet? Is it in a fashionable district? What is the city like? Are you courting anyone? Will we be presented at court? Will you hold a ball for us? Is there . . ." here she paused significantly, and Amelia immediately knew what was coming, ". . . room for me to run?"

James laughed at her and patted her knee. "I have not yet got a house of my own, but our good representative Mr. Angleford, whose work I am learning and whose home I am staying in, has a domicile ample for our needs for the moment. I am looking out for a townhouse for myself with his help, but I have not yet found something to suit me. I may well end up renting or buying Mr. Angleford's home after all, if I have not found something to suit when I fully assume the position of company representative and he moves. He has talked of moving to Bath permanently, as most of his daughters settled there, and I believe that now that you are here, he and his wife Julia have determined on this plan."

Amelia nodded; Angleford had been a fine representative, a shrewd man of business, an Elemental mage of Fire, and a clever man at getting dyes into the country through Holland or some other neutral country during the hostilities between the new United States and

England, but he was growing old, and wanted to retire. As he had no sons to train to take his place, and Amelia's father was not minded to have a stranger, even another Elemental mage, in that position, James had been appointed to take it. James was well versed and practiced in the handling of the business on the export and sales side of the ocean, and all parties reckoned it would take him little time to master the intricacies of import and sales in England. And since there was the matter of a new venture entirely, one which Angleford had not felt up to pioneering, James was the best possible replacement.

But that was business, and Serena's questions were not about business. "The house is situated in Gracechurch Street," he continued. "Which is 'fashionable' enough for those of us in trade. You will not find yourself lacking in amusements, as the Anglefords are popular guests and hosts, and intend to exert themselves on your behalf while you are here. Mrs. Angleford intends to sponsor you to regular Assemblies. I have told them that you two are out; you are both old enough and might as well be called so, even though we don't have that custom at home. I am not officially courting anyone, but . . . there are prospects. I am holding off on serious wife-hunting until I officially take over the business, which will make me a much more appealing prospect to the families in question."

"That's wise," Amelia agreed, mentally crossing one item off her list—when she got into her belongings, she'd be crossing it off a physical list as well. "Anxious mamas will be better pleased when they know you offer a girl a good situation and a steady income."

And indeed, that was another reason for James to be here. Most Elemental mages married other mages, either by choice or arrangement. It was otherwise too difficult a life; one either wasted time in hiding things from a normal spouse, or in explaining things to a normal spouse and hoping they could keep their silence about their espoused's extracurricular activities. But the United States was large, and the population thin, and the opportunities for finding mates one was not already related to hard to come by. By reestablishing the Stonecroft household in England, the Stonecrofts and their kin and allies would find far better matrimonial hunting than at home.

"As for being presented at court, no, you will not be," James continued, and smiled sympathetically at Serena's falling face. "You will not be, because you are already out, and because we are merely tradesfolk without noble connections or a touch of noble blood. Don't forget that; we 'smell of the shop' now because we are not landed *and* gentry, we are not very rich, and we have no connection whatsoever to the aristocracy. No one is presented at the queen's drawing room except those with noble blood or those who have married into the aristocracy. Nor would you want to find yourself presented—nor would any of us wish to bear the cost of such a thing." He leaned over to emphasize his points. "Do you remember those old gowns you used to laugh about, with the huge hoops and panniers and sky-high wigs? The ones you found in the attic as a child? *That* is what you are expected to wear to such a presentation, except with the high waist of modern gowns, which combination, in my opinion, makes a girl look like a fancy teapot—and which are incredibly difficult to move in. There are, I am told, several layers of petticoats as well as the hoops and panniers, and very old-fashioned tight-lacing. It's not something you can wear ever again because it must be made of materials that are not fashionable like heavy brocade, and it must be made of the finest of those materials, with a great deal of ruffles and lace, and worn with far more real jewels than both of you put together have at the moment. The expense of such a rig-out is appalling. Three hundred pounds is not considered excessive."

Serena bit her lip, and nodded her complete agreement, as Amelia had known she would. For all that Serena seemed flighty, she was the first to pinch a penny until it screamed for mercy—and Amelia knew that to be imprisoned in such a garment would be her idea of hell.

"And all that to wait for hours in your carriage, then finally be shown into the drawing room, have a curtsy to the queen as you are introduced, and then join the fearful crush with little hope of refreshment and none whatsoever of sitting down. All this so that you can announce to the world that you are out and can now attend large routs, dances at Almack's Assembly Room, be invited to the prince's parties, and consort with members of the aristocracy, who will look down their noses at you if they don't give you the cut direct because you 'smell of the shop.'" He shook his head. "Pure folly, when with the Anglefords' help you shall have balls and parties enough to attend merely by my saying 'Oh yes, my sister and cousin are both out, and have been for six months.'" Now he smiled gently on Serena. "As for 'room to run,' the Anglefords know what you are and what you need and have arranged for that. You may go out this very night if you feel rested enough."

At that, Serena sighed with relief. "You are the best of guardians," she said with contentment.

"I know," James smirked, and leaned back into the seat cushions. "And if you are very good and very lucky, some of the *ton* who are also Masters and mages may come to a ball or two within our very special orbit, and you will rub elbows with the fashionable and elite after all. And once they know your magical abilities, they certainly will not look down their noses at you, although you must not presume to approach them in public. Power is more important among our circle than rank or wealth, and they well know that one day their very lives may be in the hands of a mere commoner, so it behooves them to be as democratic as a colonial. At least in private."

But Serena had been diverted from this little lecture by the scene outside. "Oh, look!" Serena cried, sighting an imposing building out the carriage window. "What is that?"

After that, James found himself identifying anything that caught Serena's gaze. These included not just buildings, but people both afoot and on horseback or driving. In the case of the latter, James was generally unable to identify them by name, but certainly could identify them by *type*. For instance, a particularly smart-looking woman driving herself in a single-horse, bright yellow sporting carriage of a sort that neither of the girls had ever seen before was met with a raised eyebrow. "*Ladies* of that sort are not to be noticed by you," he said, a touch sternly. "They are referred to as 'Cyprians.'"

"Oh," said Serena in wonder. "They are fast, then?"

"Rather more than fast," said James.

"*Oh!*" Serena laughed. "Well, then, we know about them, but are not supposed to, and of course, must pretend they are invisible."

"Precisely."

"What is she driving, though? Do respectable people drive such things? It looks dangerous—and fun!" Serena continued.

"Respectable people are known to drive them, even women, though generally not alone. I can speak to the danger, and I assume that it must be pleasurable to be able to drive such a thing if you find danger pleasurable. But I don't personally know what it is like to drive one, as that sort of rig-out is beyond my skill," James said, patiently. "It is called a high-perch phaeton, and it takes a real Nonesuch to be able to handle such a thing. If you see a man driving one, he is either foolishly reckless, or a capital whip. If you see a woman with a groom beside her driving one, she is exceptional, and almost certainly a capital whip. If you see a woman driving one alone, she is still certainly a capital whip, but her morals are likely dubious."

Things certainly were more complicated here.

It seemed to Amelia that the carriages came in a bewildering variety, but were mostly divided between utilitarian, such as theirs, and sporting, and it was at least easy enough to judge between the category of carriage, as the sporting ones were not in the least practical.

Since Amelia and Serena had lived almost exclusively on what James now referred to as "the family estate" instead of a "plantation," and had only been to a city when they had passed through the port, virtually everything and everyone were novelties to both of them. Amelia had been about to make a caustic remark about James's coat, but kept her words behind her teeth when she saw that the number of shoulder capes he boasted was actually conservative compared to some of the men she saw driving equipages she could not identify, but which were clearly both sporting and expensive.

It appears, she thought worriedly, *that our notions of fashion are outdated. Men's fashion, at any rate.* She reflected, though without much hope, that the ladies' magazines she and the rest of the women of the Stonecroft estate had perused eagerly as soon as they arrived off the boats from London and made their way to the interior *probably* were recent enough that she and Serena would not be utterly disgraced in public. Certainly those magazines rarely featured men at all . . .

"I am sure that both of you know not to ask such questions in public," James said, finally, with just a touch of weariness.

"Of course!" Serena replied indignantly. "Of all things to say! To open ourselves to ridicule? We are not simpletons! Nor shall we gawp about us at everything that is unfamiliar! It is merely that we are safe in the coach, away from possible public censure, and we know *you* will tell us whatever we want to know!"

Satisfied, James went back to answering his cousin's questions with a better will.

Amelia remained quiet and took mental notes; Serena was asking all the questions she would have liked to, but felt uncomfortable with doing so. But then, by nature it was hard for her to put herself forward.

Serena was probably not *technically* her cousin, but almost everyone on the Stonecroft estate was at least minimally related to one another one way or another, so it was close enough to truth. She and Serena had been born within days of each other, had been raised together, thought of each other as sisters, and always referred to each other as "cousin" and their respective parents as "aunt and uncle."

The carriage deposited them in front of a handsome townhouse a bit older than some of the groups of obviously new terraced houses they had passed. Nothing could have been more unlike the home they had left, the sprawling, two-story, wooden edifice that had been added to again and again over the years to accommodate a larger and larger household, and set among spacious lawns and gardens. This was a handsome four-story construction of red brick with white plaster pillars, squeezed on both sides by its neighbors, with not so much as a scrap of greenery in front. A glance at Serena showed Amelia that her cousin was gazing upward at the rooftops. Amelia knew very well why, and it had nothing to do with guessing what room was to be theirs.

A middle-aged footman in a black tailed coat, stockings and shoes rather than boots like James, and yellow knee breeches, with his hair in a queue, handed them down from the carriage. Amelia glanced back anxiously at their trunks, but James hurried them up a set of white stairs edged with black iron railings and inside before she could ask how they would be conveyed within. Her anxieties arose again. What if Mr. Angleford was less than pleased about his visitors? True, he had supposedly volunteered to host them, but what if he had done so merely to be polite and now was regretting the invitation? It was more than enough that he was hosting James, after all, and James had a good reason to be his guest, as he was to take over the business. So far as Mr. Angleford knew, *they* were just here husband-hunting! That wasn't their main reason for being here, at least, not Amelia's, but Angleford didn't know that. What if he was scandalized if he learned what her real task was to be?

But once inside the white front door, all those anxieties vanished, at least briefly, as a distinguished, slightly stooped, gray-haired man in an immaculate dark-green coat and old-fashioned brown knee breeches, stockings, and shoes with silver buckles seized both her hands as if she were his daughter even before James could make a proper introduction. "My word! So this is Miss Amelia! You are the very image of your beautiful mother, and I should know you for a Stonecroft anywhere! Oh! How I remember how lovely Vivian Stonecroft was as a young bride, and how welcoming she was to me on my first visit to your country! You are very welcome here my dear, very welcome!"

And then he literally passed her to a plump little woman in a modish green-striped gown, beaming under her lace cap, who took her hands from his with every evidence of pleasure. "Oh! My dear! It is so good to finally have you all here!" she exclaimed. "I cannot tell you how excited I am to have young ladies in the house again! I have sorely missed all the routs, the dinners, the visits to theaters and Vauxhall, and lovely evenings in the parlor we used to have before my girls got swept up and carried off to Bath! We shall have such lovely times!"

By this time Serena had been greeted by Mr. Angleford with the same unfeigned enthusiasm, which was a great relief to Amelia, since James had said the couple were aware of her nature. The gentleman then turned his attention to James, while his wife gathered up her two female visitors and passed them into the hands of the housekeeper.

"Mrs. Jennings will see you up to your rooms, my dears. There are hot baths waiting for you; I am sure you will be glad to see them after your journey. The bell will ring for dinner, and my maid will help you dress and show you down." She dimpled. "Don't worry, we keep 'country' hours, not fashionable ones. You will not be forced to starve until seven!" Before Amelia could utter even a single word of thanks, the housekeeper bustled them away up the stairs. Two sets of stairs brought them to the third floor, and a pair of adjoining bedrooms at the rear of the house. And for a moment, with delicious aromas of cooking coming up from below, Amelia regretted taking time for a bath. But not for long.

The room Amelia was ushered into was small, as was to be expected in a city as crowded as London, but boasted a comfortable-looking bed with a brown damask canopy and curtains, a chair with an upholstered seat, a wardrobe, a set of drawers, a dressing table, a stand with a washbasin, and its own fireplace with an inset stove. She recognized a closestool behind a screen as well, which was a tremendous relief, as the existence of this object meant she would not have to take nighttime trips down dark stairs and out through the kitchen to a privy in the yard. And, as promised, in front of the fireplace and behind another screen was a deep copper tub filled with water from which the lavender-scented steam was still rising.

Amelia nearly flung all her clothing off and left it on the floor in her eagerness to get into that inviting tub, but she remembered her manners and left the clothing on the chair instead. During the voyage, their only recourse to cleanliness had been a basin barely the size of a soup bowl, a pitcher of unheated salt water, a scrap of soap, and a facecloth, and all that using these things had accomplished was to make her feel sticky. For a moment she felt all her cares melt away as the hot water enveloped her up to her ears, and she blessed the maids who had undergone a labor of Hercules to carry all that hot water in cans up from the kitchen. Not once, but twice! For Serena must have the same sort of bath waiting.

Of course, in the privacy of a bedroom, Serena had quite another way to cleanse herself—but presumably their hosts had not thought of that. *Or maybe they did, but assumed she would appreciate a bath as much as I.*

Now soaking her cares away, however briefly, she took greater note of her surroundings. The walls were a pleasant rose color, the woodwork beautifully painted in the same color. The fireplace before which she bathed had a carved white stone mantelpiece, sides, and hearth, a lovely modern stove that did far more good at heating the room than an open fireplace would. It was crowned with a picture of a fashionable young lady who might be one of the Angleford daughters above the mantelpiece. There was a fine carpet on the floor, and although there was a cloth under her bath, she made a mental note to be sure not to drip on the carpet. From what she recalled, the furnishings were a little old-fashioned, but well-made and well-maintained, and if the upholstery did not quite match the screens or the bed, well, it was close enough to maintain harmony.

From behind the screen she heard some thumping and bumping and many footsteps, which hopefully signaled the arrival of her trunks. She truly did not want to get into clothing she had lived and slept in for the past four weeks. The blue-gray merino round gown she had cast off so precipitously fortunately did not show the abuse she had put it through, but the dirt was still there, and she knew it. It would need a thorough treatment with fuller's earth, brushing, and airing before it was fit to put on again. At least it was not sweaty as well. It had been too cold on the voyage to sweat.

I'd have them all burned if it wouldn't be such a waste of good garments. But part of me hopes that the stockings, stays, drawers, and chemise are too far gone to save.

There was more activity, and the sounds of at least two people putting things in the wardrobe and set of drawers. She ignored those sounds, used a touch of magic to heat the water again, and set to actually cleaning herself from crown of head to soles of feet. When she finally emerged from the bath, wrapped in the sheet conveniently draped over the screen and fluffing out her damp curls with one hand, it was to find that her trunks had been opened, a suitable gown chosen and the wrinkles shaken out of it, and laid on the bed along with fresh undergarments and stockings. The offending and offensive dirty things had been taken away. She felt sorry for the maids who would have to clean them.

She did not bother to wait for the arrival of Julia Angleford's maid to dress; after all, she had been dressing herself all her life.

The gown waiting for her was not one she would have chosen for herself to "dress for dinner," as she had been told she would have to do before she even left home. It was a fine merino twill dyed with indigo (the sort of cloth called "superfine" and often used for men's coats) and severely styled in the manner of a Hussar's uniform. More like the riding habits that she had seen in the magazines than a dinner gown, but she was not going to complain. It was probably the one gown fit for dinner that she owned that could be shaken out with no wrinkles, so was the most presentable at short notice. And it was cold enough here in England in early March that she welcomed wool over her muslin chemise. She certainly didn't want the poor maid to add to her work by pressing a gown while she bathed, much less have to go to the effort of properly pressing out her "company" velvet dinner gown on a needle board. But she feared that her clothing was going to mark her as hopelessly rustic. The Stonecroft household subscribed to several magazines and newspapers from London, and of course the latest fashions were always of great interest to many on the estate, but the gowns described always seemed to be of fine muslin, silk, or satin, not homely fabrics like wool. Except for riding habits. Those, it appeared, were almost universally made of wool.

I hope this doesn't look like a riding habit. That would be a great faux pas, even though this was one of her favorite gowns, simple, trimmed only with silk braid, and perfectly suitable for fall and winter dinner back home. *We have not yet seen all of ladies' fashion. Surely merino wool and woolen plush would be most welcome in this cold, damp place, even for dinner!*

She dressed quickly, from the skin out, and reveled in the feeling of clean clothing against her skin again. Perhaps ships that primarily carried passengers had better facilities for them than the cargo ship she and Serena had traveled on; she didn't know. All she knew was that having to share a tiny cabin barely big enough for the two of them to stand in, with no access to their trunks, and spending the entire voyage without even a change of underthings made her resolve never to go home again if that was what was entailed. *I swear if we were rich I really would burn the clothing we traveled in.* Serena had been far more fortunate than she, but even Serena hadn't had a change of clothing. And though Serena had been able to clean herself more thoroughly than Amelia had, she had suffered the worst from confinement.

Amelia had barely gotten her shoes on and threaded a matching ribbon through her hair to confine it when Serena knocked on the door and came in before she could be invited. "Come see my room!" she gushed. "The Anglefords are *lovely!*"

Before Amelia could reply, Serena had taken her by the hand and drawn her out into the hallway and back into Serena's room. It looked very much as Amelia's room did, with the same accoutrements and colors, but that was not what Serena wanted to show her. The object of Serena's joy lay in the window, which opened easily and, as Amelia soon realized, gave access to a short roof, perhaps over a porch. "Look!" Serena said with glee. "From there I can jump to the main roof, and these houses are so close together, I can have a nice run from rooftop to rooftop without disturbing or alarming anyone!"

"So you can," Amelia agreed, trying not to shiver as that chill dampness penetrated the room. "I must say, so far the Anglefords are the best of hosts!"

Just then a bell sounded somewhere below. Serena closed the window and the two of them turned to step into the hall, just as a maid appeared at the top of the stairs. She seemed surprised, but pleased, to see them already dressed.

"If you will come with me, Miss Amelia, Miss Serena," she said with a little curtsy. "Dinner will be served shortly, and you may wait in the parlor next to the dining room."

"Of course, and thank you," Amelia said for both of them, and they followed the maid down the carpeted stairs and back to the first floor, where they found brother James perusing a newspaper in the parlor. Amelia hoped her stomach would not growl as the aromas from their dinner filled the room.

"I did not expect you two to be ready so soon," he said, not getting up from his chair. "I thought you'd certainly be still in your baths. When *I* arrived I was so crusted with salt I thought I would stay in the bath for a week." He looked very fine in his blue tailed coat of the same material as Amelia's dress, brocade waistcoat, fawn breeches, and leather Hessian boots, all tailored exquisitely to fit closely to his figure.

"My word, James," Amelia said, smiling a little. "You have become quite the macaroni!"

"They say 'tulip' here, and no, I am not that fine," James laughed at her. "I merely strive to fit in."

"Lazily lolling about as a lord?" Serena teased him. "Really, cousin, you are losing your American briskness here!"

"Nothing of the sort, minx," he teased back. "I am a man of trade; I cannot afford to be anything other than brisk. I am merely relaxing in the home of my friend, enjoying the company of my kin. But here come our host and hostess, so let us not quarrel in front of them."

"I wasn't quarrelling!" Serena objected, with a smile. "I think you look quite dashing. If I weren't your cousin, I'd set my cap at you."

"There now, see, James!" Mrs. Angleford exclaimed. "Haven't I just told you that very thing? If I were thirty years younger, Mr. Angleford would have a formidable rival!"

James blushed, which made Amelia giggle and Serena laugh aloud. They all settled close to the fire (another of those excellent stoves), presumably to wait for the announcement of dinner—something Amelia decided she would have to get used to. Except when entertaining company, there was no waiting for meals to be announced in the extensive Stonecroft family. Everyone came in to the dining room from washing up promptly at the sound of the dinner bell, which was at five by the chiming hall clock, and settled in at the table. All dishes were passed from hand to hand, with the few servants taking away the emptied plates and bowls and delivering full ones. It appeared that meals in the Angleford household were more like the formal ones the Stonecrofts sat to when there was company.

"I trust you girls are happy with your rooms?" Mrs. Angleford asked. "Amelia, you are in Grace's old room, and Serena, you are in Sophia's. Grace is Earth and Sophia is as well, so I thought the rose color would make you feel comfortable."

"We like our rooms above all things," Amelia replied promptly, as Serena nodded. "Are all your children Gifted?"

"We are all mages, but no Masters," the husband replied. "For which I am grateful. There were tempests enough as the girls were growing up. I cannot imagine adding the power—and potential for mischief among the Elementals—of one or more of them being a Master to the mix!"

Amelia gave that the polite laugh that was expected, but was busy surveying her hostess's gown. To her relief, it was of a similar mode to her own; it looked to be a good wool in a conservative style, with an embroidered bodice and embroidery down the front. *I should have known that the maids would not betray me by putting out an inappropriate gown.* Serena had opted for a sprig muslin with a red cotton twill spencer and wore her favorite pearl necklace, but then, Serena never felt the cold as much as Amelia did. This was, Amelia knew, one of the benefits of having Fire as one's Element; Fire mages never felt the cold.

It had been clear from the first that the Anglefords were pleasant, hospitable people who enjoyed the company of unaffected guests, and were genuinely pleased to be able to play their hosts. The brief interval and the fine dinner itself were enlivened by some of the best conversation Amelia had ever experienced. She learned something of what her mother and father had been like when the only child in the household had been James, and Thomas Angleford had come to meet his father's business partner. She was regaled with a bewildering menu of entertainments, both by day and by evening, which Julia Angleford laid out for them. "And, of course, there will be the visit to my *modiste* and the drapers' warehouse," she added, which made both Serena and Amelia sit up alertly. "Please do not think I am meaning to criticize your gowns," she added hastily. "In fact, the dresses you two are wearing now are suitable and unexceptional. But you will very likely want at least some of your wardrobe refurbished and adjusted closer to the current mode, and you *must* have ball gowns, which I am sure you do not have."

Amelia and Serena exchanged a look of alarm. "We have nothing like a ball gown of the sort we have seen in the magazines," Amelia admitted. "But—"

"No objections! I will not hear them!" The worthy lady actually held her hands over her ears, to her husband and James's great amusement. "You shall have ball gowns and opera cloaks. I have already consulted with your father and James about a clothing budget. We will take your things to my *modiste* and she will select the ones that need alteration and embellishment. She will show you illustrations for ball gowns, you shall pick what you like, and we will go to the drapers' warehouse to select fabric and trimmings. It will all be very economical," she added with a twinkle. "It is the warehouse. We will have the price the drapers' shops pay, not the one the drapers charge their customers. We shall *certainly* not pay the price a *modiste* would charge for supplying the materials."

"Advantage of being in the trade," Thomas Angleford said complacently. "Could never have afforded all the frills and furbelows needed by six daughters and a wife otherwise!"

Serena fanned her face with her hand. "I feared my father was about to lose every cent of profit from this consignment!" she joked.

"Don't you worry a bit," Julia laughed. "Just let visions of pretty things dance in your dreams tonight. Soon enough you'll be the ones dancing *in* them!"

With that pleasant prospect before them, they all returned to the

parlor, where, as guests, Amelia and Serena did their best to entertain the others. Amelia played the piano, choosing American songs
that she reckoned her hosts had never heard before, and so would be
a novelty. Serena sang them. Serena's voice was a low, warm con-
tralto with a sort of purring effect underlying every note. It had the
effect of making people relax without their understanding why.

James took a turn, reading the first chapter of a new novel set in
Scotland—the fact that he read a novel, rather than something "improving," greatly relieved Amelia once again. Clearly the Anglefords
did not disapprove of novels—and Amelia very badly wanted to take
out a subscription at the nearest lending library.

After that, Julia Angleford played and they all sang several old
songs familiar to all of them. When she finished, the maid came in
with chocolate for the ladies and claret for the gentlemen, which
Amelia quickly deduced was the signal for the end to the evening
and bed.

Amelia and Serena went up to their rooms, but both of them took
to Serena's first, and closed the door. Amelia made sure the door was
secure, then went to the window and opened it, trying not to shiver
too much in the cold breeze. By the time she turned around, Serena
had already changed.

In a puddle of clothing on the rug, a magnificent leopard stood,
gazing at Amelia with golden eyes. There was still the necklet of
pearls around Serena's neck.

"Hold still, you silly thing," she chided, taking the necklet off.
"You'd be bound to snap it, the pearls would be lost, and then your
heart would be broken."

The leopard bowed her head in acknowledgment of this truth.

"Go!" Amelia continued. "I'll wait up for you here. Just paw the
window and I'll let you in. It's too cold to leave the window open
until you feel like returning."

The leopard nodded and, with a graceful leap, was out of the window and into the night.

With a sigh, Amelia gathered up the discarded clothing and laid
it on the stool in front of the dressing table. She resigned herself to a

tedious, anxious hour—until she spotted a book on the bedside table beside an oil lamp burning with a fine, clear light.

She picked it up. *"Mansfield Park,"* she read aloud, and smiled. "By 'a Lady'!"

She made a backrest of the pillows and draped a blanket over her legs, making herself comfortable before starting the book. *Serena is very good about keeping herself in the shadows,* she reminded herself. *She even prowled the ship several times without detection. She may sometimes be flighty, but not about her shifting. There is no reason why I cannot enjoy some reading while I wait for her.* And after a while that was actually true.

2

THE tiny room smelled of lavender and roses, and ever so faintly of new fabric. The *modiste* eyed the contents of the two trunks of clothing spread around her without the contempt that Amelia had feared. When they had been introduced to this formidable, iron-haired, perfectly coiffed lady, in her exquisite lavender silk gown, with her aristocratic posture and her knowing blue eyes, Amelia had felt as if they were in the presence of royalty and was immediately intimidated.

Serena, of course, was not intimidated in the least—she was merely intensely interested in what the *modiste* said and did, as she was in most things, and those knowing eyes warmed slightly whenever they rested on Amelia's cousin. In fact, the *modiste* murmured a few things directed to Serena (as she examined seams and linings and trimmings) that sounded like a combination of vague compliments combined with instructions.

After examining their clothing, Madame declared judgment. "These are not bad for the amateur," the *modiste* said, with a faint French accent. "Well sewn, if inexpertly cut." She had already measured both girls with such precision that Amelia was not in the least surprised by this assessment. "And some are adequate. The muslin dresses *as* dresses merely need ornamentation, and I am sure you may do this yourselves once I direct what trimmings are needed and how to place them. Your simpler winter gowns may stand as they are, although if you have time, I suggest you improve them as you see the latest modes. Fortunately, the gowns needing my touch are all too big. Adjustments can be made easily." She began plucking garments from the chaos around her and depositing them back in the trunks. "This is adequate. This will not cause you to blush. And this. And this . . ." Amelia was very glad that the military-influenced gown she had worn the first night at the Anglefords' passed muster, as she had designed and sewn it herself. When the *modiste* had finished, half of the garments remained, in two piles, one hers and one Serena's. Now the harsher critique began. "Too missish, needs a lower neck and a more sophisticated trim. Needs a flounce at the hem and the sleeves. Too plain. *Much* too plain." And so on. When she had finished, she had a list of the trimmings that she wanted the girls to procure, specific to each dress, spencer, or pelisse. To Amelia's relief, she had not gone overboard on ruffles, flounces, and lace, at least not for her—though Serena's gowns apparently required more of all three than Amelia's did. Braids, tapes, and embroidered ribbons in specific colors were the choices for hers. It was astonishing how closely Madame had adhered to their chosen taste. Clearly she had paid exacting attention to their existing wardrobes.

We do have an awful lot of gowns, Amelia thought on reflection. But then, there was no lack of fabric at the Stonecroft estate. Clients of the Stonecroft dyes often sent large samples, or gifts as a thank-you. Amelia's father Charles had been experimenting with water-powered looms on his own, and everyone reaped the benefit of these experiments. And there always seemed to be trunks in the attic that could be plundered. Even drapes and old linens were not safe! Amelia hoped that Madame had not noted that many of the soft muslin gowns and some of the spencers and heavier gowns had once bedecked beds and windows. Another cause for worry. She felt it would be unbearably humiliating if Madame had made that observation.

Madame sent the trunks with the "acceptable garments" as well as the muslin dresses in them off to be put on the Angleford coach, to be delivered back to the Anglefords' address, and two of her "girls" were called in from another workroom to deal with the garments that had not quite met her exacting standards and needed to be re-cut and fitted.

The session was unexpectedly exhausting, and once they were through it, Madame Alexander looked up from the piles of fabric in her assistants' arms and finally smiled sympathetically. "A glass of wine, I think," she said. "And perhaps some cakes."

She bustled them out of her workroom and into her even smaller parlor, leaving behind her two apprentices to carry off the garments she had already decided needed to be picked apart, re-cut, and re-sewn. The parlor was a tiny crimson room with a single window with plush drapes, a table, and delicate chairs for four, with a fire burning in a peach-colored ceramic stove set into a small fireplace. One of the apprentices appeared with a tray on which were three glasses of wine and some unfamiliar, seashell-shaped cakes. "Madeleines," said Madame. "You will like them." She said it as a proclamation rather than an opinion, and Amelia felt that it would be a disaster not to agree with her.

But as she bit into the buttery little cake—not too sweet, so it paired beautifully with the sweet sherry Madame had served—she found herself in perfect agreement. Madame continued discussing garments with Mrs. Angleford while the two girls quietly nibbled and sipped in a state of mental exhaustion. This was very different from looking at the beautiful illustrations in *The Lady's Monthly Museum, The Lady's Magazine,* or the more lofty *La Belle Assemblee,* and trying to replicate a gown in the more simplified form that would suit their own relatively rustic living. No, apparently Madame intended the altered gowns to be in full accord with those shown in the pages of those august tomes. It made Amelia's head spin.

Her first thought was *But we don't need anything this—fancy!* But then she reconsidered. They *needed* to dress the part here, and the part was *not* that of girls who were as likely to find themselves helping to gather eggs as entertaining a visitor. The part was that of "daughters of landed gentlemen who just happened to also be in trade." Those girls would never be found in aprons chasing after hens, or slogging through mud and rain in wooden Dutch clogs to save their shoes and slippers. Their gowns needed to reflect that.

A glance at Serena told her in an instant that Serena was more than rising to the occasion, she was reveling in it. Meanwhile Madame and Julia were continuing to make notes about the trimmings that they would be purchasing at the drapers' warehouse. Only once did either Amelia or Serena speak up to contradict her.

"No swansdown!" Amelia said firmly when swansdown trimming was suggested. She'd once had a swansdown muff as a present and she'd given it away almost immediately. It had made her skin crawl.

"No indeed," agreed Serena. "It makes us sneeze."

Amelia cast her a grateful glance for the clever excuse; the truth was that she could not bear the thought of sacrificing any of those beautiful birds just to trim a gown or make a muff. True, she had no objection to ermine . . . but weasels were nasty little creatures, and it was easy enough to harden her heart against them. But swans! No.

Madame raised an eyebrow and shook her head slightly, but changed the order to a heavy silk braid. That suited Amelia just fine.

When the list was complete—and Amelia could only admire Madame's memory for color, cut, and purpose of all those garments, as well as how she intended to ornament each of them—Madame paused to have the glasses and the tray of crumbs taken away, hooded her eyes, and purred, "And now we discuss the new garments."

Julia Angleford nodded. "At least one ball gown," she said.

"Two," replied Madame. "Summer and winter. For the summer, the lightest of silk. For the winter, silk velvet or a silk twill or jacquard. We will have detachable long sleeves that will fit under the puffed sleeves for both, so that you will effectively have four gowns, rather than two. Shawls. An evening cloak for each. Your pelisses I will alter, your spencers you can re-trim. Possibly a new sleeveless overgown, fastened beneath the bosom, suitable for evening dress."

She rang a small bell on the table and another assistant appeared with a book of gown pictures, cut from many magazines, but all of the latest mode. Madame and Julia pored over it, with Serena and Amelia craning their necks to see what they were discussing. If this had happened *before* Madame had finished going through their existing clothing, Amelia would have been in a knot of even more anxiety, wondering if she was going to be stuffed into something that would leave her feeling as if she could not move without ruining what had cost so much to obtain.

And she bit her tongue to keep from protesting that they would never be attending so many balls that they would need two gowns for them. Because, she realized on quick reflection, this was *not* home and people had proper *balls* here all the time—nightly, in fact!—and not simple assemblies of just enough people to make up a set in someone's parlor, or at most, once every month or two, in the ballroom of one of the great houses in town or the surrounding countryside.

And from the way Julia Angleford kept nodding, she was in complete accord with all of this.

It made Amelia's head spin to think of how much this would cost . . . but Mrs. Angleford had brought out six girls, and already knew what such things entailed, and Amelia trusted that she would never, ever overspend whatever budget Papa and James had deemed appropriate.

Thank heavens all our muslins passed muster! Even the ones made of old sheets!

Then again, those latter muslins were, of course, meant for things like housecleaning, and Madame had probably dismissed them at first sight, knowing they would never be seen in public.

Madame finally let them go, after checking and double-checking the list that Julia had made, and sending them off with strict instructions as to what else to purchase if what was on that list happened to be unavailable.

At this point they had spent the entire morning at the *modiste*, and the wine and cakes were wearing thin. The coach was brought around and it was with profound relief that Amelia heard Julia give the order to go home.

The men were not at home, so once their cloaks and bonnets were taken away, Julia ordered a cold luncheon to be served in the morning room. Amelia scarcely noticed what they were eating as all three of them discussed what was to be done that afternoon.

"This will be much quicker than our visit with Madame," Julia declared. "Although this is not like a shop. Have you ever been to a dry-goods warehouse? No? We will have to walk through the warehouse and make our selections by ourselves, rather than having items brought to us for our acceptance or rejection. We will also be buying things that are not fabric nor trimmings: gloves, fans, shawls, perhaps a parasol for each of you for summer—I assume you are used to trimming your own bonnets?"

"Oh, certainly!" Amelia answered before Serena could.

"Good, then I will make sure to buy enough trimmings and other haberdashery that you can re-trim your old bonnets to match your re-trimmed gowns, and of course, you may help yourself to what is in my workroom." She frowned a little. "I think to economize you must make your own slippers to match your ballgowns at the very least, so I will make sure to order enough fabric for three pairs of slippers in addition to the matching gown fabric. That brings me to shoes and boots. You will probably not ride while in London, but since you will be going to inspect properties outside London for your brother's purpose, you will need a good pair of riding boots. Do you each have those?"

"Yes," Serena said promptly. "And leather wet-weather half-boots, and jean boots for the cold, and more slippers for ordinary wear and more slippers for house wear. Lots of worsted and cotton stockings, but only three pairs of silk, each. We left our wooden clogs at home."

"Just as well; no one but a farmer's wife would be seen dead in them!" Julia laughed. "Well, we must add silk stockings to the list. Madame and I think we must retire your current ball gowns to family routs; they are rather too obviously remade from your grandmama's best gowns, even though they were well made."

Amelia sighed, because she very much liked the rich rust brocade of hers, but she allowed that this was so. Clearly absolutely no one—except, perhaps, the queen's inner circle—wore the brocades of a previous generation. The queen kept the fashion that had been in the mode when she was young, and her inner circle followed suit, even to the wearing of powdered wigs!

I suppose we could remake those gowns into waistcoats for all the men of the family. Perhaps Mr. Angleford would appreciate a "new" waistcoat as a gift.

"I believe we shall be able to bring our shopping expedition well within a total that will leave your brother James smiling instead of frowning, and cause your father to rejoice that he has such frugal daughters," Julia continued.

"We know how to make silk and paper flowers ourselves," Serena put in, ever eager to make another small economy. "I'm rather good at it. And we are both very good at beadwork. So we can save that much on bonnet trimmings and hair wreaths."

"Bless you, so you can!" Julia exclaimed. "And I am sure there is plenty of crepe paper and other flower making supplies here in the house from when my girls were living here. I shall have Mrs. Jennings hunt it out."

"Flower making is easier to do before a fire than needlework, and it makes a pleasant diversion after dinner," Amelia added, feeling her anxiety about money fade back to its normal level. "We could trim our own gowns—"

But Julia shook her head. "Except for the ones that were sent home, let Madame deal with that," she said firmly. "You will have your hands full with bonnets and wreaths and embroidering new covers for your slippers."

Amelia found herself actually looking forward to the adventure in the warehouse, rather than dreading it, with Julia's promise that she would simply not allow the girls to purchase anything out of the budget. They all piled into the carriage once again, now fortified with a good luncheon, and set out into the cold.

The warehouse itself was in a district with many other similar buildings, with nothing outwardly to show what it was except for the words "Hannibal Dry Goods" on the outside.

Inside was controlled chaos amid the scents of leather, leather-oil, new fabric, and some faint hints of sandalwood and other exotics. It was just as well that Julia knew where she was going, because absolutely not a single one of the men and boys bustling about the place looked even remotely interested in helping them. But the man at a high desk at the front door recognized Julia once she identified herself, and made it known that they were now permitted to roam the premises and select what they would. He called over a young boy to help carry and, if need be, climb. This was very different from the much smaller storage houses of home, where everyone knew them, and they were, as often as not, invited to sit down with the supervisors and have a tot of rum.

The boy availed himself of a cart, and off through the towering shelves they went.

Fabric was evidently their first concern, and first they headed to the section where the bolts of fabric were warehoused. Down came bolts of light silk in white, silk velvet in scarlet and a rich brown that Amelia was immediately in love with, silk twill in a pink and pale gold. Into the cart those went, and then it was off to the trim, where a bewildering number of bolts of laces, braids, and ribbons went into the cart. Last of all, thread. Then it was all pulled to a huge table where many men stood, cutting for the customers, who were uniformly men. Amelia gathered from their talk that these gentlemen were all drapers, who sold to dressmakers, *modistes,* tailors, and those who sewed for themselves. They seemed confused and a little resentful at the presence of three women among them, but once Julia addressed a few "casual" remarks to some of them ("Oh, how do you like this year's Stonecroft indigo? My husband is the agent, and I wish you would tell me if you find anything lacking.") she was accepted as "one of them." It was rather like reciting a magic charm that made things go from frowns to all smiles. Carefully consulting her list, Julia called out so many yards of this, and so many yards of that, each piece neatly cut, wrapped in brown paper and tied up with string, and a price noted on a new list. When coming to Amelia's choice of brown velvet, the man looked over the rim of his spectacles at them and Amelia's heart sank. What mistake had she made now?

But what he said was, "This is last year's, and it has not sold at all. If you will take the lot, I can let you have it at half price."

"That is uncommonly kind of you," Julia said, with a smile that made her look half her age. "I would like this above all things."

And there is my evening cloak! Amelia thought, hardly able to breathe for her good luck.

Last of all, the cart was towed to a separate section of the warehouse, where the girls were finally able to pick out purchases on their own—fans, gloves, shawls both silk and wool, and silk stockings. "Get more gloves than you think you will need," Julia admonished them. "Unless you know how to make gloves yourselves."

Amelia grimaced a little. "Actually . . . I do," she confessed, because this was *not* something that was considered a genteel accomplishment, nor suited to young ladies. "Actual silk and other fabric gloves. We can both knit gloves, of course."

"In that case . . . well, stick to white kid, and you can make up white silk gloves to go with your gowns from the extra yardage I had cut," Julia said without turning a hair. "But get at least two pairs more of each than you think you will need. It is astonishing how badly a round of entertainments treats one's glove drawer. And someone will *always* spill something at supper."

Finally, buttons, tapes, and beads, and the cart came before a solemn-faced man in an immaculate apron over a severe black suit, who totaled up the prices. Amelia, and even Serena, were astonished by the prices—in a very good way. It drove home to her how much more expensive these things were at home. But then, everything that was not wool, cotton, or linen had to be imported, and during the last war with England, gotten across the blockade as well.

Three boys were sent with them, laboring under the parcels, to take them to the waiting carriage. This time the girls took the backward-facing seat to allow their hostess to have the forward-facing one. Julia settled the folds of her blue winter pelisse around her with every look of satisfaction.

"*Half* James's budget!" she said with the pleasure of someone who was as frugal as Serena and Amelia. "And I include Madame's fees in that. Which leaves plenty in case we discover we cannot manage without a third ball gown, or something happens to ruin your boots."

The unfamiliar sensation of anxiety melting away suffused Amelia with a sensation of warmth that was as welcome as it was unaccustomed.

Serena's eyes sparkled, and Amelia was fairly certain that hers were just as bright. It had been an unalloyed pleasure to indulge in looking at all those fine things, even in the atmosphere of a cold and inconvenient warehouse with drapers pushing their way past with barely a murmur of "beg pardon," or one of them looking cross because *they* were considering something *he* knew he wanted.

"Father will also be pleased," Amelia said. "Would you and your husband like to speak with him and Mama tonight?"

"Above all things!" Julia exclaimed, her face lighting up with a smile. "I don't like to ask James to do so too often, since he and my husband are often consulting with your father in the day and scrying is terribly fatiguing."

"After dinner, then. In place of listening to us pound your piano and caterwaul," Serena said teasingly. "Amelia has brought her mirror, of course."

"I would be astonished if she had not." Julia sat back in her seat. "Well, you two run up to your rooms; I will sort through our purchases. I will send the fabric and trimmings for your new and retailored things off to Madame, and all the rest up to you to put away."

What came upstairs, as Amelia put aside her cloak and suddenly had to sit down when she contemplated the bounty that had just been bestowed upon her was not "just" the gloves, stockings, and trimmings, it was a veritable treasure trove. Silk and merino shawls, at least two of which she could not remember selecting, fabric cut off from the larger pieces so that she could make matching gloves and slippers and probably matching reticules for both gowns, white fabric for "common" gloves, the trimmings for her "adequate" gowns, fans, and an entire box of odds and ends of fabric and pieces of very thin leather almost as light as wool cloth. There was more than enough leather for the soles of the new slippers, and there were some kid pieces too small for gloves but certainly large enough for yet more slippers with judicious piecing. Slippers were the joy and bane of her existence: so easily ruined, yet such fun to make. Mourned when they were stained or tattered beyond saving, a secret pleasure when new. Nothing made her happier than having a pair of neatly embroidered, brand-new slippers poking out from under a gown. *I shall have to make Julia at least three pairs,* she decided. It should be easy enough to get a maid to bring her a pair of Julia's so that she could trace the soles on a piece of paper.

But in the meantime . . . she selected the brown velvet and warm gold silk and extracted patterns for her own feet from her large workbox. The velvet gown was to be trimmed in gold bullion embroidery, and the silk in embroidered ribbon, so that knowledge supplied her embroidery patterns, fixed firmly in her head. She had not needed patterns laid out on the fabric to work from since she had been eleven. She took the time to cut out a pair of each set of slippers, complete with linings pieced from the scraps, and kid soles, and placed them in her small workbox, the one she actually carried with her. She had a small packet of gold bullion that she had been saving for years in there, and now was definitely the time to use it. There were probably ribbons among Julia's bonnet-trimming odds and ends to take care of tying them up; if not, she could braid some ties from embroidery floss.

She tidied everything away, her heart singing as she caressed a shawl or touched a soft kid glove. Never had she owned so many *new* things all at once. *Have I turned vain?* came the sudden, intrusive thought as anxiety attempted to spoil it all for her. But then, *No, it is no sin to rejoice in what is pretty.* Father said so all the time.

It was almost too bad that they were going to scry Father tonight.

She longed to start on those velvet slippers. On the other hand, she wanted to see Father much more than she wanted to make slippers!

Oh! I had better let Father know that I will be calling on him! A quick mental calculation told her that at about the hour of eight in the evening here, which was likely when the Anglefords would want to speak to him, it would be about three or four in the afternoon in South Carolina. He should be able to steal some time to speak, if he had ample warning.

Now to call on an Elemental to convey her message. She wasn't sure exactly what sort of Earth Elemental would respond to her summons—back home, she could count on a mix of European Elementals that had followed Elemental Masters into the new world, and the ones native to North America. Here, well . . . a brownie was the most likely. They had the least trouble with being in and around the works of humans. She sat down on the rug beside the hearth, put one hand on the stone, focused her mind so that there was nothing but a single thought in it, and sent out a quiet request for simple help. As a Master, of course, she could simply have sent out a coercive demand, or even a mere order, but that was not how she had been taught to conduct herself in magic.

And it wasn't long before there was a tiny head peeping out at her from around the fireplace surround, as if the creature was half in, half out of the wall. Which was entirely possible. It looked like a brownie to her, a fully grown human, but the size of a doll. *"What needs ye, mistress?"* asked a voice as much inside her head as in her ears.

"I need to let my father in the New World know that I will wish to scry to him between three or four in the afternoon at his time," she said, "if you think—"

"'Certs, 'tis already done!" the little thing chuckled, coming into full view. This was a male, who was dressed in a miniature version of a country gentleman's wardrobe: all brown moleskin and corduroy, comfortable oversized coat with no tails, worsted waistcoat, knee breeches, and certainly not in the latest mode. The part at odds with his appearance was that he was shoeless. He was gray-haired and had enormous side-whiskers. *"Arst something harder!"*

"Would you know where in the house there is some thin brown ribbon, or thin gold, or both, that is not being used?" she replied, feeling a bit amused. "Mrs. Angleford gave us the freedom of her workroom and supplies."

"'Twill be in yon workbox afore ye know it," the brownie replied. *"If ye needs me, Mistress, jest think me use-name. I be Natty Ned."*

"Thank you, Natty Ned," she replied, and the little fellow vanished somehow around the corner of the surround. She did not need to assure him that the usual rewards would be waiting for him on her hearth; Elementals had mysterious ways of communicating with each other, even across vast distances, and she had no doubt that he had known everything there was worth knowing about her—at least to him and the other Earth Elementals—as soon as she crossed the threshold of this house.

She sighed a little and stayed on the floor for a bit, and not just because the warmth from the stove was absolutely delicious and all the running about today had left her a bit tired. Somehow, knowing that she could still speak to Elementals here and have their help eased some of that anxiety. In fact, now that she came to think about it, most of her anxieties had evaporated in the face of reality. The Anglefords had welcomed them, and made accommodations for Serena. The cost of their wardrobe refurbishment was not going to be outlandish. Their accents had not marked them as American barbarians—although that had probably been helped by the fact that she and Serena both had an ear and a knack for languages and accents, and usually picked up the cadences of the people they were with within hours of meeting them. James was looking splendid, and neither under- nor over-worked. She had already crossed many things off her—

"My list!" she exclaimed aloud, and sprang to her feet to look for her journal.

She didn't have to look far; someone had considerately placed it in the drawer of the dressing table, along with a corked bottle of ink and a crow-quill pen. There were also some sheets of thin, light paper and sealing wafers, although she was not likely to have much need of any such thing as long as she was communicating with other Elemental mages.

She opened the journal to her lists, and began crossing things off. *Acquire the right speech. Arrange for a proper wardrobe. Make sure Serena is able to run. Make ourselves welcome and entertaining.* She had not made a sub-list for "proper wardrobe," but Madame had taken that completely out of her hands. But there were sub-lists for other things . . . the most important being the task James had already put in her hands, long before she left South Carolina. That list was headed: *Find a property for James.*

Well, nothing to be done about that for the moment. Back to the primary list. *Make acquaintances or friends within the community.* That was largely out of her hands now, too. Julia Angleford was doubtless arranging for the first of what sounded like many rounds of "entertainment" that were also designed for her to foster an acquaintance with other Elemental mages. In fact, given what she knew of Julia so far, she was probably writing invitations already!

Lists helped keep the anxiety at bay, especially when she could cross things off. But she turned somewhat reluctantly to the last list in the journal.

Husbands.

She had written this thinking she intended it for Serena. After all, her darling kitten, so full of romantic sensibilities, needed someone to keep her interests at heart, because she was altogether too likely to fall in love with someone who would not be good for her.

1. Must be an Elemental mage.

Well, one would think that went without saying . . .

But Serena, being Serena, could cry, "It doesn't matter, if he loves me!"

And it wouldn't matter . . . until it very much did.

2. Must accept Serena as she is.

Serena was quite capable of not bothering to show her beloved that she was a shifter. Until it was too late. She was also likely to withhold her breeding, but if that got out, it could mean a domestic disaster.

3. Must be kind.
4. Must be clever.
5. Must not be a fortune hunter.
6. Must be willing to come back to America if need be.
7. Must be resilient.
8. Must be a Hunter of the White Lodge.

That was nonnegotiable. Only a Hunter could understand another Hunter. Uncle Ambrose, for instance, was *not* a Hunter, and was the most peaceable and pacifistic of Quakers. He was often heard, after a Hunt, to plaintively ask if they could not have resolved the situation "another way."

9. Must love music and reading.

She knew Serena would be quite willing to do without dancing, if—for infirmity or some other reason—her husband could not dance or did not care to. But she could never do without music and reading.

10. Must not demand we be submissive.

Serena was about as inclined to be a "submissive" wife as a hawk was to walk instead of flying. Then again, so was Amelia.

Not for the first time, she had to ruefully acknowledge that the "husband" list applied to her as much as to Serena—but the likelihood of finding two such paragons of masculinity was very slim, and of the two of them, she was certain that Serena needed the helpful and supportive sort of partner that her own mother, Amelia's mother, and James's one-day wife had far more than Amelia did. *I am able to contemplate a life of spinsterhood with complete equanimity. Serena . . .* She shook her head. More than once, Serena had expressed a horror of the idea. *I can play doting auntie to a horde of Serena's children. She can't even talk about daydreams of the future without it including a mate and kittens.*

She was well aware that most women did not have the luxury she had; she could go back home and have a perfectly acceptable and ful-filling life on the Stonecroft estate without a husband. And that was a luxury indeed. For most women, from the poorest to the richest, life required a husband. If you had nothing, you needed a helpmeet just to put enough food on the table to survive. If you were merely poor, you needed a husband for the same reason. If you were middle class or rich, well, even if you had property and money in your own right, the laws were structured so that everything you did was still subject to the will of men, from your banker to your brother. And if you did not have money, the only way to make your way in the world was in the poorly paid professions of nurse, teacher, or governess. Amelia, in contrast, was lucky beyond the wildest dreams of most.

Well, all that was for later. The other lists needed to be gotten through first. There was no point in worrying about potential hus-bands when they hadn't been properly introduced into Elemental mage circles here yet.

She heard the bell ring for dinner, and came to herself with a start. *Just* enough time to dress!

After a dinner that, again, was much more formal than Amelia was really used to, they all gathered in the parlor. Amelia sat on a cush-ion on the rug in front of the stove; more than a bit unladylike, but it was the only way to balance her scrying mirror in her lap so the Anglefords and Serena could look down into it with her while they sat on the chairs. It brought back memories of sitting like this as a child; small wonder that dogs and cats preferred the hearth to a lap. Like all Earth magicians, her scrying mirror was made of a single piece of black obsidian in the shape of a shallow disk that fully filled her lap and had been polished to perfection. If she had been a Water Master, her scrying instrument would have been a literal bowl of water; if Air, she would have had to make a sort of disk out of the air itself, a feat which was quite difficult, and generally tested the skill and patience of Air Masters. James, having an unusually steady temperament for an Air Master, could conjure one up in about a quarter of an hour. And a Fire Master had it easiest: use a fire, usually the one in a fireplace.

With a heavy, polished quartz crystal in either hand, Amelia called on the magic of her Element until she felt it flowing into her body from the earth and rock on which this house stood. It was more difficult here than at home, where there would have been nothing between her and the earth but the wooden floor of whatever room she was in, but she had anticipated that. When she finally made the connection, it felt so good, she was on the verge of tears; being isolated from her Element by so much water for so long had stretched her nerves. It was like being filled with warm honey, without the feeling of sickness so much real sweet would inevitably create.

Then she reached out for her father, who was probably sitting at his own hearth, mirror in his lap, with crystals cut from the same larger formation in his hands. Making the connection felt like hand sliding into hand, and she opened her eyes to see him smiling up at her from the mirror.

"It's good to see all of you!" he exclaimed, with such warmth and enthusiasm that it might have been a year since he had last said goodbye to Amelia and Serena. His voice had a bit of an echo, as if he were talking from the bottom of a well.

"I just spoke to you this morning, Charles," laughed Mr. Angleford. "But it's good to see you, too."

"Well, knowing that my girls are safe and sound with you and actually seeing them is quite a different thing," Charles Stonecroft chided

gently. *"And I have not spoken with dear Julia in quite six months. Or is that one of your daughters, and not your wife, that I see?"*

Julia colored, and laughed. "Charles, you charmer! You'll never lure me to your howling wilderness with fair words and compliments."

"It is no longer a howling wilderness, my dear. Why, one could say it purrs. And speaking of purrs, are you getting on well, Serena?"

Serena craned her neck so Charles could see her. "Quite well, Uncle. I had a capital run last night!"

Amelia noted that Serena made no mention of the pigeon she had caught sleeping on a rooftop and eaten. Amelia only knew because there had been tiny feathers on her muzzle when she returned. *That is probably a bit too much to let the Anglefords hear about right now,* she decided. *Better not to tease her about it in front of them. Besides, they might think that they had not fed us well enough!*

They all spoke in turn, the Anglefords catching her father up on the doings since they had arrived, and she and Serena making light of the discomfort of the voyage and waxing enthusiastic about the trip to the *modiste* and the warehouse. And to her pleasure, Amelia's father made much of their frugality and complimented them on their restraint when set free in both places. *"Julia, I'd like you to give them each a hundred pounds as pocket money,"* he said when he had finished. *"You can draw on James's account. They've seldom been to a town where a lady can shop, and it's a good thing for a wench to have a bit of the ready if a tempting fan or ribbon calls to her. And there will be Vauxhall in summer, you know, and ices and lemonade to buy. Theater and concert seats to pay for. Assembly tickets. I know I can trust them both to keep track of every penny."*

Serena squealed with glee, and Amelia felt her cheeks flushing with pleasure. Oh! To be set free with *one's own money!* The prospect was intoxicating.

"Father! You are too good!" she exclaimed.

"Now, let me move over so your mother can have her say."

Amelia more than half expected her mother to follow up her father's generosity with admonitions not to make him regret it, but she did no such thing. Her face filled the bowl, looking, as Amelia well knew, like an older version of herself, and the first thing she said was, *"Now, make sure you enjoy every bit of your stay with our friends. And do your best to make friends among our sort. Try your best, even if they seem disagreeable. It will be up to you to make sure that if there are any feelings that someone is unpleasant, they are on your side, not theirs. You must not give anyone a reason to spread gossip that you are difficult. James's reputation depends on it, as well as your own."*

"Yes, Mama," and "Yes, Auntie," the two of them chorused.

"We shall make sure that everything we say and do burnishes all our reputations," Amelia added.

The faint lines around Vivian Stonecroft's mouth and eyes relaxed a bit, and she quizzed both girls about details of their gowns, gowns-to-be, and purchases at the warehouse. Then, of course, James had his chance to say a few words, although he spoke with his parents often enough that he merely tossed off a few remarks that made them all laugh.

Then it was the turn of Cheri and Samuel Meleva, who reminded their daughter that her siblings *would* be expecting presents, and advised her to get them things that they would not find at home.

"Novels," Serena said firmly. "It takes an *age* for books to come over from England to the farm, and it is unlikely that between our door and yours, someone with light fingers will be tempted by a parcel of books."

"Just the thing!" applauded Samuel, his thin face wreathed in a smile of satisfaction. "And they can all pass them about, so it will be like six presents each instead of one."

They could have gone on all night, but Amelia began to feel drained, and the faces in the bowl wavered. Thomas Angleford noticed, and decreed a halt. Goodbyes and goodnights were said, and Amelia let the magic drain from her with a sigh. For a moment she sagged over the bowl, before putting her crystals in it and handing it to Serena to take while she got to her feet.

"You look very weary, dear child," said Julia and made a shooing motion. "Up to bed with you! I shall send up some hot chocolate. You made a capital bit of work with your scrying; I don't think I have ever seen it done better, even by James."

"Mrs. Angleford!" James exclaimed, clutching his hand to his throat. "You wound me! And scrying by Air is, as you know—"

"Much, much harder than any other Element, yes, you tell us every time," Thomas mocked him. "Don't be daft. You are both excellent. She said she had never seen it done better, not that you were worse."

"*Crushed!*" James whimpered, then laughed. "Especially since I have to agree. You've matured in your magic, wench. You are likely to put some of our local Masters to shame!"

"I certainly hope not," Amelia replied, taking her bowl back from Serena. "That would be unfortunate and create resentment. We'll be in Serena's room, Mrs. Angleford," she added. "And thank you for the offer of chocolate; I am feeling rather in need of it!"

3

LIFE with the Anglefords was luxurious by Amelia's standards. Breakfast was not until *ten*. There were no hens to let loose at the break of dawn and feed, no table to set, no huge piles of mending and ironing, no eggs to gather. The Stonecrofts had very few servants as such. Most of the inhabitants of the big house at home pitched in with the usual chores, and those who didn't were out on the land at first light, tending to the crops and herds.

All were nominally Quaker, although Amelia was quite certain that if one was to make a strict assessment, the immediate Stonecroft family would have been classified as "deists," those who believed in the "clockwork God." That is, that the universe had been set in motion by the Lord, who then took a step back, obeying His own law of free will, and left Earth and its inhabitants to make their own decisions without any intervention on His part. Harsh, perhaps, but fair. And certainly better than a God that punished for very little reason with one hand, distributed milk and honey to those who shamelessly rained praise on Him, and with no logic simply allowed terrible things to happen to perfectly good, even pious people.

Washington, Franklin, and Jefferson and many of the other Founding Fathers were deists, and Amelia had found herself in agreement with them when Father had explained deism to her.

The Stonecroft "plantation" consisted of about eight hundred acres, and might reach one thousand one day. It had one enormous house that housed the (very) extended Stonecroft and Meleva families, and several standard farmhouses distributed at the further extent of the acreage. And although no one who was not an Elemental mage—and many who were!—did not realize it, there was not one single slave on the property, only tenant farmers and sharecroppers, most of whom lived in those outlying farmhouses and tended very particular crops or herds that they were quite good with.

And yet, somehow, we manage to produce enough to be considered rich, Amelia reflected, as she luxuriated for a moment in her bed while the maid—something she had never had in her life—cleaned the ashes out of the stove and built up the fire again. The household did have servants—the cook and her helpers, three men and a rotating handful of spry boys for the heavier work—but everyone, including Charles himself, was expected to "do" for themselves and pitch in as well, if they were not at work on something important, like schoolwork. If you had a bedroom to yourself, you cleaned it yourself. If you did not, you split the work between or among the ones you shared with.

The plantation had its own school . . . which, aside from reading, writing, and all the rest, taught some very sobering lessons by way of play-acting to the children of those with dark enough skin to be taken for slaves. *Head down. "Master and Mistress," always. The answer is always "yes," no matter what you are told to do. When it doubt, say you must "ask Master." Always stand back at least the length of a horse, so if someone tries to steal you, you can run back to safety. Never talk back. Never strike back. Never say what you are thinking.*

There were no slaves on the Stonecroft plantation, although there were people with dark skin aplenty. And that was a story all in and of itself. But this was why Amelia's dear cousin Serena was a shifter . . . and dusky enough that everyone deemed it prudent to claim that she and her parents were Italian.

No one challenges Father's word back home. And as for here . . . thanks to that visit from Antonio Verdi, the cochineal importer from Rome, all the Melevas speak fluent Italian.

Poor Antonio had had no idea why he had had such a restless night, and had put it all down to an unaccustomed dinner and an unfamiliar bed. He had had no clue that Elementals of all four Elements were rummaging around in his brain and stealing his beloved native tongue to impart to anyone in the house who might be in need of it.

The maid finished, having already left a pitcher of steaming water next to the basin, and Amelia slid out of bed. She had convinced Julia's lady's maid that she did not need help dressing and, in fact, that she didn't want any help in dressing. This way she could take her time, rather than rushing through things, feeling as if she was keeping the maid from doing something else important.

Last to be done was her hair, and she sighed a little at the dressing table, repressing envy at Serena's head of ebony curls. Her hair was fine and flyaway, it would never grow longer than mid-chest, and it waved rather than curled. The best disposition for it was to be gathered up in a loose knot at the top of her head and for her to thread a ribbon through it to make it *look* as if she had deliberately chosen the fashionable disheveled look, rather than being forced into it by her hair.

In fact, this morning her hair was unusually rebellious, probably inspired by the drizzle outside, and it took longer than usual to make it presentable. "Truce?" she asked it, as she looked into the mirror. Her hair declined to reply.

But there were delicious scents coming from below, in which bacon predominated, and she wasn't inclined to give it a chance for further mischief this morning.

The Anglefords did not truly keep "country hours" as Amelia knew them, because if they had, breakfast would have been at six at the very latest. And breakfast back home was served on a table that literally groaned beneath its weight, while here, the fare was so meager that the first morning she and Serena had been shocked. Bacon, eggs boiled soft in their shells, and hot rolls or toast with butter and tea! At home there would have been some sort of meat as well as the bacon and sausage, Johnny-cake and cornbread, eggs cooked several ways, bread and butter, cake, pie, jam and jelly . . . well, they were farmers at home, right down to Father, and a farmer needed a good breakfast after the chores of the morning. One thing she did admit— the tea was very good, served with milk and sugar, and often there was hot chocolate as well.

Between rising and breakfast she usually worked on her sewing; Julia took early morning callers or handled her correspondence, of which there seemed to be quite a lot. The morning light was the best light of the day to do fine work by, and Amelia was determined that the new trimmings be applied to her old gowns with the finest of stitches. This morning, it was with a sense of great triumph that she went down in a newly trimmed muslin gown. Although it was long-sleeved, she was already cold after putting it on, so she brought a shawl with her. She was very happy with her work: three rows of delicate lace applied with invisible stitches to the bottom third of the gown, which formerly had been untrimmed. Lace was ruinously expensive back home, and most people crocheted or knitted it themselves, or even made needle- or pillow-lace, but that sort of lace needed to be created with thread, not yarn, and took forever.

"Very good," Julia said with approval, when she came down to breakfast. "Quite appropriate for a morning gown."

Amelia, who had thought she was dressed for the day, blinked. "Morning gown?" she asked.

"A lady of means changes at least three times a day: a morning gown for duties at home and receiving early and informal visitors; a slightly more formal afternoon gown for receiving visitors who are not intimate friends, or in the case of you and your sister, suitors; and then dressing again for dinner. If a lady goes out for a walk or shopping or riding, she would change into a gown specifically for that purpose." She laughed at Amelia's expression. "Don't worry! Although a lady is expected to show *some* variety, you can wear the same gowns over and over, and, indeed, it would be thought a marvel of wealth or extravagance to seldom be seen in the same gown twice."

"Are there women who actually do that?" Amelia gasped.

"Certain of the Cyprian class, who, I have heard, show their power over their protectors by emptying his pockets as often as possible," Julia acknowledged. "But that is only gossip, and *not* the sort to be bandied about in our circles. We are expected to never acknowledge the existence of such females."

Amelia could not help but reflect on the slave-owners near to the Stonecroft plantation, and how whispers hinted of "favorites" certain landowners "kept." Of course, just like the Cyprians, ladies were expected to be blind to such things. Especially the wives of those landowners.

It seems to me that the Cyprians have the better life by far. Provided, of course, they have been clever enough to set money aside for the day when they will be cast off for a new toy. Then she dared to say something to Julia that would probably be unthinkable to anyone else in this society—but someone who had accepted a leopard shifter in their midst could probably be counted upon to not fall into a faint at what she was about to ask.

"But what if a Cyprian turned out to be a mage, or even a Master?"

Julia's eyes widened. "I . . . have no idea," she stammered at last. "It's never come up. But . . . obviously . . . one couldn't leave her *unsupervised*, could one? Oh, dear. I shall have to put a word about this possibility in my husband's ear."

Yes, you probably should. Because that *had* come up back home. And the entire Stonecroft plantation had been involved in rescuing the poor thing, hiding her from her incensed master, and, as soon as it could be done, smuggling her up north where slavery had been abolished. *But what would one do about a pampered, kept woman living a luxurious life who does not want to be "rescued"?*

"In fact," Julia said, as if she wanted to change the subject in a hurry, "I am expecting several people in the Elemental mage circle to come calling this afternoon to meet you and Serena. I suggest that after luncheon you wear the pale blue round gown you just finished trimming with ribbon. That would be quite suitable."

"Then I will wear the matching one in pink," Serena said, from the doorway. "I gather we are expected to be like the ladies in the magazines and spend our days in an endless round of changing garments?" She giggled and took her place at the breakfast table, after selecting some bacon and some warm rolls from the basket, and buttered the rolls. Julia poured her tea.

"Not endless, but yes. Morning, afternoon, dinner, and another change into something appropriate if you go out riding or walking," Julia agreed. "A spencer or pelisse over your gown will do if you are just going out walking."

"Well, we are not going out riding," Serena declared. "First, I don't intend to fritter my hundred pounds away on a hired horse, and second, any hired horse would take great exception to me. We had to train the horses back home to accept me, and it generally took some weeks."

Julia blinked, then nodded. "I expect that means I must cross off a visit to the Royal Menagerie from my list of amusements."

"Definitely." Serena bit into a roll. "Any lions or leopards would likely challenge me, and game animals would try to flee me in fear. I can just about manage to hide what I am from a dog or a cat, but wild animals and farm animals know what I am at once."

"Well . . ." Julia bit her lip. "If we are being open and frank . . . I would very much like to see the leopard."

Amelia brought her napkin to her lips to hide her smile, but Serena laughed out loud. "Tonight you shall," she promised. "Instead of music, I'll shift. But Amelia will have to come with me to make sure I don't terrify a maid."

Julia's eyes lit up. "I must confess, this is very exciting, and I am looking forward to it. The thought is going to carry me through what is likely to be a very boring afternoon of receiving guests who do not give a jot about me except as an extension of my husband, and who will, at any rate, be more interested in my fair guests."

"Forgive me to doubt that is the case," Amelia protested.

"Well," her hostess replied. "You can see and judge for yourself."

The parlor was crowded to capacity, and every time a visitor left, another came to take his place, as if they had all prearranged everything on a schedule. On reflection, that was probably exactly what they had done. Amelia was so torn between anxiety that they would make a good impression and a sort of hysterical amusement that she ended up mostly answering questions—oh, so many questions!—as briefly as possible, lest she burst into either tears or laughter.

Their visitors were mostly men, and she had the impression that every single Elemental mage in London and the environs had made a pilgrimage to Julia's parlor to look the two of them over. It wasn't known outside the household that Serena was a shifter; the Anglefords deemed it prudent to keep that part of the equation quiet for now, except for the Huntmaster, who would come later, and alone. But two young, female potential spouses with power, newly come to London, formed an attraction too strong to resist even for members of the *ton*. Of course, there were other considerations—like how much would be settled on them by Charles Stonecroft when they married. But being powerful enough could cancel out having no dowry and no lineage, at least according to Julia. Not that they were penniless, of course. Lineage, however, was what they didn't have. Still, much to Amelia's surprise, enough Elemental power could cancel out the "smell of the shop."

And here they are to see the fillies and try their paces.

Small wonder the magazines and novels referred to something called the "marriage market." The *ton*, or aristocrats, had the one referred to in the novels, but it appeared that the Elemental mages had one of their own.

And it was a market in every sense of the word. These men were here to see if there was something they wanted to buy, for themselves or for their sons. Any marriage, so far as they were concerned, was strictly transactional in nature. Love was for novels. In fact, Amelia had no doubt that many of these polite-faced gentlemen would much rather that the females they wanted to examine had never heard of love.

To be fair, there were plenty of parents and potential husbands back home who felt exactly the same.

Oh, that won't do for Serena. She very much hoped that these fellows would deduce that quickly. As for her—

Anyone who proposes to me had better fit my list. She didn't entirely object to a proposal being partly transactional . . . but *damned* if she was going to accept being kept like a prize breeding mare, valued only for her bloodline, and having no freedom to be herself. *And I wonder how these gentlemen will react to that!*

They were almost all superficially alike, these gentlemen who had come to gawk. Some were dressed much as James did, some far more extravagantly, with cravat arranged just *so*, collars that touched their ears, and artificially disheveled locks. They crowded together on the little parlor chairs, and differed mostly in their footwear and the color of hair, coat, breeches, and waistcoat. What struck her most, though, was the footwear, a circle of Hessians, topboots, stockings with shoes, and one or two sets of stockings with shoes with enormous silver buckles in the old-fashioned style. They could have been a display in a shoemaker's shop.

The conversation was stilted, formal, and mostly questions. "Miss Amelia, whereabouts in America did you live?" "Miss Serena, what sort of education in your power did you have?" "Miss Amelia, does your father participate in Hunts?" *As if I didn't Hunt myself!* she thought indignantly.

"We do not often need to Hunt," she said aloud. "The population in general where we live is thin, as you would reckon it, and actual wilderness is well within a day's travel ahorse. Our plantation is about eight hundred acres, and there are larger ones than that not that far away. Indeed, the smallest I know of is a hundred acres or so."

There was an intake of breath from some of the men, who apparently were not aware just how large farms in the new United States could be. From the widening of their eyes, and a new look of respect, she realized that in their eyes she had just gone from "farm girl" to "daughter of a landed gentleman." Did that put her as the equivalent of the *ton*? Very possibly!

"There are not many magicians among the settlers, and those disposed to evil generally gravitate to the large cities, like New York and Boston. But all of the magicians on my father's plantation once formed our own Hunt to dispose of something that was *not* human about two years ago."

That startled them out of their complacency. "Not human?" exclaimed one, his collar points seeming to tremble with reaction. "Good gad, what was it, then?"

"Our native Cherokee friends from North Carolina called it *uyaga*. Never human, it was a kind of evil spirit of the earth. Several of their wise men came to us on a long journey to ask us for our help. They didn't have enough mages to Hunt it by themselves, so they came to Father to ask him to lead a Hunt alongside their wisest warrior, who was their equivalent of a Huntmaster, and to bring the best of his mages with him; that included myself and Serena." The journey back up to where the creature prowled had taken quite a few days, although, thanks to mild weather that made for fine camping, it would have been a pleasure trip but for what lay at the end of the trail. That day and night of a Hunt that ended, theatrically enough at dawn, held some of her proudest memories, although at the time, she'd been terrified.

One of the men guffawed in disbelief, and Serena's eyes flashed with annoyance. Amelia took good note of him: one of the dandies with tall collar points, she recalled that he was a Mr. Anthony Danvers.

And she immediately created a mental list of "men we wouldn't marry if they were next in line for the throne."

"We consider it . . . inappropriate . . . for young ladies to join a Hunt," another said—an older man who was probably "shopping" for a son. *Though perhaps for himself, one never knows.*

"We are thin on the ground, as I may have mentioned," she replied steadily. "We use whatever tool comes to hand. As Shakespeare says, *Needs must, when the devil drives,* and as you know, what we Hunt may sometimes include literal devils, human or otherwise. And—well—allow me to demonstrate something."

Now more used to drawing power in this house, she set her hand to the fireplace surround, which was of good, honest stone, and providentially connected straight to the earth through the foundation. She closed her eyes, and let the power flow. *Immense* power, because there was a ley line nearby, near enough that she could tap into it—and she sent it all right into anyone within the protective shields of the house, including the circle of visitors. No one in this house was individually shielded; they all counted on the house shield to protect them. And it wasn't as if an influx of enough Earth power to fill them was going to harm any of them.

Amelia smiled just a little as she encountered quite a lot of power, actually; it felt as if it hadn't been tapped for a very long time, and there was a significant amount available to her. An involuntary exclamation of "By *Jove!*" told her that she had achieved her goal, and she opened her eyes to see every one of these would-be suitors sitting straight upright, with eyes like saucers. In a few cases, it appeared that their hair was close to standing on end.

Smiling a little smugly now, she disconnected herself and let the flow ebb.

"Good heavens, Miss Amelia . . ." the older gentleman managed, before any of the others could speak. "Are you . . . are you actually a *Channel*?"

"Why, yes, sir," she said simply, exchanging a triumphant glance with Serena. "I am."

"Well . . . well . . . well," blustered another. "That's very useful if one is a *farmer*, I suppose."

Because of course it would not be useful to have a Channel among Hunters to reinvigorate them when they flag. Idiot. And Mr. Quentin Holden goes on my list.

"It is also very useful if one is on a Hunt and the Hunters are running low on their own personal power," she pointed out, allowing just a tinge of tartness to coat her words. Then she softened her speech again. "But of course, I am sure that never happens on Hunts here. It's not as if this is a wilderness full of ancient, dark spirits. And you have many more Hunters in your population than we do." She tilted her head to one side, inviting an answer.

But apparently they were not used to mere females standing up for themselves. After a moment, despite being filled to the brim with her generous gift, they decided not to say anything to her. "So, Miss Serena," Quentin said, pointedly turning toward her cousin. "I understand you are . . . Italian?"

"*Si, signori,*" she replied. "Or rather my grandfather is."

He smiled in a way that Amelia did not like, and Serena narrowed her eyes. *Oh, if only he knew what that meant in a leopard. . . .*

"*E da dovi vieni? Roma?*" he asked.

Serena laughed. "*Oh certo che no. Vengo dalla Carolina del Sud. Ma nio nonna, come ti ho ditto, veniva dall'Italia, sulle colline di Tuscani, un piccolo villaggio chiamato Pienza.*"

This was fired off so naturally, and so quickly, that he was left fumbling, trying to understand her. "F-from Tuscany?" he managed.

"*Si,*" she replied demurely. "Of course, we all learned the language. It is always good to know more than one language. One never knows who a Hunt companion may be, where we come from. Well! Like my grandfather!" Amelia could tell that behind Serena's demure expression she was doing her best not to laugh at him. All this was, of course, literally true, since it was quite true that one could not count on knowing all the members of a Hunt, and, like her grandfather, not all of them could be counted on to know English. But Quentin was flabbergasted that his (probably truer than he knew) assumption about Serena had been thrown in his face and turned to dust.

And from the expressions of the other men, she got the feeling that they enjoyed seeing Quentin "put in his place." It would appear that Quentin, besides aspiring to tulip status, was a bit of a prig.

Well, all the men were now warned that neither she nor Serena were inclined to be treated as foolish "mere" girls, and it set some of them back a bit. The ones like Quentin and Anthony made their farewells and took themselves off not long after that, but there seemed to be no lack of people wanting to take their places in the little parlor. By the time everyone had settled again, the parlor held about half men and half women, and Amelia was rather more on her guard. Somehow she and Serena were going to have to dance on a line between "truthful" and "pert," or even worse, "above their place"—

Although her sharp ears caught the murmur of "eight hundred acres" passing from those who had been here already to those who had just arrived, so perhaps that wasn't as much a danger as it had been before. *Landed status seems to excuse a great many sins.*

Keeping watch so carefully over her words was exhausting, and she was exceedingly glad when the visiting hours were over, and the maid showed the last of the visitors to the door. She was already on her feet and ready to go to her room when the maid returned with one last person: an older but clearly athletic and vigorous man, dressed in the very tip-top of the mode without being as ridiculous as Quentin, with his overflowing cravat and shirt collar that would not allow him to move his head. The newcomer was a singularly handsome man, older and graying, but with the head of a Roman god, the shoulders of a woodcutter, and the general physique of a man many years younger than his apparent age.

Julia rose to her feet and extended her hand. "Lord Alderscroft, this is an unexpected pleasure and a signal honor!"

The gentleman bowed over it as if she had been a duchess, and chuckled. "Surely not unexpected, Julia, given that you have had an 'at home' with these two lovely visitors who certainly belong in our circle! Will you—"

"Oh, certainly!" Julia dimpled. "Lord Alderscroft, may I present Miss Amelia Stonecroft and Miss Serena Meleva? Serena, Amelia, this is our Huntmaster, Lord Roger Alderscroft."

Amelia was the first to extend her hand; Serena was still recovering from the fact that she was standing in front of an actual lord. *Starstruck,* Amelia thought with amusement. "A great pleasure, my lord," she said. "I am always pleased to meet a Huntmaster."

Lord Alderscroft's mouth twitched a little. "And I am always pleased to meet a Channel. Such as you are uncommonly useful, no matter what the striplings new in their powers think."

She had to smile at that. *Oh, well struck! I believe a little bird has been whispering in the Huntmaster's ear.*

"Just as a matter of record," Alderscroft said, as he waited courteously for the ladies to resume their seats before he took his own on the sofa, "what *are* your primary powers, ladies?"

"Earth Master," Amelia said promptly. "And channel."

"Fire mage, my lord," Serena told him, finally recovering, although her eyes still shone with an adoration that Amelia found a little—just a little—irritating in someone who was an American. *A lord is just a man with a title. There are plenty of us who can't trace our lineage back a thousand years and never had a monarch wave a sword at us, who have as much power, land, and money, and who might have considerably more sense!* Well, on first sight, that last didn't apply to Lord Alderscroft, but it certainly applied to the Hon. Quentin.

Lord Alderscroft nodded, sitting with his cane planted at his knees and his hands folded over the ivory knob that surmounted it. "And I understand, Miss Amelia, that you and your brother have ambitions to establish an enterprise here?"

She nodded. "You will be aware of the fabric known as *cashmere,* I have no doubt."

He mock-shuddered. "Ruinously expensive." He chuckled. "And greatly to be desired, by both sexes."

"My father has arranged for a small—very small!—flock of the goats to be purchased. Difficult to obtain, and it took all of our magical as well as commercial connections to get them. It also took all our magical connections to get them across Asia and Europe alive and intact. I believe they are waiting for transportation from a port in Spain. Our family has quite the record of being able to make things thrive that should not in our climate, and my father is certain I can do the same with these goats. And my magic will also serve to make silkworms thrive, which will be easier, because I know they can be raised here in England, and were, in King James's time."

Somehow she felt that discussing business matters with the Huntmaster would not be met with the kind of scorn it would have been with at least some of the gentlemen that had lately filled the parlor. She was not disappointed. His eyes lit up with interest. "Something tells me that this planned enterprise of yours is rather more interesting than raising and shearing goats."

She nodded. She felt perfectly at home on this topic, since she had been included in her father and James's late-night discussions of the plan. After all, it could not be accomplished without her! "We need good pasturage for the goats, but also land that has flowing water sufficient to run several small mills. We intend to spin and dye our own threads and yarn, and weave our own fabric. *Bespoke* fabric. Small amounts of bespoke fabric, of cashmere, silk, and merino, and blends. We will sell these directly to select ateliers and tailors—such as Weston—since we will be producing directly in partnership with these artisans and supplying exactly what they specify."

Lord Alderscroft laughed aloud, a pleasant laugh with no scorn in it. "Oh, American ingenuity! Not only will the men of the *ton* be competing for such rare materials, the ladies will as well." His smile turned sardonic. "You had better offer the first suit to Prinny—that's the Prince of Wales. He's likely to take offense if you don't." And he added, as an afterthought, "Don't refer to him as 'Prinny' yourself. That's only for his intimate friends."

Amelia added that to her mental list—as soon as his lordship left, it would be added to the physical one as well. Meanwhile, Selena went into another spasm of adoration at the notion that Lord Alderscroft was intimate friends with the regent. "Thank you for the warning, my lord," Amelia said, with a hint of a curtsy, although she was sitting down.

"That satisfies my curiosity about you, Miss Amelia," his lordship continued, and turned his attention to Serena. "Miss Serena, my fiery familiars have whispered to me that you are more than just a Fire mage, and I am anxious to learn just what, precisely, that means."

Ah, he's a Fire Master. That makes sense in a Huntmaster. And oh, how the Elementals do gossip! She didn't know if they had actually told him that Serena was a shifter—it was sometimes hard to predict what an Elemental might or might not do—but they had surely at least hinted that Serena harbored a secret.

Serena shook off her haze of adoration in a trice, straightened, looked Alderscroft straight in the eye, and said, "I am a leopard shifter," in a tone that bordered on defiance.

"Not a wolf shifter?" He nodded once. "I don't believe I have ever heard of a leopard shifter before now."

"There are not many of us," was all Serena said.

"That may come in useful in the future." Amelia could tell that Lord Alderscroft was wildly curious, but good manners and the unspoken protocols between two "friendly" magicians made it impossible for him to press Serena for any more information.

So instead of asking her what he dearly wanted to, he quizzed them both on their magical education and abilities, exactly as a good Huntmaster should. Julia just sat back and waited, only sending the maid for tea and cakes as the questioning continued. Finally Alderscroft seemed satisfied, and sat back a little in a moment of silence.

"Miss Amelia," he said at last, "I believe I can give you a direction in your hunt for property. Devon is perhaps the best place to raise sheep and goats. It is well-watered by many good streams and rivers, and—there is no way of being delicate about this—there are a number of young dandies from thereabouts who have inherited within the past five years or so who are rapidly running through the family fortune. I can investigate the possibility they could be persuaded to sell, and you could investigate the properties to discover if any of them suit."

Amelia did gasp at that, because this was certainly going to be far more work than his casual words suggested. And he had only just met them! "My lord! That would be uncommonly kind!"

He smiled at her, quite as if they were good friends. "My price is a cashmere shawl for my wife from your first shearing."

"Done!" she almost crowed. "Where in Devon shall we begin?" She had the vague notion that, rather than being a city, Devon was a county. And, from the sound of things, rural.

"I have just the place. Axminster. It is a market town, it is near at least one of the properties I have in mind, and unless my memory is awry, I have a small house there, currently vacant, that I can let to you."

Privately, Amelia wondered just what his lordship would call a "small" house, but this sounded very much like exactly what she and Serena wanted. "Then let us consider it a bargain," she agreed, when a glance at Julia showed her that if she did *not* accept Alderscroft's offer, her hostess was likely to leap from her chair and strangle her!

His lordship ventured a few details about this property, though Amelia was quite sure anything short of a shed would suffice, but they were interrupted by a growing noise out in the street. In the next moment all of them were staring quizzically at the window. With a frown, Julia rang for the maid.

"Send Tommy out to find out what is going on, please," Julia told her. The maid curtsied and left.

And returned, much quicker than any of them would have anticipated, with her cap half-askew, and her face alternating between flushed and white. "Oh, ma'am!" the girl gasped, both hands twisting her apron into knots. "He's escaped, he has! He's escaped!" Then she burst into hysterical tears and shoved her face into the knot of cloth in her hands.

"Mary!" Julia snapped, more harshly than Amelia had ever heard her speak. "Make some sense! *Who* has escaped?"

"The very Devil himself, ma'am!" the girl bleated. *"Napoleon!"*

4

AMELIA had often encountered the phrase "she threw her apron over her head" in novels, but she had never seen that particular action until now. Because that was exactly what the maid Mary did—threw her apron over her head, still wailing, and blundered away in the general direction of the kitchen, bouncing off the walls because she couldn't see. Lord Alderscroft said something under his breath that Amelia strongly suspected was a profanity, and got to his feet. "Forgive me for leaving so abruptly," he said, "but I will be needed—"

Julia stopped him with a wave of her hand. "Say no more," she said. "We will continue this at a better time. You must go. Duty calls."

"Your servant, ma'am," said his lordship with a pull on the brim of the high-crowned hat he had just put on and a half-bow.

From where she sat, Amelia could just see the cloak tree in the hall. His lordship gathered the many-caped dark driving cloak from it with his own hands—surely a first!—and with a swirl of fabric threw it across his shoulders. With a gust of cold wind from the door, he was gone, presumably to find the horse he had ridden here on, or the curricle and groom he had driven here with. Amelia thought it would rather be the latter; the groom could be counted on to watch over the horses until his lordship left his visit; one could not count on a horse tied up in the yard behind a house not to come to, or cause some mischief. Besides, he was probably a notable whip, who would much rather drive than ride.

Julia was visibly annoyed, probably because Frank, the footman, was nowhere in sight. "I'll be back," said Julia, as another outburst of wailing came from the kitchen. She leapt to her feet and headed to the rear of the house with a look of determination on her face. Amelia followed. It had just occurred to her that if they were to rent a house, they must have servants, and she'd never handled servants in her life. Julia could provide a very instructive lesson in this situation. Down the stairs they went, to the half-basement level, where Amelia had never been.

It appeared that the entire staff had rushed to the kitchen, which was at the back of the house in the half-basement, and full of emotional people. Amelia had been made known to them all except the tweenie, and at least she knew the tweenie's name, though she hadn't yet seen the child. They didn't have tweenies at home; for that matter, they didn't have many servants, since there were so many household members to do what was normally done by servants here.

She and Julia paused in the door to the kitchen, which lay at the bottom of the stairs. Mary (the upstairs maid), Jemma (the cook's helper), Ginny (the tweenie), and Sarah (the maid-of-all-work) wailed inconsolably while being scolded vehemently for their emotional outburst by Mrs. Gideon, the cook, and Mrs. Jennings, the housekeeper.

Amelia personally thought that Mrs. Gideon was making things a lot worse, not better. The more she scolded, the more Mary cried, and the other three were taking their cues from Mary.

Frank (the footman) shouted his fury at "Boney" and vowed to protect the women, while Davey (the coachman and groom and a much older man than Frank) shouted for everyone to *be quiet, a man can't think,* while young Tommy (the hall-boy, page, and errand boy) looked as if he was torn between joining the women in wailing or Frank at shouting.

Julia stamped her foot, and a sudden gale of icy wind whirled through the kitchen, sending dishcloths and caps flying and flour into the air, and momentarily stealing the breath it would take to shout or cry.

Well, that's an interesting use of Air magic. Useful!

Silence descended except for the limited fury of the wind, which left actual frost in its wake. Julia let it circulate for a moment or two, then dropped the wind to nothing with a clap of her hands. Cloth items fluttered to the floor, and flour settled everywhere. And blessed silence reigned.

There was still some sniffling, but her point had been made, and she stood in the door with her arms crossed, face stony. "Mary Johnson, I am surprised at you. You are a grown woman, and you should have more sense! Are you afraid Napoleon is going to crawl in through the kitchen window in the night and strangle you in your sleep? I assure you, he has more important things to do, though I am sorely tempted to do the deed myself!"

"But spies!" Mary managed, scrubbing at her face with her apron. "And them sabatoobers! And—"

"No 'ands,'" Julia said firmly. "No 'buts.' There is no reason for any soldier or agent of Napoleon to travel all the way from the continent to enter this house. And even if there was, good gracious! You all have some magic! Use it to protect yourselves from intruders while you sleep if you're afraid! And if you fear you lack the power, just ask Miss Amelia for help! Didn't you all feel her channel power to you this very afternoon? She can channel enough to you to make you as safe as if you had a soldier at the foot of your bed to guard you!"

There was some shamefaced nodding from the adults, but the younger members of the household looked unconvinced, and ready to burst into tears again at the slightest provocation. Without prompting, Serena edged her way past Amelia and whispered in Julia's ear.

"That would be very helpful, Serena," Julia said quietly. "Please do." Serena left the kitchen, and with a sudden flash of inspiration, Amelia realized what it was she had asked their hostess.

Julia's next words confirmed it. "You all know Miss Serena is a shifter, but I don't believe any of you have seen her in her shifted form, so you don't know how formidable she is. She has just now promised me to shift every night and guard the house while we sleep." She looked over her shoulder. "Haven't you, Serena?"

The leopard—complete with the incongruous pearl necklace about her neck that she almost never took off—shouldered her way past Julia, purring loud enough to be audible throughout the kitchen. The sight of her was enough to stop even the sniffling. Amelia suffered a moment of concern that Serena would frighten the youngest of the staff, but Ginny tugged at the cook's apron and begged, "Kin I pet 'er?"

"You can certainly pet her," Amelia confirmed. "You can even brush her; we brought her brushes with us, and she is very fond of a good brushing."

"Cor!" Ginny said, wide-eyed.

"Coo!" agreed Tommy.

Now that the tumult was over, it was possible to see that all of the female members of the staff wore sensible dark dresses with white aprons over them to keep them clean, and in the case of all but Ginny, white kerchiefs tucked into the front for modesty and warmth. In Ginny's case, a worsted scarf had been wrapped around her little throat—a kindness to the thin child that Amelia suspected was due to the concern of her mistress. The men all wore dark knee breeches, gray woolen stockings, dark coats without tails (except for Frank), and worsted waistcoats. All wore sturdy shoes except for Davey, who wore thick boots.

"Where would you like Serena to spend the evenings when we are all closed in for the night?" Amelia asked, as Ginny's hands twitched, as if she could not wait to touch that soft fur. "Would you prefer her to be in the parlor, in the kitchen, or—" She looked askance at Julia, since she had no idea of the layout of the "downstairs" portion of the house.

"Since there is a door to the outside yard in the kitchen, Serena, I would like you to make regular patrols from the kitchen," Julia declared. "We can fix up a bed beside the fire so you'll be comfortable." She turned toward the staff. "You all remember when Bosky was with us?"

Everyone nodded except Tommy and Ginny.

"Then you'll remember how he slept by the kitchen fire and patrolled the house at night, and how he heard *everything* going on outside and alerted Davey, Frank, and Mrs. Gideon to anything he thought suspicious. Serena will do the same thing, and her senses are keener than Bosky's were."

"Well—" Amelia temporized, "if we go to a rout or a ball, we probably will want to come home late, and it's not fair to ask Serena to come home early."

The practical and pragmatic housekeeper had something to say, and the presence of her mistress did not keep her from saying it. "Yes, but Frank and Mary stay up until you all come home when you're out of a night, and I would think Frank should be able to deal with any window-sneaking Frenchies." Mrs. Gideon sniffed. "Not to mention, who's to say if there even *will* be any routs or balls whilst that devil is loose."

Serena had padded across the kitchen floor by this time, and was engaged in rubbing her head against the three who had been doing the most wailing, plus Tommy. This was tactical; they could see her big teeth and formidable claws up close. They might have seen bearbaiting; they had certainly seen dogs fighting and would know the damage those teeth and claws could do. Mary seemed very impressed, but all little Ginny wanted to do was bury both hands in Serena's fur and press her cheek against Serena's neck.

It was very clear that Serena's promise to guard the denizens of downstairs at night had quieted most, if not all, of the irrational fears. As for the rational ones, well, that remained to be seen.

"It is not night yet, it is not even time for tea, and Miss Serena has things to do," Julia said tactfully, reminding the servants without saying as much that *they* had things to do. Serena gave a last head bump to Ginny and eeled her way around legs and table to leap up the stairs.

"Yes, ma'am," came the ragged chorus, and now that the crisis had been averted, Amelia and Julia followed Serena up the stairs. Amelia could not help but notice how much warmer it was down in the working part of the house—and very pleasant, although she knew that in most houses, fuel not intended for cooking was scant in the servants' quarters, maids were quartered in cold and drafty attics, with the warm and well-lit rooms reserved only for the housekeeper and perhaps the cook, and the idea that the basement should be lit by good oil lamps was unthinkable. Serena was not going to suffer by playing "guard dog."

Modern fashions—and the fact that neither Serena nor Amelia had any difficulty getting into and out of a pair of stays unaided—had enabled Serena to slip into her clothing very quickly, although she was still tugging at fabric to adjust things as they entered the parlor. "Who's Bosky?" she asked, slipping her stockings on, tying them up above the knee, and tucking her feet into her slippers. To Amelia's relief, Julia seemed unperturbed by her lack of modesty.

"Our last dog, of the bull-baiting breed," Julia explained. Frank came up at that moment (and Serena had finished dressing not a moment too soon!), and she desired him to find a newspaper. He went out into the cold. They gathered their shawls about themselves as he opened the front door and a cold gust blew through the house, making the lamp flames waver in their chimneys. "We got him to guard the house, although he guarded the girls more than the house. I never would have believed a dog of that breed was so intelligent, and so tender with children. The number of things he kept them from getting into was past counting. I'll never forget the time I was busy letting down Sophia's hem and he brought me little Ann, carrying her by the back of her gown, and dropping her at my feet with a speaking look and a heavy sigh—and it turned out that she had been repeatedly trying to crawl into the fire while the other four were dancing around Nursey, distracting her, and Bosky had intervened before Nursey could get to her—not once, but at least a dozen times!" Her voice grew husky, and she wiped a tear from one corner of her eye. "Bosky is why we never got another dog after he died when Ann was ten. Not because we didn't need one, but because Bosky could never be replaced."

Amelia nodded, and Julia regained her composure. "Well, even if we are not to get spies and insurrectionists invading the house, this business of Napoleon is very bad news, and it may well have a great effect, not only on the pleasures we intended to pursue, and your intentions to relocate to hunt for a property for the Stonecroft enterprises, but virtually everything. The Stock Exchange, I would imagine, is a pit of insanity right now, and I am sure my husband and your brother will have plenty to say when they get home." She took a seat near the fire, and wrapped her shawl more securely about herself while the room warmed again. "I don't know why that horrid man couldn't stay where we put him!"

Amelia, whose sentiments were torn, given how lately the British had been attempting to re-conquer the United States, simply kept her thoughts to herself on the subject. But she could not help thinking, with a touch of resentment, *Well, now you all know how it feels to fear armies marching through your cities and burning what they don't blow up or steal!* Why, the final battle of the latest war between Britain and the United States had taken place a mere three months before she and Serena had left on their voyage!

Of course, Julia and her family were scarcely to blame for that, but Amelia was not at all unhappy that those who *were* responsible were about to endure many sleepless nights.

"Then again," Serena said cheerfully, "there may be *more* parties and routs, as people wish to send off officers in their families in a cheerful fashion!" Amelia was about to chide her for being so shallow, when she suddenly understood that Serena was trying to raise their hostess's low spirits. "And in any event, now I need not hide my other self from the servants, lest they be frightened."

"They certainly welcomed your offer of protection," Julia agreed, and made a visible effort to shake off her lowered mood. "Well, if there are to be *more* parties and routs, or even a ball or two, we must devote ourselves to the construction of stockings, slippers, and gloves and the trimming of petticoats and gowns. And if there are not, well, we shall do what we may to aid where we can, and wear our finery about the house to raise our spirits. Shall we get our work-baskets?"

"I'll read while you work to speed your fingers," Amelia offered, secure in the knowledge that her stocking drawer was full, her gloves were finished, and her slippers nearly so. "Poetry or a novel?"

Julia smiled a little at that. "I have just obtained *The Recluse of Norway* from the lending library," she said, cheering up a good deal. "I very much doubt it would be to the taste of my husband or James, so we ladies can enjoy it in peace. I shall get it along with my work-basket!"

But Amelia was not to read the novel after all, at least not at first, since it appeared that Serena's transformation was much on Julia's mind. "If you do not think it impolite," Julia began, as they all settled in the parlor as the warmest room in the house—bar the ones down-stairs (which Amelia began to think of with longing), "I should like very much to know how it is that Serena takes the form of a leopard. I have never heard of a shifter taking the form of anything other than a wolf or a bear."

"Bears?" Serena said, dark eyes flashing as her interest piqued. "There are bear shifters?"

"Mostly from the north, where the Vikings originated." Julia shifted her chair closer to the fire. Frank had not yet returned with a newspaper, but it was possible, even likely, that there were none to be had yet. Amelia had opted for draping her everyday woolen shawl over her lap. Serena alone looked comfortable, but then again, Fire mages were almost never cold unless they were barefoot and in a shift in a blizzard.

"Well, we did promise you the story. . . ." Serena looked at Amelia, who closed the book in her lap and buried her hands in the wool of the shawl.

"Well, it properly begins with my great-great-grandfather, the one who started the farm when it was still a farm and not a plantation," Amelia offered. "At the time, South Carolina was about half slave-holding households and half not. Now, it's almost all slaveholders. He was nominally a Quaker—well, nominally all the Stonecrofts are Quakers—and he was extremely opposed to slavery."

"Is that the usual thing?" Julia asked, but in tones that suggested she was not sure.

"No, not all Quakers are, and there are many slaveholding Quakers—" She took a deep breath, lest she digress into the ways and beliefs of Quakers on the subject. "At any rate, when he had the money to spare, he would go to the slave market or look for indentured servants with Elemental powers." She bit her lip. "I know it sounds as if he was picking and choosing whom to help, and he *was*, but his money was limited—*our* money is limited, and—"

"No need to apologize," Julia soothed.

"At any rate, one day he went to the slave market, and to his shock there was a man up for sale literally hung with so many chains he could not move, and Elijah Stonecroft saw he was an Earth *Master*. No one wanted to buy the man—whispers in the crowd said that he was uncontrollable, even mad—so Elijah was able to buy him, even with his limited funds, which would not normally have extended to a powerful man in his prime."

"That man was *my* great-grandfather," Serena said.

"The slave dealers refused to take the chains off, so Elijah was forced to have the poor man loaded into the back of his wagon. Literally *loaded*; the poor fellow could hardly move. He wrote down in his commonplace book later that the look in the man's eyes would have terrified anyone other than an Elemental Master, but he was able to get his Elementals to get the man's native language from his mind, and he had a plan." Amelia confined herself to a strict retelling of what she knew and what she had read in the commonplace book. In her experience, embroidering a true tale tended to make it sound less true.

"You can imagine Great-Grandfather Meleva's shock when this white man spoke to him in his own language, and asked him—politely!—to remain calm while he took the chains off. And when he consulted the Elementals that had been with him since he had been taken captive, *they* told him that he was in safe hands! He didn't quite believe it, of course, so as soon as the chains were off, he shifted." Serena took up the thread. "He was shocked enough to remain where he was, however, counting on the leopard to keep the stranger from daring anything, and eventually Elijah convinced him to listen to him."

"And Elijah made him the same offer he had made to all the slaves and indentured servants he had bought. Elijah would *try* to get him home, but there was no guarantee that someone else would not abduct him on the way and make him a slave again. Or he could stay and help work the Stonecroft farm, as an equal to Elijah's other workers, be paid, and live like one of the family. Then he left Meleva standing at liberty in the yard beside the wagon to think things over, while he put the mules away."

"Obviously Great-Grandfather realized that Elijah was right, and he took Elijah up on his offer. As the farm grew and Elijah took on more land and more workers, all on the same basis as Meleva, it became obvious to him that he'd made the right decision." Serena giggled. "Especially after he married one of Elijah's daughters and became a full partner! That was when he took a first name of 'John' and kept Meleva as his family name."

"But—" Julia said, looking baffled. "Isn't that . . . illegal in the United States? The marrying, I mean."

"Of course it is. No one knew it except the people on the farm. And that's why we tell people Serena is Italian. In fact, if any of our people is light-colored enough, we tell them to say they are Italian." Amelia sighed. "It's very complicated. But you wanted to know about the shifting—"

Julia nodded, sewing lying forgotten in her lap. Amelia was very relieved that she took the news that Serena was part African and not part Italian without turning a hair. Serena took up the thread again.

"Great-Grandfather was a member of a very small tribe of leopard shifters called the Anyoto. But that gets complicated, because there are the *real* Anyoto, who can shift, and there is the much larger group of—well, they are just criminals who call themselves Anyoto, wear leopard skins and claws, and terrorize and murder the members of other tribes. The *real* Anyoto are very secretive, and try, well, just to live their lives. All of them are Elemental mages, but a Master like my grandfather only comes along once every generation or so."

Julia sucked on her lower lip. "Then . . . how did slavers manage to capture him?"

Serena grinned gleefully. "That is a very long story, and *ever* so much more interesting than a novel!"

Amelia sighed, and resigned herself to hearing a story she knew by heart . . . again . . . and accepted that she would not get to delve into the pages of what looked like a very fine novel. Not today, anyway. At least this would take Julia's mind off Napoleon.

The men came home full of news in time for a late tea, but none of it was concrete. "It's mostly speculation." Thomas Angleford sighed over his cup, and looked significantly at James. "But Parliament is in an emergency meeting, the Stock Exchange closed early, and the only people likely to find out precisely what is going on at this moment are the magicians."

"Who cannot reveal what we know without meeting with skepticism at best and accusations of treason at the worst," added James. "But we'll leave that to Alderscroft. That's his business, and the business of the other few mages in Parliament and the military. If anyone such as we even suggested we had a way to know, we'd be considered as mad as the king if we were lucky."

Well, that could be taken poorly. Amelia helped herself to one of the delicious little cakes.

Their host frowned slightly at the mention of King George's madness, but he couldn't really take exception to the statement, since it had been common knowledge even in the United States these many years.

"*Should* we try to find out?" Julia asked tentatively.

Thomas shook his head. "What would be the point? It's not as if we can do anything with the information aside from fret. Besides,

Napoleon has mages on his side as well, though he knows it as little as the prince regent does. Any attempt on our part to scry would almost certainly be blocked, and would perhaps open us up to a magical attack. What we can do is make sure James's precious goats are safe, our shippers are warned, and our men are in no danger of being conscripted. The Empire will be neither helped nor harmed by us tending to our own business." He pondered for a moment. "You might wish to secure ample foodstuffs in case there is panic buying—"

"I already sent Cook and Tommy out in the carriage to do just that," Julia interrupted. "The news had not yet penetrated far enough into the market that prices had changed much. That will certainly change by tomorrow, if it hasn't already."

Thomas nodded his approval. "Go ahead and pay your *modiste* tomorrow. Her sort operate on slender enough margins as it is. Any of her clients in the *ton* are likely to use this as yet another excuse to delay bills, and she has given us excellent service over the years. We could never have brought out six girls without her giving us truly excellent prices for her work."

Amelia wondered at the statement about the "clients in the *ton*." If she had not paid her dressmaker's bills on time—not that she had had more than two in her lifetime, since most of her clothing, and Serena's, were made at home—she would not only never have gotten work from that worthy again, she'd have had to go as far as Charleston to get another dressmaker to work with her! But perhaps the rich and the ennobled were not held to the same rules here.

Julia nodded. "Serena has agreed to stand guard in her leopard form at night downstairs, which was very good of her."

"It *is* very good of you, and I hope you will feel free to doze as much as you care to by day, Serena," Angleford said warmly. "I am afraid that Napoleon looms larger than life as a kind of devil in the minds of many, and as many of them are trembling like the crystals on their chandeliers as huddling beneath tallow lights tonight."

Amelia saw Serena bite her lips slightly, and their eyes met in a mutual understanding that told Amelia that her cousin was having some of the same uncharitable thoughts she was. But Serena merely said, "They were in such distress I could not help but offer. It will not be the first time I, and those of my extended family with my ability, have stood guard at night because of threats, or perceived threats. And I don't suppose it is entirely out of the question but that there *will* be Elementals poking and spying at the behest of their magicians on behalf of Napoleon, just as there will be Elementals doing the same on the Continent."

"True." Thomas frowned. "And I would not discount the notion that either side might order their Elementals to create as much havoc and mischief as they can, if only to keep their opposite numbers occupied."

Amelia nodded soberly, thinking of just how easily fire could spread in this crowded city. Or how catastrophic one would be among the powder magazines of the Army and Navy! That, more likely than not, was the purview of Lord Alderscroft and his set right now.

One has to wonder how much the burning of Washington was done by Fire Elementals.

Probably not a great deal, because magicians did have many ways of getting themselves out of military service, but some was certainly likely.

And Serena was right; she and the rest of her kin who shared her shifting power had, indeed, stayed on guard many nights when a much more concrete threat had prowled the countryside, either in the form of British or Hessian soldiers, or in the form of no-good troublemakers out to take advantage of the situation and blame it on the British.

Ironically, one of those Hessians had deserted and joined the clan. A good farm boy from Saxony; a desperately homesick Earth mage who had been astonished to discover an entire small colony of Elemental mages in what he considered to be a "wild" land. His homesickness had been overcome by the familiar feel of Earth magic, and since his family had been displaced from their farm by an aristocrat—which was why he was in the Hessian mercenary unit in the first place—he had no trouble shifting his loyalty.

Amelia had learned Low German from "Onkle Frederich," and he had learned good English and French from her. He was one of the shepherds living in one of the outlying cottages with his wife and some very rambunctious children. That gave them plenty of warning if someone came looking for him, though after all this time it was unlikely.

She had yet to taste anything made with apples in this country that was the equivalent of Onkle Frederich's strudel. He swore no one could replicate his Mutti's recipe like he could.

The apple tarts here are awfully good, though, she thought, and took one.

"Since you'll be up late, Serena, would you like something in the way of a late-night meal?" Julia said, when the silence had gone on a bit too long.

Serena perked up. "That would be very nice," she agreed. "If there is leftover meat from supper, that would be ideal. The cat's stomach does not do well with vegetables."

Julia laughed a bit more heartily than the remark called for, though perhaps she was just relieved to have something to laugh at. "I'll arrange it with the cook," she said. "After your reassurance to them, I suspect I may find my best beefsteaks have gone for your repast!"

Within a few days, however, the alarm had passed. Everything had gone back to normal. Canceled invitations were re-sent for new dates. The Stock Exchange returned to its chaotic self. Even Lord Alderscroft put in another appearance one afternoon, although it was a brief one.

He arrived just as several young men—this time hopeful suitors of little power and less fortune—were leaving. All of them looked as if they had bought their suits *en masse* from the same tailor at the same time—and they probably had, getting a discount in the process. Clearly their incomes—or rather, their parents' incomes—were not sufficient to grant more than thirty days before the tailor bill came due. Amelia was in complete sympathy with them on that head. And if indeed that was what they had done, all she could do was applaud them for cleverness and saving a few shillings.

And if she had felt a partiality to any of them, lack of income would not have deterred her from accepting an offer. But . . . they were also all of a type, and she suspected that if their parents knew the *half* of what she and Serena were about, they'd be horrified.

So she fed them tea and Serena pressed cakes on them, and let them at least have a few hours when they weren't getting themselves into mischief and were being reasonably entertained by stories of what life was like in America.

They looked alarmed to see Lord Alderscroft when he arrived, and made their farewells a bit more hasty than, perhaps, they had planned. Alderscroft looked at their retreating backs with amusement.

"Puppies," he said, as the footman took his hat and cloak. "I hope you are not pinning your hopes on any of them. They are mostly calling on you because their parents are in hopes that your fortunes are more than theirs."

Today his lordship's breeches were of a pale beige buckskin, his waistcoat an interesting dark red and black brocade, his tailed coat a color between black and red, his linen impeccable, and his Hessians polished to a mirror-gloss. Small wonder the herd retreated. Next to him they looked like a lot of grubby schoolboys.

"We'd assumed as much." Serena giggled. "I've no objection to an honest poor man as a husband, but those lads don't know enough to be anything, really. In my opinion, there is nothing wrong with their lot in life that some honest work could not cure, but I doubt their parents have the resources to provide that honest work. And they'll get themselves into trouble one day, if they don't get it."

Alderscroft raised an eyebrow at that bold statement, but acknowledged the truth of it with a slight nod. "If their parents don't do something about that, I suppose I will have to," he said with a faint frown. "I very much doubt that they'd do justice to a pair of colors, but appointments in Civil Service are not that hard to come by. Perhaps India. Relations with India are quite good at the moment. The Company can always muck that up, and probably will, but for now . . . that might be a good place to send them for some seasoning."

Amelia hadn't the faintest idea what he was talking about, but nodded anyway. Mostly she was pleased she was wearing something decent enough to be under his lordship's eye—her military-style gown, which had undergone a thorough cleaning under the hands of the housekeeper, Mrs. Jennings. Amelia had been intending to do it herself, but Mrs. Jennings had shooed her away, and after one look at how that good woman was working fuller's earth into every seam as well as brushing it thoroughly into the broader portions, Amelia had fled. It was clear her gown was in expert hands.

As for Serena, she would probably look glorious in a pillowcase, but today she looked enchanting in a refurbished, pale pink muslin with six pin-tucks at the knees and a new lace flounce at the hem, a rose-colored merino shawl over her arms, and a fetching little pale pink cap.

"I came today to let you know in person that I've already spoken to my man in Axminster, and the house is yours. It has been vacant for six months; there are some refurbishments he is in the midst of, and the chimneys all need sweeping, but it can be furnished and ready for you by summer. Will eight rooms and the servants' quarters be enough for you? The house is all furnished, so you won't be put to any trouble; just bring your own personal garments and move in. There is a small stable with sleeping quarters for a groom, and room for two horses and a pony to draw a light gig. The gig is already in the stable, and I can have horses and a pony brought down from my estate for you."

Amelia felt her mouth dropping open. This was the last thing she would have expected; she had anticipated having to acquire household goods and enlist Julia's help in setting everything up. Horses and ponies and gigs had not even entered her mind, although of course, on reflection, they'd need those. "Oh, my lord!" she exclaimed. "This is too much! You are too kind!"

His lordship's eyes actually twinkled, and Amelia only then noticed how tired they looked. Evidently things had not gone back to "normal" for him. "It is not every day that two eminently eligible, charming, and attractive young Elemental mage ladies, one of them a Master, turn up on my doorstep. I am endeavoring to find ways to keep you here when your commission for your brother is complete."

Amelia blushed to the roots of her hair.

"I should have had to find a tenant for it within the year anyway," he continued. "It was already furnished, and to be frank, good tenants are not thick on the ground, according to my man, let alone tenants that are mages. He was concerned that two young ladies were proposing to move in alone, but was relieved to hear of the existence of your brother." Now he was openly laughing, quietly. "I did not yet tell him that you are American, nor did I tell him that your brother is only likely to be a visitor. I want you to be settled in, and him persuaded that you are 'proper,' before I reveal that you are from a land of wild Indians and men wearing buckskin shirts and fur hats that still have the tails to them."

Serena broke into peals of laughter, and Amelia had to hide her face in her hand.

"I find myself grateful that Serena has not packed her Cherokee dress, or I am persuaded she would wear it to see the look on his face when we turn up," she choked.

"I might concoct a new one, depending on how stuffy he is," Serena confessed, still giggling a little. "Are we to look out our own servants? I assume we would outrage modesty if we did not have servants."

"You assume correctly, and the house does have ample servants' quarters. My man will take care of that; he'll find you someone reliable. A cook and housekeeper, a cook's helper, a maid, a man-of-all-work, and a groom. They will probably not have magic themselves, but they will come from households that do, and they will know about it. Or they might come from my estate; sometimes we have more young people with magic than places for them."

Amelia began to worry a bit at the expense of it all, but James walked in from the street just in time to hear all that, and quickly eased her mind. "Capital! Just the thing!" he said immediately, holding out his hand to Alderscroft, who shook it. "My Lord, we are grateful to you. This has saved me no end of trouble. When can they go down?"

"Summer. I would not ask anyone to venture on a journey of that sort in English weather until May at the earliest. June would be best. July will perhaps be too hot."

"My lord, you have not experienced a South Carolina summer," laughed Amelia. "We shall not be too hot, whatever the month is."

"I should be able to take some days off to accompany you on the post coach," James began, but Lord Alderscroft would not let him have another word.

"I will send one of my coaches," he said with determination. "Plenty of room for all their trunks and boxes. No one squeezing them into a corner, or forcing them to share the coach with a piglet or a pair of lambs."

Serena cast Amelia a look that said, plain as anything, *It would not be the first time we have shared a conveyance with a piglet or a pair of lambs.*

Amelia cast her one that said, *In some cases, I'd prefer the piglet,* and Serena could hardly contain her giggles.

"You are beyond kind, my lord," James said.

Lord Alderscroft actually grinned. "Tell me that when it is two in the morning, and we are all crouched in the heather on the moor, in mid-December, in the middle of a Hunt."

It would not be the first time we have been crouched in the middle of a—is a moor a kind of forest? In the wilderness, at any rate. At—well, we did not know what time it was, only that it was dark. In the middle of a Hunt.

She wondered what Lord Alderscroft would have thought of her had he seen her . . . in *her* Cherokee "dress," though it was not a dress at all, but a warrior's woolen leggings, knee-length woolen tunic, and moccasins. It had been far more practical than anything else they had on hand. Serena, of course, had been wearing her own fur at the time.

"We all three accept that challenge, my lord," she said cheerfully. "And we will be at your service."

"Well, I think I may need more American mages," he replied, looking as if he was willing to take her at her word. "And now, since everything is as arranged as may be until we draw closer to the day, I am forced to take my leave. There is much occurring I cannot divulge, but I wanted to make things all clear with you, so that I could devote my attention to it." He stood up. Amelia and Serena stood and bobbed little curtsies, James shook his hand and bowed over it, and Alderscroft turned to find Frank there with his hat and coat already. Frank looked as if he would have liked to say something, but of course he dared not, as a mere servant. But Alderscroft took his belongings and smiled into the footman's eyes. "I will indeed do what I can to give Boney a pasting, friend," he said. And then, to Frank's open-mouthed astonishment, he was gone, not even waiting for Frank to hold the door for him.

"'Ow did he know?" Frank finally said. "'Ow did he *know*?"

"He's Lord Alderscroft, the Huntmaster of the White Lodge of London," James said, with a certain amount of admiration in his voice. "I don't imagine there's much he doesn't know."

5

WHILE novels might have led Amelia to believe that life in London was one long round of amusements, she knew quite well that novels did not always portray the truth, and in fact, she had assumed that the chief amusements she and Serena would enjoy were walking, reading, and entertaining visitors at morning calls for the ladies who were Julia's intimate friends, and afternoon calls for ladies and gentlemen.

And one thing that *had* surprised her was the amount of leisure time having servants about gave her. Truth to tell, she was a bit dazzled by it.

But it seemed that novels were closer to reality than she could have imagined, because there certainly was a great deal more to do than walking, reading, and making calls. Once the initial fears induced by Napoleon's escape had been calmed, she soon found herself and her cousin chaperoned by Julia on a succession of more elaborate visits and quiet parties. They did indeed entertain visitors, but they were also entertained by ladies within both the trade circles and the magicians' circles, more often than they stayed at home.

Julia always warned them to watch what they said when they attended the at-homes of the former, but both of them had plenty of practice in keeping secrets behind their teeth. From those morning and afternoon excursions, they soon found themselves invited to small dinner parties, or evening parties of cards, games, music, and even dancing if there were enough couples for a set.

This was not the sort of thing Amelia was used to. The farms and plantations were so far apart that even among those who had more than ample slaves and servants rather than sharing the chores as the Stonecrofts did, it was too much effort to bring the carriage around, harness the horses, and drive for an hour or more for a small evening party, only to drive back for another hour in the darkness. Such gatherings happened no more often than once a month at the full of the moon, so the horses could see the road going home.

In fact, most parties at home were all-day affairs, beginning with a picnic luncheon, lawn games and cards in the afternoon, dinner, and more cards and dancing. One's very intimate friends might even be invited to spend the night rather than drive home in the dark. It was just not heard of that one could go to dinner and a party every night with a different family, but so it was here.

Speaking of dancing, it was with great relief that Amelia discovered that the dances in England were mostly not so different from the ones in America, and those that were—well, she and Serena swiftly found sympathetic partners at those evening parties willing to coax them through the steps. She *had* thought that the number of gowns she and Serena had been convinced to refurbish was somewhat excessive, but she soon decided that, if anything, the number was barely adequate considering all the requirements of these visits. The two of them were accustomed to rise, dress, and not change again unless there were guests for dinner, in which case, they would wear something elevated above their day gown. But here! They were to wear loose gowns in the morning, change again into something more formal after luncheon, *again* if they went out walking or calling, and *again* for dinner. And if they had been invited to dinner away, or a party, *again,* this time in one of the gowns they had formerly reserved for balls.

It was astonishing, and she could not imagine how Julia had ushered *six* daughters through the nonstop cascade of entertainments and entertaining.

In about the third week of their stay, as March was turning into April, she hurried down to the parlor having dithered over two of her gowns—one muslin, one wool—unable to tell from the weather outside if she was going to freeze in one or overheat in the other. Julia was already there, reading her mail, and looked up at her with a smile and a paper in her hand. Serena, as usual, was a little late.

"I have something to tell you," Julia said, "but we'll wait for Serena."

"My father says that Serena will be late to her own funeral," Amelia replied. "It's not entirely true—she is never late to things that are really important—but anything else—" She shrugged.

"I am not late," Serena replied from behind her. "I merely prefer to arrive last." She yawned discreetly as she entered the room. "Last night was challenging. The adults seem to have accepted that Napoleon is not going to whisk down the chimney like a witch, but the children are not so sure. They both had nightmares."

"It's very good of you to continue to stay downstairs overnight," Julia said earnestly.

Serena shrugged, and gave Amelia a speaking look. *It's probably time to say something,* that look said.

"Serena is used to caring for children with nightmares," Amelia said cautiously. "Much, much poorer and more mistreated children than your hall-boy and tweenie. You know that we are nominally Quakers; well, there is a sort of society among Quakers formed to aid runaway slaves, and we are part of that."

Julia's eyes and mouth both formed "o"s. "That is . . . illegal," she said.

"But moral, and our Christian duty," countered Amelia.

"And dangerous."

"Which is where our magic comes in. Illusions, deceptions, misdirections . . . we use every instrument available to us." Amelia was not precisely *daring* Julia to try to contradict her, but she was also not going to back down.

"Isn't that dangerous for Serena and her family?" Julia asked cautiously. "Should you be suspected, they are in very real hazard of being taken as slaves themselves."

"We would not have it any other way," Serena spoke up for herself. "Slavery is a vile institution, and should be abolished. No man should have the right to own another man." Her voice rose with passion, and her cheeks grew pink. "And the Biblical justification for it is *rubbish*. We eat lobster, we wear linsey-woolsey, we eat pig meat and veal roasted in milk, and the Bible forbids every bit of that! And the Bible allows a father to *murder* his children if they offend him! Why should we consider for even a *moment* that it is right and justified to keep slaves because the Bible allows it?"

She had risen to her feet as she spoke, and stood there looking every inch the fighter that she was. Her eyes flashed, and her hands were clenched at her sides. *It shows just how much in control of her shifting she is that there is not a leopard standing there in the midst of a tangle of clothing.* The blessing of modern fashion—especially a morning dress—meant that if Serena shifted without stripping off all her clothing, she would at least not ruin anything. At least not until she tried to rid herself of it.

Julia held up her hands in self-defense. "Pray, do not assail me further with words! I am entirely in agreement with you!" But she was laughing as she said it, not as if she was denigrating Serena, but in mild protest at the vehemence that really should not have been directed at her. "Perhaps, besides becoming acquainted with the magicians of Axminster if you settle there, you should also become acquainted with the abolitionists, and I certainly have contacts to introduce you!" She sobered. "I believe as you do, and have supported the abolitionist cause for as long as I can remember. Our early visit to your father merely confirmed both of us in that belief."

Serena sighed and sat back down. "I am sorry, but this cuts very near to the bone for me. I can't help becoming angry."

"And you have every right to be. But I did not wish to speak to you this morning of such weighty subjects. I believe it is time we all attended an assembly. We are subscribers to Payne's Assembly Rooms, and I have just gotten tickets for you in the mail this morning."

"Is this a ball?" Serena asked, entirely diverted.

"It is, of a sort. They are held weekly, and although we don't attend nearly as often as we did when the girls were with us, my husband and I usually go once a month or so. There are rules, but they are easy to follow. It will not be a crush, but it will be well attended. You will definitely meet some of the people who have called on us, young men and women in particular. I believe that you are both proficient enough in dance that you will not cast shame on any of us." That last was spoken with a twinkle in Julia's eyes and a smile on her lips. "Now that your ballgowns are here from Madame, you should get some use out of them."

Amelia could scarcely contain a rush of excitement, and Serena did not even try, and she was, for now, diverted from more serious subjects. But they both had to calm down as Julia explained the rules to them. How their places in the sets would be dictated by the number placed on their tickets by the Master of the Assembly Room. How they were to behave. How they must on no account drop out of the set unless they were ill or hurt, or there was some injury to their gown that required repair. "If you do not like the partner you have, you may not change him until the end of the set," Julia said with emphasis. "In any case, you will not have to dance with him again that evening. To dance twice with the same man suggests an attachment between you, and that is simply not done unless you are formally engaged."

It was Amelia's turn to laugh. "I wish we had that rule at home," she confessed. "There are few enough of us at balls that there is little chance of avoiding a partner you dislike." She glanced at Serena. "Donald," she said simply, and Serena shuddered.

"Ugh," she agreed. "He always looks as if he is intending to eat you. *Ugh.*"

"The dancing will begin at seven, and end at midnight, which should be quite enough dancing for anybody," Julia finished. "That is generally the rule at Assembly Rooms. It is only at private balls that dancing continues past midnight, and most of our acquaintances do not have ballrooms in their homes."

Amelia sighed a little. "And I suppose those that do would not admit those in trade to their balls."

"Well, they do, but only if the ball is composed entirely of magicians and hosted by magicians. There *may* be a chance that Lord Alderscroft will hold such a ball. He seems to be much taken with you two, and if his duties to the regent, prime minister, and Parliament allow, I think he *might* persuade himself to do so in order to give you some pleasure and the chance to attend an event that surely will be one of the highlights of this spring." She held up a hand, forestalling any shows of excitement. "I do not say he will, I only say he *might.*"

"We will not count on it. If he does, we shall be eternally grateful to him," Serena said firmly.

"And if he does not, we will say nothing of it. He has already been extraordinarily good to us," Amelia added. "All that work he has done to aid us in placing us in Axminster! He has made our hunt for an establishment for James much easier."

"I meant to tell you that he has just today also promised to look out for a place at Oxford for your brother George as well. With his patronage, there will be no difficulty in getting him established." Julia smiled at their exclamations.

"Oh!" Amelia could not help but cry. "George has *so* wanted to attend a real university! I am ashamed to say that even the best of our colleges does not come up to the academic rigor of an English university."

George was the most bookish of the great Stonecroft "herd." Amelia could easily see him settling in to Oxford to eventually becoming a don and never leaving. Especially if there was some . . . secret curriculum for magicians.

"I believe he intends to discuss all this the next time he comes to call." Julia looked as if it was all settled, which pleased Amelia no end. "So once you have all had the opportunity to discuss this with his lordship, you should ask your father to send George over in the summer."

And it is a good thing we will have that spare room, so George can stay with us until the term begins in the autumn.

That was extremely welcome news, although it paled in comparison to the news that they were to attend a real ball at an Assembly Room, such as they had read about in the ladies' journals. Not Almack's, alas . . . but Amelia knew all too well that every young woman of noble blood in all of London would have to drop dead at once before someone *in the trades* would ever be considered for one of the much-sought-after vouchers to that particularly hallowed hall. Probably not even then. The lady patronesses would probably rather send vouchers to poor little church mouse daughters and sons of impoverished vicars of "good breeding" who would have to stand up in their Sunday dress than send a single invitation to someone in the trades.

They'd probably send vouchers to people of the right breeding in prison before they sent one to us!

Why, there were plenty of people of noble birth who could not get one, for one "reason" or another. Either they had offended the lady patronesses, or they had broken one or more of the unspoken rules.

"This will be Thursday night, so you have two days to anticipate the pleasure," Julia continued. "White gloves will be required, but otherwise there are no restrictions in dress. Can you think of any other questions?"

"Will there be waltzing?" Amelia asked, uneasily. She could not imagine herself dancing in such close physical proximity to an absolute stranger.

"Absolutely not," Julia said firmly. "Payne's Assembly Rooms are *respectable*. It is all very well for Almack's to permit the waltz, but Almack's also admits people who may be of high birth, but are of low morals." She actually sniffed a little.

Amelia was both amused and relieved. Amused, because of Julia's faint snobbery. *Dance the waltz, indeed! How decadent! How depraved! We are respectable tradespeople and we will do no such thing!* Relieved, because she really did not want to find herself with the paws of some creature like Donald Evans about her waist. It was bad enough to have to stand up for an entire set with someone of the sort. It would be horrid to find oneself in its embrace. *Ew. Those slobbery lips . . . inches from my face.*

Someone like *that* would not hesitate to try to snatch a kiss. And while *she* would not hesitate to stop in her tracks and deliver a good slap with her fan, that would certainly bring an end to what had been a pleasant evening. And, for all she knew, ensure that no further tickets were forthcoming.

She shook herself out of her woolgathering and attended to Julia, who was glad to have her help in sorting through her mail, although it was clear that the only thoughts in Serena's head at the moment were visions of the pleasures to come. And who could blame her? This was surely going to eclipse every dance they had ever attended in their lifetimes!

Eventually the mail was dealt with, letters were sealed and addressed, and stamps applied. Julia brought up the subject again. "Now . . . if you merely wish to *see* Almack's, there are concerts and the like there that are not so exclusive. Samuel Harrison is well worth hearing, for instance. Perhaps we might have seemed much of home bodies because we have only gone out of an evening to friends' dinners, but we did not wish to fatigue you by adding too many things to do at the beginning of your visit," Julia continued. "But as your father said, there are many things we can take you to, depending on what you are partial to."

"Well, we would very much like to hear some proper music, played by proper musicians," Serena ventured. "An opera, perhaps," she added wistfully. "I have never seen an opera. I have only read of them, and they sound . . . glorious." *She has no more idea of how much tickets to an opera cost than I do.* But Amelia did not blame her; she felt the very same. She could count the number of times in their lives they had heard truly professional musicians on one hand. Usually, even at the rare balls, the music was provided by whoever was available at the time. Opera only appeared in the form of sheet music of arias.

"Or perhaps we could see a play?" Amelia suggested, thinking that surely a play would not be as costly as an opera.

But to her delight, Julia just nodded as if all these wishes had been anticipated, and the pleasure would be presented in due course. "If my husband is feeling fatigued, I am sure we can persuade James to escort us. Thankfully he seems completely oblivious to the charms of the sporting and gambling establishments, and he did appear to enjoy *The Magic Flute* and the plays he attended with us." She smiled, as Amelia's hopes rose. If they had taken James, who tended to abstain from such frivolities in favor of a good book by the fire, then perhaps such delights were not at all out of reach. "Well, if you have nothing you need attend to for the assembly, would you like to come with me on my morning calls?"

"Of course!" Serena said quickly, as Amelia nodded. Julia seemed to get a great deal of pleasure introducing them to her circle of acquaintances as if they were some sort of exotic beasts. And indeed, the kinds of questions people asked them did seem to reflect that. *Then again, if our positions were reversed, I would probably do the same thing.* Their hosts had been so kind that it seemed little enough recompense to be trotted around and asked about Indian raids.

They both ran up to fetch cloaks, shawls, and bonnets. There would be plenty of time later to go into raptures about what was to come.

Payne's Assembly Rooms were in a single large building, looking very raw and new among its companions, set among shops and accommodations. The front was plain brick, with Grecian columns between the tall and generous windows. Golden light shone from within, framed by curtains that appeared in the dusk to be a reddish brown color. But from here at the ground level, it was impossible to see anything else other than a glimpse or two of a crystal chandelier.

As they arrived in their carriage, it was very difficult for both of them to restrain their excitement. Other carriages were arriving—of course—and they joined a line in front of the building. The carriages dropped off their occupants, and as the Anglefords had generously arranged for them to be on the building side of the carriage as they approached, they both craned their necks to catch a glimpse of the lucky attendees. There wasn't terribly much to be seen, as the ladies at least were swathed in shawls or enveloped in cloaks, but Amelia caught the sparkle of necklaces and hairpieces, and the waving plumes of ostrich feathers. She touched her garnets self-consciously, and was at least glad that Julia had supplied them both with ostrich plumes.

She was wearing her brick-red velvet, which was split up the front to reveal an ivory damask underdress. Both were trimmed with matching blond lace and ivory rosettes. Her precious garnets were at her throat and her ears, and holding her ostrich feather in her hair. Even beneath her wool-lined, black velvet cloak, she was cold.

Or perhaps that was just excitement, because she felt as she had as a child on Christmas, almost sick with anticipation. Serena, true to her name, looked as calm as a statue, but of course, she had long ago learned to tame her emotions. It wasn't wise for a Fire mage to allow her passions free range. Perhaps that was why Fire mages rarely manifested their powers as young as those of the other Ele-mental mages. Otherwise their parents would have been replacing their houses on a regular basis. Serena's cloak matched Amelia's, but her gown was of rose-pink damask, trimmed in deeper pink satin, with a ruffled flounce at the hem, and short sleeves. She wore a set of deep golden citrines that matched Amelia's garnets. Both of them wore the required white gloves that extended almost to the shoulder, and which were the only thing keeping Amelia's arms "warm."

At last it was their turn! The carriage pulled up to the front, and it was time for them to be handed out by Frank, and enter the doors.

Julia had prompted them well. The great ballroom was upstairs, flanked by a card room and a refreshment room. The refreshments were nothing one could use to substitute for supper: bread and butter sandwiches, biscuits, fruit, tea cakes, tea (*"don't drink the tea,"* James had whispered as they left, *"dishwater is preferable"*), orgeat, negus, wine, and lemonade. James had allowed that the wine was tolerable, as was the negus (*"if you like that sort of thing"*), the lemonade was good, and the tea cakes very good, but everything else was indifferent.

But really, Amelia thought, as they climbed the internal staircase to reach their goal, *why would you come to a ball to eat?*

The stairs were broad, and *looked* superficially like marble, though her Earth senses told her immediately that they were cunningly painted wood. No matter. The stairs were not what they had come for. She and Serena followed in the wake of the Anglefords, who stepped up to a stupendously important-looking man with a list. Thomas Angleford presented them with the all-important voucher and the tickets. "These are my guests, Amelia Stonecroft and her cousin Serena Meleva. They will be taking two of the tickets assigned to my daughters for the duration of the Season."

The Guardian of the Door looked them over, and appeared pleased. He wrote something down in a great book on a plinth beside him, and wrote numbers down on the tickets. He handed two to Thomas Angleford, and one each to Amelia and Serena. "The number is your place in the first set of the first dance. Thereafter, if you are in the first set, your number goes up until you reach one. After you dance the first couple in that set, you go down to the bottom," he explained, as if to children. They nodded; it would not do to offend him, since he could bar them entirely. "If there is more than one set, you may take whatever place you find empty." He glanced up the staircase with satisfaction. "There should be five hundred people here tonight; you probably will *not* find a place in the first set all night. Still! You may be lucky. Welcome to Payne's."

And with those words of dismissal, he turned to the next in line and they were free to mount the stairs and enter the hallowed spaces of the ballroom.

Amelia was still dazzled and a little stunned at the notion that there would be *five hundred* people here tonight. *Five hundred!* Why, that was almost more people than the entire town of Cardington, South Carolina could boast. Well, not counting the slaves. No one but the Stonecrofts ever counted the slaves. . . .

But, *five hundred people* in one room. It seemed impossible!

And yet . . . after being relieved of their cloaks and coats, when they entered the room itself, it appeared that it was very much possible.

There were beautiful chandeliers hanging from the ceiling, brilliantly illuminating the room from what looked like hundreds of candles. Huge mirrors between each window reflected the light back into the room. Sofas lined the walls beneath the windows, which were framed by dark gold curtains. The air was filled with the scent of flowers, as huge bouquets decorated plinths between each sofa. An orchestra of ten or twelve musicians was tuning up at the left, and two open doors in the wall at the far right led, Amelia guessed, to the card room and the refreshment room. The air was a confusion of several different perfumes and pomades.

The first longways set of twelve couples had already formed, and they were waiting patiently in their double line for the musicians to begin. The second set was forming out of the milling crowds, who were keeping neatly to the edges of the room. There was space for a third set at the front, still. "How do we—" she began.

"You come with us," said Thomas, and, taking his wife's arm in his, swept toward the front of the room. The second set was full by the time they reached it, and the third set had two couples in it. Thomas and Julia took their place as the third couple, and he nodded to the girls to line up behind Julia. As soon as they were in place, two young men materialized out of the crowd, stood opposite them, and acknowledged their new partners with a little bow. Amelia recognized the young man opposite her as one of the "puppies" Lord Alderscroft had dismissed out of hand as a fortune-seeker.

Phillip? Paul? Oh, I remember.

"It is a pleasure to see a familiar face, Peter," she said pleasantly, as the set filled and more began.

Peter flushed. "The pleasure is all mine, Miss Amelia," he managed to get out. "I'll try not to step on your feet, word of honor."

She laughed at his attempt at a joke. "Your feet are in more danger than mine. I only hope the head couple calls something I know!"

"They will, Miss Amelia," he assured her. "Common courtesy, don'cha know. This hall ain't as stuffy as Almack's. Wouldn't go there if they'd let me in! Knee britches and white stockings and lugging around a hat under your arm all night! I ain't got the leg for knee britches," he added sadly.

This sudden burst of candor comprised more words than she'd heard out of him in three or four afternoon visits, and she decided she like this "puppy" after all. "Well," she said judiciously. "You can get the leg for knee breeches with a great deal of walking and some specific exercises for legs, but only the Lord Almighty could get either of us vouchers for Almack's."

That surprised a laugh out of him, and as the orchestra stopped tuning and looked as if they were ready to begin, she anticipated a very lively time.

To her immense relief, she heard a decisive female voice from behind her call out, "The Black Nag, if you please." The music started, and the First Lady began calling the figures.

Not only was that a dance she knew and had, in fact, danced at some of the small supper parties, but it was a relatively simple country dance. Although, at home, it was rare for there to be a full long set. Most people preferred to be dancing rather than standing and talking, waiting for the courtesy start.

In this case she rather liked it. Peter was showing himself at much better conversational advantage here than he had during his afternoon calls.

Then again, he didn't have to compete with five or six other men, and sometimes as many girls, if you counted Julia, Serena, and herself as three of them. Of course they couldn't talk openly about magic, but he was extremely adept at allusions. Finally she had to ask. "Are you at university yet?"

"St. George's," he said. "Here in London. I want to be a doctor."

Another pleasant surprise. "How is it you have time for dancing?" she teased, bouncing on her toes just a little to the music.

"Pater expects it, and I like it," he replied. "He says that assemblies are a good place to get to know ladies, and a doctor needs a wife. He wants me to take my time in studying so I don't overwork. He also said it will be time enough for me to spend long hours over books and longer ones over patients when I get closer to graduating. Will dancing give me the calves for knee breeches, do you suppose?"

"I don't see why it should not," she agreed—and just at that point, the lead couple position had passed to the one just before the Anglefords, and it was time for them to pay attention to the figures so they didn't embarrass themselves when their turn came.

They moved up in the set, and once the lead had passed to them and they had danced their way down to the bottom of the set, the conversation resumed. "I assume he wants you to be a doctor because of your special talents?" she said with emphasis on the last two words.

"Oh, to be sure!" He looked rather happy about that. "You know, there are young people, twelve or thirteen or thereabouts, with such talents, who are often diagnosed as mad, when it is only their talent coming to light and they are seeing Elementals when those around them see nothing at all. That generally happens because they aren't born into the right families to know what is going on. Pater says I'll be saving many lives by finding them and helping them. And a doctor can go wherever he likes, don'cha know." He was actually beaming with pleasure. "I ain't got the head for the business, but that don't matter, because my older brother does. I'd go into the clergy as a second choice, but I ain't got the connections for a good living, so doctor it is, and I can go practice wherever I please. Probably somewhere in the country, and if I can get it, a position in an asylum."

Peter had definitely impressed her at this point, between his ambition and his sense of humor, and he quickly proved that he had significant discernment when he noticed her narrowing her eyes at a redcoat approaching them in the set.

"Officer in the Foot Guards," he identified. "Grenadiers. Can't avoid them, Miss Amelia; they're quartered here, just outside London."

"You can imagine I have no fond memories of a redcoat," she said crisply.

"'Deed I can, but you'll have to get used to them," he said philosophically. "They swarm here when they can't get into Almack's. *They* don't care who smells of the shop. Always on the lookout for a wife with a thousand a year. Five hundred will do."

The redcoat and his partner, a young lady with an unfortunate expression on her face, danced down past them.

"Could be worse," Peter observed. "Could be Coldstream Guards. Won't touch a lady for less than fifteen hundred a year."

She almost choked with laughter. "Is life as an officer *that* expensive?"

"It is when you're mixing with the *ton*," Peter said wisely. "Getting your uniform tailored by Weston, placing bets at the fancy, or backing a pet. Barques of frailty. Buying beautiful steppers, placing bets on horseflesh, cards, dice, it all adds up pretty quickly. Next thing you know, you're in dun territory, and the general's wanting a word with you." He shook his head.

She hadn't the least idea what some of those words meant, but the general thrust was clear. Apparently, British officers had plenty of time to spend on things that were not part of their duties, and those things were expensive, particularly when you were attempting to impress a select number of the aristocracy.

They exchanged a lot more pleasantries, mostly about music, books, and where the most "painless" places in London to live were for an Earth magician. By the time the first couple had danced their way back up to the lead position again and it was the end of the dance, she and Peter were quite friends, and from indifference, she actually had admiration for him. He knew what he wanted, he knew how to get it, and he was following through on his plan.

She was rather sorry that the dance ended, because it meant she would not see him for the rest of the evening. But then something she had not expected happened. Instead of walking off, while the dancers rearranged themselves according to the rules of the assembly, he simply switched with Serena's partner. And it was only then, because she had been enjoying her conversation so much that she had not paid any attention to anything but the dance and anyone but Peter, that she noticed the distinct resemblance between them.

"Miss Amelia, may I present my brother, Edward? He'll be inheriting the business." Peter smiled at what must have been her look of surprise. "Unlike me, he has no time for afternoon visits, but he very much wanted to meet both of you. Also," he added, "he's a much better dancer than I am."

"Why, yes, I am," Edward said, and grinned. "Miss Serena, my I present my younger brother Peter, who is studying to be a doctor?"

Both of them bobbed a little curtsy, and Serena looked pleased with her new partner. Amelia was perfectly prepared to like *hers*. Unlike Peter, his collars did *not* reach to his ears, and there were none of the marks of the dandy about him. Although after her long conversation with Peter—nearly a half an hour!—Amelia was more in sympathy with his sartorial ambitions, since he balanced them with his intellectual ambitions and a good heart.

Edward grinned broadly at her, and passed his gloved hand over his hair. "It is just as well that I am the better dancer, since if what I just heard is correct, the Prime Lady for this evening has just called for a reel, and a complicated one at that. Peter might be able to converse well, but no one can fault my superior footwork!"

Edward must have been correct, for the long sets were subtly dividing into smaller groups of three couples. Well, at least this time there would be more actual dancing! She looked forward to doing something besides standing for ten minutes at a time.

There was always one idle couple in each group of three, so Amelia did get to talk a bit with Edward as well. Though he teased Peter about being the "bookish" one, she soon learned Edward wasn't stupid. He managed to convey that his Element was Water, that his abilities were limited mainly to scrying and seeing to it that the household water supply was pure—no mean feat in London, she suspected—and all without actually *saying* anything that could not be taken for anything but commonplaces. And as for the rest, she actually found out much more about the family business, which turned out to be supplying victuals for the Army.

Or at least, as much of the Army as was stationed near London.

"It's a job of work, I can tell you," he said, and by the time the reel was over, she had a pretty sound notion of just how *much* work it was, without any means to preserve foodstuffs outside of salting. "Don't blame the poor rankers for complaining about victuals," he said. "Nothing but bread and tea for breakfast, and boiled beef or mutton with potatoes for dinner. No supper, and if you can believe it, this all comes out of their pay, just to add insult to injury. It's as unfair as expecting your maid to pay you for her victuals! If a man wants to eat better, he's got to buy it himself, which means somehow getting the time to go to a market."

This was all in bits and pieces while they were the passive couple; most of the time they were hard put to show their footwork, which in this reel was intricate and energetic. It was easy to tell that the "family business" was as much a passion with him as medicine was with his brother, and it was really no surprise that was the case, given Peter's Element. Earth magicians had always been tied to the land and its bounty, and unless they had gone to the bad, they were excellent stewards of the land and the people living on it. Healers generally tended to be Earth mages, though not always.

"Least we can do is make sure what we sell them isn't adulterated, isn't diseased, is honest weight, and as good as we can get. Consider it my duty, as does Pater, though there are plenty of crooked merchants out there who pull every trick they can to cheat the Army out of the last groat," he continued.

"Well, I commend both of you," she said, which made him blush a little—and then the dance was over and he and his brother had to make their bows and seek new partners. She was feeling a little warm, but not at all tired, though she was very glad she had not opted for the detachable long sleeves for this gown.

And just at the moment she decided that she was going to stay in the set and not seek something to drink, that detestable redcoat approached, and bowed. Cursing etiquette, she curtsied in return, although of all things, the very *last* was that she wanted to dance with an officer of the same army that had spent the last thirty-seven years attacking her country and trying to bring it back into submission!

"Captain Harold Roughtower," he said with a bow. "If I may?"

Well, she had the right to refuse, but it would not put her in any good light, and *might* get her barred from any further balls if she did refuse him, since she had no actual reason, besides instinctive dislike, for being so rude.

"Miss Amelia Stonecroft," she said shortly.

"I know who you are, Miss Amelia, and I regret my duties prevented me from calling on you and your cousin," he said, startling her a little, and making her suspicious, since there was no good reason why an Army captain should know anything about the Anglefords' guests. "We share certain interests, even certain abilities, if you were curious."

The Prime Lady called for a cotillion. That would be enough dancing to keep him quiet, so she only said, just before the music started, "I had no idea such as you were in the Army."

"Oh," he answered lightly, as they passed and circled one another, "we seem to be everywhere."

If anything, her dislike only increased as they danced, even though he said nothing that could conceivably give any offense. Perhaps it wasn't so much what he said, it was how he said it. He had an air of superiority about him that she would have expected out of a member of the aristocracy—and he lost very little time in letting her know he had an estate in Devon, which certainly explained that air.

Landed gentry, then. But not good enough for Almack's, she could not help thinking, a little smugly.

He also made slighting comments about Peter and Edward, which did him no great favor in her eyes. And it was not long before he began making passing inquiries that could not be taken in any other light than that he was trying to ascertain if she had some sort of portion, and if so, how much it would be when she married.

Well, that explains his interest.

So this was one of the fortune hunters she'd been warned about. Likely Peter knew exactly who he was and what his aim was in coming here in the first place, and that was why he had told her about rapacious Army officers, making his comments general so he couldn't have been accused of slighting the captain.

Thank you, Peter, she thought, as they passed and repassed in the figures of the cotillion.

He was a cursed good dancer, however. Good enough to at least give her grudging enjoyment.

Finally, in a brief moment when they were idle rather than dancing, she said, with false gaiety, "Alas, we Americans are poor country cousins! My talent is all my fortune, although Lord Alderscroft certainly values *that* highly!"

"His lordship's opinion is to be valued," the captain replied, though it was clear her statement had put a death blow to his interest. "And everybody knows he has a discerning . . . eye. And knows what he is looking at."

But when the dance had ended, he could not get away from her quickly enough, and for her part, she was equally glad to be rid of him.

"What an *odious* man," said Serena with distaste. "Clearly hanging out for a fortune! What did you think of Peter and Edward?"

"Rather too young for me," Amelia replied, taking her fan from her wrist and fanning herself briskly. "Why, Peter is at least two years younger than I, and his brother one. Other than that . . . they do seem to tick off most of the particulars of my list, at least superficially. I'd have to interrogate them at length to know for certain."

Serena laughed. "You and your lists!"

"My lists have proven their worth," Amelia had to remind her. Then the Prime Lady called for another dance that required a longwise set, and she and Serena waited to see what sort of partners fate had in store for them.

She got a gentleman about her father's age, and Serena got one old enough to be her grandfather. Apparently either neither man had come with a spouse, or, unlike the Anglefords, their wives and they preferred to dance with other partners. She had nothing to regret, however, for the Honorable Walter Bedshire engaged her in a lively discussion of music and the musical joys to be had in London during the Season. He was an amiable sort of gentleman, happy to please and be pleased, and more than eager to describe what was currently available. And a side glance at Serena showed that while her partner was elderly, he was as intriguing as hers was. Serena was already deep in a discussion about hunting, of all things.

The Anglefords bestowed friendly and familiar nods of greeting to both the new partners as they all settled into the dance, which, along with shifting her vision momentarily into the mage sight, told her that her partner was an Air Master, and Serena's was a Fire mage. Which certainly explained her partner's enthusiasm for music, and Serena's for hunting—and explained Serena's compatibility with him.

"It is a pity that *Love in a Mist* has just closed," Amelia's partner said regretfully as the lead couple danced down between their upraised arms. "It was a pretty thing, and gracefully performed. The Theater Royal has a Grand Concert of music at the end of the month, which I believe you would enjoy ever so much. If your hosts cannot procure you tickets, I would be happy to exert my influence for you."

"That is uncommonly kind of you!" she exclaimed. "And it does sound like the very thing I would enjoy."

"There is also a fine Spanish guitarist just come to London, Fernando Sor; I shall make inquiries for you if there are any concerts he is performing at that are open to members of the public, or which I might procure invitations for my wife and I and include you. He is quite sublime." He seemed so eager to please, like an affectionate hound that willingly bestows his regard on anyone inclined to offer attention, that she was quite touched. And so refreshing after the odious captain!

But his interest was explained in his next sentence. "My dear wife is a treasure, and I am lucky to have her, but she cannot tell one note from another, and only comes to musical events to gossip and look at fashions." He sighed. "Even at assemblies and balls, she only comes with me for cards. She is in the card room even now, and will be there the rest of the evening. It is wonderful to find someone of *our sort* also interested in music, and I would like to make your time in London one of enlightened pleasure."

"Then, by all means, I would welcome your help," she told him. "And I would enjoy the company of yourself and your lady wife above all things."

She caught the eye of Thomas Angleford, who indicated with a nod that he had overhead this conversation and approved. That made her very happy.

"Capital! I shall make up a list! Then you and I can discuss music in the intervals, and my dear wife can flit off to gather the nectar of *crim con* to cherish and mull over without a care." He chuckled. "Bless her! She is the dearest creature on earth, and won't leave me to go off to concerts alone, but whenever we go I can see her vibrating with the urge to indulge in what is, I must admit, her only vice. With you to occupy me, she will get as much enjoyment out of the affairs as I do for a change!"

It's a great shame I am not permitted to repeat partners, she thought as that dance ended, and he bowed himself away, professing delight in the dance and the intent to send his wife along with his card on the morrow. *Among Peter, Edward, and the Honorable Walter, I would have an evening drowning in pleasure!*

6

THE next day, Mrs. Beatrix Bedshire called at precisely the correct hour, armed with her husband's card and her own hearty good wishes and enthusiasm for the plan. She was a tall, still-handsome woman who had adopted the best parts of current fashion while retaining those things of the previous generation that best suited her age, dignity, and person. Despite being indifferent to music, she had a lively sense of humor, knew every bit of the best gossip without being in the least cruel or reveling in others' misfortune, and had a very forgiving nature. Her magical ability was extremely minor, which didn't seem to bother her a whit. Her sons were long out of the household and her husband amenable to her fancies, and she, Amelia, and Serena hit it off from the beginning. And thus began a round of delights that satisfied Amelia and Serena's wildest fantasies and took a great deal of entertaining pressure off the Anglefords. Walter and Beatrix were an utter delight to be with; theirs, so they confided, had been an arranged marriage from very young, but they had been raised closely together, and as a result, felt as if they were wedding a best friend. "Which," Beatrix said decidedly, "is a great deal better than all this harum-scarum running off to Gretna Green with somebody you only know says lovely things to you, dances well, and shows a scarlet coat to perfection!"

Since it didn't appear that either of them knew the captain except in passing as a fellow mage, Amelia didn't think they had him in mind, but she couldn't help but take note that the description certainly matched him.

So thanks to "The Honorables," as Serena insisted on calling them even to their faces (to their delight), their weeks were full without putting the Anglefords to any stress. They attended the ball at Payne's Assembly every Thursday night, which they got vouchers of their own for, now that they were known to the master of ceremonies; they attended two or three concerts a week with The Honorables, many of them private. Then there was generally one excursion a week with Julia, usually of an educational nature, such as a visit to the Tower of London, to Montagu House to tour the British Museum (as arranged by Lord Alderscroft, Amelia suspected), a special tour of Hampton Court Palace (definitely arranged by Lord Alderscroft, although The Honorables actually knew some of the impoverished "grace and favor" aristocrats that lived there, and as a result they got a rather good tour of every part of it, including the somewhat neglected gardens). There was shopping, of course; the search for exactly the right shade of embroidery thread could be a delightful excuse to walk and browse and see if they could catch sight of some of the *ton*. And of course, for a guaranteed look at the *ton*, there was always a walk in Hyde Park, to observe them as they rode or drove their carriages or trotted along on their exquisitely bred horses. There they could see the very peak of fashion, as well as the peak of fashion foibles; the former to be admired if not aspired to, the latter to provide a great deal of amusement when they got home.

To be sure, those beautiful horses did not much care for Serena, so she was careful to stay well away from the bridle path. They sensed something of what she was, and their instincts strongly urged them to bolt if she got too near. She found this hilarious, but she never risked anybody's safety by getting within that distance.

Except once. And the rider had only himself to blame for it.

An obviously vain and very handsome tulip caught sight of them watching the riders and drivers from that safe distance, and they later guessed that he had immediately decided with no reason whatsoever except for Serena's beauty that they must be a pair of "convenients" accompanied by their lady-keeper. And in order to ascertain their price, he made for them, despite the increasing unease of his poor horse, who began to curvet, sidle, and foam.

This almost immediately attracted attention, and several riders, both male and female, stopped to watch. No one offered to intervene, however, and as soon as they were aware of what he was about, they all tensed. Obviously the horse was in growing agitation. Obviously he had missed his mark in his judgment, because all three ladies were not wearing welcoming expressions, and were, in fact, backing away. And obviously something bad was going to happen. But whatever it was, they were going to let it happen and be entertained by it.

He was halfway to them, the horse growing more lathered and showing his distress by the moment, and Julia Angleford getting ready to send him angrily on his way with a setdown, when the horse decided he had had enough.

With a dreadful neigh of terror and desperation, the horse performed a maneuver that would have delighted the heart of any dressage trainer had it been by command, rearing, hopping forward a few steps on his hind legs alone, dropping to all fours again, whirling, leaping into the air, frantically kicking behind him with both hind feet at the top of his leap, and taking off at a full gallop once he had landed.

The young tulip was extremely lucky that he slid right off his horse's back as soon as it reared, and landed safely, if ingloriously, on his behind. And he at least scrambled out of danger before the horse executed the rest of its maneuvers, or he could have easily been killed, because that backward kick had a great deal of energy behind it. When the beast galloped off, he looked as if he was torn between swearing and stamping, or pelting off after it. A glance at the growing audience decided him; better to pelt off ingloriously than to face an unsympathetic crowd of people who, without a doubt, outranked him in every possible way.

"Mushroom," said one gentleman dismissively, as Julia plucked at each of their sleeves, and indicated with a glance that they should move along before someone put two and two together and tested the theory that the horse had spooked at *them*. Or, specifically, at Serena.

"Too much horse for the rider," opined another. "May not be a mushroom, but these young fellows *will* make a mull of it by buying a high-stepper they can't handle."

"Likely brought up from the country," said an older man. "Not wise to buy a green 'un, then slap a saddle on him and bring him straight to the Park to show his paces. Poor dumb creature was *that* lathered. Boy should have noticed and taken him straight back to the stables."

"I'm going after him," said a third, a gentleman in immaculate and expensive riding gear, with ill-concealed glee. "He doesn't deserve that beauty, and he'll probably take the first offer I give him." He picked up his reins and headed off in the direction of the fleeing horse and pursuing rider at the fastest pace that protocol in the Park allowed.

As they moved discreetly out of earshot, Amelia was just relieved that no one had noted that the cause of the altercation had been them. "Well," Julia sighed, "at least no one *else* thought we were incognitas."

"That *was* the prettiest piece of hubris rewarded I have ever seen in my life, though." Serena giggled.

"At least now we know we are safe from unwanted advances on horseback as long as Serena is with us," Amelia added, trying to sound calm and amused, although in truth this had set all her anxieties into as frenzied a gallop as that poor horse.

"Do you girls wish to return home?" Julia asked.

Serena tossed her head. "What, and let a—what did that man call him?—a *mushroom* spoil our day?"

"A 'mushroom' is someone who is trying to crowd his way in where he is not wanted, but not in the way you mean," Julia corrected gently. "It generally means one of *us* trying to emulate and crowd into the *ton*. But I take your meaning. There is no reason to let one young fool who certainly got his comeuppance ruin our walk."

So they proceeded as normal, but now Amelia was doing more than looking at the fashions—and sometimes, with just a tinge of envy, at the one or two daring Cyprians driving their own spanking phaetons, and looking so beautiful and so perfectly turned-out that they literally turned heads. Male ones, and a few female as well. The ones lying back languidly and being driven by a coachman with a little tiger she did not envy nearly as much. They made it look as if the business of being beautiful and entertaining a gentleman in the evening was too utterly exhausting. But the others, well, they certainly earned the name of "adventuress," because they *looked* as if they found life to be an adventure.

And she very much wanted to try her hand at driving one of those phaetons herself. Not the high-perch variety, to be sure, but she loved horses and she like driving, and this was the closest thing she'd seen to the kind of freedom she was used to on the plantation.

But after the incident with the importunate young man and his horse, Amelia was now looking as much for signs that Serena was affecting other horses—and that people were taking note of that— as she was looking at the fashionables with great interest.

It was, frankly, exhausting, and much of the enjoyment she had been taking from the walk on the Row had been extinguished.

Amelia was just happy to be back to the house, and excused herself to go to her room and get her composure back. After she mentally hammered her borderline panic into submission, she was able to admit that even if someone had guessed *they* were the cause of the horse bolting, not one of the onlookers had any way of proving *why* it had bolted.

Most people did not know about magicians, and those who did were overwhelmingly magicians themselves. Of magicians, most of them thought shifters were a myth. So even if—by some impossible coincidence—one of those people watching had been a magician that Julia did not know (which seemed unlikely), there was no reason to think they'd presume Serena's status. *They'd probably just assume it was a shawl, or a bonnet, or our dresses blowing in the breeze that spooked an already nervous horse,* she told herself, as she stood at the open window and let that same breeze cool her cheeks. *Just as that one rider said—someone had brought a green and nervous horse straight from the country into the bustle of Hyde Park without conditioning him to all the London traffic first, and he acted accordingly. Still. We need to be careful. Even among the mages there are not many who are as accepting as the Anglefords.*

There were other reasons to feel anxious, of course. Napoleon continued to gather up support as he and his forces rolled across France with very little opposition. And Amelia sensed the undercurrent of nerves even within the walls of this house, although there was not the level of sheer panic there had been among the servants when he first escaped. A not-inconsiderable amount of anxiety was caused by the ever-present fear that the Army would commence the same sort of brutal conscription that the Navy was guilty of—literally snatching men off the street by press-gangs. It was a practice so brutal that they even impressed American sailors into British slavery whenever they got the chance! The manservants of the household other than the coachman refused to go near the docks for that reason, and nobody blamed them. But nobody knew whether the Army would resort to similar conscription, and if that happened, the servingmen would not dare leave the house. No one was talking about it, but Amelia sensed it as an underlying current of unease that never went away. Not unlike her own anxieties, to tell the truth.

Finally, rather than fret herself to pieces, she closed herself in her room, set up a summoning circle, and called on Natty Ned. She had not invited him to come talk—which was more like what her "summoning circle" was, an invitation rather than the rather ruder version that *compelled* an Elemental to come to you—since he had so obligingly found her those bits of ribbon she had asked about.

But what she *had* done was to make a tiny pair of boots from some of the kidskin she was using to make gloves, and leave them next to the buttered scone she'd gotten for him on the hearth. Since both were gone the next day, she assumed that he was pleased.

She spun out the magic to extend her invitation and sat down on a cushion on the floor to wait.

She didn't have to wait long, and when he appeared inside the summoning circle she was tickled to see he was wearing the boots.

"And what can Natty Ned do for you, lady?" the brownie said with a wink and a nod. *"It's little enough you've asked of me. The cook has asked more, and she can only ask, not compel."*

"You should know that I never compel. I wouldn't even if my life was in danger," she corrected. "Compulsion is a sister to en-slavement."

"Oh, aye, and we know how you and your cousin feel about that.*"* Ned chuckled. *"Favor for favor, like the cook. And what would be the favor?"*

"Can your kind keep a watch on Lord Alderscroft?" she asked, as what might be a brilliant thought struck her. "There are two things I'd like to hear about. The first is if there are any complaints about Serena—anything that suggests that people suspect she is a shifter. The second is what he learns about Napoleon's actions and what the government is going to do about them. Particularly if they are going to start conscription for the Army."

Ned nodded. *"Aye, that can be done, and aside from that, the likes of him, Huntmaster and all, don't pay no heed to the likes of me. We're Earth and he's Fire, and he'd have to stretch his gaze a good way to see us in the first place. Fire don't have much use for us'n; it's Air they want in a pinch, and it's Air he'll be gettin' his Masters to call on to spy on Boney."*

She heaved a sigh of relief. She could, of course, have asked Lord Alderscroft herself, but—as had been made very clear over the past few weeks in her interactions with those of the nobility—she was "shop" and he was *ton,* and the former did not put themselves for-ward to the latter. Not that his lordship himself hadn't been all geniality whenever they had met him here in private, but in public was likely to be a very different matter. Despite all his willing help, it wasn't wise to assume that his egalitarian attitude was more than a polite ruse. Besides . . . she was a Channel, and that, without a shadow of doubt, informed all of his interactions with herself and her cousin. She was *potentially* useful, but had not yet proven herself. Until then, he owed her nothing.

"Then I shall leave you and your friends some good things on my hearth every night," she promised. "Favor for favor."

"We're partial to Cook's pancakes," the brownie said, with an avaricious look that briefly replaced his affable expression. *"She leaves us biscuits now and then, and bread, sometimes a scone, but almost never pancakes."*

"Pancakes," so she had learned, were very different from the sort she knew in America. They were much flatter, often eaten folded into triangles, and could be eaten as often cold as hot. Truth to tell, without the leavening agent that American pancakes used, they didn't get tough when cold, so they were rather good that way.

"I can get you pancakes," she promised. The cook often offered the treats to both her and Serena along with a "nice cuppa" at bedtime. Serena, of course, had no interest in pancakes, since part of her evening "romp" included ambushing a fat pigeon or two. She would get *her* treat before settling down on guard in leopard form in the kitchen. She still did that, for the servants were still wary of Napoleonic incursions into the house of a night, though now they were concerned about magical spies rather than physical presences. Why they didn't worry about the same thing during the day, when spying Elementals might reasonably be supposed to overhear or see something marginally worthwhile, she did not understand. And why they didn't think the Elementals that were attached to the household, like brownie Ned, wouldn't at least come and rouse their attention if a foreign creature intruded, made no sense either. She hadn't asked Julia about it, but she was fairly certain every magical household had their Elementals on guard as a matter of course. All the Elementals on the Stonecroft plantation were *specifically* tasked to do that very thing, because there were just as many Elemental magicians who were perfectly happy with keeping other humans as slaves as there were those who were against the practice, and while it was legal for the Stonecrofts to employ freedmen, it was illegal to marry them—and extremely illegal to facilitate the passage of runaway slaves to free states.

"Ah, you're a grand lady, you are," sighed Ned. *"Anything else?"*

"Nothing that I can think of," she said, and Ned gave her a little bow and vanished from the circle.

A few pancakes? A small price to pay for *knowing* rather than guessing. Now if only she could progress a little farther with her lists.

But that was, infuriatingly enough, going to depend on what Napoleon did. *Wretched man. Why couldn't he just rot in Elba as he was supposed to do?*

All the world—or at least London—seemed divided between being terrified of what Napoleon was doing and what it might mean for England, and intent on ignoring what he was doing and acting as if nothing had changed. Or, at least, allowing themselves to be distracted from what he was doing. The Angleford household was by no means immune to this. On the one hand, the servants still begged Serena to keep a watch belowstairs at night, even though they knew she did a great deal less *watching* and more sleeping. (Possibly, of course, since the cook kept an "open pantry," and if hunger struck in the middle of the night, they could help themselves, each of them had gone tiptoeing across the darkened kitchen only to find themselves looking into a pair of shining eyes in a spotted shadow, and hearing purring, they knew she could awake on the instant.) On the other hand, they themselves apparently slept soundly, and went about their daily work with none of the hysterics the word of Napoleon's escape had engendered. On the one hand, Julia and Thomas scanned the morning and evening papers faithfully and with looks of concern, and not a day went past without Thomas or James asking her if she "had heard" anything. (This had puzzled and somewhat alarmed her the first time it happened, since she hadn't told anyone she was keeping a discreet eye on Lord Alderscroft, but then she gradually decided that it was because she was the only Master in the house and they might reasonably assume she was using her powers to keep apprised of the situation on the Continent herself.) On the other hand, she and Serena were encouraged to attend concerts and musical entertainments with The Honorables and go to the Thursday balls at Payne's, and Julia still held regular visiting hours as well as going out visiting herself. And as far as Amelia could tell, for Thomas and James, the business of the business was going on as usual. That seemed to hold for the rest of London as she saw it.

But, to be sure, she was not seeing more than the smallest slice of it.

There *were* fewer redcoats at Payne's, which as far as she was concerned was an improvement. And some of the young bucks she danced with had begun vaguely and wistfully talking of purchasing a commission. But the talk never got past how expensive it was to do so.

(She had to wonder just how expensive it was likely to be if Wellington began pulling troops from England to fill out and match the ranks of their Prussian allies. And if conscription became a reality, would these same fellows be paying someone *else* to take their place? Or did that only hold for the rank and file, and not the officers?)

The twice-weekly scrying-talks with her parents—and often Serena's—touched on none of this. Instead, their initial concern had been to make sure that the monies intended as their marriage portions had been transferred safely into the Hoare's Bank, the same bank in London they did all their business with. While modest by the standards of the *ton* and even by the standards of the wealthiest merchants and bankers, it was still a considerable amount to have transferred across the vastness of the Atlantic. And now that this had been settled, the calls mostly concerned whether they were *sure*

Lord Alderscroft was sincere in his offering of an accommodation to let, and what the status of it should be. And since his lordship's chief London steward was keeping James apprised of progress on a regular basis, and of course James dealt with all the business questions on his own calls, all they cared to know about besides that was whether there were any *prospects*.

Amelia bore this regular interrogation without complaint. Serena teased them about it, once even going so far as to pretend she was interested in an officer in the Coldstream Guards (Alarms! Excursions! Horrors!) before letting them know she was teasing.

But on their fourth ball at Payne's, at the end of April, there occurred something Amelia had never expected.

She had taken her usual place next to the Anglefords, with Serena one place below her. The Anglefords had secured the place of Lead Couple in the third long set to form. Serena had already secured a partner—her beauty and good humor made her popular—and Amelia was waiting for someone to come pay his attentions, when she found herself being accosted by Master Payne himself.

"Lady Sophia sends her regards," the master of ceremonies said deferentially, "and wonders if you would care to join her as fifth in her set."

Since Lady Sophia was *clearly* of higher rank than Amelia was, and had secured to herself the position of Lead Lady of every single ball here that Amelia had attended, this was not so much a request as a demand, and everyone in their party knew it. "Go!" whispered Julia urgently, as Serena reached over to give her a little push.

"Why, yes, certainly. It would be my honor," Amelia said, managing not to stammer. She followed Master Payne to the top of the room, where the first set had formed up—almost. There was one very plain but very well-dressed young man fifth in the set who did not have a partner.

"There she is," said the formidable-looking—and equally well-dressed—older lady at the top of the set. "Thank you, my dear," she said to Master Payne before turning to Amelia. "You would be Miss Amelia Stonecroft, I presume?"

"Yes, my lady," Amelia said, with a curtsy, wondering how on earth this woman knew who she was. Surely not an acquaintance of Lord Alderscroft. . . .

She hooded her eyes a moment and invoked mage sight for a moment. *No, not a hint of powers. So unless this is some social acquaintance of his—*

But what the lady lacked in magical powers she more than made up for in sartorial and social powers. She was dressed in extremely expensive azure silk with even more expensive cobalt silk lace trim—which Amelia recognized on sight as handmade and bespoke. The patterns were *nothing* she recognized, and must have been created specifically for her ladyship. She wore a matching blue silk turban with a sapphire brooch pinned to the front that must have cost an eye-watering sum of money. A matching brooch ornamented her corsage. For all of this display of wealth, however, it was clear she was dressed to dance: no train to have to pin up or trip over, and fetching azure kid half-boots that would take a great deal more abuse than Amelia's slippers.

As for the lady herself, she was not, as so often was the case, "mutton dressed as lamb." No art concealed the gray in her hair, and her gown was tailored precisely to the dignity of someone in her late middle age. Her most striking feature was her very blue eyes, which nearly matched those sapphires for brilliance.

"I make the point of keeping track of the best dancers here," the lady continued, with more than a touch of proprietary arrogance, as if it were she and not Master Payne who was in charge of the assembly.

But maybe she is. Maybe she's the equivalent of the lady patronesses of Almack's.

"My nephew is without a partner tonight. We can't have that, can we?" A lesser spirit than Amelia's might have wilted under that draconic gaze, but Amelia met her eyes with confidence, or at least, the confidence of an American who couldn't care a fig about lords and ladies.

"Certainly not, my lady, and I shall do my utmost to come up to his skills," Amelia agreed, and at the lady's gesture, took her place opposite the young man, giving him her best smile. Like his aunt, he was dressed well and expensively. Silk-satin knee breeches, silk stockings well-embroidered with clocks in gold thread, black kid dancing shoes, formal black tailed coat, silk waistcoat in gold and white brocade, white linen shirt, and a conservatively tied linen stock. His collar points were conservative as well. All fit him as perfectly as if it had been molded to him—and he might be plain of face, but he was quite handsome of figure.

While they waited for the rest of the sets to form up, the young man, visibly nervous, introduced himself to her. "Mathew Davis, at your service, mum," he said in the oddly slangy accent most young men of rank seemed to have adopted. "Fiancée's a bit unwell. Didn't find out till I arrived. Aunt's set on me dancing."

"Amelia Stonecroft," she replied, with a hint of a curtsy. "From America," she added, putting a little defiance into her words.

"Oh, I know," he said, surprising her. "Everyone in Auntie's set knows. She ain't fibbin', she keeps track of every good dancer at Payne's an' makes it her business to know all about 'em." And before Amelia could take alarm at that, he added, "She don't care if you're a duke or a candlemaker, all she cares about is if you know how to foot it."

At that, Amelia decided that for honor of president and country, she was damned well going to "foot it" and foot it proper!

"Good luck," the young man concluded, with just a touch of alarm. "The sets are all made up, and I reckon she's going to try your paces."

And as some of the chatter in the room died, the lady's voice rang out, loud and clear, "Lord Nelson's Quadrille, if you please."

Oh lud, a quadrille! He wasn't joking!

Quadrilles required exacting attention to the steps and the figures. Although there were only five figures and no changes, the steps of the quadrille were complicated and French, and each different quadrille had different figures and steps. She didn't know "Lord Nelson's"—she had the feeling that her ladyship had chosen it with exactly that in mind—and she was going to have to *pay attention* as strictly as she ever had in magic.

At least she got one form of relief—besides calling the dance itself, Lady Sophia called the figures and the steps. It took a great deal of proficiency in a dance to call and dance at the same time, and it was unheard of back home for a lady to call the dance—that was usually reserved for the master of ceremonies or the bandleader. But this was apparently unexceptional behavior for Lady Sophia here at Payne's, because Amelia had heard her clear, sharp voice calling out dances before this.

Her partner eyed her anxiously through the first figure, relaxed a bit by the third, and looked to be enjoying himself by the fifth. For her part, Amelia's determination carried her triumphantly to the other side of the dance, and a glance up at the Lead Couple as she and her partner bowed to each other showed her that Lady Sophia was bestowing an eagle-eyed nod of approval at her.

The unspoken rules of behavior were, of course, that no one was to dance with the same partner twice in an evening; Amelia wasn't sure how this was going to be enforced in the Lead Set, but suddenly all the men moved down a partner, and the man at the end of the set moved up to stand opposite her ladyship.

Now she was partnered with a plump, middle-aged man with a twinkle in his eye and a look of great good humor. He was nowhere near as expensively dressed as Lady Sophia and her nephew; in fact, he could have sat in the Anglefords' parlor without standing out at all. "Passed your test with flying colors, Miss Amelia," he opined. "Welcome to the Lead Set. Hope you like dancin'—Lady Sophia frowns on anyone who dares to sit out a dance!"

"I like dancing above all things," Amelia declared with truth. "I'd rather dance than anything else! Except perhaps reading."

"Well, you'll get your fill of it with us," he declared, as Lady Sophia, perhaps taking pity on everyone, declared that the next dance would be a reel.

She only caught up with her cousin in the brief interval for the orchestra (and everyone else) to take a rest, when Lady Sophia allowed everyone to partake of refreshments—and in Amelia's case, a glass of lemonade was sorely needed!

"This is a triumph!" Serena gushed, when they found each other at the punch bowl. "Everybody is talking about it! Lady Sophia almost *never* lets anyone new in her set, and obviously, you're American, so—"

"I hope I showed well for the flag," Amelia teased back.

"I'm serious!" Serena insisted. "Lady Sophia *could* get vouchers for Almack's, but she doesn't even bother, because she says the dancing is indifferent, the music is insipid, the company is boring, and the refreshments are abominable!"

"Well, I had better hurry back to my set, then," Amelia replied. "I can't keep her ladyship waiting!"

But she realized, as her heartbeat quickened a little as she neared the forming lines, that she actually hadn't been sarcastic. This was *challenging* in a way nothing had been since they arrived here. Challenging physically and mentally, and overcoming that challenge was exhilarating.

Challenging enough to drive everything else out of her mind.

Hang Napoleon. Tonight she had been made a member of Lady Sophia's set at Payne's!

It had been a quiet morning at the Anglefords on the Saturday following the ball. There were fewer visitors than usual; in fact, the only people in the parlor were Amelia, Julia, two older magician friends of Julia's, a Mrs. Hulmorton and her daughter, and Peter, who was actually there to loan Amelia a book. So it was with a sense of shock that Frank announced, "Lady Sophia Dutton," and the formidable lady herself sailed into the room like a miniature warship.

This morning she wore a white silk gown and blue spencer of twilled silk, another matching turban, and only a simple string of pearls. She had with her a walking cane with an ivory top, which she consigned to Frank's care. Julia hastened to rise, and offered her the best chair in the room, which she declined. "I came to interrogate your charming guest, my dear," she said, with a hint of humor. "I've never met an American. If they can all dance as well as Miss Amelia does, I might import a few!"

Amelia took that for the joke that it was and laughed. "We are not *all* living in wooden cabins and dancing with bears," she replied with spirit. "I'm told that Ambassador Benjamin Franklin made quite a splash at the French Court before the Revolution!"

"Good for you! Stand up for your country! I won't pretend to know what started the war. Don't follow politics; never did. Treaty's signed, there's an end to it. So tell me what brings you here?" Her ladyship sat back in her chair, folded her hands, and prepared to listen.

Amelia made her explanation as brief and entertaining as she could, then, acting on the intuition that Lady Sophia might be amused, added, "And since my brother James is deeply embroiled in the business here in London, I am undertaking finding that property for him."

"Are you, then!" Lady Sophia chuckled. "I find it in my heart to feel sorry for any agents who dismiss you out of hand, or think to take advantage of you! Do you intend to stay once that task is completed?"

"Yes, my cousin and I will manage the property for James until he commences the construction of our silk, spinning, and weaving facilities on it. Then, well, I suppose we can manage house for him until he finds a wife."

"Hmm! Hmm! And are you two misses in equal search for husbands?" The lady seemed actually interested at this point.

"Less so than perhaps one might think. We have a small income, quite enough to live comfortably upon if we economize, especially in a market town like Axminster, where things are likely cheaper than in London." She sighed a little. "I *shall* miss the excellent dancing here, though I suppose there are assemblies and even a ball or two a year in a market town."

Lady Sophia chuckled, sounding like Serena when she was

purring. "I like to see independence in the right sort of gel. You're clever, you've got a good bottom to you, and your education is good. Well then, don't *settle*. Worst thing you can do in a marriage, *settle*. Better no offers than the wrong one. Meanwhile, let me give you a bit of advice. Consols."

Amelia blinked, wondering if she had heard wrong. "Consuls? Like ambassadors?"

"Con*sols*," Lady Sophia corrected. "Consolidated annuities. Government bonds. Get 'em on the Stock Exchange. Pay three percent twice a year. Safe as houses. If you've got any money, put it in them."

"That's good advice," Peter ventured.

"My father put my dower in 'em, and since my dotard of a husband didn't understand the Stock Exchange and didn't want to, he didn't touch it. Now I've got a solid fifteen thousand a year that's mine, free and clear of the estate, that no one else can touch. Not even my son, at least until I'm under the sod." She actually grinned. "You've got good sense. I assume that pretty cousin of yours does, too. Don't *settle*."

Amelia smiled. "I have a list," she offered.

"Stick to it." Lady Sophia rose. "Now, the other reason I came here was to say, you're not only in my set at Payne's, you're in my *set*. Regular invitations will come. Accept them if you're free; won't harm my feelings if you send regrets." She looked over at Julia. "Includes the household. Understand you know the Honorable Bedshires. Friends of mine. Just stopped by and let Beatrice know. Bea and I can cackle about *crim con* while you and Walter get lofty over Handel. Everyone goes home happy."

Amelia stood and offered her hand, which Lady Sophia took and shook. "I can sincerely say that making your acquaintance has been a very, very great pleasure, Lady Sophia, and I am relieved to intuit that you understand I have no designs on your nephew."

Lady Sophia barked a laugh. "I like you, gel, demned if I don't. You couldn't pry him from Miranda if you wanted to. Neither of them *settled*. Looking forward to actually meeting your cousin. Pleasure, Mrs. Angleford."

And with that, she was off, leaving Julia bemused. "I think I may like her," Julia said at last. "She certainly is a force of nature."

"I feel as if I have been run over by a wagon," Peter said faintly.

"She has a reputation," opined one of Julia's visitors. "Earned, apparently. But if you're on her right side, she doesn't give a crumb about rank or wealth, and she is very loyal."

"She's *terribly* kind to animals," added the other. "She has taken in many abused horses and dogs. She once beat a man in the street with her cane for whipping a downed horse in front of her."

"'Struth," seconded Peter.

"Well . . . where were we?" Julia said, after contemplating this for a moment. "Oh! Yes! Peter, what were you saying about the wells?"

"Typhus," he said succinctly. "Coming from the wells. It's a certain thing, traced it myself. Either use magic to purify your water, boil it, or start a cistern for rainwater on the roof and keep it *clean*. Make sure birds and rodents can't get into it."

Julia *tsk*ed. "A consequence of all the building and all the backyard latrines put in without consideration of drainage, I suppose," she lamented. "Thank you for the warning. I'll let belowstairs know."

"At least your people are mages too, and won't bob and agree to your face and put unboiled water in your lemonade." Peter sighed. "We're going to see a lot of typhus this year, I fear. Oh! Remind them about hand washing."

"I don't have to remind *them*, they remind *me*. It helps that we don't economize on soap." Having used Julia's beautiful, soft, and soothing scented soaps, Amelia knew what she meant. The same soaps—bar the harsher ones for cleaning things like floors—were used by everyone, from Julia herself to the tweenie. There was no one nursing soap-burned hands in this household! And there was no need to encourage the servants to wash; indeed, thorough washing was considered a must in this household, and time allowed for it. And with those beautiful soaps came Julia's equally fine lotions, freely shared with the rest, including a bay-scented one even the men would use.

"Well, with that depressing news, I shall take my leave." Peter rose, and made his bow. "It is with hope that this will be the worst news you shall hear for some time."

"One can hope," Amelia replied, as he kissed her hand in farewell. But of course, that immediately set her anxieties in motion again. Typhus! What would be next?

7

WHAT came next was not a bout of typhus in the household, nor the decision to conscript for the Army. It was the strange lack of warm weather, which should have set in by May, and the brilliant sunsets but hazy skies. No one knew what was causing this, which everyone thought would soon "blow over," but which Elemental mages eventually knew, a bit grimly, would not.

An enormous volcano had erupted in the South Pacific, spewing vast amounts of ash into the air. Thousands died in the initial eruption. Hundreds of thousands were dead or dying of hunger as the ash blanketed their land and water, killing rice crops and fish alike. Because it was so far away, Amelia had not even noticed this eruption, except, perhaps, in the form of an uneasy dream, easily dismissed by day. Volcanoes were erupting all the time. Earthquakes happened all the time. And these were on the other side of the globe. Even if they occurred "relatively" nearby, as in Italy, or Turkey, she probably would not have noticed. It was only when the weather failed to improve, when flowers failed to bloom on time, when the chill air stayed chill, did any of the Elemental Masters think to "look" into this, and discover what was going on. Even their own Elementals had not noticed, because in general, their reach was purely local, and it took some effort for them to consult with others further away.

This was a global catastrophe, and the results would persist for, it was reckoned, at least two years. The Air Masters all knew now that this ash had flown high above the earth, where it was likely to stay for the next two years, and the British ones had advised Lord Alderscroft that this was very likely to be a "year without a summer." Crops would fail, not only in Britain, but around the world, at least in the Northern Hemisphere. There would be famine and food riots. But what could anyone do? The Earth mages would do their best to counter what could be countered—Amelia had already volunteered— but there were only so many of them, and many millions of acres to cover. And it would be worse next year, since the ash spread slowly.

A hasty call to her parents had proved that there were already effects showing in America as well. They hadn't known what was wrong, either, until Amelia told them. They immediately put plans into action: ways to keep the soil warm, changing what crops they intended to grow this year to account for the cold, protecting the precious indigo plants and the cactus. The Stonecrofts would be all right—but their neighbors would not, unless they followed Charles Stonecroft's advice. And farther north than South Carolina would be much, much worse. How many mages were there that could help their neighbors? Much fewer than in England—if you only counted white ones. And thanks to how the majority of white people in the United States had treated the native tribes, Amelia would not blame the natives at all for being disinclined to help.

"We picked a terrible year to start a new enterprise," Amelia said, when Lord Alderscroft came to consult her on what, if anything, she could do. "I will do my best, and as a Channel I will bolster all the Earth mages I can reach, but we cannot help the whole of England, and my powers will only stretch so far."

"Napoleon picked a terrible time to break out of prison," he replied dryly. "When the weather worsens, which it will, he'll be fighting our allies—and us, of course—in bitter rain and mud."

"He is as likely to be prepared as we are," Thomas Angleford warned. "There are Elemental mages in France too, you know, and surely some of them support Napoleon."

"All I can do is advise, and that as circumspectly as I can," Alderscroft said helplessly. "Above all else we want to keep the number of people in the government who know about us to a minimum. I *hope* that soon the news of the eruption and its effects will reach our shores, and when it does, my colleagues in the Royal Society can point out what is likely to happen to our weather, but by then, it may be too late to do anything about the food shortages. It will be difficult to convince farmers that they need to plow crops under that they have already planted and plant the few things that are likely to produce. We may have more luck with the Army."

They all sat in gloomy silence for a while—a silence made more gloomy by the overcast outside. *All that time I spent remaking my muslins,* she thought, wryly. *Well, I cannot do much about feeding the country, but at least I can help this household stay warm. I believe I shall ask one of the maids to take me to where secondhand clothing is sold. I am certainly not going to spend an extravagant amount of money on woolens and flannels when I can remake things long out of mode. And since we are likely to be spending our days by candlelight, no one will even notice that the fabrics have been re-used.*

"On another note . . . I picked a terrible time to hold a ball," Alderscroft said with a snort. "But the depth of this disaster will not be understood until midsummer or even later. And we cannot hoard or preserve enough from a single ball to make even the smallest dent in the hunger that will occur by fall. . . ." He shrugged. "I came to also tell you that I am not canceling it. It is whistling in the dark, or dancing on the edge of the precipice, but the ball was already planned, and we might as well dance. I was hoping this ball would raise spirits deflated by Napoleon's continued victories. . . ."

His voice trailed off.

"Well," Amelia said. "At least we are warned. Where we can, we can put in crops that can sustain themselves over the cold summers. You can advise people in Parliament on that subject, I presume, without revealing us for what we are."

"It would be a good idea to encourage the preservation of fish, I believe," put in Serena. "The Indians of our home make great use of smoking and drying of fish; New England has an entire industry based on barrels of salted cod, and a starving man will not turn up his nose at a dried herring, where now he might sneer at something less than fresh."

"Both ideas are good. I'll consult with our Water mages on the coast and Earth mages in Denmark, Sweden, and Finland." He sighed. "We'll do what we can to soften the blow. And there is another good reason to hold this ball; I'll be able to consult with mages who do not scry well or at all about what is coming." He looked at Amelia, Serena, James, Julia, and Thomas in turn. "At least, I can advise those who are within a day or two of London by post coach that we can expect to attend. For the rest, I fear I will be working my horses hard to cover the rest of England. I shall have to leave Scotland, Wales, and Ireland to Masters there."

"You would not want to encroach," Thomas pointed out. "MacPherson in particular gets thorny about the Sassenachs running roughshod over his Scots."

"You might as well sweeten the sour news with dancing and dinner," Julia said. "You are right in thinking that a few gallons of white soup and some cakes are not going to make a particle of difference in a year of crop failures. Think of it as a ball on the eve of a great battle. No one knows how the battle will turn out, but having a little joy beforehand will help us deal with the hardships to come."

"I should consult with you more often, Mrs. Angleford," his lordship said with a wan smile. "I forget that you have sound common sense and an outlook that differs quite a bit from the dwellers in stately homes."

"You are always welcome to do so," Julia replied, taking not a whit of offense from what could have been taken as a very backhanded compliment. "And at least *we* have warning, and can do what we can to soften the blows for those who depend on us."

"Beets," Amelia muttered to herself. "Turnips. Rye, barley, oats, especially rye. There may be some forms of wheat that tolerate the cold. Cabbage. Kale . . . kale can even grow in the snow. Peas, brussels sprouts, potatoes . . . if there is no blight. . . ."

"Make me a list," Lord Alderscroft said instantly. "Send it to me as soon as you finish it. I cannot tell you how useful it will be."

"You shall have it this evening," she promised. "I will send it by Elemental. I need to consult with my father. He has probably already spoken with our Cherokee allies, who will have, by now, spoken with tribes in Canada, and will know what will survive these next two years. But by all means, talk to the Danes, Norwegians, Swedes, and Finns. If they cannot add to the list of crops, they can certainly give you techniques for protecting plants from freezes."

Alderscroft took his leave of them, and Amelia, for one, felt very sorry for him. Not only was he burdened with Napoleon, now this! And there was only so much he could do. It wasn't as if he could go to the average farmer and urge him to replant all his fields with cabbages and leeks—the man would think him mad, and possibly drive him off with dogs. All he could do was warn the other mages of Britain, let *them* know what to do, and hope they could persuade their neighbors.

Many would not be able to persuade farmers of this wisdom, or the farmers would not be able to change their crops. And as a result, many would starve.

So she voiced her earlier thought aloud. "We, personally, need to go to somewhere that good, gently used, old clothes are sold," she said, bringing the subject back to their own little family. "Then we can remake them into clothing that will at least be warm. All those heavy furs, woolens, and flannels that are no longer fashionable— there will be yards of fabric in those old skirts we can make into flannel petticoats and woolen gowns."

Julia laughed a little. "And all those old ladies like the Queen who refused to give over the fashion of their youth will be laughing at the poor misses in muslins who are freezing at midsummer. But yes, you are right. I'll ask Mrs. Jennings; she will likely want to go with us to acquire similar stuffs for everyone on the staff."

"The men will do all right. They have their woolen coats and breeches already," Serena pointed out. "But we should be knitting everyone scarves, gloves, and extra stockings. At least yarn is not too dear." She sighed. "Oh, my pretty silk stockings! I think they will not be seeing the light of day for some time!"

"At least our prettiest things will be saved from wear," Julia said, as cold comfort. And then, with more cheer, "But there will be such a crush and so many candles at Lord Alderscroft's ball that we can safely wear our summer ball gowns."

"I am going to find someone's old beaver-skin cape and line a day robe with it," Amelia declared. "It won't matter if there are touches of moth's tooth, no one will see it on the inside." And at Serena's giggle, she glared at her cousin. "All very well for *you* to laugh! You are Fire, and you are never cold!"

"And I grow my own fur!" she replied, pertly.

"So you do. In*fur*iating," James punned, making them all groan.

On hearing their news, Mrs. Jennings declared that she was *very* glad that she lived in this household. "I shall want an increase in household money so that Cook and I may put by as much as we can," she said. "I fear you will all be sharing your rooms with bags of dried peas and beans, and possibly with hams and sausages! It is too bad that we are not in the country; the price of flour is likely to be very high before this is over."

"We will make do," replied Julia. "Perhaps I can find other things that can be used instead of flour. But you are right, we should put by as much as we can. Tell Thomas what you need, and he may be able to purchase it at wholesale rates." She sighed. "Our 'bread' may be ship's biscuit for a while; we should get some barrels of it. At least it will be kept drier than on a ship."

"In the meantime, we'll go to the Jewish Quarter, Mrs. Angleford," the housekeeper continued. "There are good, honest clothes brokers there. It is *very* likely we can find some good crape gowns as well as wool; those will be nice and warm, made over, and will not shame you to be seen in at your concerts and theater adventures. When would be convenient?"

"When will be convenient for *you*, Mrs. Jennings?" Julia smiled. "I can put off afternoon visits; you cannot put off all the work this household requires!"

"You are too good; no other employer I know would think of that," Mrs. Jennings replied. "Well! Between Cook and Mary, I believe I can count on my afternoon being free tomorrow. We should take Tommy with us to carry parcels. Frank can mind the door while he is gone."

"Tomorrow it is. You and Cook put your heads together and make a list of foodstuffs to store. We'll want to buy it as soon as we can, to avoid prices going up, but we'll do so over the course of a few weeks. Oh! Is Sally going to kitten soon?"

"The little minx! Yes. Shall we keep all the kittens this time?" Mrs. Jennings clearly knew where this conversation was going. "She's always taught her kits to be excellent mousers, and if we are going to store vittles all over the house, we'll need more than one cat."

"Good; that's all I can think of. If you see anything that takes your fancy on this shopping excursion, for you or the girls or Mrs. Gideon, we'll get it."

"Lots of good worsted; we'll all be knitting till our fingers bleed, I expect." Mrs. Jennings waited to see if her employer had anything more to say, and retreated to the lower floor to impart the bad news to the rest of the staff.

They all wore their oldest and most-worn things for the trip to the Jewish Quarter, and they wore plain, unornamented bonnets with big brims. As ready as she was to economize, Julia Angleford was not prepared to be *recognized* while doing so, and even Mrs. Jennings dressed "down" in an old calico, layered with several shawls, and an even older cap. It appeared, however, that she was not at all averse to bargain-hunting, because the owner of the first shop she took them to recognized her on sight, and welcomed her gravely. He was a fine-looking man, with long locks at his ears, dressed conservatively in a black coat, gray waistcoat, old-fashioned breeches, and a tall hat.

"And what is your pleasure, ladies?" he asked, after finding and dusting off four slightly wobbly chairs, and making a great show of gesturing that they should sit.

"We need winter gowns well out of the present mode," Julia said. "Wool, crape, flannel, heavy linen. *Very* heavy silk, if you have it."

"As it happens, I may have just the things that you are looking for, and it may be that you will not need to look further. Josef!" he snapped, calling into the depths of the rather dark shop. "Bring out the latest consignment!"

"It is still in trunks, father!" came a plaintive call from the rear.

"Then bring out the trunks!" the merchant said impatiently.

And at length, a be-locked youth in an impeccably tailored waistcoat, linen shirt, and long trousers dragged the first of three enormous trunks out to the front of the shop. Truly the trunks were as tall as he was and, lying down, came to his mid-thigh. The proprietor opened the first trunk with a flourish, and began pulling out tightly packed garments redolent of cedar and lavender.

They were, in fact, nearly identical to the queen's favored garments, panniers and all, and the first lot was completely unsuitable, since they were heavy brocades that could not pass as fashionable except as waistcoats. But the next trunk was full of what had obviously been day dresses, and they came in a selection of heavy, soft, embroidered linens and silks, figured crape, and fine merino wool. There was so much fabric in the skirts of a single one of these garments that Amelia reckoned each of them could get two gowns and perhaps a spencer and other odds and ends out of each. And there were some flannel "lying in" gowns, completely unused, that would make excellent, warm petticoats. It was obvious from looking at them that these things had all come from the estate of some wealthy woman whose heirs could not be bothered to reuse any of her garments, and for some reason, none of her servants had been gifted with any on her death.

The lying-in gowns must have been from her trousseau, but why were they never used? Was she childless? If so, and if her estate had gone to some nephew, then perhaps that explained why the clothing had ended here. He might have just peeked in the trunks, saw it was clothing, and ordered it off to the clothing merchant. And if this had all been in storage when she died—and it looked as though it must have been—Amelia could not imagine what had been in the woman's wardrobes.

Well, perhaps not much. She might have been a recluse, and lived in petticoats and a dressing gown.

They all made their selections; Amelia took a heavy embroidered yellow linen, a figured rose crape, and a blue wool with a lot of heavy silk braid that would have to be unpicked and taken off. Serena confined herself to one silk, one linen, and one crape, all various shades of red and brick. Julia chose green and green-blue in crape and wool. They took all of the lying-in gowns. Mrs. Jennings expressed her satisfaction with the two black wool gowns she got for herself, and some gently used flannel petticoats. Amelia urged her to take a black silk, and she refused. "Silk! What use is silk to me?" she asked.

And for the other downstairs ladies, she acquired brown wool and gray linsey-woolsey garments from the merchant's inventory, all with voluminous skirts ripe for remaking.

"Is there anything else?" the gentleman asked, with great dignity, but the obvious desire to make the most of such affluent customers as he could.

"I don't suppose you'd have any fur cloaks?" Amelia asked without much hope. Because the trunks were all but emptied except for the brocades.

"Well . . . Persian lamb," he said disparagingly. "Alas! I have no seal, no beaver. Most people keep such things for themselves. It is easy to make muffs and collars and cuffs."

"Lambskin! The very thing!" Julia exclaimed. "Let us see them!"

Two were gold, one was brown, and the fur, which Amelia had

never seen before, had a silky sheen to it. All three were women's cloaks, and very well cared for, with the exteriors being matching velvet. Voluminous to fit over the voluminous gowns of the previous century, which meant they, too, could be cut down, and the remnants made into muffs, hats, or collars and cuffs, or a lined shawl. The velvet was badly rubbed, quite bare in some places, but some might be saved, and if nothing else, Amelia judged she could make some nice caps as gifts for downstairs.

Poor little Tommy was appalled at everything he would have to carry. But that was simply solved. The proprietor threw in some embroidery supplies that had been in the last trunk, and gave them two of the trunks themselves, he was so delighted with his good luck. Then Tommy and Josef took the trunks to the carriage and loaded them there, and with Josef's help Davey got them onto the roof of the carriage, where they were secured. They haggled just enough over the price to make the good man sure he had gotten a great victory, and before tea time they were on their way back to the house.

"I have never met a Jew before," Amelia said thoughtfully. "He was quite nice. I do not know why Shakespeare was so disparaging of the race."

"Because Shakespeare suffered from prejudices that are common to this day," Julia replied, and sighed. "There is a fine family of Jewish mages here in London, but sadly, you will not meet them at Alderscroft's ball. Those prejudices are why you only find them in moneylending, or secondhand dealing, or tailoring, or in businesses where they only have contact with their own kind." She paused for a moment. "I shall invite them to come after dinner in the next week. They won't eat with Gentiles, but they are all musical and we can have a musical evening."

"Aaron is as honest a man as one would ever want to meet," Mrs. Jennings said stoutly. "His family has been in this business since before the king took the throne. When I went into service, my mama took me here to find clothing to remake for my new position, and though his father knew we were poor, he treated us as if we were duchesses, and searched until he could find something good that we could afford, and charged us half because it had stains that needed to be cut out. A good man, and the son is as good as the father," she repeated.

"Well, he was good to us, and we are going to have our hands full with all of this," Serena said with unconcealed glee. "Why, now I feel quite at home, to be making my *own* clothing rather than letting a *modiste* do it! I confess, though, I am very glad we won't need these things until winter. That will give us plenty of time to create some very nice gowns indeed. By the time we bring them out in public, the other ladies will be wishing they had something as nice and warm, rather than looking down at us because woolens are not modish enough."

"Sadly, if his lordship is correct, we shall be working on these gowns in summer weather chill enough to make it no hardship," Amelia said sadly. "I was hoping so much to see real May Day celebrations here, and a bluebell wood! But from all he says, the flowers in May might be scant. But if we are not to be frolicking out of doors, we can at least have something to fill our hands."

Julia sighed. "I had rather have the gowns made by someone else, but I fear that I would blush for shame to have Madame Alexander know I was sending her *used* fabric. It is all pride, I know, but there it is. So you must help me; it has been many a day since I made my own gowns!"

Amelia's once-tidy room now had an entire corner piled with voluminous gowns. It would be neater once she had picked them apart and laid the fabric flat, but at the moment they were a giant untidy heap, for there was no room for them in the wardrobe. And knowing she would not be able to rest until that unmanageable pile had been reduced to something reasonable, after dinner she decided to do something about it. She had gone up to her room after a somewhat gloomy attempt to read aloud to the group, but the men were preoccupied with plans to weather this crisis and weren't heeding, and

Serena and Julia clearly had *their* finds on their minds. So the ladies left the men to break out the brandy and try to think of all the possible outcomes the months ahead might bring.

Once upstairs, she immediately got her scissors and began her deconstruction. After all, she had done everything she could; the promised crop list had been gotten from her father and sent to Lord Alderscroft by means of Natty Ned, who had consented to appear in the front parlor.

For Mrs. Gideon, there were suggestions from her mother from their old receipt book, which was full of recipes using very limited ingredients from the colonial days. And there were even a few for substitutions for flour if flour became too dear—although her main suggestion was "just get used to the taste of rye and barley bread, dearest."

It had even been hard to enjoy dinner, despite Mrs. Gideon doing her uttermost to produce something unusually good, a lovely, thick soup with crusty rolls and a delectable cake, because all Amelia could think of was that this time next year there would be people starving and there was nothing she could do about it.

At least she could take out her frustration on seams.

The lovely thing about those huge skirts was that, aside from the bodice and sleeves, there had been very little *fitting* involved in their construction. The huge skirts were nothing but pieced-together rectangles, all of the same size, and a great deal of pleating. That left her with the fitted bodice and tight sleeves, and that neat pile of folded fabric she had hoped for. She took the fitted bodice to pieces as well, thinking that if nothing else, she could use it to make a warm spencer for Ginny, the tweenie, as none of the other servants would fit it. The original owner had been very slender!

The gowns had been expertly made by a good *modiste*; the stitching was practically invisible, and every potential weak point had been reinforced with tiny diamonds of matching fabric (probably left over from cutting the fitted bodice and sleeves). She learned a bit in taking the first gown apart, and used that to tackle the deconstruction of the velvet cloak. That was when she discovered that this "Persian lamb" certainly *was* lambskin, and probably very young lambs at that, the pelts were so small. The hide was quite delicate and would need to be sewn carefully, probably with a silk thread, and definitely with a very sharp needle in order to avoid tearing it. But this was no different than sewing rabbit, and she had done enough of that in the past. The number of baby swaddles, baby booties, and mitten linings she had sewn was past counting.

The cloak was enormous, as one might expect, given that it had to go over one of those huge dresses. There would be more than enough fur to line that morning gown she was planning, and there would be plenty left over for other projects.

Sadly, most of the velvet was badly rubbed, with the foundation fabric showing, especially on the back. But . . .

There might be enough for that morning gown. If not, there would be enough for a muff, and a hood and shoulder cape, not just for her but for someone else. And the threadbare stuff would not be wasted; she could use it to line the spencer for Ginny.

With one gown and the cape reduced to parts, she at least felt tired enough to sleep.

New anxieties notwithstanding.

New worries need new lists, she thought as she fell down into sleep.

Within a few days, Lord Alderscroft's invitation arrived, and even though it was expected, it still caused a flurry of excitement in the household. Gowns were inspected for dirt, wear, or the tiniest of tears, sent downstairs for cleaning and freshening up, and came back upstairs for mending and darning. Having learned from that gown she had taken apart, Amelia not only reinforced her own dress against accidents, she showed Serena how to as well.

Then came the visitors, because, of course, everyone in their magical circle had also received an invitation, and all of the ladies felt it needful to confer with all the other ladies.

There were debates in the parlor every morning by all the lady mages that could cram into it, all of them chattering about trims and minor changes of style to update a gown that might have been seen once too often in its current state.

Amelia could tell, however, that all this was in an attempt to stave off varying degrees of anxiety about what was to come. Every mage in London knew now about the volcano-winter that was going to descend on them. Every magical household had begun preparations to survive it.

But there was an equal amount of uncertainty and anxiety about what Napoleon would do. Would he actually have the temerity to do what he had not before, and invade Britain?

The weather, and Napoleon. The two things loomed over them like Gog and Magog from the Bible, giants of strength and doom that none of them knew how to counter.

Amelia hovered between wishing she was home—where at least there were no worries about Napoleon—and wondering if she should just consult with James and take passage on the next boat going there.

But if she did, if *they* did, for Serena would not let her go alone, what could they do there that the rest of the family could not?

And the family had already gone to great expense to send the two of them here. James *did* need their help. The bitter weather would not last forever, and there were places where their dyes would be in demand if the demand fell off in England. Charles Stonecroft had barely begun to explore trade with places like Jamaica and the Caribbean, for instance. And eventually the new British enterprise still needed to be established.

And it won't establish itself.

Two years of cold would certainly put fine wool, silk, and cashmere in vogue. The rich would still want these things, and they would not want anything drab, which meant that the market for dyes would still be strong. Silk, despite being light, was warm, and certainly the lords and ladies of the court would still be ready to pay for beautiful things to wear—again, that meant a market for dyes.

Reminding herself of this eased her anxiety just a little, made her chest and throat relax a little, took a little of the furrowing out of her eyebrows.

Then there were James's goats, still languishing in Portugal. *Perhaps I can find a farmer near Axminster who will rent us a pasture so we can bring those wretched goats over sooner. . . .* That was another worry and one she did not have an answer for.

Serena poked her in the ribs with her elbow. "You are woolgathering again."

She sighed. "Literally. Worried about James's wretched goats, among other things. If the weather is going to be cold, I want to get them *here* where we can care for them and not leave them to the whims of a hired shepherd."

"Who is an Elemental mage. And a friend of James," Serena reminded her. "How you can worry about so many things at once brings me to astonishment."

"How you can worry about so few astonishes *me*."

Serena did not take offense. She never took offense. "Think about nice things. Think about the ball! Just think, this ball might be where we finally meet someone truly eligible!"

Amelia found herself smiling a little. Of all of her cousins, Serena was the one whose ambitions were the most conventional. She wanted—truly *wanted*, and not because she was told this was what proper young women wanted—a good husband and a swarm of children. For herself, Amelia was . . . not so sure. She felt, vaguely, that there were other things she could do. Be a scholar perhaps, or . . . or . . . well, she just wasn't sure. She didn't want to be an explorer; that would mean going to uncomfortable places and risking life and health, and not having pretty things to wear. A scholar would be fine, though; she could read as much as she liked, visit great libraries, and be comfortable. Learn things. Teach them to others? Perhaps . . .

But she didn't actually dislike the idea of having a husband. Children, on the other hand . . . certainly not as many as Serena wanted or her own mother had.

Perhaps I could be a lady author? I would not have to worry about where I lived or having enough to eat, since we'll be living on James's property. Certainly she could write better fantasies than some she had read. Would the novelty of reading about people in America be enough to sell books in Britain? If she wrote something like an American version of *Pride and Prejudice*, she could even use her old friends and neighbors as characters and no one would be the wiser.

But for now . . .

"I am tired of worrying and making lists," she admitted. "I would like to dance until I am too weary to think. I would like to have a glorious dinner in a fine home before we are reduced to lentil and cabbage soup. I would like very much to meet interesting people who have done interesting things and gone to interesting places. I would like to hear music I have never heard before and be surprised by it."

"You would like—" Serena summed up "—to be taken out of yourself for an evening."

She squeezed her cousin's arm. "You know me too well."

"Think about small things," her cousin urged her. "All the little things we can actually do. If Napoleon beats the allies, we can go home, after all, and our home is much better situated to deal with the coming weather. Set yourself small goals! For one thing, there are many ordinary people that we can warn, delicately, that the summer is likely to be very cold and the winter very bad. That nice Jewish clothes merchant, for instance. We can say—oh, that we've seen exactly this kind of thing in America. We know there will be two summers that will be frightfully cold, and winters that will be bone-chilling, and make up all kinds of signs that the Indians allegedly told us to tell us this is so!"

"My goodness, that's right, you can!" exclaimed one of their guests, who had overheard her. "And we can do the same—Banbury stories about sailor brothers or fathers, or that *you* have told us these things about the Indians." A spot of color came into their visitor's cheek, as she brightened with pleasure. "What an *excellent* idea, Serena!"

It was Serena's turn to color up, as the rest of the ladies heaped praise on her for being so clever. Truth to tell, Amelia was terribly proud of her for it, too. Sometimes she forgot that Serena was really quite clever; she just didn't trot out everything she was thinking as some people did.

That led them all to start discussing whom they could tell, what tales they could make up that would be believed, how to warn other members of their families to back up those stories. By the time they all left, they were genuinely more cheerful than they had pretended to be when they arrived.

"Are you going up to dress for the afternoon?" Serena asked, when the last of the visitors had been shown out. "Were you or Julia planning to make calls?"

"I suppose so? We had not planned anything, but it is what we usually do. Was there something you wished to do this afternoon?"

"Yes," Serena said. "I found the most *ravishing* music, and I want both of us to learn it in time for the ball. Let me run up and get it."

Before Amelia could say anything, Serena had already left the room, and came back almost immediately. "I found it in that second-hand book store Julia took us to last week," she said. "It seems to be from a larger score—perhaps an opera—but this duet is all I could find. It is for soprano and counter-tenor, which means you can sing the counter-tenor and I can sing the soprano part. It will show both of us to perfection, if you don't mind playing the piano part."

With that, Serena opened the pianoforte and arranged the music on the rack, and began playing little bits of melody. "Come! Try it! You will be Nerone, and I will be Poppea!"

"Nero and Poppea?" Amelia furrowed her brow. "But . . . they were very wicked. How could there be beautiful music about them?"

But she could not help but be drawn to the piano, where she saw the words *"Pur ti miro, pur ti godo"* at the top of the page.

"'I gaze upon you, I desire you'?" she gasped.

"I told you it was ravishing! Now, don't be all missish. We have certainly sung worse!" Serena was all smiles. "Only listen, and try!"

Serena asked so little of her that she could not help but give in, and stumbling a little over the unfamiliar notes and Italian words, they began.

Pur ti miro, pur ti godo,
Pur ti stringo, pur t'annodo;
Più non peno, più non moro,
O mia vita, o mio tesoro.
Io son tua, tuo son io,
Speme mia, dillo, di.
Tu sei pur l'idolo mio,
Si, mio ben, si, mio cor, mia vita, si.

Within moments, Amelia knew that Serena was right. This was the most ravishing song she had ever heard in her life, even stumbling through it as they were. "Who wrote this?" she said when they came to the end, Serena carefully turning the fragile old pages as she played. "It is a work of genius!"

"It doesn't say. And we should have these pages copied so we don't destroy them utterly in trying to learn this," Serena replied. "This will *certainly* reinforce my Banbury story that I am Italian!"

"No one but an Italian could have written this," Amelia declared. "I hope we can do it justice. But I want to make one change, because 'I desire you' puts me to the blush, and makes me very uncomfortable. I will happily sing '*ti adoro,'* instead, because I *do* adore you, my minx, and it scans better anyway."

"Then you *will* sing it with me!" Serena clapped her hands in glee.

"I think it will sing itself, but yes," Amelia replied with a smile. "Now let's beg Julia for some music paper and make copies before these words and music vanish before our very eyes."

It took them the afternoon to make copies and put the originals in a safe place. Then they practiced after dinner, to the astonishment

---

* *Pur ti miro, pur ti godo,* the final duet and conclusion of Monteverdi's *The Coronation of Poppea.* The opera itself was neglected from 1651 until 1888, but I've taken the liberty of having Serena discover this one, singularly beautiful aria.

of Julia, Thomas, and James, who all declared they had never heard anything so delicious.

And finally, for the first time in days, Amelia went to sleep with something other than worries racing around in her head. No, her mind was full of music.

I gaze upon you, I adore you,
I embrace you, I enchain you;
no more grieving, no more dying,
o my life, o my beloved.
I am yours, yours am I,
my hope, tell it, tell.
You are truly my idol,
yes, my love, yes, my heart, yes.

8

THE morning of Lord Alderscroft's "magician's ball" dawned clear and bright, if unseasonably chill for the middle of May; if you looked, you could see a sort of gray haze high up in the sky, above even the clouds. Amelia tried not to look at it, since this was the harbinger of worse to come. She was trying, very hard, to follow everyone's advice: *enjoy this, and make good memories to hold us in the hard times.*

This was to be more than just a ball as Amelia understood the meaning of the word. Lord Alderscroft had decreed that the festivities would begin in the early afternoon, with a concert for those who wished to arrive that early, then a light meal, a hearty afternoon tea, which would be laid out in a room next to the ballroom. Amelia and Serena had gotten used to that particular meal, substantial enough to tide one over until dinner, since they had been living with the Anglefords. Mealtimes truly were different than the ones at home. Instead of a hearty breakfast featuring almost anything one might want, there was tea, toast, boiled eggs, perhaps a little bacon. Then something small at luncheon, rather than another hearty meal of the sort working farmers needed. Then tea, which was more like lunch at home, except hot foods were rarely served, then dinner, which was the main meal. Then, sometimes, supper, which was generally soup. The Anglefords rarely took supper unless everyone had been out late, in which case they all gathered for soup, or perhaps more toast (*yet* more toast!) and boiled eggs, or sometimes oysters and a bit of chicken.

So they would be fed after the concert. Then when the meal was over, the room would be used for refreshments for the dancers; given that this was a private ball, and it was Lord Alderscroft, Amelia knew there would be more than biscuits, lemonade, and negus; if someone drank his lordship's wine until they were tipsy, or ate entire plates of tiny sandwiches, no one would be impolite enough to complain.

Then there would be dancing from seven until ten, with a card room for those who were not dancing, then a fancy dinner, followed by a short concert by those of the guests who cared to participate, then more dancing until four in the morning. Naturally Serena had placed both their names down as part of that second concert, and after hearing an *a cappella* rendition of the first few bars, his lordship declared that he would rather not have the concert if they were not in it. Boldly, Serena had asked for a harpsichord. Just as boldly, his lordship promised one would be present.

"I hope there is really a harpsichord," Amelia fretted, characteristically. "Our song will sound so much better with a harpsichord. I hope people like it."

"He probably already has one in the music room," Serena declared, as they got into the carriage, their winter cloaks folded around their gowns.

"But what if it is out of tune?" Granted, a pianoforte was nearly as quiet as a harpsichord, but now Amelia had managed to fixate on it. And she knew it. This had happened before, when there were so many worries on her mind that it seized on something trivial to obsess over—possibly so that she didn't obsess and panic over something so large and potentially terrible that it would paralyze her. "I hope no one thinks we have gotten above ourselves, putting ourselves forward in an unseemly manner, by doing this."

But Serena had seen her get into this state before and always knew how to soothe her. "Don't worry. It is Lord Alderscroft! I am convinced that he could conjure a harpsichord up out of scraps and strings at need! And so far from putting ourselves forward, remember his lordship practically demanded we sing!"

The Anglefords had never mentioned if they had been to Lord Alderscroft's London home, but Amelia assumed that they had. Since he was the Huntmaster, it would make more sense for mages to gather there, where presumably there was plenty of room and privacy, than somewhere like a coffee shop or a tavern. When her family had Hunted with the Cherokee, they had gathered in the Cherokee Council House. Otherwise, well, there were enough mages in the family that they had never needed to call in outside help for a Hunt, and they usually gathered in the threshing barn.

"Lord Alderscroft's home in Chester Square," she heard Thomas say to Davey, as he and Julia got into the carriage, taking the forward-facing seats. James entered last, and she and Serena made room for him between them. They all settled, and the carriage moved off with a rattle and jingle of harness, and a lurch.

"Is this anywhere we have been on our walks?" she asked. Julia shook her head.

"It's in Belgravia, and we would be very out of place there. Probably mistaken for servants, if we went walking about! People like us do not call on people like his lordship!" she said cheerfully. "That's why he always turns up on our days 'at home,' rather than risking snubs for us if we went into Chester Square. The house is a ridiculously imposing pile, and I cannot imagine living in it. His lordship and his wife are alone there now that their sons are all at Oxford, and I think the echoing emptiness would drive me mad!"

"It's not that empty," Thomas protested. "It's full of servants."

Julia just shook her head.

Amelia shivered with anticipation. *This* was the sort of thing she had privately longed for when she first heard that she and Serena were to join James in Britain. It would be like living in a novel. Mansions! Balls! Lavish dinners! *So stop worrying for once. Take a deep* breath. *Do what even his lordship said, and for once, live in the moment.* She was going to take Serena's advice and try not to think about what they all might be subsisting on this time next year. She would try not to think about anything but dancing, music, and company she would probably enjoy a great deal.

After all, next we'll be in our own rented cottage, there should be a bit of land and a garden with it, and we can have forcing frames to grow vegetables. Low ones. Pumpkins! Pumpkins will be perfect! There are so many things that can be made with pumpkins! And we can have chickens. Perhaps a hutch of rabbits, or a cote of pigeons. We won't starve. No matter how many times she told herself she would *not* be thinking about and planning for utter disaster, she just kept coming back to it. *Fiend seize it! I am worrying again.* She forced herself to pay attention to what Serena and Julia were talking about.

". . . seven stories tall, twenty bedrooms, a ballroom of course, a library, a music room, a study, a card room, a breakfast parlor and a guest parlor, and probably ever so many things I can't remember," Julia was saying, and Amelia realized that she must be talking about Lord Alderscroft's mansion. "It has *grounds*, and multiple gardens, even a small orchard. He built it for his wife; she is London born, and is not comfortable in the country."

"Fire?" Serena asked. Fire mages tended to be the most comfortable in a city. Fortunately, where the Anglefords lived, it was *just* new and uncrowded and unpoisoned enough that she and all the Elementals of her power were still comfortable. Presumably the same held for where the Alderscrofts lived. . . .

You silly thing. It has grounds and gardens and an orchard. Even the most sensitive mage will be comfortable there, an oasis in the city.

Julia nodded.

"Well, it sounds as if it is almost as big as our White House," Serena said. "It must certainly bigger and better than any house I have ever seen, even our own. Perhaps there are mansions in New York City or Boston that are that big, but we've never been there that we would know."

"The homes in Chester Square are all very much like this," Julia continued. "He is quite important in the House of Lords, and often advises the queen and prince regent. Many very important people live in Chester Square, in Belgravia in general."

Amelia nodded; Alderscroft had implied as much, but had never once actually said anything about it.

"So many of his fellows in the House of Lords live in Chester Square as well, although we will not see any of them at this ball. I don't know how he explains to them that he has balls with all us commoners, but I suppose he is held in such high esteem that people ignore such a social *faux pas*, if they even notice that the conveyances coming to his door are more like what would come to the *servants'* entrance than to the front."

Novels have made this rather clear. To be honest, when Lord Alderscroft had first turned up at the Anglefords' home, she had been a little shocked. According to those novels, unless one was a Poor but Honest and Beautiful and Good Young Woman—well, rather like the fairy tale where a goose girl married a prince—no one from a lower class ever got a glimpse of the upper unless they were servants in a great household.

But that is true for anyone who is not an Elemental mage. "Smells of the shop," and all. And I am certain most households treat their servants as invisible. It was a truism, at least where she came from: if you are a mage, then surround yourself with mages, and treat them well, because you may be relying on each other for your lives.

She had managed to lose the thread of the conversation Serena was having with the others, and began listening again only as Julia was saying, "His lordship belongs to all the important clubs, but for us, *the* most important one is the Exeter Club. It's the one almost all the mages in London belong to, regardless of their social status—not unlike a club devoted to boxing and boxers, where men of all classes are welcome and treated alike. The *male* mages, that is," she said, a bit tartly, with a glance at her husband.

"Don't blame *me*!" he said. "*None* of the London clubs allow women!"

"You'd allow a street urchin in, an actual pickpocket, if he was a mage, but you won't let a woman in even if she's a Master," Julia replied, stiffly. "I do not see the logic."

Amelia glanced at her brother, who was carefully hiding a smile. Thomas had a cornered look. Evidently this was an old grievance.

Not that she blamed Julia in the least. For all the ease and delights of living in Britain, the women seemed to have much less freedom here than she had at home.

Fortunately for everyone's comfort, they arrived in Chester Square shortly after that statement in the not-quite-argument, and both girls gawked through the carriage windows at the huge houses, five, six, and seven stories tall, all made in the same elegant, simple style, all constructed of the same white stone, and all of them with walls around them over which trees and tall, manicured bushes peeked. Amelia marveled and wondered if grand houses in America really did look like this.

Possibly. Enough of our most prominent people from the largest cities have been to England and even the Continent, and they bring back fashions in all things, even houses.

"I don't think these mansions are as big as the White House," Amelia said thoughtfully, as they drove through a black iron gate in a white stone wall onto a circular driveway with a portico over the drive at the door. "But they are certainly big *enough*."

The carriage door was opened by an actual liveried footman in dark red satin, complete with powdered hair, who extended his hand to Julia. He assisted all the ladies out; the men got out by themselves. As the carriage drove off, the footman turned his attention to the next carriage, and a liveried doorman gestured silently that they should come inside.

"Is Davey going back home?" Amelia asked anxiously, gazing after the carriage as it drove around the corner of the building. *What if something happens and we need to leave? Someone being unpleasant, or, oh, I don't know. Something very off-putting. Or worse, what if someone makes Serena so angry she shifts? Lord Alderscroft did say he was not going to tell anyone about her, so no one is likely to realize you anger her at your peril . . .*

"Not at all. He's taking the carriage around to the back of the property where the stables are. The horses will get nose-bags, blankets, and water. All the coachmen will have food and drink directly from the kitchen while we disport ourselves. That's why you didn't hear a word of complaint out of him about how long the entertainment will take," said Thomas. "Lord Alderscroft has a reputation for purchasing exceptional beer. And the coachmen will all have plenty of food as well, and someone to keep an eye on how much they are drinking. There will be no drunken coachmen driving home from here!"

Once inside, they found themselves confronting a rotunda, a round room framed by thick columns, painted blue and white. In the center was what appeared to be a Greek or Roman statue—whichever it was, the subject was a woman, perhaps a nymph or goddess, and she was nude except for a wisp of carved fabric across her lower parts. Amelia hardly knew where to look, so she settled her gaze firmly above the figure, gazing at the fine crystal chandelier lit by what looked like a hundred candles. Serena glanced at her, the corners of her mouth twitching. Amelia was well aware that the Elementals of Fire were seldom more than half clothed at best, and as for those of Air and Water, well, they often wore no more than the stone statue did. But at least her Earth Elementals had some grasp of modesty!

She was a bit surprised that there was not some representation of Fire in this rotunda, but perhaps his lordship would have considered that a touch gauche. Or perhaps a semi-nude classical statue was acceptable to his peers, but a djinn or a salamander would raise many questions.

Another footman directed them to one of the doors in the rotunda, yet another footman relieving them of their cloaks and coats as they passed him by. They found themselves in a large room that had been set up for a musical presentation: rows of delicate-looking gilded chairs, facing six more chairs and both a pianoforte *and* a harpsichord. Less than a third of the audience chairs were occupied, but all of the musicians' chairs were. Two violins, a viola, a cello, a harp, and a flute, plus a player at the pianoforte. Amelia followed the others to a set of chairs near the front, and prepared to be happy.

While they waited, Amelia examined the room. It appeared that this was a dedicated music room. Like the rotunda, it was painted in blue and white, with paintings of the Muses around the walls, and plaster decorations of harps, trumpets, lutes, and scrolls ornamenting the crown molding and the pilasters. There were windows along one wall only, but a fireplace at either end of the room. Blue drapes hung in the windows, and there were cushioned bench window seats at each. Silver candelabras had been mounted to the wall beneath the paintings, and there was another huge glass chandelier in the middle of the ceiling. Although there were no flowers in this room, the faint scent of flowers lingered in the air. Roses, mostly, although she thought she scented peonies as well, and the spicy breath of carnations. Lord Alderscroft was very rich; he likely had a forcing-house just for flowers, and very likely had an orangery for citrus fruits and perhaps even a pinery for pineapples.

They could not have been there but a quarter hour, when Lord Alderscroft himself entered the room and nodded to the musicians. The first violinist rose.

"We will be performing a concert of Mozart transcriptions from his larger works," the young man said. "The first will be scenes from his opera *The Magic Flute*." Then he sat back down. Amelia perked up immediately. She had not heard much Mozart before she arrived here, and she had adored every bit of what she had heard.

We are such bumpkins, she mourned a little. In her life she had never heard a musical ensemble larger than a quartet unless it was a band playing dance music. And even then, the members of said quartet were generally amateurs. She had only once heard singers who performed anything but common songs. True, there was sheet music that came over, just like novels did, but it really took expert musicians to play anything that wasn't slow, like the song she and Serena were going to perform. She wouldn't have dared if it weren't slow.

She was not disappointed in what she heard. Well, maybe a little disappointed, but not in the performance. The music was so wonderful she only wished she could see and hear the entire opera and was sad that the opportunity had never arisen.

More people entered the room as the musicians played, but at least they did so quietly and respectfully, and did not unduly disturb anyone's pleasure as they took their own seats. Somewhat to Amelia's surprise, one of them was Captain Roughtower, and with him was another man she did not recognize. They took seats immediately behind the Angleford party, but did not interrupt their pleasure.

When the pieces were over, the first violinist stood. "We will have a brief interval. The next selections will be from *The Abduction from the Seraglio*."

The musicians stepped away from their chairs, and the audience members began to talk among themselves. Thankfully none of them had behaved badly during the music, as some people did at the public concerts Amelia and Serena had gone to—talking right over the musicians, eating, drinking, and generally behaving in a way she considered very disrespectful.

"Good evening, Thomas, Julia," came a low but cultured voice from behind them—*not* the captain's voice. "I would like very much to thank you for warning us all of what we are to expect for—two years, you believe?"

They all turned in their seats. The speaker was the man with the captain, of course. He was dressed simply, but impeccably: blazing white neckerchief tied in an ordinary knot, gray and white waistcoat, black coat, and black breeches of the sort James assured Amelia were called "inexpressibles" for the way they clung to the legs. He was lean, with very dark hair, a face like a hawk, keen blue eyes, and a nose that would not have been out of place in the face of a bird of prey.

"Mr. Nightsmith, it is a pleasure to see you here," Thomas said, warmly. "You can thank our guests for that warning. This is James Stonecroft, his sister Amelia, and their cousin, Serena Meleva. James is Air, Serena is Fire, and Amelia is an Earth Master and a Channel."

Amelia nodded at her name; she had been surprised to see the captain here, but on closer magical examination—something she had not been able to do in the bustle of the Assembly Room—it appeared that he was an Earth mage. So that explained it.

"I believe Amelia and Serena are about to become your neighbors next month, at least for a while," Thomas continued.

"Oh! Then they are the reason Alderscroft has been refurbishing his little house in the village." Nightsmith turned his sharp eyes on Amelia and her cousin, and she tried not to squirm under that hard gaze. "Well, I shall be greatly obliged if I may prevail upon you to channel for my fields. And offer any more advice on the crops we may be able to bring out under difficult conditions."

"I will channel for any mages to protect and enrich any fields that I can reach; I do not intend that anyone should starve if I can help it," she replied. "And as for advice on crops, if you have not already plowed your wheat under, try to force it along before the weather worsens, and you may still have a crop. Otherwise, if you do not think it can be forced in time, and you decide to plow, cabbage will be extremely useful, as will mangels and other root vegetables. Pumpkins and similar autumn vegetables also will certainly be useful, and of those, pumpkins keep well. Food for your animals in quantity, food for people in quality. And cut wild grasses and marginally edible shrubs and the like for silage."

"Really, Phillip, *must* we discuss plantings and the like as if we are at an agrarian fair?" laughed the captain. "Alderscroft brought us together to enjoy ourselves before whatever doom befalls us, whether it be Napoleon or volcano weather!"

Mr. Nightsmith turned his unsmiling face on what Amelia presumed was his friend. "Not all of us get our income from timber, Harold."

"And a scant income it is, too." The captain waved dismissively. "Pray, have you any good horseflesh coming along?"

Nightsmith's face actually showed some animation. "Four or five good hunters, actually. Brave, willing, and good spring. They'll be ready for their first hunt in the fall, and I would be obliged if you'll try them all. You are a good judge of horseflesh."

"I shall, if my regiment isn't packed up across to the Continent," the captain promised. "I am grateful to you; the sad nags I can actually afford are bone-rattlers."

James lit up. "I love riding to the hunt above all things," he exclaimed. "Although our gray foxes will not give us the run that a red fox will." He made a face. "They will run up trees, if you will believe me, or lose themselves in swampland, and even dig themselves safely into a rabbit warren with astonishing speed if they are not near their den." He did not ask for an invitation to a hunt—no polite person would—but Amelia knew how much he longed for such a thing. He was a fine rider too, and in her opinion, it was a great shame that he was unable to ride in London. Unable—or perhaps unwilling to sit the kind of hard-mouthed, played-out beast that was available for hire.

"As a fellow magician and soon to be my neighbor, you shall have an invitation," Nightsmith said immediately, earning her reluctant gratitude. "And you shall ride out of my stable. In our hunt club there are no ranks and no precedence based on anything but the ability to stick a horse, keep with the hounds, and treat a sweet goer with the respect he deserves. But . . ."

"But?" James prompted.

The captain laughed. "Phillip will not allow us to ride a hunt to the kill," he said, "unless the fox is known to take his depredations into people's coops and pens."

The slightly . . . *mean* way in which the captain had said this reminded Amelia that her first impression of the captain had been that she did not like him. And now, her second impression was that she did not like him.

But Nightsmith just shrugged. "I like a good, long hunt, with riding over as many obstacles as possible. Foxes who are chased and live to be chased another day learn to be clever, and can give the hounds the slip enough times to make a hunt interesting. They also learn to be wary of hounds and men, which means to be wary of the keepers of coops and pens. I have plenty of game, enough to share with an occasional fox, and I consider a few pheasant and duck to be worthy pay for my amusement. Any fox that will not learn to confine itself to my game, well, that is why I have a gamekeeper. Better the fox meet a clean death at the end of a rifle bullet than be torn apart by hounds."

"So you always say." The captain sighed. Amelia was taken aback. *Does he actually* enjoy *watching an animal ripped to death by hounds?*

"I love a good hunt, I love a neck-or-nothing ride on a generous horse that is willing and giving, but I, too, have not much stomach for the 'view to a kill,'" James admitted.

"And shooting?" Nightsmith asked. This was the most animated that Amelia had yet seen him. "Do you shoot?"

"Every boy, and some girls, learn to shoot and shoot well, where we are from," James replied. "It is a necessity. We are not in a howling wilderness, but there are wolves, bears, and catamounts. We hunt game, and if you could see the abundance of game we have, you would stare your eyes out. What's more, the natives are *our* friends, but that doesn't mean there aren't what we call 'nasty, two-legged varmints' about. If a man will not come up to my door and offer to work in order to eat, but skulks about, looking for what he can steal, then he should not be surprised if I show him off with a bullet." James shrugged. "There are few constables and fewer magistrates."

The captain made a wry mouth. "If so many of you are cracking shots, it comes as less of a surprise that—" Then he shrugged. "It is over now, the treaty has been signed, and there's an end to it."

"There's an end to it," really? I wonder how he would feel if our army overran his estate every year or so and looted it?

"The musicians are returning," Nightsmith announced, and turned to Amelia. "Perhaps we can continue our discussion later. Over dinner, if we are seated together. Or if there is no further occasion, when I welcome you to Axminster."

He says that as if he is the prince of the entire town, Amelia thought, not sure if she was amused or affronted at his hubris. But she did not, she hoped, show her reaction, and she settled again in her chair to enjoy the music.

At the end of the concert, servants came to announce "a light, cold collation," the expected afternoon tea, which proved to be a buffet table laden with all manner of delights, and small tables at which to enjoy them. This was presented in a handsome room she was told was "the breakfast parlor," painted a cheerful yellow, with white drapes, and more candelabra on the walls between the windows. Landscapes adorned the walls, and the windows looked out into a garden. The table was staffed by a half-dozen servants, the men in the gray-and-white livery of the Alderscroft household, the women in gray gowns, over which snowy aprons had been tied, hair neat beneath white caps. Amelia held back to observe, and discovered that one did not help oneself; one approached the table, indicated to a free servant what one wanted, and was rewarded with a full plate when done. Nor did one carry one's own plate; younger servants carried it to the table, then came back with one's chosen beverage. Tea, mostly, and lemonade, although there was wine and many gentlemen were enjoying it.

Amelia did not particularly want to speak with Mr. Nightsmith, in part because he would probably bring the captain with him, but mostly she did not want to talk about the very things that were giving her so much anxiety, and *he* looked as if he was going to quiz her on what she knew and what she could do to help his property. So it was with great relief that she heard herself hailed by some of the "morning callers" who were always welcome in Julia's parlor. These were the Misses Sumner, two young ladies of eighteen and nineteen, and their aunt of "indeterminate age." All three wore lovely silk-satin gowns in shades of rich, golden yellow, which suited their blond hair to perfection and made them look as if the parlor had been fitted around them. Amelia selected a random assortment of things that would fit on a plate—most of which she did not recognize—and joined them, after looking about and seeing that Serena had been similarly claimed by another small group of morning acquaintances.

"Well!" exclaimed Miranda Sumner as she sat, her blue eyes sparkling. "In the midst of gloom and doom we have some good news!"

"Tell!" Amelia demanded, taking her seat and preparing to be amused. "I am wearied to death of bad news."

"Penelope's Jasper has declared himself!" the older sister said happily, as her younger sibling blushed and examined a cucumber-and-butter sandwich as if it were the most interesting thing in the world.

Well, this was news indeed, and very good news! "But I thought his salary was inadequate to support—" Amelia began.

"He has been promoted!" Penelope murmured proudly. "Full barrister! And Mr. Jenkins told him *strictly* that he must find a wife at once and marry, so that young lady clients will not disrupt the work by attempting to flirt with him rather than concentrating on their problems!"

"*Surely* he was jesting—?" Amelia gasped, for she could not imagine either that Jasper Melleneck would be flirted with, or that young ladies would come to a law office expecting to flirt. Or that the lead barrister of the firm would *order* his newly raised subordinate to wed!

"*Surely* he was not!" Miranda declared. "It is a fact." She rolled her eyes. "It is also a fact that this is the only way such as *we* will ever be accepted in polite society—unless we marry a clergyman. That makes a barrister a *very* desirable *parti*. I am sure that many young ladies of our lack-of-rank would be very happy to marry Jasper."

By "polite society," Amelia knew, Miranda meant the *ton*—the greater *ton*, the *haute ton*, that mass of many hundreds of Londoners who boasted rank, land, or both, which included the ultra-select group who received Almack's vouchers. If your income came from your land and you yourself were not farming it, or if your income came from investments or some other form of not-actually-working, and you had aspirations to take part in polite society, then by default, you were a member of the *haute ton*. The only exceptions to this unspoken law were officers in the military (who might have little to no income but what the Army supplied), the clergy (who were by definition "gentlemen" but who might also be poor as the proverbial church mouse), and barristers and attorneys (who were by dint of their profession in the law considered to be gentlemen and could style themselves "esquire"). "Esquire" was, as she knew from her reading, a title formerly held by a knight's attendant, who was himself in training to become a knight, so it was near to nobility.

But for someone who actually *worked* for a living—like James and Thomas, or Alfred Sumner—the only chance to be accepted by the *ton* was to marry into a landed family. And even then, it was even odds that the spouse would be snubbed. Still it was a chance, and from what she knew of him, Lord Alderscroft would probably assure that the new bride was *not* snubbed by paying one or more public calls himself. Amelia was fairly certain that the calls he had made to Julia and Thomas had *not* been public.

But the Anglefords would not want those calls to be made public, either. The peace and safety of Elemental mages lay in the appearances that they were normal members of society.

"I would not marry Jasper if I did not love him," Penelope said softly. "But I *do* love him."

"But how wonderful that you found someone you love who will also raise you in society!" Amelia exclaimed sincerely. "*And* he will be a good companion to you and make you happy, and you will have a good income as well! What excellent news! Please tell Jasper to call so that we can wish him very happy!"

"We're marrying as soon as we can post the banns," Aunt Emily said with complacence, quite as if she were the one getting married, tucking an errant curl under her gold silk turban. "If you have not gone to Axminster by the time of the wedding, you and your cousin and brother and the Anglefords will certainly get invitations. If you *have*, we shall rely on James to show for your family, and Thomas and Julia to show for theirs." She twinkled at Miranda. "Perhaps you and James might conceive of a *tendre* for one another!"

Miranda laughed dismissively, but she didn't look displeased at the idea. *We could do worse for James, and I like the Sumners very much,* Amelia thought, then chided herself for acting like a matchmaking mama.

"Thomas, Julia, and James will at least be here, and I know they will be delighted to come, and James can indeed do the honors for all of us," Amelia replied, nodding, and doing her best to show nothing but light interest in the other implications.

James came to collect her with Serena on his arm just before she had run out of interesting subjects with the Sumners. Since *she* had always considered it to be better to leave while the conversation still delighted, rather than lingering until one was stifling yawns, she was happy to see him. James took her on his other arm, gave friendly greetings to the Sumners, and took them from the refreshment room out yet another door and into the ballroom.

The six musicians that had entertained them with Mozart selections had been joined by four more: another flute and three clarinets. They were setting up on a low dais next to the door they had entered from. James paused just out of the way so that Amelia and Serena could properly admire the room.

The high ceiling boasted *four* massive chandeliers, and more of those silver candelabra were placed at intervals along the walls between beautiful mirrors, for there were windows along only one wall of this room. Handsome plaster half-columns framed windows, mirrors, and candelabra; the walls were painted a pleasant rose, with white plaster festoons and garlands in the upper parts. Beneath the mirrors were plinths upon which stood silver vases overflowing with flowers—the real ones she had already guessed at, by the scent that filled the air. At the far end of the room was a sort of balcony, where those who were not inclined to dancing and preferred to watch could sit, and low couches lined the walls for those who *wanted* to dance, but were suffering from momentary fatigue or lack of a partner. Beneath this balcony were doors leading to other rooms. The card room, perhaps, or the dining room, or neither.

"Now, I must take you to meet Alderscroft's wife," James said. "She will see to it that you are introduced to plenty of partners."

Amelia quaked a little in her shoes. It was quite one thing for Lord Alderscroft to be so easy and intimate with mere commoners. *Men* could do as they liked, and befriend boxers or jockeys or tradesmen. But women. . . .

And yet, for politeness, she would *have* to be introduced to the lady of the house. And, if need be, suffer a snub. Hopefully not the cut direct! Surely not even a lady would do that to someone they had not even been introduced to yet!

James led them to one of the couches at the head of the room, where an exquisitely gowned woman was chatting to three more very like her. She had raven hair put up behind with a few curls artistically escaping, the whole held in place by a small and elegant tiara of diamonds. Diamonds encircled her neck and adorned her wrists over her gloves. Her gown was of blond lace with a rose silk dress beneath it.

And it was very clear by the way she blazed up to Amelia's mage sight that she was a Master of Air, and a very skilled and powerful one.

Now she quaked even more, although Serena only appeared interested and pleased to make her acquaintance.

Her ladyship's eyes wandered momentarily from her companions, and she clearly caught sight of James. Her gaze brightened.

She stood up, and gestured to him to come forward.

"My dear tiger!" she exclaimed fondly. "I have been looking for you this past hour or more! And these are your sister and cousin?"

"My cousin Serena Meleva, Lady Alderscroft." He let go of Serena's arm, and nudged her forward. Serena curtsied and dimpled. "And my sister Amelia." Amelia made the best curtsy she could manage, though her knees shook with anxiety beneath her dress. "Serena is a Fire mage and Amelia—"

"Is our very precious Earth Master and channel," her ladyship said warmly, and reached out and took a hand from each of them. "Welcome! I wish our circumstances were better, and that we all did not feel as if we were dancing on a cliff edge, but I am determined that we shall have good memories from tonight to sustain us through harder times. I make you acquainted with *my* sisters, Lady Cherborne, Lady Turnbridge, and the awkwardly named Lady Ladysmith."

The three were gowned as beautifully as Lady Alderscroft, the first in blue silk trimmed in swansdown, with ostrich feathers in her hair and blue aquamarines at her throat, the second in ruby velvet with rubies, and the third in a stunning gown of white silk trimmed in black ribbon and black ribbon rosettes, with more diamonds on her wrists, at her throat, and in a magnificent tiara.

The last of the ladies in question laughed heartily. "Aura will *never* forgive me for that!" she said, all smiles. "And you must call us Chloe, Penelope, and Ariadne. And of course, the queen of us all is Aura."

"I beg that you will call us Amelia and Serena," Amelia replied, steadying her voice. "Your father admires the Greeks?"

"How astute of you! Yes, very much so. And our poor Nursey never *could* get her tongue around Ariadne, and always called me 'Airy-dairy!'" This made both the girls laugh, as it was meant to.

"Now, before you all leave town for Axminster, we must have a good, long, cozy chat," her ladyship continued, still in the same warm tones. "I shall send a note so that we can find a time convenient. But for now, Ariadne and Chloe are going to take you all around this ballroom and make sure you are introduced to every gentleman here. If you do not dance every dance because you have not got a partner, I shall hold them responsible!"

"Horrors!" Ariadne chortled. "Whatever shall I do! Come along, American cousin," she said to Amelia, slipping her arm into Amelia's. "Let us take a few turns around the room before she insists I find you a husband instead of just a dancing partner!"

Amelia sighed with relief to find herself with someone she would have found utterly delightful even if the lady had *not* been about to make her first private ball a success.

"Now, tell me whom you already know," Ariadne demanded. Amelia obliged, ending with Mr. Nightsmith and the captain.

Ariadne made a face when the Captain's name was mentioned. "Oh," Amelia said, feeling emboldened. "I know. *So* obviously hanging out for a fortune."

"To be fair," Ariadne said thoughtfully, "he *does* need a fortune. His father was not a gambler, but he might just as well have been; he and his wife spent far beyond the income from Heathcombe. And the house is in shockingly bad condition. But that is no excuse for the way he snubs ladies as soon as he discovers that they have only a modest portion to their names and no hope of inheriting more."

"He has not snubbed me," Amelia admitted. "Not exactly."

"Well, you *are* an Earth Master, and as such, in our circles, that is someone very much worth—Frederick! The very fellow! Allow me to make you known to Miss Amelia Stonecroft. You know, the American Earth Master!" She gave the startled Amelia a little nudge and Amelia gingerly extended a hand, which was seized and kissed.

"My very great pleasure," the portly, balding, middle-aged man said, with every evidence that he felt what he was saying. "I believe you know my daughter; she has called upon you once or twice? Caspia—"

"Oh! Of course! You must be Mr. Bevins! It is a pleasure!"

"And you will, I hope, save me the first cotillion? I do love a cotillion." He beamed at her, and she could not resist.

"It is promised to you, sir, with all my heart!" was her enthusiastic reply.

Ariadne smiled graciously at both of them, and with an apology that she "must get Amelia introduced so that she would never need to sit out a dance," she whisked Amelia away.

Ariadne was more than as good as her word; by the time the musicians had finished setting up and tuning their instruments, Amelia had been taken all around the ballroom, introduced to so many men her head was in a whirl, and brought back to Lady Alderscroft for further instruction. She was only grateful that she had had the good sense not to promise any more dances, or she surely would have promised to multiple gentlemen, which would have been unforgivable.

"Now, you'll allow me to give you a little instruction, I hope, my dear? I am assuming that in America balls are not . . . quite like ours." Her ladyship patted the couch beside her as Ariadne swirled off in search of Serena and her escort, and Amelia took the seat gratefully, feeling a little dizzy at the honor.

"I would be most obliged, your ladyship."

"Aura, please! Just a little, since Ariadne sometimes has more hair than wit, and forgets that not everyone is of the *ton*. You must not dance with your brother. You must not dance more than one dance with a gentleman, particularly if the gentleman is married. It is assumed that if you accept a second dance, he is interested in courting you, and you are interested in being courted."

Her ladyship raised an eyebrow at Amelia's startled *"Oh!"*

"I thought you might not know. Now, the first dance will be a Scotch reel, and if you do not object, William—that is, Lord Alderscroft—is most desirous of partnering you as the second couple. I shall make free of partnering with my dear tiger, your brother, and we will be the first couple. That will set the tone for the evening, and everybody will want to dance with you, once he has."

Once again—that odd nickname for James. "My lady," Amelia ventured. "Why do you call my brother your tiger?"

And once again her ladyship produced that charming, deep-throated laugh. "For several reasons. The first is that at our first Hunt with him, William and I were separated by a pack of hell-hounds, and James defended me like a veritable tiger. He brought with him an Indian weapon—I believe it is called a tomahawk? And the hellhounds fell beneath it like wheat before the scythe. Secondly, when William believes I need an better escort driving than one of the footmen, and James can get free of work, he rides up behind me like a tiger—that is what they call those little boy grooms that the Corinthians like to employ. He says he does not want any *hint* of impropriety, which is *so* considerate of him."

"That sounds very like him," Amelia said thoughtfully.

"And third, he is very . . . springy in the dance. Like a tiger."

Amelia had to laugh. "He does *bound*, does he not?"

At that moment Serena and Chloe appeared, and Chloe gave her sister a very military salute. "All introduced and instructed, General," Chloe said. "Ariadne gives her regrets and says to tell you that Andrew Slatkin has captured her ear and is giving her some very useful instructions about forcing-frames and hothouses."

"Then in that case, let him pour that wisdom into her shell-like ear," said Aura Alderscroft, quite seriously. "She will remember every bit of it and write it down before she goes to bed. I cannot *believe* she got Andrew Slatkin to impart his wisdom!"

"She promised to ask Amelia if he may call. She said she would, and that opened the floodgates."

"Well, then, they can talk during the dance," said Aura, rising, as Lord Alderscroft and James somehow appeared like magic. "Let the ball begin!"

9

THE next few hours flew by. Since Amelia had a very good view of her host and hostess, she noted with no surprise that both of them were superb dancers, and Lady Alderscroft called the dance with the aplomb of a professional caller. The next dance was a cotillion, and Mr. Bevins showed up to claim it; they remained in Lady Alderscroft's set, while his lordship claimed a dance in another set with sister Chloe. And after that, in the interest of being fair, Amelia took the first gentleman to ask as her partner—if need be, promising the others, "You may have the next, and you the one after that, and you the one after that," and hoping she could remember their faces. Between needing to keep track of the figures being called and to whom she had promised dances, and doing her level best to dance well, she quite forgot her troubles. No one snubbed her—at least, not that she knew of—and if anyone *had,* the snub certainly did not deter potential partners. And such a variety! From the jolly Mr. Bevins, to a lad barely out of school; from a young physician to a smart naval officer; from an actual *duke,* to a cheerful, cheeky gentleman who told her directly he worked in the haberdashery warehouse and had seen her there with Julia and Serena, "And I've got me eye on your cuz for the next Scottish reel!" So far, this ball was everything she could have dreamed of, and more! The concert had been perfect, the room was neither too cold nor too warm, and here she was with as many partners as she could have wished, and if they were not all up to the high standards the Alderscrofts' set, well—*she* was not up to those standards either.

Almost too soon—*almost,* because she had begun to feel the number of dances she'd had affecting her legs, and her stomach reminded her mournfully that the cold collation had been *quite* some time ago—the last dance before dinner was called. That was when the young physician turned up again, with a card that proclaimed he was to partner her in to dinner.

"If you don't mind—" he said, diffidently.

"Good heavens, I am glad to see a face I at least recognize!" She laughed. "And you can tell me all sorts of medical horror tales. I promise I will not flinch. I have dressed game *and* putrid wounds with my own hands."

"Ah!" he replied, not at all taken aback. "So it is true what they say about the ladies in America!"

Does he think we all wear skins and chase deer with the Indians? That amused her more than anything.

"If it is complimentary, then yes, it is true." She smiled, saving him from having to tell what it was "they said."

"As we are both Earth, and from that statement, we both have some experience in medicine, I would like to ask you about what you have learned from Indians about medicine. If you have time . . ."

"Infinities! Multitudes! I will gladly tell you all I can in the space of the dinner, and if there are herbs you wish to try to cultivate, I will have Father send seeds—if he can. There are some wild plants that grow poorly from seed, and resist domestication. Even at the hands of an Earth Master."

At that point, the signal was given for them to go in, and they did, with James accompanying Lady Alderscroft, Serena accompanying Lord Alderscroft, and the charming Dr. Edward Trevor taking her in. That set the tone for the rest of the evening; anyone who wasn't too stupid to live was now aware that the Stonecrofts and their cousin were highly valued by his lordship, regardless of rank, or lack of it.

The beautiful rose-pink dining room was as long as the ballroom, and not as wide; the table going down the middle of it could easily seat all of the guests. The darkened windows along one side acted like mirrors, reflecting the light from the chandeliers overhead, the sconces on the walls, and the candelabra on the table. There was a lot of cutlery on the snowy tablecloth, but Amelia was fairly certain she could get through the meal without disgracing herself.

Dr. Trevor drew her attention to a sheet of paper on the tablecloth between them, inscribed in a neat hand. "This is a menu of *every-thing* that will be brought out," he told her, and even though she was exceedingly hungry, her eyes began to glaze over before she had gotten halfway down the page. He chuckled at her expression. "Don't worry, you are not expected to eat everything! The menu is here so you can see what will be brought at each remove. You can ask a footman specifically for what you want, and when he brings it around, he'll make sure to offer you some."

She sighed with relief. "This is far more than I am used to, even when we have guests or a party. This is more like a Christmas feast, when we gather all the families on the plantation together and everyone brings a dish!"

Dr. Trevor's eyes looked amused behind his glasses, but he *tsk*ed a little. "And this is why so many gentlemen have gout, I fear, because some of them *will* try to eat some of every dish. Well, for your future grand suppers, this is called *service a la russe*, which is bringing courses in and clearing them before the next. *Service a la francaise* is when all the dishes are brought to the table at once."

"That is how we do it at home. Well, with much more abandon, and no footmen; we are a lively family, and we simply pass dishes from hand to hand." She finished perusing the menu, having decided what she wanted. The first course, of course, would just be a soup and breads; this one seemed to be a vegetable soup. The next course consisted of several kinds of red meat: beef, mutton, ham. She decided on beef, since most of the cattle on the plantation were dairy cattle, and she seldom got beef at home, though it was quite common on the Anglefords' table. However, they had never once served this dish, *boeuf en croûte,* and she was very curious to try it. Then came a course of salad, pickles, vegetables, cheese, and jellies. No question there; she had *never* had asparagus, so that and some pickles would be lovely. Then came the fish course, which consisted of several sorts of fish, and eels and oysters, which apparently counted as fish. She decided she had no preference and would just take what was first offered. Then another meat course, this time of meats in pastry of various kinds. Then four different sorts of fowl: two chicken dishes, a pheasant dish, and partridges. For both those courses she couldn't decide and again determined to try whatever came her way. Then at last came the dessert course: a strawberry tart, a lemon soufflé, and an almond cake—along with nuts, cheeses, fresh fruit, wafers, and jellies.

By that time, I think all I will be able to manage is fruit or a little jelly.

The sheer amount of food that was about to be presented was stunning. And concerning. Once again, she found herself wondering if they would all regret indulgences like this in a year, when they would be glad for pease porridge and a little bacon.

Some of that must have shown on her face, for Dr. Trevor said soothingly, "Nothing will go to waste, not in this household. What can't be preserved for other meals for the family and staff will immediately be sent by a cart to a soup kitchen. And you may be sure that the staff have already feasted before us and the coachmen will be partaking in some of this largesse as well."

Well, she had made enough soup in her time from various odds and ends to know that practically anything could be incorporated into a tasty soup. And it was good to know that Davey would have a share of this bounty.

Dr. Trevor chuckled, then. "Normally it is the privilege of the cook to augment her income by selling leftovers out of the kitchen door. But everyone in his lordship's household either *is* a mage or knows about mages, so he pays them a very good wage, more than enough to make up for that loss."

"It also keeps strangers from prowling about. And mages who have gone to the bad from spying out their enemy by pretending to be such a buyer," she observed, and Dr. Trevor nodded.

"Meanwhile, downstairs is kept very content, because they eat what the family eats, and their quarters, while relatively small, are very comfortable. Their free hours are one full day a week off, and a half day on Sunday, which is far more than anyone else gives their servants—at least, those who are not mages. *And* time spent learning and practicing their magic is counted as household duties. Then, once a year, they may take a week's holiday, to spend it as they like, although obviously they cannot all take Christmas or Easter. It's a shame we can't all do so much for our staff, but because *we* have so much to lose by exposure, you'll find that all of us treat our staff so well that many of them are reluctant to retire even when they can scarcely carry a tray across a room." He smiled. "As Burke would have it, 'enlightened self-interest' tends to steer our fragile barques as mages. Now—oh, the soup course has come. Will you have some? It is a soup of spring vegetables."

She nodded, and discovered that Dr. Trevor was not the sort to tediously quiz her on Indian medicine or the rough sort of doctoring she knew how to do. He let her enjoy her food and did not ask anything while they were both still eating. Then he would satisfy his curiosity on some point or other, then invite her to ask him whatever she should choose.

For the most part, she asked him about customs here that she did not entirely understand, secure in the knowledge that he would not laugh at her ignorance. And indeed, he did nothing of the kind. So involved was she in this conversation that she paid scant attention to her seatmate on the other side—but that was all right, because he was half deaf, very old, and quite content to slowly enjoy his lordship's excellent food. In fact, very early in the dinner, if he needed her help getting the attention of a footman, he would gently tap his fork on her wineglass, and when she turned to him, he would whisper what he wanted in a hoarse voice that could not have been heard more than a foot from his head. She would obtain what he needed;

he would pat her hand and say, "You're a good little gel. Very kind," and go back to enjoying his dinner.

"You know," Dr. Trevor said, after the third time she assisted him, "that's Grand Duke Pevensky, the Archmage."

Even in America they had heard of the grand duke, a Russian who had resided in England most of his life. He must have been over a hundred years old!

"Why—think of all he has seen!" she marveled.

"I believe he is dictating his memoir. It will be several volumes, and the White Lodge is having copies privately published for all of us. What he does not know about Water magic is not worth knowing." Dr. Trevor indicated that she should lean backward a moment. "Your Grace, have you any need of anything from me?"

The old man turned slowly and stiffly and smiled. "Very kind, doctor. It is a good day for me. I am enjoying the feast, and the dancing, though I am a mere watcher. And the music! Oh yes, the music! This little gel is a kind child. If she is an example, Americans are fine stuff. Have her to Briarhold Manor one day soon." He looked at Amelia. "Yes, you'll come to Briarhold. Before you leave for the country."

Then he went back to his meal.

"Will he remember?" she asked, very much in awe that he even *considered* inviting her to his home.

"Mind is as sharp as a saber. He'll remember, he'll tell his secretary after dinner, and you'll get an invitation. You do realize you *must* go, don't you?" The doctor raised an eyebrow.

"Of course! I am not some silly miss with more hair than wit! This . . . this is like being invited to Merlin's tower!" she replied.

"That is a very good analogy. He knows far more than just Water magic. Odds are he can tell you something about Earth magic that you don't know, and will give you such a clear explanation that you will ever after be impatient of people who aren't gifted with such clarity. And he will probably give you some antique trifle as a gift. He is slowly disposing of his property, but only to people he believes need or will cherish the thing he gives them." He helped her to some fresh strawberries—she was fascinated by how large they were; at home strawberries were no bigger than the fingernail of your pinky. She was afraid they would be tasteless and wooden, as large fruits often were, but they were delightful.

A different wine had been served with each course, and she had been careful to accept only two or three tablespoons worth of each in her glass. The concert was very soon, and the last thing she wanted was to be tipsy.

When it looked as if his guests had had their fill of sweets, his lordship rose to his feet, and tapped his glass with his knife to get their attention.

"For those of you who prefer conversation, the dining room and my lady's parlor are open and prepared. For those of you who are musical, there will be a short concert in the music room." Lady Alderscroft rose and prepared to lead those ladies who were not interested in the music to her parlor; his lordship delegated the task of passing out port and brandy to his chief butler, and nodded to Amelia. She went a little cold at her own temerity of thinking she could amuse all these people, who had surely heard much better singers than she. But she got up, said a brief word to the doctor and the Archmage, and joined Alderscroft. As she approached, she noticed that there were several more people coming from the table to where Alderscroft and Serena waited. All in all, about eight of them, not counting herself and Serena.

"Amelia and Serena I know wish harpsichord accompaniment. Are there any of you who would prefer professional accompaniment?" his lordship asked, as they gathered about him. Two people, a stately, if stout, lady and a dark, sardonic looking man, indicated that they would prefer that option. Serena had already raised her hand eagerly, so Amelia did not object. A professional at the keyboard would sound better than she ever could!

His lordship handed out a prettily calligraphed program; Amelia saw that he had placed herself and Serena as the last performers. *Oh good, that means if the others run over the time allotted, he can cut us out.* She felt that as relief, rather than insult. *And anyone likely to be bored will have left before we sing.*

"Let us go to the music room, and you can give your scores to the keyboard player," his lordship concluded, and more or less herded his little gaggle of "artists" before him out of the dining room, through the ballroom, and into the music room.

The harpischord player from the little ensemble providing music for the previous concert and the dancing was waiting there already. He jumped to his feet and bowed.

"Mrs. Chesterton, Mr. Archer, and Misses Stonecroft and Meleva have asked if you will kindly accompany them," his lordship said.

"May I have your scores?" asked the musician, a thin, energetic man of middle age, his blond hair still bright and untouched by age, worn long in defiance of current fashion and pulled back behind his head in a tail, though it lacked the powder that would have been necessary thirty years ago. He looked first at Mrs. Chesterton's. "Ah! I know this by heart. 'Where E're You Walk' is an excellent choice." He set the score down on the music rack on the harpischord. "And you, Mr. Archer?"

The sardonic-looking man proffered his score. "You are *brave*, sir!" the musician said, with a look of astonishment. "The Bach 'Chaconne' is a challenge!"

The gentleman nodded. "Easy to learn, difficult to master. I hope to do justice to it."

"I hope to do justice to your playing," the musician replied.

Mr. Archer barely cracked a smile. "Oh, I intend to lean upon your sturdy arm. Be prepared!"

And now the musician turned to Serena, who held their score to her chest. "If I may?" he asked. With a little giggle, she handed it to him.

And for the first time, he appeared taken aback. "What is this?" He leafed through the few pages. "A duet—but from *what*?" He looked at the first page. "*Nerone e Poppea*. So this must be from—an opera? But one I have never heard of—" He leafed through the pages again, eyes flashing back and forth as he scanned the score. "Monteverdi, perhaps? I must say, I am glad this is a relatively simple duet, because I shudder to think I may be premiering a piece long lost!"

"I have been playing it in our practices, so it cannot be too difficult," Amelia said diffidently.

"Oh, my dear lady," the musician groaned. "It is the simplest pieces that are the most difficult! But I will do my poor best."

They took their seats in the little "performer" section at the front of the room, next to the piano and harpsichord, along with the rest of the people performing. It appeared that they and the stout lady were not the only ones singing. There was a guitarist and another violinist, and since there was a harp with the other two instruments, at least one person would be playing the harp. Probably the rest would play the pianoforte and perhaps sing to their own accompaniment.

A strange, contented calm settled over Amelia as a surprising number of the guests filed in to listen—it appeared that port and snuff, and tea and gossip, were less attractive than music right now.

Oh, but I think I know why. Extended talk will oscillate between Napoleon and the weather, neither of them pleasant subjects, and yet, difficult to avoid. Better to listen to even the worst of amateur performances than spoil the good feelings the evening has brought so far.

She and Serena had been part of many an amateur performance session, both when it was just the family, and when friends and acquaintances would join. Indeed, both here and at home, it was considered necessary for a young lady either to have some musical accomplishment to use to amuse company, or to be an excellent reader. So she was prepared for the worst and had her practiced "I am very interested!" face on.

But she needn't have bothered. The guitarist played and sang first, three rollicking sea shanties, which got everyone's toes tapping. Then came Miranda Sumner on the harp, who played and sang a lugubrious ballad called "I've Given My Heart to a Flower"—but it was clear from the start that she was aware how silly and sentimental it was, because she tossed her head and emoted with such exaggeration she had everyone in stitches. The violinist came next, and he was truly excellent, and somehow managed to imbue his piece with a universe of pain and sorrow to the point that there were tears in more eyes than just Amelia's. But the next up took to the piano and played a lively mazurka that drove those tears away. The stout lady did a very creditable rendition of "Where E're You Walk," without resorting to any exaggeration or over-sentimentality.

Though it did occur to Amelia that perhaps she was restraining herself, given that Miranda had done such a fine job of lampooning that sort of performance.

All in all, she would have been very happy if the concert had ended with the next-to-last, a girl who was, perhaps, the best amateur harpist she had ever heard. But then the musician took his place on the bench before the harpsichord and nodded to them, and they stood up. Serena started for the right side of the harpsichord, and Amelia started for the left.

They hadn't planned it that way, but the musician immediately began the opening bars while they were still far apart. Serena immediately turned and faced Amelia after the first three bars and held out her hands to Amelia.

"*Pur ti miro,*" she sang, the notes as pure as larksong.

Amelia responded by holding out her own. "*Ti adoro,*" she responded and lost herself in the beauty of the song.

Slowly, they crossed the distance between them, still singing, until at last they held each other's hands in a clasp, each of them concentrating so hard on her response or their harmony that energy practically crackled between them.

And out of the corner of her eye, Amelia saw an astonishing sight. They didn't just have an audience of people . . . no, from out of nowhere (as was their habit), what could only have been described as a *horde* of Elementals filled the sides and the back of the room. Besides the usual brownies that you would find in a home, there were dozens of little grotesques, creatures that appeared to be part bird or part insect, walking mushrooms, or tiny doll-like creatures that seemed to be made of twigs or other forest bits and bobs. And on Serena's side were salamanders, fire fae, and firebirds.

Now, she was quite used to seeing Natty Ned and the household Elementals sneak into the parlor to hear them practice or perform—

but never so many as this! It looked as if there must be over a dozen Elementals for every single person within these walls! And the little grotesque fae were almost never seen outside of wilderness, or at least, gardens.

Rather than making her nervous, she felt a rush of gratitude and relief. If they were entertaining enough to bring throngs of these fae creatures to the music room, then surely they couldn't be boring the humans.

So she closed her eyes and put every bit of her heart into the music, just as Serena was. Because they really, truly, did adore each other, with all the fervor of people who had fought beside each other under the worst of circumstances, and who quite literally were prepared to die for each other.

. . . though I really would rather not . . .

Their voices wrapped around each other like a jessamine and a trumpet vine, or like the "rose and the briar" in common songs about dead lovers, twining so closely together that you could not distinguish where one left off and the other began. Their vibratos matched so closely it almost sounded as if it was one, impossible voice.

It wasn't a long performance, of course. The song was short, and could not have lasted for five minutes. But there wasn't a single sound in the room but the harpsichord and their entwining voices, until the very last, languid, beautiful, *"Si, mio ben, si, mio cor, mia vita, si."*

Then there was a silence so profound that she looked up at the audience, afraid that they had somehow created an incredible social *faux pas.* But surely Lord Alderscroft would not have asked them to sing this specific song if he thought it would offend!

But then the harpsichordist stood, the legs of his stool scraping a little on the floor, and began slow, deliberate applause.

That seemed to break the spell, and every person in the room leapt to their feet and began applauding wildly, some with actual tears on their faces. *"Encore!"* shouted someone—the guitarist, she thought. And that unleashed a flood of *"Encore! Encore!"* until she and Serena looked at each other, then turned to their audience, nodded, and went back to their original starting places. The keyboardist sat down, and they began again.

They had to sing it again twice more before their audience released them, and that only happened because people came to the music room looking for their promised partners in the dance or the card room.

Amelia was not certain exactly how Serena felt, but she practically floated back to the ballroom.

"Sir Roger de Coverley" ended the evening, as it did at many balls; it was a country dance, and not too terribly difficult or energetic, since by that point feet and legs were nearly worn out, and eyes and heads were drooping. Amelia was both glad and sorry that the evening had come to an end, because it had felt like something out of fairyland. The others had retrieved their coats and cloaks and gone to wait at the entrance hall for Davey and the carriage. Not being as immune to the cold as Serena and the others seemed to be, Amelia had gotten her cloak and waited, out of the way, in the shadows of one of the columns, still buoyed on the memory of what could only be called a splendid success. She had had partners not only enough for every single dance, but had there been twice as many dances, she would still have had partners. And there was no doubt that their song had gone well. More than well. She caught bits of conversation from where she was: "—you should have heard the Americans—" "—absolutely ravishing song, I was quite carried away—" "—no, completely unknown to me, never heard the melody before—"

And she might, just possibly, have gotten a little bit of a case of swollen pride, had not something else brought it crashing down.

Someone began speaking quite close to her, but on the other side of the pillar, and she recognized Phillip Nightsmith's voice. He sounded irritated. "Yes, Roughtower, that's all very well, but I find it most unbecoming for females to put themselves forward in such an . . . unmannerly fashion."

"Dash it all, Nightsmith," laughed the captain. "You're never satisfied. If girls won't put themselves out to entertain, you call them simpering and missish, and if they do, you call them unmannerly! Make up your mind!"

"Decorous harp playing, a little on the pianoforte, there's no harm in any of that," replied Nightsmith. "But this! Emoting the song to the point where one would have thought they were lovers, not cousins! And *two* encores! Disgraceful."

If there had been the slightest doubt in Amelia's mind that Phillip Nightsmith meant her and Serena, that would have dashed that doubt on the rocks. There was not another pair of women in the entire party that matched his description.

"Stuff and nonsense. That was no worse than a dramatic poetry reading. Besides, they're Americans, and no doubt they're used to more freedom than our English girls."

"Then someone needs to give them a sound lecture on decorum." Nightsmith sounded *very* cross.

"Well, it won't be me. And Alderscroft himself asked them to perform that very song, aye, and stood at the back of the room listening with a smile on his face! You're too nice, Phillip. Inside, you're an old lady railing about 'the youth these days.' You've got more high-flown notions of manners than the queen herself."

Amelia felt herself going hot and cold by turns, and she did not dare move from behind the pillar. They would certainly know that she had been listening, and lud! She would be damned if she was going to give that black-clad *prig* the satisfaction of knowing she'd heard him!

She might have remained there for the rest of the night, except that someone hailed them both from the door, and as she shrank further back into the shadows, they moved off.

She gave them to the count of twenty, then headed in that direction herself, praying she did not encounter them. But the hail must have meant that their conveyance had arrived, because they were nowhere in sight, and to her relief, Davey was just pulling up to the front steps.

But she was trembling with contained rage as she got into the carriage, so much so that even the Anglefords noticed.

"Amelia, what has set you—" Serena began.

"Of all the *impudent, self-satisfied, conceited, blue-stockinged, arrogant ASSES!*" she burst out, and let what she had overheard out all in a torrent.

When it was out, she felt a little better, although she was still fuming. "And to think we are going to have to be *neighbors* to him," she continued. "Oh! Mr. Nightsmith! He is *quite* the most *eligible* bachelor in Axminster!" she simpered. "Well, it's no wonder he's still a bachelor! It's clear nothing but a saint would satisfy him as a wife! I should like to box his ears!"

"Would you like me to break into his chicken coops and eat all his hens?" Serena asked, chortling.

"The temptation is very great!" she exclaimed, then settled down a little. "Well, I will be polite to him, because if anyone is going to be the leading gentleman in Axminster, it will be him. He's also, most likely, the leading mage in Axminster, and we will have to work together as the weather turns vicious. And it would be *too* mortifying if he knew I had overheard him. But lud! I *almost* came to like the captain for standing up for us!"

"I would rather like to eat his chickens," Serena mused. "But you are right, we will have to be polite to him. *But* if we cannot find land for James around Axminster, then the night before we leave, I *will* go and eat them. Two or three at least. And I will leave the feet and wings at his front door."

"Oh, my bloodthirsty little cousin!" James exclaimed, as the Anglefords chuckled. "Why not leave the head too?"

"Because the head is the best part, you goose," Serena said complacently.

Julia and Thomas did their best to soothe Amelia's bruised feelings, assuring her that absolutely nobody else had thought she and Serena were somehow *forward* in their performance. "Nightsmith is a prig," James said, dismissively. "You'll see tomorrow, when people come visiting. People will *want* to come visiting, and when they do, they'll be dangling for an invitation to a little private party so they can hear you two sing that song again."

Amelia allowed herself to be soothed; after all, that was just one solitary sour currant in an otherwise delightful bunch, and she wasn't going to allow the man to ruin her experience of the kind of ball she had only ever read about. She considered complaining to Lord Alderscroft about it, but by the time the carriage rolled up to their front door, she had decided that would look petty and weak, and she did not want to tar herself with that particular brush.

Part of her wanted to resolve to get revenge on him *somehow*, but as she cast her mind over all the things she needed to do, she realized that pursuing revenge was just not going to be worth the effort. Besides, it was already the end of May, and sometime in the latter half of June, they would be moving into that as-yet-unseen house that his lordship had promised, and there were still many things to be done.

Besides, if, after we have moved, he still proves to be a prig, Serena might just get her chicken dinner.

After returning home at nearly four in the morning, no one was inclined to get up at their normal time, not even Serena. But considering that anyone who was likely to call on them had also been at the Alderscroft ball, sleeping in until noon did not seem so great a sin. Especially as today was a Sunday. They would miss morning services at the church the Anglefords usually attended, but Amelia doubted that God would mind.

In fact, Amelia was down first, to find that the servants had considerately set up a cold collation in the dining room, ready for whoever needed food.

That is, she *thought* she was down first, only to discover, when she raised the covering cloches, someone had been there before her, for inroads had been made in the food.

A yawning Julia entered the room as she contemplated a cold egg pie with a pronounced gap in it. "I feel like the three bears," Amelia said. "Who's been eating my porridge?"

"James and Thomas," Julia said, regarding the pie thoughtfully. "They went down to the docks to see if the ship from America is in yet. Your father promised crop seeds."

"I remember, but I had forgotten she is due."

Serena came in at that moment, looking very catlike as she sometimes did when she was pleased with herself and the world. "Who is due?" she asked, then answered her own question. "Oh, the ship. Well, the sooner we can get those crop seeds to his lordship, the better. Is there any clotted cream?"

By the time they were done eating, the men were back with the welcome news that the ship was indeed in. They had hired a carter, and all the precious seeds were in their warehouse.

"And that is how we repay Lord Alderscroft's kindness," said Thomas with immense satisfaction. "I sent a message by errand boy that he can collect the seeds at his leisure."

"It'd best not be too leisurely, or it will be too late to get them in the ground," James said, chuckling.

And before anyone could respond to that, young Tommy came rushing into the dining room. "His lor'ship's askin' to see you!" he said, all aquiver with excitement. "I took't him to the parlor! He gimme a sixpence!"

"And you can certainly keep that sixpence," Julia said warmly. "Dear heavens, am I a *frightful* mess?" She patted at her cap in dismay.

"You are fine, and let's not keep Alderscroft waiting," her husband replied, and offered his hand for her to rise.

Amelia was just grateful that she had taken the time to actually dress, and not merely throw a dressing gown over a morning dress. *Good thing my old habits die hard. At home, I would not have known what a "morning dress" was.*

They all descended on the parlor in a group. His lordship was waiting there in what, for him, must have been casual attire. Riding boots, buckskin breeches, a plain waistcoat, a coat without tails, a stock tied with a simple knot, and a soft cap. He looked none the worse for wear after the ball.

"I have come to collect my seeds!" he said cheerfully. "I had one of the farm carts and two of our cartage horses brought up from the estate when you told me Charles Stonecroft was sending them, so I can get them into the ground as soon as possible!"

"Well, then, you will need this," said James, handing him a fat envelope. "All the information you need on each plant. The seeds themselves are inside hessian bags, which are inside waterproof barrels. Father wasn't taking any chances."

"Wonderful! And I realized that I was not entirely clear on the cottage—that is, it is a *furnished* cottage, and I am sending staff over from the estate after all. They are all young people due for a promotion, and restless at being so far from anything like a town, so this was a double pleasure for them."

"I believe we should give them an additional evening free every week," Amelia said to Serena. "If they are young, they will want to go to a tavern—"

"Pub," his lordship corrected. "That would be both wise and kind. It's clear you know how to handle servants."

"Mother often put me in charge, and I have been learning your ways from Julia, so yes," Amelia agreed. "But we are keeping you. I just want to thank you for a delightful evening last night."

"Oh, you two ladies were quite the triumph, let me assure you," Alderscroft chuckled, standing. "I suspect you will be getting more invitations to evening parties than you know what to do with! But we must be off; I want to get those horses on the road while it is still Sunday and the streets are uncrowded."

Thomas returned, having collected his coat. "Come along, my lord," he said cheerfully. "I'll have Davey take us there, and your cart can follow. Then I can leave you at your doorstep and return home myself."

"Excellent plan!" Alderscroft pulled the brim of his cap at Julia, Serena, and Amelia. "Ladies, adieu."

"Did you hear that, Amelia!" Serena crowed when he was gone.

"We were a triumph! You should not give a *fig* about what that odious man said!"

"You're right, and I won't!" Amelia agreed heartily. "What's Mr. Nightsmith after all, and what is his opinion worth?"

A triumph! Take that, Phillip Nightsmith!

10

AFTER the excitement of Lord Alderscroft's ball, things went back to normal—or at least, as normal as it could get when May temperatures were chill indeed, and Napoleon was romping his way across France with little to no resistance. Amelia and Serena reduced their gigantic dresses to more manageable piles of fabric, and even went so far as to cut projects out and take all the pieces of each and package them neatly in brown paper, together with the right thread and trimmings, to keep each project together. Sewing would have to wait until they were established in their new home in Axminster.

Downstairs, in the odd moments of idle time, needles were clacking incessantly as even Davey and Frank were knitting warm stockings, gloves, and scarves. Amelia suspected that wool was about to become fashionable again, and advised Thomas of this. That caused him to acquire skeins of silk, lambswool, and merino wool, have them dyed in cochineal and indigo and every color the two could make together before anyone else could think of doing so, and offer them to the haberdasheries. The skeins practically flew out the door, according to his gleeful report. The ordinary people of London might not know about the volcano, but no one could deny the weather was unseasonably cold, and warm accessories were required.

The downstairs household reaped the benefit of this experiment, in the form of skeins of common wool and linen dyed in the last dregs of the vat—which made some very nice pastels. Amelia had expected the men to reject such colors, but on the contrary, the women of downstairs had to battle the men for the pale lilac, blue, and rose.

On reflection, she should have expected that. The men of the *ton* enjoyed silk stockings dyed in similar colors, so why shouldn't Davey and Frank do the same with wool?

Amelia now shared her bedroom with sacks of dried peas and beans tucked under the bed and the space beneath the little table beside her bed. Rat-proof barrels had been bought and carried up into the attic with much swearing, and bags of ship's biscuit, oats, barley, and rye stored in them. At the moment, they only rimmed the area, but Amelia had very little doubt that by the end of summer the entire attic would be full. So would the loft above the tiny stable where Frank slept. And probably parts of the cellar. The hoarding had begun.

Mrs. Gideon had carefully read all of the instructions that Amelia's mother had sent on drying various foodstuffs to preserve them. This was a technique used by the Indians to great effect, but Mrs. Gideon, having always been a cook or cook's helper in a city, had never had occasion to use it. She had been astonished when presented with the instructions for making jerky, and rendered speechless by the directions for making pemmican. But she made a try of it, using currants for the fruit instead of the blueberries and cranberries the Indians used, and when everyone in the house decreed the experiment to be "edible," she declared she would make no more objections to these alternatives to potting meat. It certainly made efficient use of meat scraps.

Lord Alderscroft had gotten a second round of seeds, this time mostly "hard" or "field" corn, with the caution that "they might not produce ears, but plant all three of the Sisters so you'll get something out of the plot." The Stonecrofts had long used the Indian practice of planting the "Three Sisters," corn, beans, and squash, in the same hill to maximize the amount of food they could grow in a garden. And while Alderscroft predicted a rebellion from his gardeners at such an unorthodox method of planting, he agreed that this should be given a fair trial and was confident he would prevail over his gardeners and tenants. If the corn *did* produce this year, that would be one more thing horses could eat, saving the oats and barley for people.

Most people had no idea, of course, that lean times were coming, and went on about their business with no concern except for Napoleon.

And Napoleon was a legitimate concern. Amelia had asked Miranda Sumner—who it turned out had an astonishing head for business—why people were so fixated on the man.

"Because without actually threatening our shores, he can absolutely *ruin* our economy," Miranda said wisely. "If he defeats Wellington and our German allies, the Stock Exchange will be crashed. Or at least the consols will."

"Why? I thought consols were safe?"

"Because the consols depend on government spending being *reasonable*. And if Napoleon manages to defeat our initial forces, there will be massive military spending, something . . . well, no thanks to the Prince Regent, something we can ill afford. And once that happens, an invasion by the French will seem more likely than not." Miranda shrugged helplessly. "And if the consols are devalued, many people's incomes will vanish, and *that* will mean there is less money all around." She sighed. "I wish Papa would listen to me about this. But at least he is doing what Julia and Thomas are doing, and investing in foodstuffs. If the consols crash, we might not have money for much, but at least we will eat. Oh, *why* did these things have to happen at once?"

Amelia agreed with her. Sometimes Amelia wanted to shout warnings from the roof—but what good would it have done? Who would believe her? And not many people had money to spare to "invest" in foodstuffs. All she could do was resolve to be generous to the poor, and advise all the mages she could reach.

Life was not all worries and hoarding. Serena and Amelia continued to attend the Thursday Assemblies at Payne's, there were more invitations than ever to dinners and after-dinner parties, and generally before the evening was over, Serena and Amelia would be asked to sing their song.

"It's a pity that you didn't find more of that opera," Amelia said in the carriage after the fourth such party and entreaty. "Not that I am going to complain, because our song is still the most ravishing piece of music I have ever heard in my life! But it would have been pleasant to offer something besides it and 'Mary's Tears' or 'Meet Me By Moonlight.'"

"At least we are able to give them something besides 'A Son of the Desert Am I.'" Serena giggled. "I am *sorely tempted* to give them a rousing 'Star-Spangled Banner,' however."

Amelia almost choked, as Julia and Thomas looked at the two of them in bewilderment. "What is that song?" Julia asked, and Amelia explained.

"Well . . ." Julia said, slowly, as the carriage rumbled over some particularly rough cobbles. "Most people would not recognize what the song was about, although they *would* know the melody as coming from 'To Anacreon in Heaven.' At least, they would not understand it is about a decisive battle against the British until they thought about it. I don't think anyone would be *offended*, but they might ask for an explanation." She was quiet for a moment, and they could almost hear how thoughts were buzzing about in her head. "You two are now possessed of reputations high enough, and with talents desirable enough, that I think you could venture that song without causing any trouble. Unless a member of the military was there."

"Oh, we should do that, then," Serena continued. "But we should save it for some occasion where Captain Hightower is present."

"I am quite in charity with the captain at present, despite his behavior whenever we are in the same room as him and an heiress,"

Amelia told her. "I am better acquainted now with his circumstances, which are difficult; he cannot sell the estate, because it is something called *entailed*, which I do not quite understand—"

"If an estate is 'entailed,' it means it cannot be legally sold, as it is meant to be carried on to owners in the next generation," Thomas told them. "The purpose of entailment was to ensure that properties could not be broken up, and that they were kept in the family in the main line of succession. Entailment is often used with primogeniture. Sadly, it is often done to keep the estate from passing to a female, even when there is no direct male heir. And in that case, the nearest male heir takes it even if he is a total stranger to the rest of the family. This also prevents a father from disinheriting his eldest son."

Since this was the first cogent explanation that Amelia had heard of the practice, she found herself taken aback by the injustice of it. "Do you mean to say that if a man with an entailed estate dies with only daughters, some distant cousin can come along and throw them out into the street?"

"That can happen," Thomas said gravely. "And indeed, even a *son* can cast mother and sisters out when he inherits, as he is under no legal obligation to support anyone except those in his own personal family."

Amelia found herself a little short of breath. "I—have no words," she finally said.

She could hear Julia and Thomas shifting in their seats uncomfortably.

"About the captain," James prodded gently, to get the uncomfortable subject laid to rest.

"Well, the estate is apparently given over to sheep and timber; mutton is cheap, and common wool is cheap, so there is not much income from either. Those who can afford it prefer cotton, linen, and merino. He hasn't the servants to convert to some other form of income-producing agriculture; the only food besides mutton that the estate produces is just for him and his few servants, and he has no tenant farmers that might give him a little more income. That leaves him with timber, which is not . . . *useful* as a regular crop. The house, to hear him speak about it, is practically collapsing except for the outer walls and a few rooms in the east wing, which is where he lives when he is not with his regiment. There are some Roman ruins on the property, but alas, they have not produced anything like a hoard of silver and gold, or even valuable statuary. So he limps along in damp rooms, impossible to heat, and for personal servants has but a single old woman who serves as his cook and housekeeper and a man for his garden, the pig they fatten every year, and the chickens. So you see why I am more in charity with his fortune-hunting. He lives in what one could call 'genteel poverty,' with a millstone of an old house about his neck."

"There has to be more of this story," James said. "Otherwise you would not have reversed your opinion so drastically."

"He has partnered me regularly at Payne's," she admitted. "So he is not *snubbing* me because I have no fortune, which is more than I can say for some. We've conversed on magic, and it is enlightening to hear from someone with minimal power to understand the frustration they feel. Only imagine! He is an Earth mage, and yet is powerless to help his own lands in any substantial way! And if he *could* do what I can do, he could, within the space of one growing season, turn the property into a veritable Garden of Eden!"

"Well . . . that certainly is the basis for being more in charity with the man," Julia agreed.

"And . . . he *did* defend me to Phillip Nightsmith, on the evening of the ball," she admitted. "It was not so much a defense as it was laughing at that odious man's antique notions of what a lady should be and act like, but it *was* an effort that he needn't have gone to. Neither of them were aware I could hear."

"Well, I still don't like him, but for your sake I will not snub nor cut him, then," Serena declared.

"And perhaps when Nightsmith realizes how much pleasure you two have given others through singing—*and* understands just what a work of genius that song is—he will revise his opinion of the song and you," Julia suggested mildly.

"Well, *I* think the next time he is at a gathering with us, he must be subjected to 'I Have Given My Heart to a Flower' rendered as a serious ballad, and we will see if he changes his tune about *our* song," Serena declared in a voice full of mischief.

"Oh, that does have some merit," Amelia agreed, trying, and failing, to hold back laughter.

She laughed, but always behind her laughter lurked anxieties. She no longer feared that she and Serena would not be accepted—thanks to Julia, Thomas, and his lordship, that fear had been erased from her lists. But now, of course, there were twin menaces—the remote one of Napoleon, and the very immediate one of the weather. *That* was always there, lurking, in the back of her mind. And whenever her hands or feet were active and her mind unoccupied with any other thing, she was thinking, thinking, trying to generate solutions that could be applied largely, rather than just within her circle.

This had been a particularly long evening; the Sumners had invited them for dinner, cards, and lottery playing, and a little supper of sandwiches and wine afterward. Some people laid on entire meals of oysters and eggs, fricassee of chicken, mushrooms in cream, sliced meats, and so on, but at least in the households Amelia had visited, consideration for downstairs took prominence, and supper was generally something cold that could be held for hours on trays with tea towels laid over them, and brought up by a couple of maids while the company was to help themselves. That way Cook and her helper could go to bed at a decent hour, any dishes could wait for morning for the tweenie to clean while breakfast trays were made up, and the maid that stayed up to serve could nap until she was needed. But this meant that the party generally extended to midnight and no further.

So when they entered the front door and there was a small parcel waiting for her on the card tray, Amelia was much too tired to think about opening it. Since it did not have the look of something that had traveled further than across town, she assumed it was some trifle she had bought in advance that the shop had just sent over. There had been a few of those over the past few weeks, things that a shop was temporarily out of, and which there was not enough urgency about that she wanted to go to the effort of finding them elsewhere.

She picked it up as they all said their goodnights, and took it up the stairs with her, leaving it on the top of her bureau.

She spotted it in the morning as she was brushing her hair, and as soon as she had put her hair into a loose chignon, she fetched it. There was no writing on the outside of the brown-paper-wrapped package, so that meant it must have come by messenger.

She unwrapped it, revealing a pasteboard box. Opening the lid, she found a folded note, and a small ball of absolutely clear amber, with a simple, three-legged brass stand it could rest in.

Well . . . this isn't something I purchased!

She opened the note.

Repairs on the house in Axminster are nearly finished. This is a focus, currently purposed as a scrying anchor, matched to its twin that is currently placed on the mantel of the parlour. In this way you can view your new home and let me know if it lacks anything or there are things you would have otherwise. Alderscroft.

She almost dropped the amber, she was so shocked. This was astonishing! How had he thought of this clever way for her to tour her new home without ever moving from London? And why had he done so?

Silly goose, she chided herself. *This is his way of saying you earned such a thing because he has noticed your efforts regarding the coming weather. As for the rest, it means that you and Serena can object to anything you'd rather not have.* Something else occurred to her that made her laugh a little. *I suspect he has had his servants go through the attics of his manor and furnished the rooms with things that are* much out of mode. And he is afraid that either those furnishings will offend our taste, or there will be too much furniture or not enough. Well, being out of mode didn't matter to her, and it wouldn't matter to Serena. In fact, it might be preferable! Especially if there was anything in his attics, or the house, that was from the days of the Tudors. She didn't much care if her house was bang-up to the mode; what she cared about was that it was comfortable, and properly padded. Tudor furniture was amply comfortable.

She could not help but note that an examination via scrying

would allow her (and Serena of course) to go places their physical bodies could not—to examine a suspect patch of damp up near the ceiling, for instance, or get behind shelves in the cellar to look for rat holes. That was probably something his lordship had thought of as well.

She brought her prize down to breakfast, rather than taking a cup of hot chocolate and some toast in her room and writing a letter of thanks. Better to put off the letter and kill two birds with one stone by thanking him while addressing any concerns.

Serena was already there, having discovered the joys of "toast soldiers" dipped in soft-boiled eggs. To Amelia's mind, this sort of breakfast was still very inferior to the kind of breakfast they had at home—and when they were established in their own place, she was *definitely* going to shock downstairs with her orders for the morning meal. But then, as the inevitable privations began, she would shock them anyway with some of the barbaric recipes she was going to order. *And I'll probably have to teach the cook how to cook them,* she thought with resignation.

"Alderscroft sent me a twinned scrying anchor so we can scry the new house," she said as Serena looked up from her meal, a lock of curling black hair falling down across her forehead from her loose chignon.

"What a clever man he is! Sit down and eat, and we'll do it straight away when we have satisfied ourselves. I have nothing I cannot put off for two or three hours." Serena's movements became less languid as she set to finishing her breakfast with a will.

Julia was already preparing downstairs for the food privations to come by ordering oatmeal porridge every morning—real thick Scots porridge, of the sort they ate at home, and not thin gruel. And they were *all* eating it, too, downstairs as well as upstairs. Serena and Amelia were used to it, from breakfast in the winter back home, but it was taking the Anglefords some time to decide how they liked it. Salted, as the Scots did? With fruit and cream as the Stonecrofts did? With cream, cinnamon, and honey, which was Serena's choice? With jam or fruit preserves? They'd tried it once with gravy from the previous night's roast, and . . . well, that had not been a success, though to their credit, they did not waste it and ate it anyway. There was a pot of it on the table right now, in fact, and Amelia helped herself to a bowl full, topped with cream and currants.

It wasn't breakfast as she knew it at home, but it was very filling. And pleasant, on this cool morning, when there had even been a fire lit in the dining room.

Serena examined the amber orb on the table between them as she ate, and nodded her approval. "Amber is probably even better for scrying than obsidian," she observed.

"Yes, but it is a very small ball. I could use it by myself, but you would be craning your neck until you got a cramp to see anything. We'll get a better viewing if I use my mirror and link it to the amber." She finished her meal with a cup of strong tea; she missed coffee, but Mrs. Gideon didn't know how to brew it, and after the first effort of bitter, boiled liquid full of grounds, she had opted for tea. Perhaps the fur traders found such a drink pleasant, but she did not.

By the time she finished her tea, Julia had come down, and Amelia told her of their plans for the next couple of hours. Julia nodded. "I think surveying your new home is an excellent idea, and now is as good a time as any to pursue it. I can get on with my shopping alone, which is for nothing interesting today, just orders for the kitchen. How kind of Alderscroft to have thought of this!"

"How trusting to have given me something intimately connected to his own magic," Amelia replied, holding up the little sphere and looking at the upside-down reflection of the breakfast table in its warm depths. "I could do a great deal of mischief to him if I were inclined."

"Then guard that carefully," admonished Julia, and Serena finished the last of her toast and eggs, and the two of them went back up the stairs to Amelia's room.

Mary had already made the bed and tidied the room; the two of them sat cross-legged on the bed with Amelia's scrying bowl between them. Amelia extended her hands out on either side of the bed, willed power into herself from the earth, and energized the protective circle around the bed that she had put in place the day they arrived. Warding where you slept was the first thing any mage did, whether they were stopping for just the night, or intending to stay for a while. It was impolite to impose *your* house wards over your host's unless they requested you do so, so she had not warded the whole house. She and Serena would certainly ward this new place as soon as they arrived in Axminster.

With mage sight, the effect was of a golden ring around the bed, which "grew" upward and inward until it met at the top, forming a golden, glowing dome over the two of them. She tested it, and found it sound. Then she narrowed her concentration to a spot on the counterpane between her and Serena, and called on Natty Ned. *That* was a matter of picturing him in her mind and forming a sort of mental invitation. *Will you call on me?* Though not in words, but in feelings. Most Elementals responded more quickly to feelings than anything else.

Since he already had "permission" to cross her wards, there should be nothing impeding him—

"And what can Natty Ned be doing for you, my lady?" One moment, there was nothing on the counterpane. The next, there was the Elemental, as if he had winked into existence at that moment, or stepped through a door in the air. She had no idea how the Elementals did that. But neither did any other Elemental Master she'd spoken to. It was as if Elementals moved from wherever they were to wherever they were wanted, without going through the intervening space.

"Serena and I are going to scry, and I wanted the household Elementals to know about it and not be alarmed," she said.

"Ah! Looking over your new nest, are you then? Thanks to you for the warning." And with that, he bowed and was gone.

Serena—who could, of course, see and hear all that—just shook her head. "How do they *know things* like that?"

Amelia laughed. "Eavesdropping on us at all times, of course," she pointed out. "And then probably gossiping incessantly about what they learn." She took the amber ball in her right hand, moved the obsidian bowl between her and Selena so that they both had an equally good view of what was in its depths, and cradled the ball in her palm with her left hand supporting the right. Once again, she pulled power from the Earth and gingerly fed it to the amber sphere.

It reacted *instantly.* It pulled in power hungrily as she turned her attention to the flat obsidian bowl and fed it power in turn. Orb and bowl took on auras of light, of the same golden color as the ward. Then she reached out physically and touched the sphere to the bowl, muttering a few words of power under her breath, repeating them three times, until the auras ceased being two spheres and fused. The result looked like a fat figure eight, glowing the same amber color as the sphere.

Now what appeared in the ball would also appear in the bowl.

Show me where your twin sits, she commanded silently, and a thin golden mist filled the bowl then retreated, so that the bowl reflected the view from the twinned sphere.

The scene in the bowl was that of a pleasant parlor, with two mismatched sofas and two chairs in the Rococo style, their elaborate wood frames cushioned by leather over padding. Someone had gone to the trouble of freshly painting them and touching up the gilding along the high spots of the carving. The chairs were arranged with their backs to the fireplace, and the sofas facing them, with a fire screen that matched the rightmost sofa next to the rightmost chair. Nothing else matched, which made Serena giggle. Amelia raised the viewpoint and saw a third chair in the corner, snuggled up to a little Rococo table. There were mismatched tables beside each sofa and chair, and candleholders on every table. Bookcases lined all the walls. The room itself had wooden wainscoting up to about head height, then painted plaster, but the heavy wooden beams that were crossing the ceiling overhead and showing above the wainscoting betrayed the cottage's age. So did the windows, with their tiny glass panes carefully fitted together with lead. This was a Tudor house.

"Oh, my!" Serena laughed. "You were right! He has raided his attics for us!"

"I rather like it," Amelia said, tilting her head to the side. "He's had the things refurbished so the cushions all match—restuffed, too, I'll wager. The bits of carpet all match, and the curtains are new, and match the gold in the carpets. If the fireplace hasn't a draft and doesn't smoke, I suspect we'll be spending a lot of time in that room. Look how the sunlight falls through the windows! It is really quite pleasant, and looks warm." She allowed Serena a moment more to take it all in, then moved the viewpoint, checking for damp spots up near the ceiling, then mouse holes down at floor level. Everything was as it should be, and the wood and buckskin-colored walls gave the room quite a welcoming and sunny look. She moved their viewpoint, then turned it around to show a gray stone fireplace that took up fully half of the wall. *Yes, in winter we will definitely be spending a lot of time here.* That was when she spotted the two benches inside the fireplace itself, built into the walls, tucked in under the brick mantelpiece and covered in sheepskins. "Look! It's an inglenook fireplace, like the one in our parlor at home!"

"And there will be no one to fight us for the seats in the winter!" Serena said gleefully. "I already like this place too much to want to give it up!"

"Let's see what's next," Amelia suggested, moving the viewpoint out through the door.

It became very clear that on this floor, at least, there were no hallways, which further confirmed that it was centuries old. The parlor emptied directly into the entryway, with stairs going up to the right, the front entrance appearing to the left, and another doorway directly in front of them. The narrow entry boasted nothing more than a strip of carpet, a narrow, upholstered bench, very plain, and a coat rack and stand for canes. No need for a hall boy here!

"I wonder how the ladies of Queen Caroline's time managed with those enormous skirts and panniers in this entryway," Serena said aloud.

Amelia laughed. "Probably one at a time!"

Also blessed with golden wood wainscoting, the predominant color of the plaster in the entryway was the same buckskin as the parlor and the wood of the stairs. The stairs were plain, but sturdy.

The next room proved to be the dining room. More wainscoting, more heavy beams. Rococo was the theme again here, with a massive sideboard displaying tableware of designs long out of style, the gilded edges much rubbed, the scenes of shepherds in the wood a bit faded and scratched.

"Those plates are pretty," Amelia observed. "And I don't care if they are mismatched, though it looks as if Alderscroft sent us his grandmama's second-best china. It's still china, and I will not blush to serve visitors on it! Secondhand but good is much better than new and cheap."

There was a Rococo dining table large enough to seat ten—a very nice touch, as it meant they could invite people to dinner—and amusingly, the chairs were of two different patterns, five of each. "Oh, that's clever," Serena said aloud. "They've arranged the chairs so there are no two matching chairs touching each other. It looks like a deliberate choice now, instead of hand-me-downs."

Under the diamond-paned window, opposite the sideboard, was a long, narrow table, quarreling violently with the Rococo style of the rest of the room, since it was quite plain, and would not have looked out of place in the Stonecrofts' home on the other side of the ocean. "Ah, that's so we can have meals with all the courses brought in at once!" Serena said. "What do they call it?"

"*A la francaise,*" Amelia supplied.

Worn but clean carpet on the floor again, and here the walls above the wainscoting were painted a slightly darker gold. And there was another fireplace, which meant the dining room should not be cold. Although keeping so many fires lit at once was going to cost in terms of coal or wood.

There was a door to the right, and Amelia moved the viewpoint through it. She was unsurprised to find the kitchen there. Here the difference with the other two rooms was stark. There was no wainscoting, and the plastered walls had simply been whitewashed; the heavy, dark beams were visible across the ceiling, and the floor was practical stone tiles. There was a counter of stone over wood, and two stone sinks, one with a pump, under the windows in the left wall, and a massive standing cupboard on the wall they had come in through, which displayed copper and iron pans, pots, and flat grid-dles. But to the right, where the fireplace was, there was an iron cookstove of the very latest kind. It fit easily inside the absolutely enormous fireplace, which was big enough to roast not one, but two pigs in it simultaneously, and also boasted two ovens.

"I think we shall have *no* problems keeping our cook," Serena said, a little in awe. "Why, mother would walk through fire to have a stove like that!"

In the middle of the room was a big wooden worktable. To the far right in the back wall was a door, left ajar, and another door just past the cookstove on the right-hand wall. That door proved to lead to a storeroom, with a trapdoor in the floor.

"That will be the cellar, I think we can skip that," said Amelia, and took them through that intriguing door at the rear. There were three plainly furnished rooms there, and a door that led outside. One room was larger than the others; held a single bed, a desk and chair, and a wardrobe; and would be for the cook/housekeeper. The other two held two beds each—maid, cook's helper, tweenie, and perhaps another maid. Instead of a wardrobe there were two clothes chests, and two stools in each room, and a rack for holding blankets or drying underthings. The furnishings looked good, if plain; the beds had good mattresses, good pillows, and an abundance of folded linens and blankets atop each. There was a small fireplace in the larger room, but nothing in the smaller rooms, which would have to get heat from the kitchen.

"No fireplace for the maids," Serena observed. "But back home *we* don't have fireplaces in our bedrooms either. At least I don't."

"I don't either. It just makes you dress faster, and then you go wash up in the kitchen," Amelia agreed.

Amelia moved the viewpoint back to the entryway, and deter-mined there was another door there under the stairs. That led to a small storeroom that must be partly behind the parlor and had a door that also probably led outside. "That could be how *we* get to the privy," she decided. "But let's check the parlor again."

Sure enough, there was another door at the back of the parlor that led to what looked like a workroom with large windows giving lots of light. Again, this was plainly furnished, with no wainscoting, but had three enormous cupboards for storage, and two worktables, along with several plain chairs stacked on top of each other. This room had another brick fireplace. It, too, had a door leading to the back.

"Have you noticed all the fireplaces?" Serena said with approval. "Every room but the storeroom and the maids' rooms has one."

"We'll probably need them." Amelia sighed. "But I think this cottage must have been built during the reign of Queen Elizabeth, when there were very cold winters like we are about to face. All those heavy beams and whitewashed plaster give it away. That would account for it. Let's go up the stairs."

The stairs led to a landing where there were four doors and a trap in the ceiling. One bedroom for each of them, plus a spare? The doors looked to be a later addition; they were not the heavy, pegged plank doors of downstairs. Amelia wondered if they had once been open doorways with nothing but a curtain, or just open to the landing. Did no one in Tudor times require privacy? The floors were wood, and paths had been worn into them, betraying the cottage's age.

She looked up at Serena, who was gazing with interest into the bowl. "So far, I have nothing to quarrel with; have you?"

Serena shook her head. "I would have said that 'beggars cannot be choosers,' but nothing in this house is in the least objectionable. It might be mismatched, but it is all of good quality. I would not be ashamed to entertain anybody here."

"Nor would I." She moved the viewpoint into the first bedroom. Here there was no wainscoting, just the painted plaster and heavy beams. Blue walls, blue curtains, worn but good carpet, and very plain, solid furnishings. But old, much older than anything downstairs. The pieces were substantial, the wood dark with age. Bed, wardrobe, chest at the foot of the bed, a chair and writing table, small tables on either side of the bed, washstand, and closestool. And fireplace; if all the bedrooms had fireplaces, that would be most welcome. From about head height, the outside walls slanted inward at a steep angle. "James's room, should he come stay for a while?" Serena hazarded. "Is this Tudor furniture?"

"It's blue, and James is Air, so it is probably meant for him. And Tudor vintage likely, but it is the kind of furniture the most important servants would be given, I think. Something like a personal secretary or a governess. Or perhaps a grown child."

She moved to the next room. There was no doubt whom this one belonged to; it could only be for Serena. Rococo burst forth in all its glory in a royal red room: bed with a massive headboard and footboard covered in caved curlicues and gilded, with landscapes set in roundels in the headboard and footboard. Fainting couch, gilded, and upholstered in faded red brocade. Rococo washstand, desk, chair, dressing table and stool, enormous wardrobe, closestool, screen, blanket chest, and red curtains at the windows. More good, faded carpet on the floor, and a fireplace with a stack of huge flat cushions next to it. A Fire mage would be completely at home here.

Serena purred. "I don't know which I like better, the fainting couch or the fireplace cushions," she said.

"Both suit you, my little kitten." Amelia laughed.

Third room; this was a mirror to James's, except the wardrobe was smaller, and the walls and curtains were green. "George," they both said instantly, for George's element was Water, and he would be with them at least until the autumn term began at Oxford, if Alderscroft got him a place by then.

Amelia wondered what she would see in the fourth room. The anticipation drove every other thought out of her head.

She moved the viewpoint and sighed happily. The room had been painted a warm, light gold, and there were darker gold curtains at the window. But the furnishings *had* to be Tudor. The bed was huge, canopied, and bed-curtained in brown. Brown carpets lay at either side of the bed, to ensure warm toes in the winter. There was a padded bench at a table that had been repurposed as a dressing table, a Tudor writing desk and matching chair, a massive blanket chest at the foot of the bed, a pair of massive Tudor wardrobes, a Tudor closestool and wooden screen, and side tables to the bed that were also Tudor. She could not have been happier if Alderscroft had consulted her on her ideal bedroom.

It was a pity she and Serena were going to have to share their bedrooms with foodstuffs—but then again, the Tudors had probably done that. Hams, sausages, and cheese in wax hanging from the beams, bags of pulses and grains under the beds, and anywhere else they needed to go. Still! There was that storeroom, and a cellar. Perhaps they wouldn't need to pile food everywhere.

"How did they move all that in here?" Serena gasped. "That bed would *never* fit through the door, and must have taken six men to move!"

"I don't think they did," Amelia replied after a moment. "I think this is the original furniture for the Master of the house. Part of it, anyway; more might have been brought in. I think that bed has been here since the house was built, and was built in place. Possibly all the Tudor furniture has been here all along. This wouldn't have been a cottage when it was first built, it would have been the house of some important man in Axminster. Which means—I think—that we will probably have our own kitchen garden, an herb garden, and a flower garden or a shrubbery or even a small orchard. I believe it was uncommon for the houses of prominent people to be without some land around them. Why, we might even have room for a henhouse or a piggery! The storeroom just off the kitchen would have been the stillroom. And the workroom off the parlor would have belonged to the lady of the house. It might even have been her summer parlor."

"With all the dressmaking we plan to do—not to mention magic—we had probably better keep it as a workroom," Serena suggested. Amelia nodded her agreement.

"Well, I have not seen signs of damp or vermin," Serena continued. "But if a cat does not come with the house, we must get a pair, a tom and a queen."

"Better we get them in Axminster than uproot the poor things from London and force them to travel. Cats do not like travel. Let me see if I can get as far as outside without losing our anchor," she suggested. The best way to do that would be to proceed as if she were there in person, using a door, and not merely walking through an upstairs wall. The more one believed in what one was doing, the easier scrying was, and it was hard to believe in walking through upstairs walls out into the air.

She went out through the front door, to find three stone steps brought them down into a delightful front garden with a paving-stone path. Enclosed with head-height, thick stone walls, it contained plots of flowers alternating with what looked like herbs. She gasped with delight. As kind as the Anglefords were, she dearly missed greenery, and this looked like heaven on earth to a mage like her. A break in the wall had been fitted with a pretty little wooden gate that opened onto the road.

She moved the viewpoint deeper into the garden, and turned so they could see the house. As she had expected, it was completely Tudor, but not the kind with whitewashed exterior walls and black beams. No, this was sturdy, gray stone, matching the chimneys, of the sort that made those stone walls that marked individual fields outside the town. That accounted for why the walls were so thick. And it was a slate roof! All she could think was to thank God that their bedrooms had ceilings, because she'd heard from other people that while slate was excellent in winter and summer, and easier and cheaper to repair than thatch, slates had been known to crack in a fierce storm, and fall down inside to land on one's head.

But I do wonder what might be in that attic.

She took the viewpoint out through the gate to find herself on the main road. There were several more "large" houses such as this one on either side of the road, also in the Tudor style, all in good repair, and a few of earlier or later vintage. So this would be the "good" neighborhood in Axminster, where the prosperous came to live— not unlike this neighborhood. The "best" neighborhood was probably further along the road, where residents could have even more extensive gardens and significantly larger homes. Or, perhaps, right in the middle of town, where the owner of a big house could flaunt his prosperity.

Beside the gardens there was a graveled drive bordered by more walls leading to the rear of the house. She took her viewpoint along that drive, and found a small stable of more modern vintage, also made of stone; it looked as if it had a loft above, which would be where any manservants would live. And next to that were much bigger gardens than in the front, enclosed in yet more stone walls. They were all neatly laid out with raised beds. Impossible to tell what, if anything, had been seeded in those beds, the spring had been so cold, but they definitely had been tilled and seeded, and small green plants struggled bravely in them against the chill. And there were hens! They were picking their way along the beds, diligently searching for bugs. A henhouse lay at the bottom of the garden, and a little bit away from that, a beehive. And, of course, a stout stone privy. No piggery, but she reckoned she could pay a farmer to raise and butcher a pig for her.

"Anything you want to see?" she asked Serena.

"No, you won't be able to take your scrying out into the road for long, or into the neighbors' gardens, so that will have to wait until we are there in person." But Serena was smiling. "I am *quite* in charity with this house! I would not in the least mind leasing it from his lordship for quite some time! It wouldn't be a bad thing to bring some of our brothers and sisters over, two at a time, once we find James his property."

"And cousins. We are about to outgrow our plantation," Amelia mused. "That *would* be no bad thing. There must be more of them other than just George who are interested in coming here."

"You know what this means, however, do you not?" Serena asked, archly.

Amelia felt her mind go blank, because she could not fathom Serena's meaning. "No?" she replied tentatively.

"Now we are going to have to go out of our way to cultivate Mr.

Nightsmith and Captain Roughtower so we can quiz them about Ax-minster." Serena grinned at Amelia's expression.

"Oh, no," Amelia moaned.

"Oh *yes*," said Serena gleefully. And continued to grin as the prospect caused Amelia to lose control of her scrying, and the vision of the back of their house dissolved into mist and was gone, leaving only the gleaming obsidian bowl.

11

JUNE was finally here, and significantly warmer, though everyone that was not an Elemental mage informed Amelia that it was not as warm as it should be. It was only a matter of weeks now before the move to Axminster, and some things had already been sent on. All the fabric and cut-out pieces from the winter clothing, for instance, each project neatly packaged in brown paper, each packet including the correct color of thread and all the trimmings. Those in turn had been packed as tightly as possible into wicker hampers and marked with a label designating Amelia's projects or Serena's. Julia had insisted on sending on more linens, and all manner of needful things besides that: buckets, pails, and mops; knives and cleavers; spoons and large forks for the kitchen. Soap for washing and soap for cleaning. An entire hamper of rags. Some of the foodstuffs had gone on too, though except for the pulses and grains, which were still blessedly cheap in London thanks to Thomas Angleford, Amelia intended to purchase most of her stores at the weekly Axminster market, where they would be cheaper still. Or grow them; as cool as this month was, it was still time to grow a few things like pumpkins that didn't mind the cool. And much of their American wardrobe had gone on too, since they hadn't needed it much here. Two cats had been obtained, and been given the run of the house once their paws had been buttered. Serena's mama swore this was the way to keep a cat from wandering back to its old house, and it seemed to have worked.

Amelia looked at her lists as she sat at her desk in her room; it was good to find some things crossed off, but there were so many to go! And the husband list—well—so far there was nothing to say on that score.

1. Must be an Elemental mage.

They had met *so very many* Elemental mages, but none that seemed to fit. Many of them were too old, or too young, or too married. The only two that were obvious choices were Phillip Nightsmith and Harold Roughtower, and . . .

Her heart sank a little, at the idea of being tied to either man. *No. No, no, no. I shall not consider them yet. I would rather be a spinster!*

Perhaps Axminster might broaden their prospects. Perhaps when sons came back from universities for their vacations . . .

And perhaps Napoleon would be defeated, all those soldiers would come home, and there would be prospects among them. Roughtower could not be the only mage in the Army, could he?

2. Must accept Serena as she is.

Well, there had been no prospects to test that on . . . and they did not have the permission of Lord Alderscroft to reveal it to anyone else. Amelia got the feeling that they should obtain his consent before they pulled back the curtain on that particular aspect of her cousin.

3. Must be kind.

Many who were kind, but all too old, too young, or too married. And some who were *not* kind, although they kept the snubs and little aggressions well out of sight of the Alderscrofts, and to tell the truth neither they nor their attempts to irritate the American bumpkins mattered much to Amelia. But *must be kind* was imperative, and that flag remained furled.

4. Must be clever.

So far everyone they had met was clever. Even Nightsmith and Roughtower were clever. Roughtower was even clever enough to realize she knew what she was talking about, and sat down with her one day at a card party and quizzed her about "all this planting rigmarole." And took notes! And said he was going to send them all to his gardener so they wouldn't be eating dead leaves come winter. But he wasn't *kind*. Many things, but not kind.

Well, he is handsome. I would not mind helping him fix his property, and I would not mind living roughly until we did. As a Master there is a great deal I can coax from my Elementals, and dwarves and gnomes are good builders. I wonder if he could be taught to be kind. . . . She shook off the thought and looked back down at the list.

5. Must not be a fortune hunter.

The fortune hunters had eliminated themselves. They probably would have returned, Roughtower with them, if they knew how big the plantation back home was. But, like Serena being a shifter, this was something that would only be revealed when the prospect had proved to be able to hold his tongue. Besides, neither she nor Serena would tolerate a fortune hunter; their bride portions might only supply about five hundred a year together, but thanks to shopping with Julia, she knew that the two of them could live on that.

6. Must be willing to come back to America if need be.

Absolutely *no one* was a prospect there. Even when a potential prospect had spent hour upon hour of interested questioning about

America, the end had always been, "Lud! I'm glad I don't live there!" *And that eliminates Hightower. As an officer he cannot leave unless he resigns or sells his commission, and if he does that, the income from his position ends.*

7. Must be resilient.

Too many prospects. An Elemental mage had to be resilient, when they might be called to a Hunt at any moment. Frankly, Amelia was surprised that she and Serena hadn't been yet! There had been three "feral" ghosts within the city itself, and outside of it, a ghoul, a troll, and something creating tangible nightmares that Alder-scroft had *thought* was a mage gone bad, but which turned out to be a child born to an ordinary family who had sent him to Bedlam because he would not stop crying about the things he was seeing that no one else could. Incarcerated among the truly mad, the poor mite had summoned creatures to keep him safe from them. But they were not *nice* creatures, and the child did not know what he could do, so they were not bound to stay with him. So off they went a-wandering and at least three of them had made it past the gates, alerting the Master of the White Lodge that there was something that needed to be Hunted. Now the child was properly with an Earth-mage family who were teaching the poor mite how to handle his powers.

I am woolgathering. She turned her attention back to the list.

8. Must be a Hunter of the White Lodge.

Everyone they met here was a Hunter of the White Lodge. Likely everyone with magic who knew Phillip Nightsmith would be. And anyone without magic whom they met in Axminster would not be. So, at the moment, that could not be considered a concern. All magic here in England derived from a single source—not like in America, where there were people of varied beliefs and nationalities, who had their own ways of dealing with inimical forces and beings. The

Hessian mages, for instance, had their own version of the White Lodge, and rarely interacted with the Stonecrofts.

9. Must love music and reading.

That did not matter until they had gotten through numbers one through eight.

10. Must not demand we be submissive.

Unknown, except for Nightsmith—his little tirade about *females putting themselves above their place* made it very clear where his sentiments lay—and Roughtower was a military man, and military men tended to demand submission of their spouses. But then again—that afternoon with Roughtower—he had been more than willing, eager even, to rely on her expertise. Perhaps?

Resolutely, she shut the book. There were other—

Her thoughts were interrupted by a growing noise in the street. A noise she had heard before, a noise that made her heart sink, even before her head recognized it for what it was.

Surely everyone else in the house knows that sound! It was the noise of people in a panic. Many people; probably every master and servant from every house on the street. Every single one of them going "have you heard" and "what shall we do?" and similar unhelpful things. Every one of them in a panic and every one of them doing nothing to assuage that panic.

It *had* to be something about Napoleon. Nothing else made people lose their heads like he did.

As she dashed out of her bedroom, she nearly ran into Serena, and as the two of them leapt down the stairs like a pair of hoydens, they had to stop before they reached the bottom of the stairs, for virtually *everyone* in the house had crowded into the entry.

At least they aren't all in the street.

"What?" gasped Serena. "Why is there a row?"

"We've sent Tommy out to find out!" said Mrs. Jennings.

At that very moment, Tommy burst through the door. "Wellington!" he sobbed, shaking like a leaf in the wind. "Wellington's in retreat! He might be dead! Boney's won!"

And just like that, Amelia watched an entire group of normally sensible people fall to pieces.

The words sent a tremor through the people packed into the entry. Mary started to sob. But before an uproar could start, Amelia said, sternly, *"Stop."*

Perhaps it wasn't her place to command them, precisely, but in the absence of their proper master and mistress, she was going to exert some authority before the hysterics that had happened when news of Napoleon's escape broke out.

To her great relief, they unconsciously accepted her command. Responding to the calm and authority in her voice, everyone except Mary got themselves under control, and even Mary stifled her sobs in her clenched hands.

"Just because someone has run through the town spreading a story, it does not follow that the story is true. I have a better place to get news than people running about in the street. You know I am a Master, and I already have Elementals watching Napoleon," she said, soothingly, if not precisely truthfully. "And I will ask one of them directly." She held out her hand and circled her palm with a glowing ring of power, and called, "Natty—"

And there the brownie was, standing on her palm, before she could finish his name.

"Hey now, hey now, hey now," said the brownie. *"Can ye all see and hear me?"*

There were either nods, or looks of envious delight from the servants. All except for two. Davey and Mrs. Jennings looked from Amelia's palm to her face and back again, quizzically. Amelia obligingly sent power into the brownie until their eyes widened.

They must be Air. Air has the hardest time seeing Earth. When their eyes widened, she knew they could see the brownie. And if they could see him, they could hear him.

"There now," Natty Ned said with satisfaction. *"Miss Amelia has*

been clever, and arranged for me to look in on his lordship on the regular, because his lordship has Elementals that do nothing but keep watch and report back. That news in the street is a day old! Why, there was even a ball last night for Wellington and his generals! Then they smashed Napoleon at a place called Waterloo! Boney's nose has been tweaked and Wellington gave him a thrashing and clapped him in irons! It's over! Victory!"

At first the staff looked at the brownie in disbelief. Then in growing hope. Then Tommy gave a tentative cheer, which might have sent the rest into a happy riot. Which would have been bad, because even if people didn't believe them now, when word came in the next day or so, those same people would remember, and start to wonder how the Angleford servants had known the truth long before anyone else did. So Amelia put a stop to any celebration before it could happen.

"Here now! Mind what we are!" she snapped. "No one can know this! That's why Lord Alderscroft has done nothing about the panic out there! Remember that we can never do or say something that might make people think we are not what we seem!"

There was a silence, a collective sigh, then Mrs. Jennings said, sadly, "Well, 'tis going to be an uneasy night for many. And the panic in the Stock Exchange—well, my poor consols will be all right in a day or two."

From out of nowhere, Amelia heard the voice of Miranda Sumner in her mind.

"Consols. Get 'em on the Stock Exchange."

And—"If he defeats Wellington and our German allies, the Stock Exchange will be crashed. Or at least the consols will."

That was when it struck her: a great and glorious way to increase their fortunes without having to do anything except spend that fortune wisely. "Davey!" she gasped. "I need to send a message to James and Thomas! Can you get to the warehouse quickly?"

"Oh, if you can lend me power enough, I can call a sylph. We can send her," Davey advised. "The sylphs like James, even without him being a Master. Mrs. Jennings can help too, if you'd rather."

Mrs. Jennings looked about her, and reasserted her authority.

"Everyone except Davey, back to work, please. Just because the world is losing its head, it doesn't follow that we can lark about. Remember, by tomorrow when news comes for ordinary folk, this will all be over. Oh! And make sure to leave a nice custard tart on the hearth for the brownie, for being so good as to ease our minds." As the others shuffled back to whatever task they had abandoned, Mrs. Jennings turned to Amelia as the one to give permissions. "Might we use the parlor?"

"Of course," she said, and she and Serena came the rest of the way down the stairs and joined Mrs. Jennings.

"Have either of you ever called an Elemental before?" she asked, as they settled around one of the round tables they used to play cards and lotteries on. Natty Ned still rode on her palm, so she placed him on the table, where he regarded them all with interest. Serena took a seat on the opposite side of the table from the two servants, and Amelia seated herself beside her cousin.

"A round half dozen times," Davey said with confidence. "When Lady Ladysmith's coachman helped. He's a Master."

"More than that, I think," replied Mrs. Jennings. "There's a witch—" She blushed. "Well, she's my friend, and she *calls* herself a witch; I don't rightly know if that's true, but she does. But she's my friend, and she helped me call a sylph when I needed some answers about some of my cousins." Mrs. Jennings didn't elaborate, and Amelia was not about to pry. "You know, there is no reason why we cannot do so together, Davey. Two of us will be surer than one."

"Why, that's right!" Davey exclaimed. "Well, soonest begun is soonest done." He put one hand on the tabletop. Mrs. Jennings covered it with hers. Amelia took Mrs. Jennings' hand and touched the ley line. She opened herself to it, and operated strictly as a Channel, allowing the power to flow from her into the others. The room was utterly silent—but the crowd out in the streets was not. It sounded as if people were really working themselves up into a frenzy.

At least this was a genteel neighborhood; there were parts of London where it would not be safe right now, and darkness would only make things worse. Frightened people often lost their heads, and there were always others who would prey on those who were in a state where they were reacting, not thinking.

There will be broken windows and broken heads before the night is out. As the power flowed into Mrs. Jennings and Davey, she watched them take it and twist it from Earth to Air, from gold to blue. Between them, they created a summoning circle much faster than a single mage working alone could have. Because she was a Master, she could see and hear Elementals from every Element, so it was no surprise to her when the blue-glowing ring on the table shimmered once, and a sylph appeared in it.

Even if the creature did make her blush hotly.

Most sylphs wore little to nothing except their long flowing hair, and never used their wings for modesty. This one was no exception in that regard—but she was a little different than the sylphs Amelia had seen at home in America. She had green wings with darker green veins—a butterfly type she was not familiar with, so it must be peculiarly English.

"How may I assist, my dear friends?" the sylph said, in a breathy voice, looking at the four of them.

"Geniver, do ye ken the tall lad from across the salt sea what lives here?" Davey asked. *Ah, he knows this one, then.*

The sylph nodded enthusiastically. *"I do. He is at his place of labor."*

"We need ye to take him a message," said Mrs. Jennings.

The little thing smiled and twirled her hair swirling around her like skeins of gossamer thread—which did nothing to hide her naked little body. Amelia blushed more. *"'Tis easy done. Give it me, and I'll take it to him straightaway!"*

I prefer the talking birds that are the Indian Air Elementals. Even if the jays always steal something from me.

With that assurance, Amelia took a pencil and the smallest, lightest strip of paper she could find, and wrote on it in her clearest, smallest letters. *Take all money and buy consols,* she wrote. *All. Trust me. A.*

James would not fail her, even if his first thought was that she was mad. But his second thought would be that she must have accurate information from *somewhere*, and he would realize that what was being touted in the streets was not true. He was clever; he'd intuit that she must be getting information either from her own Elementals or from those of another Master. And he would know that they could take great advantage of that.

Then she rolled it up and handed it to the sylph, but she let Davey give it orders. No stepping on another mage's toes, here!

"Fly as fast as ye can, and give it to the lad," Davey urged.

"I go!" she responded instantly, and vanished from the ring. Amelia let the power drain, and the ring faded.

"Well," she said. "I hope he believes me."

"Why?" Mrs. Jennings asked bluntly.

"Because," she laughed weakly. "I might just have given Serena and myself a fortune for fortune hunters to long for."

But then she turned to Natty Ned. "Can you find Julia outside these walls?" she asked the brownie.

"Oh aye. I see where ye be goin'. 'Tis no time for her to be out in the street."

"Davey, get Frank, and Ned will guide you to Mrs. Angleford," she said, once again appropriating authority. "Get her back safe."

"I'll get something to use for cudgels," Mrs. Jennings said, a bit grimly.

"Who'll guard the door?" Davey asked, his brow creased with worry.

For answer, Serena just snarled a little. Davey startled, then smiled thinly. "Right you are. Find me a stout one, Mrs. Jennings. If trouble comes, I'll break its head for it."

Julia had fortunately taken to the back alleys to avoid the mobs forming, and thanks to Frank and Davey's escort, she had gotten home about an hour after the first hysterics began.

The first thing she had done when she got home and took off her bonnet was to take out the whiskey and pour her helpers a stout drink by way of thanks.

The second thing she did, after leaving Frank and his ax-handle at the front door, and Serena at the back, was to effortlessly command the rest of downstairs to pretend there was nothing going on outside. "They won't get in," she said, calmly. "So do your best to ignore the poor benighted things and get on with your day."

And she herself did just that, throwing herself into doing the account books for the household.

Thomas and James came home late. Their somewhat disheveled appearance made Julia fly into Thomas's arms, then pat him all over to reassure herself that he had come to no real harm.

"It's a riot out there," said James, doing his best to tidy himself and failing utterly. "I am glad you thought to send hired guards with Davey, or we might be lacking a carriage and horse just now."

"I didn't—" Julia began.

"I did," said Serena, who had gone back to being a girl once the men were safely home. "I still had some pocket money, and it was enough. Davey knew just who to hire and where to find them. We Americans are prone to expressing our emotions with cudgels, so it occurred to me that a carriage and horse might be tempting to the weak wanting to escape London."

"Oh, bless you!" Julia and Amelia cried as one. Then Julia laughed weakly. "Come to the dining room," Julia said, "and you can tell us what happened. Over a good meal that we have kept warm for you; we have been subsisting on tea and toast this evening."

"Ah, you kept dinner! I am utterly famished," Thomas said with gratitude, as Amelia hugged her cousin in thanks. "Indeed, this will go better over dinner."

Against all custom, all of downstairs, including Davey, had crowded into the dining room to hear what was said. Neither Julia nor Thomas admonished them—and it *did* mean that there were plenty of hands to serve.

"James understood what you meant, and rushed to the 'Change when the sylph brought him your note," said Thomas. "I followed after about two hours, and we stayed there until the closing bell. It was a dreadful sight." He shook his head. "The fear—one could taste it. It was clear that all these men had but one thought: *liquidate, get what you can, and flee.* Grown men were practically coming to blows every time a potential buyer appeared. Some men were *weeping* in public! I dare say that under normal circumstances, they would rather have been seen naked than weeping. I lack adequate ability to describe the chaos, but it was, in its way, as terrible as a battlefield."

"I was initially inclined to buy immediately, but as soon as I saw the panic, and how the price of consols kept plummeting, I decided to hold out until the last minute. Providentially, I had the Stonecroft chequebook with me, so when Thomas arrived, I took my courage in both hands and plunged."

"How much did you venture?" Amelia asked, breathless.

"All of it," he said gravely. "Might I have more roast mutton? And potatoes?"

"*All* of it?" she gasped, as three sets of willing hands passed him the food.

"Every liquid cent. Your marriage portion, Serena's, and everything that was in the account that we were not going to need in the next several days. If ever there was a time to plunge, and plunge deeply, this was it." The silence in the room was portentous. "By the time I bought, consols were down to a fraction of the value they had held this morning, and only the closing bell stopped the fall."

"I ventured as much as I dared—" said Thomas. "We aren't as liquid as James, but we *have* been saving to buy provisions, so I used that. I'll sell once the consols go back up enough. People were alternately blessing us for taking their paper and cursing us as fools."

Amelia felt her breath catch in her throat, and there was a hollow feeling of fear in her heart. She had only ever intended James to invest their marriage portions, not *everything*! And Thomas! "But what if I had been wrong?" she gasped, visions of just that swarming her thoughts. "What if the consols don't go back up?"

"You said to trust you. We trusted you," Thomas said simply, since

James's mouth was full of roasted potato. "Now, both of us would like to know precisely why you told us to do this thing."

"Obviously Wellington didn't lose," James added. "We assumed that from the beginning. But how did you know?"

"Well . . . I have a . . . spy, of sorts, in Alderscroft's household," she said, a bit embarrassed. "I asked Natty Ned, the household brownie, to ask one of Alderscroft's brownies to help me keep an eye on what his lordship learned about Bonaparte. Just to let me know if Bonaparte did something!" she added hastily. "I knew *he* must have Elementals all the way over to Belgium that were keeping him apprised, and I just wanted us to have some warning. Lady Dutton told me all about consols, and about the Stock Exchange and what would happen if Bonaparte won, and when we heard the news I knew at once that the price of consols would fall. And . . . well, it seemed like a good idea." She faltered, but said no more.

"And you knew that when the *real* news came home, the price would rise again!" James slapped his hand on the table. "Well played, Amelia!"

Thomas and Julia looked just a little appalled at the notion that she'd had an Elemental spy in Alderscroft's very household . . . well, she was ashamed, but only a little.

"So what *is* the news?" Thomas asked, as James applied himself to his plate. "Obviously it's that Wellington did *not* lose."

"It's better than that! He won! And Bonaparte is captured again!" she crowed, and was pleased to see the Anglefords' expressions return to approval. There was obvious relief in the way the men's shoulders suddenly relaxed, as if they had been holding themselves tensely this entire time.

"Well, I think we can expect to see the value of our purchases return to normal by midday tomorrow at worst," Thomas mused. "Those that sold them will be eager to buy them back, and the frenzy to repurchase might even drive the price higher than yesterday's. And considering that when we bought them, consols were a tenth of the value that they had been yesterday—"

"*What?*" Julia gasped. "A *tenth*? How much did you buy?"

"Quite . . . a lot," James confessed. "I'm not even sure of the exact number. I would have to look at our receipts. But the important part is that you and Serena can each count on a thousand a year without lifting a finger. And when I sell what I bought with the company money, even after I have repaid the company coffers, I'll have what I need to set up the spinning and weaving and silkworm farm immediately, instead of doing it all piecemeal."

"You'll save money on that, certainly," Thomas said calmly, as if the news wasn't good enough to make Amelia feel faint. *A thousand a year! Each! Why, that is more than four times what we'd need to live on!* "If you can offer a crew work on three buildings instead of just one, you can bargain with authority." He turned to Julia, and patted her hand. "Tomorrow or the next day I will sell enough to put all the company money back in the bank. And we will have enough interest money coming in yearly from consols that you will never need to worry about money again."

Julia didn't burst into tears, but she did seize her husband's hand and hold it tremblingly to her lips.

"Do you suppose Alderscroft took advantage of this?" Serena wondered out loud.

"There were several on the floor who did, and I am sure his lordship has a man to manage his Exchange dealings for him, so the answer is 'maybe,'" James replied. "I have great admiration for the men with the nerves to do so without *our* information. They are either highly patriotic or playing a very long game indeed."

"Where are these consols?" Serena asked. "You didn't bring them home with you, I hope!"

"No, they are safe at the bank, for now." Thomas did something he had *never* done before: he chased the last bit of gravy around his plate with a bit of bread and popped it in his mouth. He must indeed have been starving. Julia was either so stunned by all this, or so amazed at the news, that she didn't chide him for such a lapse of manners.

"Coming back, we ran into a mob that was trying to take any sort of conveyance they could away from its rightful owners. Somehow the news had transmogrified from 'Boney has beaten Wellington' to 'Boney is sailing up the Thames with an army,' and people were try-ing to flee. That was where Davey's cudgel-men came in very handy. Thank you for thinking of that, Serena, and sending the money to hire them along." He grinned ruefully. "I did not have a feather to fly with."

It was clear that both men were exhausted; in fact, everyone looked drained by the day's events. Amelia certainly felt that way. And when the last of their euphoria wore off, by common consent everyone went to bed.

But Amelia could not sleep.

She stared up into the darkness, listening to people rushing aim-lessly to and fro in the street, chasing rumors, looking for news—possibly looking for victims. And she felt a deep sense of shame over her work today. Not leaving a brownie as a spy on his lordship; that was nothing much, really, since all the "spying" she had intended was to make sure they all knew about Napoleon's movements. No, it was shame that she had personally orchestrated the means to profit at the expense of others.

"Ye've got your mind a-churnin' like the Thames at tide-turn, lass," came Natty Ned's voice from the headboard above her head. *"Tell old Ned, speak it out afore it sinks claws in ye."*

"I'm afraid what we did—wasn't right," she said, letting her an-guish pour out. "We took advantage of people who didn't have our information. Tomorrow or the next day, when the Exchange returns to normal, they are going to be angry and unhappy."

"If ye be thinking practical, that they'll be comin' to get back their consols, well, they won't. At least not the way some 'un in yer America would, with fists or a stick or a rifle. They'll just slink away and try to cut their losses." She could hear his little feet hitting the headboard as he swung them. *"The 'Change is a kind of gambling hall. And them as go there every day are like gamblers at the faro table. Except the big difference is that at the 'Change ye can't cover yer bets with vowels."*

"With—what?" she asked.

"I-O-U," he spelled out. *"Vowels. Ye cannot buy consols or stocks*

with promissory notes. *So they lost, but unless they had nothin' but consols, they didn't lose everything. They'll swallow their pride and get on."*

"But I'm not sure this is *moral*," she explained. "We took advantage of them. It doesn't seem fair."

He laughed. *"Life isn't fair in the Exchange, lass, nor at the gaming table. People who expect* fair *don't go to either place."*

She pondered that for a good long while. "How do you know so much about this?" she asked.

"Thomas dabbles on the 'Change, and gets mages what do it on the regular to give him advice. I think you made a dream come true for him. He was hoping to have a big win, so he and Julia can move to Bath without worrying."

Hmm. Maybe she hadn't done a bad thing.

"It still seems . . . exploitive."

"I cannot swear to ye that ye harmed none. I can swear ye didn't harm anyone that wasn't expecting harm, and who is cursing himself— or will be—for being so rattle-pated as to be spooked by rumor."

"Fair enough," she replied. Then asked her question again. "Did Alderscroft profit by this?" Because if his lordship had . . . she wouldn't feel it was unethical.

Natty Ned burst out with a laugh. *"Lud! Didn't he! Sent his man to the 'Change with orders for* plenty *of things besides consols. He'll be a damn sight richer in a week."*

All right, then. And no harm in not bothering to tell him, either. Pot and kettle, after all.

Now *she* could relax, and think about the move that was only three days away.

12

"WHAT do you think it will be like?" Serena asked, gloved hand caressing the vellum envelope that held her invitation to Briarhold from Grand Duke Pevensky, a beautiful handwritten piece in round hand that even included ornamental capitals and flourishes. Except for the name, Amelia's was identical to Serena's, and she was touched beyond words that not only had the grand duke thought to include Serena in the invitation, he had sent her a separate invitation—because obviously they would include these beautiful pieces in their scrapbooks, or even in frames on the wall. Neither of them had ever seen a true example of what James had referred to admiringly as a Stately Country Manor before, and Amelia had not dared to try scrying from the invitation to see what it looked like. If the grand duke was as powerful a Master as people had implied he was, he might detect her and be offended. She already was touched by the man's kindness, and suspected that before the visit was over she would be more in awe of him than she was of Lord Alderscroft.

"We'll find out soon enough," she replied, looking out of the windows of the carriage at what had just appeared in the window on the right side. "I think these walls are around Briarhold." Walls a good six feet tall, made of local red brick and surmounted with tops and column caps of sandstone, looking more than ample to discourage invasion by the uninvited. Beyond them were glimpses of treetops and even hills, none of it agricultural, suggesting that the grand duke did not need an income from agriculture on his personal property surrounding his manor.

The formidable red brick walls continued for quite some time before they came to a gate, a massive piece of ornamented ironwork framed by two creamy stone pillars, with a red brick, slate-roofed gatehouse just inside. It was a proper, lived-in gatehouse too, as betrayed by the presence of a gatekeeper who emerged from the front door, still buttoning his livery jacket, to open it for them.

There was some brief conversation they could not hear between Davey and the gatekeeper; the latter was quickly satisfied, and they were on their way again. "Can you see anything?" Serena asked.

"Not without sticking my head out of the window like a child," Amelia replied, since there was nothing to be seen at the moment except a vast expanse of perfectly manicured lawn, some trees and shrubs, and a hill. How did all that property get mowed? Did the grand duke use sheep? "It seems this is a very long driveway . . ."

Serena put her invitation away in her reticule, and clenched her hands on it. Amelia almost had to sit on her own hands to keep from sticking her head out that window by the time the first bits of Briarhold came into view, and she held her breath as the first glimpse of a two-story, flat-roofed, red brick and cream stone wing came into view. She glanced to the right, and saw a bit of what looked like an identical wing on the other side. This was a *new* home, probably built no earlier than the beginning of the reign of the king. The simplicity of it was as elegant as an expensive modern ball gown, where sheer cost of materials spoke, rather than trimmings and spangles.

It wasn't until the carriage made a wide turn to the right and took the curve of the driveway that part of the whole of the main building spread itself in Serena's windows, and only when they were handed out by a footman in blue and red livery that absolutely dated to the beginning of the king's reign that they saw it in all its glory.

The center part of the main building was crafted of that creamy stone; the rest was of red brick. Ornamental frames ran around each window in stone, and stone pillars ran from ground to roof, separating each window from the next. The main building was three stories tall; the two flat-roofed wings were two stories. It managed to be imposing and beautiful without any towers, statues everywhere, or other fanciful architecture. The whole made up a "U" shape with the wings embracing the gravel-paved courtyard in the middle. Six wide stone steps led up to the wooden double door, and there was another footman in red-and-blue livery and powdered wig waiting to guide them inside.

He nodded to them in a friendly fashion and indicated with an outstretched hand that they were to proceed in through the open door. The front entrance made them both gasp, with its pale pink plaster walls and gilded plaster decorations, and the massive portraits in gilded frames on either side. One was of a beautiful woman in a scarlet and gold gown of the previous century; the other was of a handsome man in a scarlet satin suit of tailless coat, knee breeches, white stockings, and scarlet shoes in a white, curled wig, in whose face Amelia could detect signs of the grand duke's features.

A doorman bowed to them gravely after he closed the door behind them. "Who may I say is calling?" he asked, in respectful tones.

"Miss Amelia Stonecroft and Miss Serena Meleva," Amelia said, as Serena touched her reticule, ready to produce her invitation at the first sign of resistance.

"Ah!" the doorman said. "You are expected. And precisely on time." He smiled as if to indicate that being "precisely on time" was admirable and courteous. And slightly raising his voice, he called, "Ivan!"

A little boy in livery identical to the adults' and a miniature periwig popped out of an alcove to one side of the entry hall.

"Take the ladies directly to the grand duke. They are expected." The doorman bowed and retreated to his post. The boy bowed to each of them, and then gestured that they should follow.

Amelia would have liked for the boy to saunter rather than trot briskly as he led them through the wonders of the place. Pastel-painted walls with snowy plaster Rococo decorations were every-where, as were paintings that deserved to be studied, and furnishings worthy of a king. But the boy was in a hurry, and restrained him-self from running only because doing so would inconvenience the girls. Amelia was extremely glad they were wearing their best sum-mer afternoon gowns, delicate and tasteful constructions of silk gauze rather than muslin, and even then she felt severely under-dressed.

At length they came to what could only be the library, since it was floor-to-ceiling and wall-to-wall books, except for the window wall, which was only half books. The other half was taken up by an ample, stone-framed fireplace and the window. This wall was painted a warm red, and had another portrait, this one of an older grand duke and the old king standing together.

Sitting in a comfortable chair near the fireplace, in which a cheer-ful fire crackled, was Grand Duke Pevensky himself. As apparently was his custom, he wore a suit of the previous generation nearly identical to the ones in his portraits, of fine black satin, with blin-dingly white silk stockings and black shoes.

He looked up alertly as they entered.

"Miss Amelia Stonecroft and Miss Serena Meleva, come to call upon you, as arranged, my lord!" the boy said clearly.

"So I see, so I see." The old man chuckled. "You may go, Ivan. Tell Ekaterina to send in the tea service. Ladies, please seat yourselves. I hope you will forgive me for not standing."

"Certainly, your highness," Amelia said, having been schooled on how to address a grand duke by Julia. She and Serena went to com-fortable, brocade-upholstered chairs that had been pulled close to the grand duke's in anticipation of their arrival. She bobbed a little curtsy to him before seating herself; belatedly, Serena did the same.

"I am very glad you took the time to come all this way to amuse an old man," he said. Now that he was not trying to speak over the cacophony of many voices at a dinner, Amelia detected a very faint accent in his words. More "f" than "v," and more "d" than "th," for instance. Just enough to betray that English was not his first language.

"How could we not, when it is a handsome man who has invited us, and not an old one at all," Serena dimpled at him. "Also, a fascinating man! We could not have kept away!"

He laughed. "Oh, you are a charmer! I like charming ladies. I particularly like charming ladies who have come all the way across the great ocean, from a place where I have never been! Will you indulge my curiosity and speak with me about your portion of America?"

"Of course!" they said together, then looked at each other and laughed. The grand duke joined in the laughter.

"Well! Tea shall be here presently. My people are very fond of tea; I think you will like how we make it. You will like my Russian tea cakes, and the tea shall make your throats smooth for much talking. Tell me about your home, if you please. Your actual *home*, and not just your region of America."

They took turns. He seemed much more alert than he had been the night of the ball; perhaps that had been due to the lateness of the hour. Serena was far franker than Amelia would have been; and he asked many questions. Inevitably, as Amelia had guessed it would, the subject turned to slavery. When he learned that many of the tenant farmers on the plantation were freed slaves, and that there were no *actual* slaves in their employ, he blinked and nodded in approval. They took a moment to savor his truly excellent tea, brewed on the spot by the maidservant in red and blue, out of a formidable contraption he told them was called a *samovar*. "I think that a mage, who had gathered about himself other mages, could not have done otherwise. Even though I did not have nearly as many mages among my serfs as you have among your tenants, my family acted in a similar fashion."

"It seems we cannot help ourselves, sir," Amelia smiled. "Dr. Trevor, my partner at Lord Alderscroft's dinner, called it *enlightened self-interest*."

"That is a good name for it. Now, the Lion of London has told me, Miss Serena, that you are a shifter," he said, startling them both enough to make the teacups rattle in the saucers in their hands. "Some of my people in my home of Russia are wolf shifters. My late, beloved wife came of that blood, although she did not possess the power herself. And you are a leopard-shifter?"

"I am, highness," Serena said, recovering her equilibrium. Then she turned her head to the side. "There is a good screen behind you, which will preserve my modesty and your sensibilities; would you like me to shift for you?"

"Oh, *would* you, my dear? I would be most obliged! I have only seen a leopard in the Tower menagerie, and those poor creatures were—" He shook his head. "Sad and bereft and near mad, I think. I should like to see a leopard as they are meant to be seen."

Serena leapt to her feet. "With all my heart, highness!" she exclaimed, and ran to the screen (which probably concealed a closestool or a chamber pot for the grand duke's convenience).

Amelia was used to how quickly Serena could slip out of her clothing and shift, but this would have been the fastest *she* had ever seen, for it was not very many moments before Serena bounded out from behind the screen and circled around the grand duke's chair, her pearls still around her throat, purring. She sat down at his feet, tail curled about her paws, and regarded him with widened eyes, which made her look like a giant spotted kitten.

"*Krasivyy!*" he exclaimed. "*Slavnyy!* Beautiful!" He hovered his hand near to her head. "May I?"

Serena purred louder and shoved her head under his hand.

"Like silk, your coat! Muscles like steel! Eyes like amber! Ah!" His own old eyes sparkled in their nest of wrinkles. "It is not often that I experience a new thing, and I thank you for bringing your dear self to me and indulging me. Would you like to be a girl again?"

Serena looked at Amelia, who correctly interpreted the look. "She would be happy to sit at your feet and warm them, but it might frighten your staff should anyone come in, so yes, she had probably better be a girl again." Amelia smiled. "Besides, leopards do not appreciate tea cakes; they would rather have a nice fresh partridge for tea."

Serena *whuffed* at her playfully. She got up, circled around so the grand duke could see every part of her, gamboled and rolled like a kitten for his entertainment, then bounded over to the screen. It took her longer to get into her clothing than it had to get out of it, and by the time she did, the maid had returned with new treats.

"You must try these," the grand duke urged, as Serena approached the chairs again, using her ribbon to tie up her hair in a loose chignon. "They are also from Russia. The little pancakes are called *blini*. You do so—a bit of cream, then a spoonful of caviar, then fold, and eat. Do not chew!" he added. "Chewing makes the caviar bitter."

They followed his example, using a tiny, mother-of-pearl spoon to put a dollop of what looked to Amelia like tiny black peppercorns on the pillow of cream; Amelia thought the taste was interesting, but over-salty. But by the widening of Serena's eyes, she found the treat delicious.

"Ah, now!" said the grand duke, with a chuckle. "Perhaps Miss Amelia has a sweet tooth. Try with strawberry preserves. That leaves more caviar for us!" he added to Serena, who was quick to take up another warm, pillowy miniature pancake and add more cream and caviar.

Amelia *much* preferred the strawberry preserves and the currant jam with the cream. But she was very careful not to look greedy, though it was hard. The tiny pancakes were very good. Between them, Serena and the grand duke demolished the little bowl of caviar. Amelia had heard of caviar, of course; it figured as an indicator of the height of luxury in some of the novels she had read. In her mind, it did not live up to its promise, although it was clear she was outvoted on the subject.

Once Ekaterina had cleared away the remains of the feast— nothing but crumbs, a few little black specks, a smear of cream, and the pots of jam and preserves—the grand duke settled back in his chair. "Now, it is your turn to question me. What is it you would like to know? I know a great deal about magic and politics, and magical politics."

Amelia was only too happy to take advantage of his knowledge. On the subject of magic, his answers were clear and concise, which was more than she had gotten from the few books her father owned. In that afternoon, she learned more about her own powers, and what she could expect to do with them, than she had learned in the rest of her lifetime. He gave her simple-to-follow, basic instructions on how to heal, cleanse the earth of poisons, banish inimical Earth spirits, and break curses laid with Earth magic. She realized just how haphazard her education in Earth magic had been up until now: a great deal about some things, like being a Channel and combative Earth magic, and nothing or almost nothing about others.

Serena got just as thorough an education in fire. Dr. Trevor had been right; what this man did not know about magic was not worth knowing. Finally, after almost two hours, Amelia sighed.

"My head is full!" she exclaimed. "I wish I had brought a notebook!"

"Ah, my dear, I have the remedy for this." He gestured to the bookshelves. "Go there, yes, just there. Fourth shelf up from the bottom. Do you see all those books in identical binding? Red, green, blue, and yellow? Those are all copies of the same books, one color for each Element. Take a yellow for yourself, a red for Miss Serena, and take home a blue for your brother."

She took the slim volumes, then hesitated, her hand hovering over the green. "May I? To complete the set? My brother George is Water."

He laughed. "Of course, of course! My wife and I wrote these books, knowing how often knowledge is lost as we spread ourselves across the world. I am hoping you have, or can get, the equivalent information from the Indians you know so my secretary can make similar volumes."

"We shall devote ourselves to it," Amelia promised. "I shall quiz my father, and Serena can quiz hers about similar knowledge from the former slaves who are mages on our plantation."

"Excellent!" He actually rubbed his hands together. Just then, the clock chimed, and he looked up at it. "My dear gels, I will not keep you longer. I am growing weary, and you will be wanting to return for your dinner. But just one thing."

He rang the bell standing on the table next to him, and one of the footmen appeared as if conjured. "Bring my little presents, will you, Peter?"

The footman vanished and came back with two little wooden boxes, whose tops and sides were brightly painted in glistening lacquer with beautiful stylized flowers. He gave one, featuring golden flowers, to Amelia, and the other, featuring red, to Serena.

"Why, this is ravishing!" she exclaimed, assuming these were the presents, for she truly had never seen anything like these boxes.

"From Russia, of course," he said, proudly. "But the gifts are inside."

She opened hers. Inside was a silver disk, very worn, held in a silver frame that allowed both sides to be seen, and allowing it to be worn as a pendant. She peered at it. There were vague indications of some sort of figure on each side, and possibly the remains of letters, but she could not make anything out. "What is this?" she asked.

"It is very old. Roman," he said. "It was found in some ruins near the Black Sea. I have used it successfully to . . . I would not put it as 'banish' spirits of Romans or associated with Romans. I would say that what this amulet does is awaken the spirits in question to what they truly are, and allow them to become their true selves. In the case of the ghosts, it lays them to rest. In the case of the diminished avatars of gods, it depends on the avatar. Most seem to choose to fade, some to ascend or descend, presumably to their rightful homes, and once, to merge with a more powerful native spirit of the equivalent orientation. In that last case, it was an avatar of Hecate that chose to merge with the Morrigan here in England. You will probably have occasion to use this, since as a Channel, you may sometimes awaken these old Roman spirits."

She picked it up, and realized it was hung on a very stout chain. She put it around her neck. The pendant fell just between her breasts, and she felt immediately warm, and welcomed.

"And this?" asked Serena, holding up a pendant of her own. It was an arrowhead made of opal, which flashed red as she turned it.

"That will succeed where your own senses fail. When the leopard loses the scent, use your magic on the pendant, think of what you need to find, and a guide will appear from within it. It is not an Elemental, it is a spell. It was made by my dear, late wife."

"Oh, but I can't—!" Serena protested.

"On the contrary, she made many such fire amulets over the years; this is but one of many. I am always pleased when I can pass one on to someone who can use it." He shook his head. "I will not take 'no' for an answer, my dear gel." His smile was positively angelic. "You have given this old man so much pleasure this afternoon! But now I must dictate all I learned from you to my secretary, and you must be on your way back to London."

"Your highness, you have been too, too kind!" Amelia exclaimed.

"I have amused myself and given myself the pleasure of your company," he replied. "And this will, the good God willing, be but the first of many visits. When you come back to London from Axminster, send word that you are here, and we shall have another visit and share blini and caviar again."

Amelia could tell he really was getting tired now, so she and Serena tendered their thanks once more, and when the footman responded to the bell, followed him out to the front door, where Davey was waiting with the carriage, carrying their precious gifts with them.

Three days later, that visit was much on her mind, as the amulet was a constant, comforting presence about her neck. And at last they were on their way to Axminster. The journey that would have taken almost a week, had they only traveled slowly by hired carriage with frequent stops to rest the horses and overnight stops at inns, took just less than a day with changes of horses on the road. This luxury was unthinkable to most people, and once again, she had Lord Alderscroft to thank. Like the Royal Stage, they would travel at night as well as by day; like the Royal Stage, they began their trip in the evening, about sunset, for two reasons. First, the roads were better nearer London, and those roads would be clearer, and easier on the horses traveling at night; and second, the nearer London they were, the less the risk of highwaymen there was, so it was best to make their night-time travel from London to Bath, rather than from Bath to Axminster.

They could not take Davey and the Anglefords' coach away from them for such an extended period of time, of course, and Amelia had been determined that they *not* go to Lord Alderscroft yet again. . . . So she had planned to hire a coach and driver and suffer through the slow trip. Despite sending things on ahead, they still had too much baggage to take with them to travel as passengers on a commercial stagecoach.

But it appeared that his lordship had already made his own plans. Before she got further than an inquiry, a brief note from Alderscroft informed her that he had staged horses already for the initial leg of the journey and that he had arranged for everything else—she need only decide on a day, and one of his traveling coaches would turn up in late afternoon to carry them off.

"Don't bother to object," Julia advised her, as she agonized over how much she owed him already (while inside she rejoiced at the money she would save). "There's no point. He's taken you on as his current pet project, and until you all are fully settled, his project you will remain. Send him a note saying you plan on leaving Thursday."

And so it was. On Thursday evening just before sundown, the coach arrived. The coach was pulled by six matching bays, and was painted in dark green, which was all she and Serena got to see before they were bundled inside and told to settle in. In a trice, their trunks were loaded up top by the two coachmen and two guards, they had said their goodbyes out the window, and they were rattling down the street, heading for the road out of London to Bath.

Inside, the coach was pure luxury; the inside was upholstered as well as Serena's fainting couch, in red wool with red plush accents, and it had red woven silk bands of stylized flames as decorations and as straps to secure whatever items they might need at hand. There was an ample hamper of food on the floor between the seats, which included wine, cold ham and chicken, potted meats, fruit, bread rolls, and cakes. Amelia's sharp eyes had spotted a second hamper up beside the active coachman; she reckoned this was to ensure that they stopped at posting inns for no longer than it took to change the horses and not for a possibly lengthy tipple.

The coach was well sprung, provided with plenty of lap rugs for both of them, and indeed, was comfortable enough for the girls to sleep in, accustomed as they had come to be to sleeping under difficult circumstances. And since there were only the two of them, with nothing but the hamper of delicacies and two bandboxes with important or valuable things in them inside the coach, there was plenty of room to curl up on the wide seats.

There would have been even more room if Serena had taken her leopard form, but Amelia thought that inadvisable.

"But what if there are highwaymen?" Serena asked yet again, as they finally rolled onto the highway, leaving the cobbled streets behind.

"Then you will transform, I will cut your dress away if need be, and you will deal with them. But there will not be any highwaymen. We will be too near London for them while it is dark, and besides, it is the full moon. The coachman and the guards will see any highwaymen as soon as they see us, and you may be sure that since they are in his lordship's employ, they have magic enough to make the use of their pistols moot. Or," she added thoughtfully, "magic enough to guide their pistol shots, as we sometimes do."

Serena sighed, sat back in her place on the rearward-facing seat, and pouted a little. "I wanted to run alongside the coach."

"And terrify the horses into running so fast they exhaust themselves?" Amelia teased. "That is a fine way to thank Lord Alderscroft for his kindness!"

They were out of London by the time actual darkness fell, and the novelty of peering out the windows into the darkness, straining their eyes to catch glimpses of the lights of dwellings, or trying to guess, as they rattled through villages, what the place looked like by daylight, quickly palled.

And it was much colder inside the coach than inside a house. It was mid-June, and yet it was as cold as April, a month notorious for cruel winds. This did not bode well for crops and beasts, though Amelia tried not to think too hard about that. There was only so much she could do, and she was, by Heaven, going to work her magic with a will once they arrived in Axminster, but she was only one channel and Master, and there was an entire country at risk here.

They seemed to pause every few miles, but not for long, and for no reason that Amelia could discern, though after each pause she thought she caught glimpses of small houses right on the edge of the road.

The oil lamps on the outside of the carriage had been lit by one of the guards; the lamps on the inside might have been tricky to light if it had not been for Serena, who simply placed one hand on the lamp and the wick ignited. They were moving so much that it simply wasn't possible to read, so they got out their knitting, talked about everything and nothing, and eventually ate and drank from the hamper.

"Oh! We are a couple of barbarians!" Amelia laughed, as Serena passed her the open bottle of wine she had just drunk directly from.

"I would not undertake to pour *anything*, the way this coach is rocking," Serena countered. "Unless you want to have to have your lovely things dyed to disguise wine stains!"

"I think I will be a barbarian," Amelia responded, after a gulp of wine. She had intended it to be a sip, but the movement of the coach made that impossible. "I am very glad Julia had Mrs. Gideon cut these bread rolls before wrapping them up. I fear I should have sliced my hand open if I tried now."

"You *could* have been a *complete* barbarian and torn them open. Here—" Serena took the wine bottle from her and handed her a very safe butter knife, two of the rolls, and a little round wooden box that held butter. "Do you fancy chicken, or ham?"

They got a respite every ten miles or so when the horses were changed. It did not take long, however; in fact, Amelia was both fascinated and startled by how quickly six new horses got put to the rig. After the first stop, the horses were no longer Lord Alderscroft's; that would have been impractical. They were hired post horses supplied by the posting inn, and with them came a postilion boy to ride the tired horses back to their original inn at the next change. Each change came about every hour or two, more or less, apart. The sheer cost of this almost made her a little faint . . . but then again, as Thomas had pointed out, it was true that Alderscroft had turned the same trick with consols that he and James had. And Alderscroft had far, far more to spend than they did. *No wonder he is so rich he has more influence than many dukes! This is probably not the first time he has acted on his foreknowledge!* And indeed, why shouldn't he? There was no question of morals and ethics here: Alderscroft would never withhold information unless giving it would betray the existence of mages. His first loyalty must lie with the mages he led, just as a priest's first loyalty, after God, was to his congregation. Alderscroft certainly was not laggard about spreading his wealth among "his people," either—look what he had done and was doing for them!

I can be loyal to Alderscroft. As for this country I am in . . . I will serve its people, for that is my duty, but I do not give a fig for its government or its king.

The journey was giving her a lot of time to think these things out. This was not a bad thing. It was also giving the two of them a lot of time to nap. Also not a bad thing.

As for the two coachmen, Amelia had no idea if they changed with each change of horses, or somehow slept in shifts. But they had looked like hardy gentlemen who knew their business, so she minded hers and did not go craning her head and neck out the window to see what they were doing.

After eating, they chatted a while, and knitted, but the excitement of travel wore off, and full stomachs and dim light were more inclined to nurture sleep rather than speech. After the third time finding herself slipping sideways in her seat, Amelia just gave up, took off her bonnet and put it safely atop the hamper, and drifted off.

She woke, still in the dark, aware that she needed to use the privy, to find Serena looking at her. "The next time we stop, I want to get out and use the inn privy," her cousin announced.

"I suspect the coaching staff will agree with that idea," she said. "How long do you think—"

"Soon," Serena said confidently. And indeed, she already had her bonnet on. "I'll get out first and get the coachman's attention."

Serena was right—she usually was when it came to time and distance. The coach slowed—the sure sign they were coming to an inn—then pulled into a square yard full of light and the sound of people. And while Amelia was still organizing herself, Serena did indeed hop out.

"Sir!" Amelia heard her call, as the sounds of harnesses jingling and hoofbeats marked grooms bringing up a new team. "May we—"

"Sure-eh-ly, Miss," one of the coachmen called down from the box. "We'll be doing the same, since you are. Take your time, lads!" he added, raising his voice. "We'll be sending our beer on its way!"

Rough laughter met this sally, and the coach swayed as guards, coachmen, and postilion climbed down. Amelia opened the coach door, to find herself assisted to the ground by a strikingly handsome fellow with a rifle across his back. "In through that door," he said, pointing to a door in the building in front of her. "Straight on through to the other side. You'll see the privies. It's considered mannerly to buy a cup of tea after."

She blushed a little, and thanked him, then scampered off, not willing to make them wait just for her.

The thick mug of indifferent tea was a small price to pay for the comfort of *not* using a certain oddly shaped basin she was already familiar with—not to mention the hazard of spilling its contents in the coach—and she rejoined her party to find she was *not* the latest to return; that went to the guard who had assisted her down. She found Serena chatting to the two coachmen like an old friend.

"Hello!" she said, coming up to them rather than trying to get into the coach, because at just that moment, walking about felt better than sitting. "Thank you for an uneventful journey!"

Both coachmen guffawed; one was noticeably older than the other, and a similarity of facial features made her think they were father and son. They wore Lord Alderscroft's livery, though the guards did not. "Thenkee for noticing, miss," said the older of the two. "Not one in a hunnert would know the skill it takes t' bring a coach along the road by night."

"Well, Pa . . . ." said the younger. "A top-sawyer like his lor'ship does. But not many as travels inside."

"Which is why we're *here*, and not sleepin' the sleep of the blest," the older man replied, and laughed. "It's good t' get a round shakin'-up now and again, keeps the moths away and stirs up the blood. Wouldn't like it if it were *too* often, but it ain't, and never in rough weather 'less it's an emergency. I do recall the time we was at his lor'ship's estate near Chard—Amberly House, y'know—an' her ladyship was 'bout to have Master Harold all early—" He stopped. "Well, we'll just say we had a wild drive in half rain, half snow, and all in the dark to get a . . . a, *you* know . . . *special* doctor with *special* skills." He winked, and Amelia realized that a good part of this gentleman's skill, and his son's, came from them being Earth mages, probably ones with a special affinity for animals. "'Twas my cuz's duty to ride on the fust off-hand horse with a lantern, and him no more'n—I'll say ten year'n old, since young Master Harold's twenty now, same age as my lad here, and at Oxford."

"All wuth it, though," said the younger man, proudly. "Couldn't get us to work for anybody else, not for five thousand a year."

"Lord Alderscroft is a nonpareil," she agreed. "May I ask a question about the drive tonight?"

The older man made a gesture as if to invite questions.

"Why do we pause every so often?" she asked.

"We're traveling turnpikes as much as we can," the younger man said quickly. "There's gates and fees, but we've got a paper that says we're paid ahead, so all we need to do is stop and show the paper. His lor'ship does this trip often enough his secretary has it all done and ready for us, and papers in our jackets, when we leave the stable."

"Oh!" There were turnpikes—a *very* few—in North Carolina, but there was talk of opening many more. "How convenient! Back home we have to stop and fumble with money, and sometimes the toll-man wants a bribe as well as the toll."

"And here comes our last man," said the older coachman. "And the postilion." He raised his voice. "Buck up, lads!"

"I'll help ye into the coach, miss and miss," said the younger one, and handed them both in while the men distributed themselves over the top of the coach.

And off they went, into the night, where despite the rolling, bouncing, and clattering—and perhaps because of just a *little* more wine—both girls were asleep, confident that both skill and magic were working together to keep the journey safe.

They woke up as the coach rolled through Bath in the very early morning. They looked out of the windows and refreshed themselves by giving their faces, necks, and arms a scrub with a water-moistened handkerchief in turn. Amelia was much impressed with the famed watering place. "If we cannot find a place near Axminster, finding one near Bath would be most agreeable," she said to Serena as the latter rummaged through the hamper for the makings of a breakfast.

"I don't know that we'd have the luck in Bath that we did finding lodgings in Axminster, but . . ." Serena adjusted her bonnet after placing it on her head without benefit of a mirror. ". . . well, we are not exactly *poor* anymore. We could afford to pay far more than we are paying his lordship, and still have plenty to live on, without touching your father for more."

"That is *quite* true!" Amelia smiled at the thought of all the entertainment to be had in Bath. True, there was plenty in London, but so spread out across the great metropolis that one had to have a carriage to reach everything. Bath, or so she had been told, was perfectly arranged so that everything was within walking distance. "And people lease for short terms all the time; there should be plenty of furnished properties!"

"That is putting the cart before the horse, however," Serena reminded her. "We have every reason to think that we *will* find a good property near Axminster, and Bath is not so far from Axminster that we cannot afford an extended pleasure trip now and again." She laughed. "After all, now we are quite spoiled! We never thought of assemblies and balls and concerts when we were at home!"

No, we thought of homely entertainments, and card parties amongst ourselves, dances in the threshing barn, and more often than not, using these entertainments to hide the presence of escaped slaves, she thought, and it seemed as if that life belonged to another girl entirely.

But they had only a brief stop in Bath for everyone to relieve and refresh themselves, and soon the resort city was behind them. Now there *were* things to look at, and both Serena and Amelia watched the countryside with an eye to brother James's needs. Now that he, too, had more money to work with than they had dreamed possible, finding a property seemed all the more urgent.

It seemed that his lordship had been correct when he named this part of England as ideal for James's ventures. The rolling hills, deeply green despite the unseasonable weather, argued for good pasturage for their merino sheep and cashmere goats. There was plenty of shade for them in the summer—once summer truly came— in the form of lines of trees bedecking those hills. The mulberry trees for the silkworms wouldn't care for the cold, but they would need several years to grow before they were producing leaves enough for silk production (unless they were lucky enough to happen upon a property where the white mulberries supposedly imported for that purpose by James I existed), so the "volcano weather" would have abated by then. What they needed for the sheep and goats was not warm pasturage, but *dry* pasturage, and with all these rolling hills, that should be easy to arrange. What was not so easy to arrange would be the swift running streams they would need to power the spinning and weaving mills.

It was beautiful countryside, what her father would have called "soft," meaning that the soil was rich and stone-free, there was exactly the right amount of rain, and the sort of pests that could make a sheep or goat's life a misery either not present or easily controlled. James had done all that sort of research before he even thought about embarking on the task, much less bought a herd of goats. Even before Lord Alderscroft's recommendation, Devon had been high on the list of places they wanted to look.

So they were free to look out the windows as they rolled through tiny villages that looked as if they had been there since the days of King Arthur. It was a great contrast to home, where almost everything was raw and new, and scarcely anything was more than fifty years old, because people had a habit of tearing down and replacing, or just moving elsewhere and building anew, in a country where the resources seemed inexhaustible.

They spread out the map they had brought across both their knees, and tried to identify each tiny hamlet in the distance, on top of a hill or nestled in a valley, and marked, even if you could not see the buildings themselves for the trees, by the tell-tale of its church tower or spire. The fields were separated by robust hedges rather than fences—but those hedges had had hundreds of years to grow, and they looked the part.

And it was shortly before they were starting to think about luncheon, and wonder if there was still enough in the hamper to put together a meal, that the traffic on the road caused the coach to slow. Shortly after that, houses near the road put in an appearance, and the road turned from earth to cobbles. Not a surprise, since it seemed that there was a *lot* of stone used in building here. Perhaps those fields weren't quite so "soft," after all; with all the stone walls, all that stone had to come from somewhere, and it was likely it had been grubbed out of the fields centuries ago.

The carriage slowed to a crawl, as it caught up with local traffic, and then she heard the coachman call to the horses, and it began to turn.

And not onto a street, but onto a driveway. She and Serena crowded onto the right side of the carriage, and saw with relief and delight that it was, indeed, *their* driveway, and their new home. And running out to meet them from the back entrance were an older woman, two younger, a girl, and a boy, and coming up from the stable was a man.

The coachman knocked on the roof of the carriage. "Time to get out, miss and miss! Come and see your new home!"

13

THE older lady, graying brown hair tucked into her cap, was their cook and housekeeper, Mrs. Sawyer. The two younger, both blond, square-faced, with round blue eyes, and nearly alike as two pins, were the housemaid and the second housemaid, Bessie and Sarah. The skinny brown-haired girl was the cook's helper, Rosie. The raven-haired boy was Jackie, "the general dogs-body," as Mrs. Sawyer said. And the man, Ethan, weathered as an old shoe, most of his mousy hair hidden under a cap, was almost as much of a "general dogs-body," as he would take care of the pony (and the horses, once they got them), drive the cart on errands, chop wood, carry water, make repairs, and haul whatever needed to be hauled. According to Lord Alderscroft, they had all come from his employ at his vast estate, and thus, were either Elemental mages or knew all about them. That was a great relief. It would have been the first time Serena and Amelia would have had to hide what they were, and Amelia was not entirely sure they were up to such an exhausting task.

"You poor tired lambs get right inside," said Mrs. Sawyer, establishing herself from the beginning as a motherly sort, once the introductions were made. "Would you rather eat first, or tidy up?"

"We'd like to tidy, please," Amelia said before Serena could answer.

"Bessie, take them to their rooms and bring up hot water. Ethan, Jackie, you help the gents get the trunks down and to the rooms, then take the gents to the kitchen for a good bite and a sit-down on something that ain't moving." She turned to the coachmen, who were just getting down off the box. "We're not much on beer here in Devon, but we're that proud of our scrumpy, and there's a breeched cask in the kitchen."

"Ho!" said the older coachman, rubbing his hands together. "I'm that fond of scrumpy! You watch yourselves, lads," he added to the two guards. "'Tis stronger than beer. One glass and the world starts to glow. Two and it starts to go!"

"Well," said his son. "If they commence to fall over, we can bide and rest the horses till they can stand on their own two feet again."

Amelia would have been amused to hear more of this manly gossip, but Bessie was anxiously waiting to take them to their rooms, and she didn't want to provoke nerves in the girl, so she waved to Serena and they followed through the gate and the front garden and into the "cottage" itself.

It was all as it had appeared during the scrying. In through the entry they went, then up the stairs, where Bessie flung open each door as if presenting the rooms to royalty. Amelia went straight to hers.

And Bessie had every reason to be proud, because it was obvious by the smell of fresh polish and oil and lavender that she had been hard at work up here. Great changes had been wrought since Amelia did her scrying. Every bit of wood shone, the beds were made up and looked like heaven, there was a very small fire in the fireplaces that Bessie proceeded to heap with wood, and what hadn't been polished had been scoured to within an inch of its life. Amelia took a deep breath and let it out in a sigh as she stepped into the room that would be hers; it felt as if she had had a huge burden taken from her, and never, except at home, had she felt more welcomed. There were two huge trunks already here, both marked by inlaid squares of golden leather upon which had been written "Amelia."

What she *wanted* to do was lie down on that bed and not get up until morning . . . but a grimy feeling warred with her wish to really sleep, and that in turn warred with her empty stomach, and the arrival of her last trunk and two bandboxes—the latter carried by Jackie—precluded lying down. Right on Jackie's heels came Rosie, with a pail of hot water. That decided her. When the luggage had been put down, the hot water poured into the pitcher, and everyone cleared out, she closed the door, stripped to her chemise, and had as good a "bath" as one can get from a basin and pitcher. There was a slop pail under the table holding the basin to pour the dirty water into, so she even had a good rinse as well.

Perhaps it was de rigueur to have a lady's maid, but she had made it very clear to his lordship that neither she nor Serena wanted one. Now she was glad she had, because as tired as she was, being fussed over would have made her insane. And it wasn't as if she needed help. Tight-laced corsets were a thing of the past; her short stays were not laced in the back and neither were Serena's.

She was washed, brushed, and in one of her refurbished old gowns from home—a cotton broadcloth heavier than her more fashionable muslins, suited to the cool weather. It was one of her favorites, and was printed in little flower sprigs in a warm brown, and after its re-styling, trimmed in brown braid. She brushed out her hair and pinned it up again—and, assuming that fashions here would be more modest than in London, topped it with a little cap she was very fond of. Then she dug deeper into the trunk and pulled out a superfine brown shawl with gold fringes made of ribbon.

She practically ran into Serena, who had opted for one of the muslins from home, the same printed flower as Amelia, but red, rather than brown, and no shawl. "One day you will have to teach me the trick of never being cold," Amelia sighed, as the sounds of contented men talking echoed up the stairway.

"Be born into Fire," Serena teased, and skipped on ahead of her. They both knew where the dining room was, of course, and on entering it, found Mrs. Sawyer laying out an actual *hot* luncheon of the substantial sort they were used to, not a little nuncheon of cucumber sandwiches and chicken salad! Taking pride of place was a meat pie with gravy bubbling up through slits in the crust. Next to that was a still-warm cottage loaf, pots of preserves and butter, a plate of cheese, dishes of pickled vegetables, and bowls of pea soup.

Mrs. Sawyer looked up as they came in. "In good time, and good appetite, I hope, my ladies! 'Tis sorry I am that there's no new peas, but—" She shrugged. "Since I am told 'twas you that sent out the warning that the weather will not be what it should, you know better than I why that is."

"And it is nothing you could remedy, Mrs. Sawyer," Amelia assured her. "This looks *glorious*. And much nearer to what we are used to in America than those thin little noon meals of London."

"I could never cook in London," the housekeeper declared. "'Tis either tea and toast, or so many courses it takes three cooks to make it all. Pray, do you prefer a London *ton* breaking of fast, or a farmer's country one?"

"Country!" they both exclaimed, which caused the good lady to smile.

She poured out the tea, then departed, leaving them to do ample justice to her handiwork.

The sounds of happy men in the kitchen made Amelia wish wistfully that matters between servants and masters were more equitable here, the way they were at home. She would have liked very much to have partaken of the same meal as their coaching companions, joked and laughed with them, and bid them a proper farewell.

But that wasn't how things were done here, not even among Elemental mages. Familiarity was discouraged. As kind as Julia was, she would have been scandalized to sit down to a meal with downstairs, and they would have been just as embarrassed and uncomfortable as she was. Even here, in a very provincial town, that was true. Familiarity went one way only, from high to low. Never from low to high. In fact, if she had tried to socialize with them, they would have been very uncomfortable.

But the same holds true of us, she reminded herself, reveling in mutton, carrots, and rich gravy. *When it comes to the* ton, *we are the low and they the high. We can't just turn up at Lord Alderscroft's—or even Mr. Nightsmith's—without express invitation, and they initiate all conversation, not us. They would never sit down to eat with us at our table. Not with shop-scent all over us, and never mind how powerful our magic is.*

At length, the tramping of boots leaving the back way told her that their recent companions had departed—evidently the warning about the strength of the scrumpy (whatever that was) had been taken to heart. Then came the sound of metal-shod wheels and steel-shod hooves on gravel, the carriage was turned around, and off they went. Hopefully to make Alderscroft's estate between here and Bath before sundown.

Rosie came in shyly to collect the dishes. "Mrs. Sawyer wants ter ask if you'd like a bit of somethin' sweet for puddin'?" she asked, her voice scarcely louder than a whisper. "There's treacle tart and cream. Or there's apples."

"Treacle tart! Please!" Serena said immediately, never one to turn down anything sweet.

Rosie trudged off with the remains of the pie, returned with a huge wooden tray and two pieces of tart with clotted cream atop them, and collected everything except the tea service. Serena closed her eyes with pleasure at the first taste of the tart. "I hope there's enough of this for dessert at supper," she said.

Amelia laughed. "If I poured honey on a brick, you'd eat it," she said.

"Yes," Serena replied. "Yes I would."

When luncheon was over, and they had retired to the drawing room, Mrs. Sawyer presented them with a basket full of calling cards. Amelia looked at it, a little askance. "What are the rules for calls here?" she asked. "These people—" she lifted the basket—"have obviously called or sent their cards, but do we return the visit? Or do we wait for them to make a second call?"

"I've sorted them into packets," the housekeeper told her. "This one is tradesmen; you'll want to just look through them and decide which you fancy patronizing. This one is the local magicians; *you* are the only Master here in the town besides Mr. Nightsmith, so they need to call on you. This packet is the people of the same social rank as you; there is some overlap with the mages, and I have assumed that you are the same social rank as the doctor, and not as high as the parish priest."

"The priest would be same rank as Mr. Nightsmith, would he not?" Serena asked.

"Yes; he is considered a gentleman—" She stopped for a moment, and flushed. "I hope I am not speaking out of place, but as you are Americans, his lordship wanted me to explain the social rules of a market town like this one most explicitly to you."

"By no means! We need such explanations," Amelia said immediately. "Social rules are very much different in North Carolina."

"Well, I confess I am a bit confused. Your father is landed, is he not?" Now the poor woman was indeed very uncomfortable. "And yet he is also a merchant. So . . . there is some confusion as to whether you are the same rank as Mr. Nightsmith or, say, Mr. Evans, the butcher. I decided on my own that you are the equivalent of the doctor, which would permit you to call on Mr. Nightsmith and him to call on you, but you must not call on him before he has first called on you."

Amelia laughed. "Yes, we are landed. And Serena and I each have our own independent income from consols. The Stonecroft plantation is eight hundred acres, but if Father has his way, it will be expanded to a thousand."

"Eight . . . hundred . . ." This overcame the poor woman, and she sat down rather abruptly. "My goodness gracious. *Eight hundred acres.* And an independent income for each of you. This puts you *above* Mr. Nightsmith!"

"Oh, I think we can reasonably claim to be co-equal with the doctor," Serena told her. "Any man jack can go carve out a hundred acres or more for himself in America; land does not have the same meaning there as here."

"Mercy. *What* is your income?" As she seemed to need the information, Amelia gave it. "About a thousand a year, each. From consols."

"Equal to Dr. Partridge then. That settles it." Mrs. Sawyer seemed relieved to have that settled. "Now, the first call to non-mages you *must* make is to Reverend Podding, although it is very likely he will not be in, nor his wife, for they have their parish duties. After that, you should return the calls to as many of your equals as you can fit in an afternoon. Make calls again the next day, then be at home to receive callers on Friday."

"I think we will make calls on mages on Tuesday, and non-mages on Wednesday, then fit in whatever we can until we have caught up," Amelia said, with a glance at Serena, who nodded. "Can we walk, or will we need to take the pony and cart?"

"Everyone is within easy walking distance," Mrs. Sawyer assured her. "I have walked it out myself to be sure. Except for Dr. Partridge; he is at almost the opposite end of town from you, and it is mostly uphill."

"At home everything is uphill." Serena laughed. "But we shall follow your advice! Do you expect anyone to make morning calls today?"

What an absurdity to refer to them as "morning calls" when they happen between three and six in the afternoon!

"I think not. You must make it known that you are in residence by making calls yourself. And it is perfectly agreeable that you not be 'at home' today, since you have only just arrived." Mrs. Sawyer paused. "Perhaps, if you are inclined, you will be 'at home' for Reverend Podding, Dr. Partridge, and—well, we cannot expect Mr. Nightsmith to call."

I would be just as happy if he did not, Amelia thought, but schooled her face not to show anything. "I believe that is a sound plan," she said instead. "Serena and I would like to unpack our trunks and put what is appropriate to the weather out for airing, and then into the wardrobes—"

"Oh, you mustn't do that. That is Bessie's work," the housekeeper corrected, and flushed. "I'm sorry, but Lord Alderscroft was *very* particular that you needed careful instruction on what is due your station." She paused again. "Begging your pardon, but you really *should* have had a lady's maid, but no one will know that you don't, if you don't tell them direct. We're used to keeping secrets, as you well know, and this is just one more."

"Please don't apologize. I am aware that what seems like our over-familiar ways could lead to unfortunate misunderstandings," Amelia soothed. "We are grateful, are we not, Serena?" And she kicked Serena in the ankle when Mrs. Sawyer's attention was elsewhere.

"Yes, of course we are!" Serena said promptly. Then she perked up. "We can teach Bessie how to do our hair, and she'll be helping with our gowns anyway, so if for some reason something *must* be divulged, we are training her to be a lady's maid. If that suits you."

"A fair compromise," Mrs. Sawyer said with relief.

More instruction poured from Mrs. Sawyer; Amelia took careful note of it. It wasn't *greatly* different from what they had learned when staying with the Anglefords; it was just that it seemed that people were even more meticulous about rank and society here in this little market town than they were in London. *Or actually, they are just as nice about it in London, but the circle of mages was wider, they are more equitable, and that was mostly what we saw.* It wasn't precisely a quagmire that they needed to cross safely, but it was certainly going to be a chess game.

Well, I like chess. Poor Serena does not, but she is very good at cards, and this is not at all unlike a card game.

"What days do you suggest we be 'at home'?" Serena asked.

"Saturday and Tuesday. Lord Alderscroft had cards made up for you." Again, Mrs. Sawyer faltered. "It seemed . . . more convenient . . ."

Serena burst into laughter. "For heaven's sake, Mrs. Sawyer, please do stop apologizing for what Lord Alderscroft has arranged!

He is making our path smooth for us, as are you, and we are everlastingly grateful for every thing!"

"Thank you, Miss Serena," the worthy lady said. "I confess, I am walking upon eggs—"

"Well, don't be." Amelia met her eyes squarely. "You may be as familiar with us in private as you like, simply reserve what we call 'Sunday manners' for times when others are about. Now, how are we to find agents to interview about venues for my brother James's venture?"

"His lordship has assigned one of his men of business to do that, but you must walk the properties for yourselves to determine if any of them will do. Agents have been instructed to call on Monday mornings only." Mrs. Sawyer's voice went up on the last word, suggesting that she was not sure about that.

"That is perfect. As long as this doesn't violate some convention?" Mrs. Sawyer shook her head.

"Then Monday mornings it is. And that gives us Monday afternoons to drive out to see these properties. Is his lordship's estate within driving distance?"

"You had better borrow horses from Mr. Nightsmith and ride them until you have a chance to visit his lordship's estate and choose horses for yourselves; the pony won't be fast enough. But yes, why?"

"Because I am going to channel some protective Earth power into his estate, and work some other Earth magics, to compensate for this volcano weather," she said decidedly. "And I wish to do so at the earliest moment there may be. It is the very least I can do to repay him for all his kindness."

"Then you should write to his housekeeper and tell her what day you intend to come. She can offer you appropriate hospitality and refreshment," Mrs. Sawyer said, her expression becoming one of awe. "I . . . have never met a Channel. My power, too, is Earth, and I could not undertake a fraction of what you propose to do."

Amelia shrugged. "My father taught me that great power must be paid for in undertaking great responsibilities. I shall do the same for the town—tomorrow night, I think. Today I will reserve for our own little property here." She winced a little. "I would not have thought a simple carriage ride would make one so fatigued!"

"In that case, let me get Bessie, and you can put your things to rights so that you may rest a little before teatime." Mrs. Sawyer stood up. "Oh! I meant to tell you that a pianoforte is being delivered today. The gentleman delivering it will also assay to tune it."

"Oh, well then," Serena said saucily, "Then there is no point in pretending to read whilst I nod off for a nap, for the whole house will be full of *plink, plink, plink!*"

Bessie made short work—*much* shorter work than Amelia would have—of the trunks and wardrobe. Some garments merely needed a good shaking out. A couple she wrinkled her nose at, and decreed a good airing; and two she declared need the touch of a sponge and an iron before they were fit to be seen. The ball gowns were handled with the reverence reserved for holy relics, and carefully put in pride of place in the wardrobes. The offending articles were swiftly carried off to be refreshed and cleaned, leaving Amelia to dispose of her personal items where she chose.

Fortunately most of these were already in boxes packed within the third trunk, and those boxes merely needed to be placed where she wished. Good strong light came in through the many-paned window in her room, and since she knew the placement of furniture because of her scrying, she had been able to plan where everything would fit ahead of time. During this pleasant task, the pianoforte and the tuner arrived, and the house was, indeed, full of annoying *plink, plink, plinks*. Since the sound could not be avoided, she gathered some of her sewing and went out into the gardens.

The sewing was merely an excuse to take a turn about the grounds that were now hers, by rent, if nothing else. This house— she was more certain than ever it had once rejoiced in the title of "manor"—was pleasingly called Honeyrose Cottage, and indeed, the poor rose vines struggling against the unseasonable cold had

managed to produce some white blossoms that combined the intoxication of rose scent with a powerful undernote of honey. She resolved on the spot to pick some of these and distill the scent from
them for herself. And now was just the time for her to make sure the
vines would produce enough blossoms that she could do so.

She found a cluster of garden benches near the roses, and sat
down on one, putting her sewing basket aside. Closing her eyes, and
opening her senses, she sought out the nearest ley line, and found it
at the opposite end of the town.

*That's probably where the doctor's house is, which, since I know he
too is an Earth mage, is why his house is there. Well, this line is strong
enough he won't notice that I am sipping from his cup.*

Besides, this was only a very small working. A deep one, but small.

She gathered power; carefully, so as not to disturb anything the
doctor might have in motion. She created a minor line from the
major one to this location, and channeled the power into the earth
under the property, creating a kind of magical, self-sustaining furnace that would only take power from the ley line if it was needed.
It infused power gently into everything in and on the property that
was living: the earth itself, which she trained to sip power to warm
itself; the bees in their hive, which she strengthened against cold
and disease; the hens, which she offered the same to; and all the
little Earth Elementals, whom she directed to their new source of
magic, since there hadn't been one here natively. Last of all, she
touched Mrs. Sawyer, now that she knew the good lady to be Earth,
and linked her to the source as well.

For her, this was "timeless," as in, she felt no time passing while
she worked. But when she tucked in all the "ends," tidied her work,
and opened her eyes, she found Rosie hovering anxiously at her
elbow.

"Mrs. Sawyer would like to know, miss, if you want your tea in
the house or in the garden, miss. Also, miss, we was all wondering,
miss, if Miss Serena would be so obliging as to shift for us, on account of we want to know what to look for and not shoot her for a
stray dog, miss."

That last nearly made her laugh out loud, which would have been dreadfully embarrassing for the poor child, so she restrained herself. "If Miss Serena is having her tea in the parlor, I will go there too and ask her," she said kindly.

"Aye, she is," said little Rosie, obviously a little sick with excitement.

Well, this has to be the most exciting thing that has happened to this market town in quite a while. She knew very well what had happened; Alderscroft had taken it upon himself to tell their staff of Serena's nature, and quite rightly too. There could have been all manner of unpleasantness if she'd come in from or gone out on a run, and startled someone.

The repast laid out in the parlor was exactly what was wanted; not just some lovely scones, clotted cream, and strawberry jam, but nice little ham-and-butter sandwiches and other more substantial and less sugary fare. After all the work of channeling, she was hungry enough to eat a bear.

"I felt you working," said Serena, as she entered. "And so did everyone else. So while you were doing that, I warded the place so you wouldn't have to."

Since Fire wards were *always* more "offensive" than Earth, whether they were set by Master or mage, Amelia thanked her heartily, and began making earnest inroads on the bounty.

"Do you feel like shifting for the staff?" she asked, when the first fires of hunger had been fed. "They want to see you."

That certainly got Serena's attention. Not that it was difficult to get her to shift. Amelia had the feeling that she was more comfortable in her leopard body than her human one. "Idle curiosity, or they want to know my size and shape so they know what to expect at night?" Serena asked, around a ham sandwich.

Amelia had to swallow before she could answer. "Both."

Serena raised an amused eyebrow. "Now?"

She knew what Serena was thinking: she'd be happy either way, but preferred to finish eating. "If it's convenient."

Serena grinned. "It will be when Bessie comes in to clear away."

As Serena said that, movement out of the corner of her eye caught Amelia's attention, and she saw some of the little Elemental grotesques, and a brownie, creeping into the room.

"It seems we are going to have an Elemental audience as well," Amelia told her. She saw Serena unfocus her eyes to invoke her mage sight, and saw her grin even harder.

"Well, make their acquaintance formally, since they've likely been hovering, hoping you would ask them to introduce themselves, since you did that Work in the garden." She took a long sip of her tea. "I'm just waiting for Rosie to come in here to collect the tea things so you can tell her to tell Mrs. Sawyer to assemble the household and I can shift for them."

The protocol for establishing a relationship with the Elementals of a particular place was to create something her father called a "welcoming circle." This was a magic circle of the sort usually created for summoning something, but without all the guards and extra wards on it, something that said wordlessly, "I am here to protect you, not exploit you, and I would like us to be friends and help each other."

So she twirled her finger about her head, creating a little golden thread of power that expanded to fit over her, then over Serena, then to fill half the room. As the Elementals stared at it with all their eyes, she made a little coaxing gesture to them, and they slowly, shyly, began to come into her personal space.

But then she held out a biscuit, and the shyness vanished.

The one thing that Earth Elementals loved was human food, particularly milk and baked goods. They didn't *quite* push and shove to get close to her to get a share of the teatime leftovers, but they certainly did crowd up to her, and more arrived with every passing moment. Soon there were not one, but four brownies, a garden gnome and his family, two fauns, and an entire menagerie of grotesques, most of whom only needed a small piece each, of a size she would have called a "crumb," because they themselves were so small. She was a little surprised at the fauns; they didn't have such a thing in America, though she had read about them in the two magic books the household had, and none had appeared in London, probably because it was so built up with stone and iron. Axminster must have been small enough that fauns could visit from true wild lands. When everything had been distributed, she folded her hands in her lap and addressed them.

"I am Amelia," she said. "This is Serena. Serena is Fire, and a shifter. She can become a very large cat. We want you to know that we will *never* compel you, not even if our need is very great. Is there someone you would like to be your spokesperson?"

They all looked around and finally settled on a lady brownie, who cleared her throat self-consciously, and stepped up to the hem of Amelia's skirt. "Master," she said, with a little bob, "I be Sarah Small."

"Thank you, Sarah, for speaking for the others. If they need something from me, they can either go through you or appear directly to me if it is urgent. If there is an urgent problem, do not hesitate to come to me for help. And if I need anything, I shall say your name, and if you would be so kind, come to me so I can make my needs known."

Sarah nodded her head solemnly; Amelia had the sense that it had been a very long time, perhaps hundreds of years, since they last interacted with a mage. That argued for the idea that there were no Masters in Axminster now. The closest might be that odious, pompous ass, Mr. Nightsmith, and Earth Elementals did not like to travel too far from their own territories.

"You can *always* tell me 'no' if something is beyond your powers, and we will find a solution together," she added, and saw relief on many small faces. "And I generally trade food for favors." And now she *really* had their heartfelt interest. "You probably saw I have warded this space within the boundary markers. You have also seen I created a power source. It is to be shared by all." She tapped her lips with her finger. "I think that is all. I hope we will all be very happy together."

"Shall we go, then, Master?" Sarah asked diffidently—still clutching half a biscuit. She was so adorable that if Amelia had been much younger, she would have been tempted to ask Sarah to play along with her two dolls. Sarah had a round little face, with apple cheeks, big brown eyes, and brown hair in a single plait down her back. Her hair was covered modestly with a cap of a style at least two hundred years old, and she wore what would have been an Elizabethan common woman's dress: full brown skirt, spotless white chemise with full sleeves and tiny lace on the end of the sleeves, a bodice that laced up the front in black, and a white apron. Unlike Natty Ned, she *did* have shoes, soft leather ones. Brownies *had* come across with their magical human families—and for that matter, were still migrating, whenever a mage moved households across the Atlantic. Sometimes they stayed with a "place," but more often than not, they went with a family, particularly if the alliance was of long standing.

"Yes, you may go," Amelia told her, wondering how long it had been since this brownie had what she would have considered "her" family.

And just like that—the room was empty again.

"That went well," Serena observed. "Ah! Hello, Rosie!"

Rosie twisted her hands in her apron, but her expression reflected awe rather than anxiety or fear. "You been talking to the Pharisees," she stated.

Now, Amelia had learned, from the book that the grand duke had given her, some quite modern and very useful information, and one of those bits of information was that country folk, who were aware of the presence of the Elementals even if they couldn't see them, had alternate names for them. It was common lore that to say a creature's True Name was to invite it to come calling, and very few of them wanted the attention of Elementals. A list of some of those alternate names had been in the book, so Amelia knew very well that Rosie was not talking about ancient Hebrew priests, but "fairies."

She nodded. "Yes, I have, because I have established that I am a friend, and although I am a Master, I will not harm them, but I will not put up with any nonsense. So there will be no stealing or souring of milk, no tangling the pony's tail, or putting toads in your bed, or any other mischief."

Rosie sighed with relief, and reached for the tea things. "And Rosie? Will you please tell Mrs. Sawyer to assemble the staff here so Serena can shift for you all?"

Poor Rosie almost dropped the teapot as her eyes went round, but to her credit she nodded, and left with the pitiful remains of their meal.

"I should go upstairs and shift, then," Serena said, and her eyes narrowed as she teased, "I could just do it here—"

"That would mean looking ridiculous, tangled up in your clothing, or it would mean scandalizing the entire staff by removing everything until you are nude." Amelia raised an eyebrow. "Don't try to bluff me, we have been together too long."

"So we have!" Serena laughed, and got up to race up the stairs.

The staff turned up at the door to the kitchen and shuffled into the dining room, shooed along by Mrs. Sawyer like a bunch of hens. They all had a half-apprehensive look; Amelia wasn't sure if it was because they were about to see a shifter in her beast form, or because they felt that they didn't belong in the dining room. Amelia felt a little sad; it seemed a pity that—given they all had some magecraft—they couldn't treat each other like equals.

Then again . . . we aren't the equals of "our betters" in this country either.

Amelia gave a sharp whistle, and Serena came bounding down the stairs and into the room.

Rosie gave a little yelp; Jackie's eyes went round as his mouth made an "O" without any sound coming from it. The rest of the staff had expressions that varied from astonished to more than a little fearful.

Mrs. Sawyer wasn't having any nonsense. She stood there with her fists on her hips, and gave them all a withering look. "Come now! It's Miss Serena! You can see she still has her pearls on!"

That slightly absurd touch changed the fear to respect. For her part, Serena played the Leopard Princess, stretching, then sitting, then yawning hugely, all the while emitting a deep purr.

"I din' know leopards purred," said Jackie in wonder.

"It's 'cause they just be big cats, goose!" said Rosie, who had regained her composure.

"Manners," Mrs. Sawyer said, darkly. It was very clear at that moment that Rosie, who was older, considered herself to be Jackie's superior.

"You ain't a-gonna go for my hens now, are ye?" Ethan asked Serena directly, eyeing her with challenge.

Serena shook her head so hard her ears rattled.

"She'll probably poach rabbits, perhaps pigeons," Amelia explained calmly. "She'll leave pigeons in roosts alone. She likes to go for a run every night and hunt, so leave the door unlocked for her. She'll lock up after herself after she changes back."

"Better nor a mastiff," was Ethan's calm verdict.

"We'll want to get the pony used to her, starting when she is in human form," Amelia continued, as Bessie's fingers twitched as if she would like to stroke that soft coat. "The best way, Ethan, is for you to hold the pony firmly while Miss Serena grooms it as a human. The pony will know she is a shifter, even when human, and be very nervous."

Very nervous is an understatement, considering the behavior of that poor horse in Hyde Park.

"Then we'll move to her holding its head and giving it treats. Once it's calm with her in human form, we'll have her stand near the pony, shifted, then when it lets her approach, she'll come with a carrot in her mouth for it. If it's a clever pony, this shouldn't take long."

Ethan nodded, as if this all made perfect sense to him, which it probably did.

"Is there anything any of you want to know?" she asked.

"Kin I pet her?" Jackie asked boldly, as Mrs. Sawyer snapped, *"Manners!"* and Ethan took off his cap, *thwapped* Jackie in the head with it, and put it back on.

In answer, Serena stood up, strolled over to them, rubbed her head against Jackie, allowed whoever wanted to to pet her head, then left the room and ran up the stairs. Serena came back down in a trice, tucking her cap onto her head.

"You must be powerful magic. Never seen a lady get dressed that fast afore," said Jackie, and got another *thwap* for his troubles.

"I *am* better than a mastiff, Ethan," she said seriously. "And if there is ever trouble, I am good for protection. I have done more than mere protection in America."

Ethan did not ask what she meant, but he looked very impressed. Possibly he had been on a Hunt, and understood what she was implying.

"Curiosity is satisfied," said Mrs. Sawyer, briskly. "And you all have work to do."

That was all it took; they all shuffled out. Mrs. Sawyer stayed behind just long enough to say, "Thank you, Miss Serena, Miss Amelia," and left herself.

"Do we have anything we *must* do in the remaining hour or so before supper?" Serena asked.

Amelia shook her head.

"Then I am having a nap. I think you should, too. It feels as if we stepped down out of that carriage yesterday." She stretched. "I cannot account for the fact that merely *riding*, in a very luxurious conveyance, should make me so tired!"

"We have done a great deal," Amelia admitted, and could not stifle a yawn.

"That does it. I may not have been doing actual work, but you certainly have. Come upstairs with me. Anything else you think you should do can wait."

Serena took her hand and pulled her to her feet, and she did not resist.

It turned out that not only was Mrs. Sawyer's visiting card system admirable, but by morning she had organized the cards by which day they should return the visits, and put them in little baskets with a label. Even better was the hand-drawn map of the town that the girls found by their breakfast things (at last! A proper farmhouse breakfast!) in the morning, with all of the homes of the Elemental mages marked on it. They both studied it as they ate. "Well, I think we can get all the mages called upon in one journey, except for the doctor," Amelia said, as she perused the map with one finger, the other hand occupied with a sausage roll. "Fortunately there are not many of them, and except for this one old woman here—" she tapped the map at a square that said "Mrs. Brightman, Mouse Cottage"— "they are all people who have left cards. Mrs. Brightman did not leave a card, she left a very lovely bottle of lavender water, and Mrs. Sawyer says she believes she might be the local 'wise woman.'"

"You mean witch?" asked Serena, her eyes dancing with mischief.

"Very likely," Amelia admitted. "There is a disadvantage to having staff supplied by Alderscroft; they aren't locals and they don't know the town the way locals do."

"True, but as outsiders, they haven't made any enemies yet, and the local people aren't likely to try and take one of them aside for a beer or a nice cup of tea and try to extract information about us from them," Serena observed. "All the townsfolk will have to guess what we are made of; except, perhaps, for the mages. What the mages know will depend on how close they are to Alderscroft's circles."

"Or to Axminster's 'most eligible bachelor,'" Amelia observed wryly. "Although Nightsmith is such a cold fellow, I have difficulty imagining him being convivial and gossiping with anyone. Except the captain; he probably shares as much as he ever does with the captain. The captain hasn't a feather to fly with, so I expect he would put up with quite a bit of off-putting from Nightsmith in order to keep drinking his port and riding his horses."

"Well, let us plan our calls, follow this excellent map Mrs. Sawyer made for us, and see how we are treated." Serena toyed with a bit of fringe on the end of her sash. "I propose our complimentary cotton twill spencers over simple muslins. Nothing too out of the ordinary or showy, but good quality. And if you need something to make you certain these outfits will be appropriate, remember that we have bonnets and reticules that match."

"I think those are excellent choices. If we are going to be doing that much walking, though, we had better use our jean half-boots and not slippers," Amelia agreed. She very much liked that particular spencer, and if it grew too warm, they could always remove the spencers and carry them like shawls. Both spencers were made of a heavy twilled cotton; hers was a golden brown that had been dyed with tickseed flowers, and Serena's the same cheerful scarlet as a soldier's coat, dyed, of course, with their own cochineal. The jean half-boots were identical, of a striped dark brown.

They both retired upstairs as the entry clock chimed two, to change into muslin dresses suitable for walking, and the spencers. The day looked to be fine—the sun a little dim, thanks to all that volcanic ash in the air, but there were very few clouds.

Amelia was down first, and Mrs. Sawyer presented her with the calling cards that had been made up for both of them. They looked very fine, but not *too* fine, on good paper, but not *too* good, and displayed simply their names, the words "Honeyrose Cottage," and "At Home: Tuesday and Saturday." When Serena came down, Amelia offered her cards for her card case as well. It looked as if Lord Alderscroft had ordered a hundred for each of them!

Well, at least we are in no danger of running out.

So armed with calling cards, booted and bonneted, they set out on their first calls in England on their own.

The first lady they called on was the wife of a gentleman who owned the largest dairy in town; socially he was somewhere between "trade" and "gentry." He made his living selling milk, cream, butter, and cheeses of several kinds, which made him "trade," but he owned his land and herds outright, which made him "gentry"—in fact, he was in the exact social gray area that they were. So not only was he the nearest to Honeyrose Cottage, he was also the nearest to their exact, nebulous station.

There was a gravel path beside the roadway, a nicety that allowed them to stay out of the way of drivers and riders, and avoid the dirtier road. It seemed to Amelia that Serena had picked exactly the right outfits for them to wear, for she was neither too warm nor chilled. She was conscious, however, of eyes on them as they passed—from within houses, and from the yards outside. Those who watched from behind their curtains she would not acknowledge, but if someone dressed as something other than a servant was keeping a covert eye on them, she did her best to try to catch their attention, then smiled and nodded, but did not stop. It pained her to not acknowledge the presence of servants, but to do so would have marked them both, socially.

Such a delicate dance they were doing. But if James did indeed settle hereabouts, then what they did *now* would make his life harder or easier in the future.

The house they sought was a large and prosperous-looking one, easily twice the size of their cottage, and with a handsome front garden, and glimpses of a substantial coach house behind. They were met at the door by a maid smartly attired in a brown dress with a starched white apron and a white cap, tendered their cards, identified themselves, and asked if the lady was "in."

She was, indeed, and the housemaid ushered them inside, leaving them for only a moment in the hall to inform her mistress before escorting them into the parlor. So it would appear that the lady was expecting them to call and had informed her maid of that fact. That boded well.

The lady in question, a Mrs. Brisley, rose from her seat and extended a kindly hand to each of them. She was stout, and wisely did not slavishly follow the fashion of light muslin dresses for day wear, appearing instead in the same sort of figured linen calico that they often wore at home, a fabric more forgiving and less revealing than a clingy muslin. It was a handsome gown, of a dark cream with tiny dark blue bouquets, and just a single frill at the hem and the wrists. She wore a conservative cap with lace lappets covering her hair.

The parlor was ample, with handsome, modern furniture, everything that could be wanted for such a room. All the upholstery matched, a fine plain blue plush. It was papered, rather than painted, in an ornamental floral in blue. *Quiet good taste,* Amelia thought approvingly. The one thing that clearly *was* expensive was a tufted wool carpet in blue and cream that extended nearly wall to wall. *Of course,* she thought, belatedly putting her facts together. *Axminster is known across the world for its fine carpets.* Only Moorish carpets were finer.

"How exciting to have not one new mage in Axminster, but two!" the lady said, after the two of them took seats side by side on a sofa near her chair. "What has brought you here? No one has been told anything, my dears! All that anyone knew was that Lord Alderscroft refurbished and staffed his old cottage, which has been vacant since a reclusive gentleman tenanting Honeyrose Cottage departed."

"Not 'dearly departed,' I hope," Serena said mischievously, before Amelia could stop her. "I should not like to encounter a gentleman ghost in the hall at night!"

"Oh no, nothing of the sort!" Mrs. Brisley hastened to say. "No, he decided to go live in Bath, for the sake of his health. He did not much care for the new doctor." The last was uttered in a kind of whisper, as if she was afraid the "new doctor" would overhear.

"Is the doctor so very disagreeable?" Serena prompted, making Amelia kick her discreetly in the ankle.

"Well . . . I would not say *disagreeable*, exactly, and one does not like to be at odds with a fellow mage, but he is . . . very *nice* in his ways. He never seems to have time for a cup of tea or a chat, and he is quite . . . *professional*." She said that as if being "professional" was to be avoided. "A visit is always the same with him. One explains what is wrong, he makes an examination *each time*, as if one had not already *told* him what was wrong, and he writes out his instructions and a receipt for the apothecary *if* he thinks it is warranted, even after one has already *told* him what was wanted! And often he disagrees with our previous doctor, dear Dr. Longate." She patted her cap self-consciously. "I am not sure he is doing me *nearly* as much good as Dr. Longate."

Amelia got the shrewd notion, from the aggrieved manner in which this was all stated, that Mrs. Brisley judged herself to be the sole arbiter of her health, and expected her physician to comply. But she murmured something about how these *modern men* were all trained to treat all patients as if they had never encountered them before, and not with the cozy comfort of fellows of the previous generation, even if this was the latest of several visits.

That seemed to satisfy Mrs. Brisley. "Of course you have a perfect understanding of the situation!" she exclaimed. "No one that Lord Alderscroft accepts as a tenant could be otherwise! Now, I expect you will like to know our Elements. My dear Mr. Brisley is a Water mage—just enough to be sure that our beautiful cattle are producing only the *purest* of milk—and I am Air."

Of course you are, Amelia thought with amusement, for no one could have exemplified the sometimes flighty nature of an Air mage more than Mrs. Brisley—blurting out opinions about the doctor to complete strangers, and confiding things that probably had better not be confided on such short acquaintance.

"It must be a great comfort to both of you to be married to fellow mages," Amelia continued.

"Oh, indeed," the lady said, as if that thought had never crossed her mind. She continued to prattle on about the other mages of Axminster, with frequent asides about "our *notable* Mr. Nightsmith" and some prodding questions about whether the two of them had met him "in Town," meaning, of course, in London. At no point did she actually get around to asking them why they were in Axminster, how long they intended to stay, or any other thing about themselves. It was clear that the sun rose and set on Mrs. Brisley's comfort and self-importance, but she was so ingenuous about it that Amelia could not find herself to be irritated with her.

"We did meet Mr. Nightsmith at a ball Lord Alderscroft held in London just for mages in his White Lodge," Amelia told her, without mentioning that she had met him at the Payne's Assemblies as well. "But of course, there were many other people we met as well, and we only took note of him because we understood that he must be the leading mage of this area, as well as the most powerful. So, of course, if a local Hunt is required, he must organize and lead it, and that is to be noted."

Take that, you officious prig.

Mrs. Brisley gave an exaggerated shudder at the mention of a Hunt, opined that she was sure that no such thing had been needed within her lifetime, but added, "But I am sure if such a disagreeable event were to come to pass, it would, indeed, be Mr. Nightsmith that would lead it. Just as he takes the lead in truly delightful events, such as balls."

But that gave Serena the opening to ask about assemblies in Axminster, and to Amelia's joy, it turned out that they were twice-monthly affairs, held in the largest room of the guildhall on Saturday night, by subscription, no vouchers required.

"The master of ceremonies is Mr. Thomas Witty, the owner of the carpet manufactory. He will be in his office at this time of day, and he will be happy to arrange for everything," Mrs. Brisley told them, then her voice trailed off, and she looked doubtful.

She is trying to work out if we are too high above a carpet manufacturer to get a subscription and tickets in person. I suspect she cannot tell, because she has no idea why we have rented this small cottage, and we might merely be holiday visitors. Now she is regretting not asking us more about ourselves.

"I'm sure we can arrange to obtain everything needed before the next assembly or even the same day if it comes to that," Amelia said before Serena could jump in. "Would that be this week, or the coming week?"

It amused her to keep Mrs. Brisley in doubt as to their actual status. The poor woman's bird-like thoughts obviously fluttered about in her head for a moment before she answered the question. "That would be this week. Oh, I am sure there would be no difficulties if you presented yourself at the guildhall and arranged it all then and there! *Obviously* two ladies such as yourselves would be welcomed immediately!"

They both smiled at her; Amelia was not sure what *her* smile looked like, but Serena's looked like a cat in cream.

"Well, my Element is Earth," she said, changing the subject. "I am a Master, and a Channel." And before Mrs. Brisley could jump in with a request for her garden or her husband's herd to be fortified, she continued. "As soon as I have met and gained consent of all of the mages in Axminster, I intend to fortify the entire town. It would not be right to fortify the property of *only* the mages, and leave everyone else out. The duty of a Channel is to the entire community, after all."

"Of course," Mrs. Brisley murmured.

"And my Element is Fire," Serena said cheerfully. "I'm very useful if your wood is too damp to burn!"

That got a laugh out of the lady, and all was well again. They chatted another few minutes, then the maid appeared at the door with the information that "Mrs. Chetham is here, ma'am." And by the rules of calling, this signaled the time for their departure, since this was a first visit, and they could not be expected to participate in a good session of gossip. And of course it was entirely possible that Mrs. Chetham had turned up only because she had seen the two strangers to Axminster entering Stonebrook House, and had held off as long as she could, planning to have a good cozy talk with Mrs. Brisley and find out what she knew. They rose and took their leave, and left with a nod to Mrs. Chetham, who was *not* a mage.

"Well, that was a near miss. I was afraid she was going to ask you to fortify her garden then and there!" Serena giggled, when they were back out on the street. Now that they were out there, it was clear that the common building material here in Axminster was stone. Even the minster, from which the town took its name, was made of stone. A square-towered church, it probably dated back to before Tudor times. Imaginatively called "the minster," it was, of course, Anglican. And Amelia had been pondering whether or not they should attend it. *She* had no particular objections, despite being nominally a Quaker (and if this was known, she probably would not have been welcome!), but Serena might feel differently.

Wait until we meet the—priest? Rector? Vicar? Parson? How vexatious that I don't actually know which this is. Well, wait until we meet him. That might make all the difference. Serena probably would not care if the man in question was Anglican, as long as he was a good man and cared about his parishioners.

Of course, if he doesn't sermonize too long, and has good music, neither of us will care. Good music and short, apt sermons put me in better charity with my fellows than the opposite do. God cares about what is in one's heart and how one treats his fellow man, and not about mortal titles and meaningless nonsense about which prayer book one uses.

They were almost to their next destination, "Froglet Barton," so she put her woolgathering out of her head, and prepared to see what was in store.

"I am *not* looking forward to the trudge home," Amelia said to Serena, as they neared their final call, a cottage called Mouse Cottage that didn't seem to be bigger than a couple of rooms—the one that belonged to the "local wise woman," Mrs. Brightman. They had not received any set-downs; at two of their calls, the lady had genuinely not been at home, and an elder daughter and a spinster sister had imparted in what seemed to be genuine distress that said lady would be *devastated* that she had not been there to meet them. This had been met with sunny smiles and the invitation from both of them to "look in at our At Home day." The rest of the calls had been generally successful—probably due to the fact that Amelia was a Channel and a Master, which was, it seemed, the equivalent in local circles of being gentry. That information had been greeted with awe, which was quite gratifying. Unlike Mrs. Brisley, the called-upon had done their best to give genuine information about the town, ask appropriate and polite questions about the girls themselves, and confide an equal amount of information about themselves. A couple had cooled a little on learning they were Americans, but that was only to be expected, and they had run into that in London as well. While Amelia felt that being the injured party in multiple attempts at invasion should take precedence, she could see that people who did not understand what had been done *to* America could have a different outlook.

The rest had ranged from polite and cordial, to, in the case of Emily Stockton of Hutton House, warm, convivial, and clearly eager to make friends. But again, being as powerful and learned as they were did help. No one had even the same amount of magical ability as Serena, much less Amelia.

They turned down a graveled path between houses that led between tall, somewhat ragged hedges, with no hint of what lay on the other side of them. At the end of that path *seemed* to be another hedge, but a narrow gap encased an even narrower, stone-lined path that ended at a tiny little stone cottage, as old or older than their own, but single-storied, much smaller, and without a stable. On either side of that path were herb gardens that made Amelia's heart rejoice, for they were healthy despite the unseasonable cold, protected, and beautifully cared for.

But as they neared the door, startling sounds came from the two open windows, in one of which sat a very large tabby cat—a cat which, unaccountably, did *not* take exception to Serena's presence.

First came the noise of smashing crockery.

A female voice. "And I do not care *what* you think, you old quack! Tincture of silver is going to do *no good*, and will turn that silly goose *blue* if she takes it too often—which she *will*!"

Smash. The cat remained unmoved, but blinked at them with enormous copper-penny eyes.

A male voice. "Look, you old witch, what makes you think—"

Smash. The cat yawned.

"What makes you think I haven't *tried* it? Back when I was young and foolish, that is! Save it for a salve, but keep that garbage-water on the *outside* of your patients, unless—"

The cat uttered a startlingly loud *meow*, as they both stood there, frozen in place, then jumped down inside.

"And that's my visitors, you daft baboon! Answer the door before they take fright!"

Amelia really was on the verge of turning on her heels and running away, although Serena looked more amused than startled, but before she could move, the green-painted door, adorned with cheerful painted flower sprigs, opened in her face.

Standing there was a young man—in his mid-twenties, if Amelia's judgment was good—wearing a good, but rumpled, blue suit coat, brown pantaloons and waistcoat, unfashionable *brown* Wellingtons whose surface was so abraded they could never have taken a polish, and a white shirt and plain stock that suggested his laundress needed to be changed—or his housekeeper required a sterner hand than his. His square face bore an amiable look, his curly brown hair was tousled, and he was hatless.

"Well, let them in, you gurt booby!" said the female voice from within. "Don't just stand there with your bare face hanging out like the village idiot!"

Far from objecting to this characterization, the young man stepped aside and waved them into the cottage.

There was, to Amelia's eyes, a pleasing confusion about the interior. Pleasing, because while on the surface it might seem that it was disorganized, she could easily tell that it was not. Rather, it was full to bursting with all manner of useful things: overcrowded, yes, but perfectly organized. Many things hung from the rafters: in one place, bunches of drying herbs, then strictly separated, sausages and hams, then cheeses in wax and nets; apart from all of these, hanks of freshly dyed, drying yarns, and apart from them, pots and pans. Except where there were small windows, with both the outer shutters and inner, metal-framed glass standing open, the outer room was floor to ceiling shelves and cupboards. As much as could be had been crammed inside, and yet there was still room to move. Not a great deal of room, it was true, but adequate for one person.

And presiding over a makeshift table composed of boards over trestle horses in the center of the room was a most remarkable woman. She was old, but vigorous. Neither lean nor fat. Hair tucked so completely up in a cap that not a strand of it could be seen. She was dressed all in browns and creams, not unlike Sarah Small, the brownie who made her home in Honeyrose Cottage—farming fashions that went back a century or more. And most remarkable of all, she had a cloth bag in front of her on the table, and a hammer in her hand.

"Mrs. Brightman?" Serena hazarded, before Amelia could speak.

"The same! And you would be the two gels that young Alderscroft rented Honeyrose to." She pointed the hammer at Serena. "You'd be the shifter." She pointed the hammer at Amelia. "You'd be the Master."

They both stared at her, gape-mouthed. Mrs. Brightman laughed heartily.

"Don't look at me befogged! My brownies talk to yours, of course, and as soon as you shifted, Miss Meleva, one of yours came running to me to tittle-tattle. Don't worry, no one else will know, unless you tell them."

"Well . . . that is comforting," Amelia said. *And it is comforting to finally find someone in this town that has enough magic to be able to see and talk to their Elementals.* "Oh! Your lavender water was delightful, thank you!"

"It should be, I've had enough practice making it," Mrs. Brightman said complacently. "Come in, sit down. Tea? Jam and bread?" She ducked down underneath the table and became invisible.

The cat meowed loudly from the left, where it sat on one of a pair of stools. Taking the hint, Amelia led Serena over to them, where they sat down.

"Partridge," the old woman ordered, "feed the poor gels. I need to put my smashings with the rest."

With that, the young man picked his way across the cottage to what seemed to be the designated "kitchen" area, where he fished two thick pottery mugs off the top shelf of a cupboard, plucked a teapot off the hearth where it was keeping warm, poured both mugs full, and plucked a plate of brown-bread-and-jam sandwiches from somewhere. He balanced the food in one hand and the two mugs in the other and brought both to them.

"That's honeysuckle tisane, you won't need sugar," said the disembodied voice under the table, followed by the sound of crockery shards falling into something.

Well, now I know what she was doing, I just don't know why. Amelia relieved Partridge of one of the mugs and a sandwich, because it was very near their own teatime and all the walking had made her famished. Serena took the other mug, and two sandwiches. Amelia took a sip of the tea, very perfumed, and tasting faintly of nectar, then a bite of sandwich, which had a robust gooseberry flavor without being sweet.

"Partridge," ordered Mrs. Brightman, emerging from under the table with a slat bucket in one hand. "Bring the teapot and the sandwiches, and let's all go out into the back garden. It's too crowded in here for five."

Five? Oh! She is including the cat.

Obedient as a child, the young man took the pot and the plate, and picked his way back to the front door. Amelia and Serena followed, and in turn were followed by the old woman and the cat.

Once out in the front garden, the young man led them around the side into a "back garden" that mixed flowers, vegetables, fruits, and herbs in what looked like chaos, but to Amelia's eyes and knowledge made far more sense than any garden she had ever seen other than the ones back home. Plants that had deep roots were planted near ones that had shallow; plants that repelled insects and animals were grown next to ones that were far too attractive to both. Plants that needed shade were grown in the shadow of plants that needed full sun. Edible flowers mingled with vegetables. Sunflowers loaned their tall stalks to beans and peas. Fruit trees glistened in the sun with the webs of thousands of spiders—which, of course, kept insects and birds off the ripening fruit. Ladybirds were everywhere.

And now Amelia saw without needing to ask what it was that Mrs. Brightman wanted with pottery shards. Narrow paths of crazy-paving made of hundreds of thousands of colorful bits of pottery set into what must have been cement wove their way through the beds, and four bench seats with curving backs, arms, and sides were placed around a central, circular table. Three of the four benches were covered in more cement and crazy-paving; the fourth was half-covered, showing its rough wooden skeleton. Amelia and Serena took their places on one of the finished benches, the young man took a second, and the old woman the third. The young man put his burdens down on the table, produced a leather cup from a hanger at his side, and poured himself tea.

"Just a touch of fire on the teapot, will you, my dear?" Mrs. Brightman asked Serena, who was happy to oblige. "Now, a proper introduction. This is Dr. Partridge, who fancies himself learned because he not only went to university to absorb Greek and Latin and precious little doctoring, but also studied with a surgeon and an apothecary. Which, if she but knew those latter two, would send Brisley into fits." She cackled.

Because a doctor is gentry, but an apothecary is trade, and a surgeon is no better than a barber.

"Oh! That's very clever of you, Doctor!" Amelia said, admiringly. "Especially in a small town like this one."

The doctor shrugged. "My father is a surgeon. My mother *would* be an apothecary if men had the wit to admit females into the profession. She studied with *her* father. I don't take trade from our local apothecary, but I know what he can do, and I know what he knows. It's easier to prescribe than if I had no notion of his bag of tricks. And, of course, when it comes to herbs and quite a few other things, I can rely on Mrs. Brightman."

"And they both had the mother-wit to warn him off nonsense like mercury salts and *tincture of silver*," said the old woman warningly. "And why you didn't listen to them about the silver, I will never know!"

"Because it is useful in a salve!" he exclaimed.

"Well, *naming no names,* but it won't do anything about a *certain person's* dyspepsia," Mrs. Brightman said crossly. "'Tisn't a *sour stomach* she ails with, 'tis eating too much sugar. *You* know that, *I* know that, and *she* knows that, if only she would leave off. *And* she would lose a pound or two in the bargain."

"Birch sap," Amelia said instantly.

"I beg your pardon?" said the doctor.

"Take birch sap, reduce it to half its volume, and give it to her to use in place of half the sugar she uses," explained Amelia. "Tell her it is a special sweetened tonic she should use in her tea. Likely the worst thing that will happen will be she gets thirsty—or if she uses too much, she'll be using the closestool a good deal. If that happens, she'll likely send for you."

The doctor pulled a little notebook from a pocket and made notes. "So you are a healer as well as a Channel, Miss Amelia?"

"I am. And you?" she asked boldly.

"Healer by learning, not by power. Earth, but not a great deal. I can see Elementals, but they generally ignore me unless I plead with them for help, and I have a few magical tricks in my budget I can use to make my medicines more efficacious. I have a little more power than anyone else here except Mrs. Brightman," he said modestly. "I have enough to tell when none of my remedies will prevail, but not enough for true Healing."

"That must be . . . intensely frustrating," she said sympathetically.

He shrugged, as a sparrow landed on his shoulder. Absently, he held a jam sandwich up to his shoulder; it pecked a bite and flew off, sending a dropping with uncanny aim onto the cat, who snarled and ran off after it. "I take comfort in the undisputed fact that I do more good and less harm than anyone I matriculated with." He ate the sandwich in quick, neat bites. "I have Lord Alderscroft to thank for my position here."

"It's to his advantage," corrected Mrs. Brightman. "Having someone like you within reach of his estate, and more to the point, to Nightsmith's, is as valuable to him as the place is to you. And you could never have lived in Bath."

He shuddered. "Good lud, no."

"City poisons?" Amelia asked with sympathy.

"Well-bred idiots," he corrected, acidly. "At least *here* the people that count themselves as gentry are so in awe of my learning and exalted status as a gentleman that they generally shut up and do as they are told, as long as I coat it in enough Latin to choke a prelate."

Amelia very nearly choked, and Serena startled all the birds into silence with her peal of laughter. "I can see we are going to get along," she said merrily. "So let us tell you about ourselves."

14

THE rest of the week was pleasant, in a much different way than living in London had been pleasant. They did not go to the shops—such as they were—except for a single hour when they made the rounds of all of them, bought trifles, and ensured their welcome. They didn't actually *need* anything that they hadn't already bought and brought with them. It was clear to both of them that most of the shopping would be for foodstuffs and household goods like candles, and that was part of Mrs. Sawyer's job. Mrs. Sawyer arranged for milk, butter, and cheese deliveries, which left only the grocer, greengrocer, and butcher to be patronized on a regular basis. Mrs. Sawyer was a shrewd bargainer, so all that was left to her. Amelia made a single morning visit to the minster, because it was central to the entire town, and pretended to pray while in actuality she was infusing the entire area—a circle she judged was about a mile across—with what she hoped would counter the volcano weather. It took about two hours before she was too tired to continue. On coming out, she met the vicar—it *was* a vicar—and his wife, bringing in fresh flowers to decorate the church. The Right Reverend Mr. Podding ("like Pudding, you know, but with an 'O'") was a pleasant, middle-aged man, blessed, as he said, with "two of each," all of them adults. His daughters were still with him ("But there are prospects! Good prospects!"), while his sons were at Cambridge. Mrs. Podding smiled and said very little; Amelia got the impression that she was intelligent, but sweet and shy. Neither had a hint of power. Both said they would call on Saturday. He said some encouraging things about music that made her think attending service would be tolerable.

Calls were made, calls received, winter gowns cut out and projects packaged together. At least the cool weather made working on wool actually pleasant. Amelia worked in the garden, which Alderscroft had had planted . . . and she suspected Mrs. Brightman had done the planting, for it looked very like the "witch's" own garden, but more regimented. If the effects of volcano weather could just be ameliorated, there would be a great many nice things to come out of it. She had been very pleased to discover that there were plenty of vegetables, blackberries, strawberries, gooseberries, currants, an apple tree, and a pear tree at the bottom of said garden.

Then came Saturday, and before they could set off on foot to the assembly at the guildhall, Ethan pulled around to the front gate with the pony harnessed to something that seemed very familiar.

"Oh!" Serena exclaimed. "It's a cheer!"

"We call it a *chaise*, mum," Ethan corrected. But it was very like the "cheers" or "shays" that both of them knew how to drive. A two-wheeled cart suitable for two people, with a hood that could be put down if the weather was fine, as it was today; it was far more suitable for transporting two ladies in dance finery and slippers into town than the dog cart that went on errands with Mrs. Sawyer. There was even a stand for a footman at the back. The pony was a fine little fellow, big for his type, with a knowing eye and a chestnut coat. He was the apple of Ethan's eye, and it showed in his beautifully brushed mane and tail.

"Are we driving ourselves, Ethan?" Amelia asked. "We both can."

"That'll do, then, mum," Ethan replied. "I'll just take the footman's place at the back, and take the chaise home. I doubt such fine leddies as you will leave afore the last dance, so I'll be back and wait-ing at midnight." And he pulled a nice silver watch out of his waist-coat pocket to display with all the pride as if it had been the Crown Jewels. "His lor'ship done give me this, sayin' I'd need it. Set it by minster clock, I did."

"That's capital, Ethan!" Amelia beamed at him, and he flushed with pleasure.

She presumed that Serena had been going out to the stable to get the pony accustomed to her; the pony eyed Serena with some suspicion, but gave no trouble as they climbed into the chaise. But just to be sure, Amelia took the reins. The pony settled when she did that. With a chirrup and a flick of the reins on his back, she got him moving, turned around, and headed up the road to the center of town.

They arrived at the guildhall in fine style, and to the envy of some of the other maidens, who had to walk, escorted by mother or brother, or more rarely, father and mother together. They alighted from the chaise; Ethan got down from the back, took up the reins, and smartly turned the rig and sent the pony home. Amelia admired his driving style; their "man of all work" had hidden depths!

There was no trouble securing a subscription on the spot, espe-cially since Amelia had taken pains to have the exact fee for two on her person. She noted that Mr. Witty, wealthy carpet manufacturer that he was, seemed more than a little in awe of them. Perhaps it was the pony chaise, perhaps it was the way she and Serena had been conducting themselves since they arrived. It seemed that he was in-clined to put them on the "gentry" side of his mental ledger. Amelia got the impression from his manner with them—extremely respect-ful without being obsequious—that if she had demanded it, she could have been made prime lady and a patroness on the spot.

Well, that won't be happening unless we come into a great deal more money!

The assembly was held on the ground floor, in a broad, plain room with many windows, some rather plain iron chandeliers with-out any ornamentation, and an area at one end that had been made into a stage. Currently that stage was occupied by a pair of male fiddlers, a male cellist, a female flautist, a pianoforte with a gentleman at the keys, and a damsel with a tambourine. Amelia noted with pleasure that they were actually tuning their instruments to the piano; too many times back home that had not been the case.

Padded benches and a fair number of chairs lined the walls, and there was a table beside the stage that held a punchbowl and cups. This, apparently, was all the refreshment that would be provided, unless someone else turned up with more, later. Still! *We've danced on less,* Amelia thought.

"Miss Meleva! Miss Stonecroft!" she heard behind her, in a very familiar voice, and turned to meet the greetings of Captain Roughtower with far more welcome than she might have back at Payne's— especially when she saw that Mr. Nightsmith was with him. "Alderscroft informed us that you had finally moved to Honeyrose Cottage, and we hoped that you would grace the assembly this week!" he said with enthusiasm. Nightsmith just looked solemn, but not altogether unwelcoming.

Perhaps he intuited from my frost at Payne's that he displeased me, though he does not know how.

"How do you come to be here, yourself?" Amelia asked. "Did your regiment move to new quarters?"

"Oh, now that Boney's on his way to prison again, I've been granted long leave," the captain said, and sighed. "Mostly it's to see if there is anything that can be done cheaply about the house on my estate. And to see if there is any way I can raise more money from it. Nightsmith's been kind enough to invite me over for an extended stay."

"If I allowed you to stay in that drafty barn, and you caught pneumonia and died, people would blame me," Nightsmith said, with such an unreadable expression that Amelia could not tell if he was joking.

"It is delightful to see familiar faces here," Serena said cheerfully, while Amelia held her tongue. "Do you come to every assembly here?"

"We shall *now*," the captain said, taking Serena's hand and bowing over it, then doing the same for Amelia. "How could we stay away? Oh, I meant to tell you that partners are not so thick on the ground as they are at Payne's, so the rules are different here; it is perfectly permissible for a lady to dance *twice* in one night with a gentleman without any impropriety. And if the company is particularly thin, as many dances as one would be allowed at an evening party."

His charm had the effect of loosening her tongue. "Then will you claim your two dances from us now?" Amelia asked archly, holding *just* back from actual flirting.

"I believe I shall!" the captain replied. And with a glance at Nightsmith, added, "Don't be so Friday-faced, Phillip, and claim yours too, or you shall be left on the sad sidelines with the mamas, and you know what that means."

Nightsmith smiled thinly. "I have been fending off marrying-mamas for quite some time now, Harold, I know how to defend myself." But he turned to Serena and said, "If you would oblige me by dancing the first dance this hour, and the first of the third, I should consider myself happy."

"I shall be most obliged!" Serena said, dimpling.

What on earth does she see in him? Especially after what he said about us?

"Then I shall beg of those same dances with Miss Amelia," the captain said. "And for symmetry, may *I* claim the first dance of the second hour and the first of the last hour from you, Miss Serena?"

"With all my heart," she replied, faintly smiling.

"Then if you would be so kind, Miss Amelia, might I beg those same dances with you?" asked Nightsmith.

She was tempted to deny him—but if partners really were not that thick on the ground, well, he *did* foot it well, and she didn't *have* to tender him any more conversation than she would a stranger.

I came here to dance, not be a wallflower.

"That suits me, Mr. Nightsmith," she said with cool courtesy.

There had been no assigning of numbers for the sets; apparently

this assembly proceeded by the rules she was used to in America—
everyone formed up as they found partners, and since there were
two more couples at the stage, waiting for a set to form behind them
to the right of the stage, that was where they went.

Amelia contrived to get a couple between them and Serena and
Nightsmith, just in case she wanted to say something to Roughtower
that she didn't want overheard by his friend. But Serena had welcomed Nightsmith like an old friend, and was chatting to him amiably while they waited for the dance to start, so probably he would be
occupied with her and paying no attention to anyone further down
the line.

"How bad is your house, really?" she asked Roughtower.

"It's pretty bad," he admitted. "The roof leaked in Father's time,
and we protected the furniture and paintings as best we could
while closing down the parts that had leaks and living in the more
habitable sections, but nothing was actually done about the leaks.
I'm also afraid that woodworm has gotten in there, too. Right now,
there's two rooms and the kitchen that can still be lived in, nothing
more." He grimaced. "It's just as well that I can't afford but the single
servant, plus the man that serves me as gardener, stableman, and
gamekeeper either; there's nowhere to put them. I haven't dared to
go up on the roof to see what the damage is. I'm afraid I'd fall
through."

The fact that he had even mentioned going up on the roof himself
put her even more in charity with him. She hadn't met a single person that considered himself "gentry" who would have done this sort
of labor.

"Well," she said. "I did promise Lord Alderscroft to use my powers
on his estate and Mr. Nightsmith's. I can extend that to you. And 'use
my powers' is a very broad sort of promise. If you'll permit me to, I
might be able to do something about your house. Everything that is
wood, that is. Rafters, and interior walls, and such. At least then
someone can go up on the roof without fear of falling through."

The dance began then, and he nearly fumbled the first steps, his eyes wide with astonishment. "But—how?" he asked, as they turned together.

"I am a Master," she reminded him, and the dance took them apart again. He had to wait for his next question through the next few passages, and they danced down to the bottom of the set.

"What does that have to do with fixing my roof?" he demanded.

"I won't *coerce* Elementals, but the fact that I am about to protect this area from the volcano weather will win me many allies in this part of the country," she admitted. "There are a great many of the Earth Elementals who are not only capable of fixing a human home, they are willing to do so for the proper exchange. I assume your housekeeper is a reasonable cook and baker?"

The dance separated them again, and he was clearly on tenter-hooks until he got back to her. "She's not up to dinner parties, but she's a good plain cook," he said.

"Well, dwarves will work on stone, which should take care of your walls, and your roof if it is slate. Dwarves like savory baked goods. Breads, rolls, anything of that sort. Brownies can be per-suaded to work on wood. They prefer sweet things. Kobolds, who work in mines, can tend to foundations. Dairy goods suit them. I have good working relations with all of them."

"Did you ever try this on a house before?" he asked, and the dance moved him away again.

"Yes, it was another rafter situation like yours with one of our tenants," she told him. "It took time, but when my allies were done, the rafters and the roof had been replaced, the stonework made whole and sound, and some instability in the foundations was ad-dressed."

"How have I never heard of one of us doing something like this?" he asked.

"Probably because in these days, no one but me is daft enough to try it." She laughed as they passed and re-passed. "People assume that you either have to coerce the Elementals, in which case they will all desert you and never work with you again, or you have to spend long hours bargaining with them. But their weakness always has been human food, and if you aren't stingy with it, and you can keep non-mages off your property while they are working, they're willing."

The dance parted them, then brought them together again. "I would be greatly obliged, Miss Amelia, if you were to exercise your power on my house," he said. "Though first, of course, you must discharge your primary obligation."

"Oh, I have done," she said. And once again, the dance parted them. "And I am now free to fortify your estate and Mr. Nightsmith's. I have fortified the land associated with Axminster in a circle roughly a mile across, centered on the minster. That should cover most smallholdings, farms, and the Brisleys' dairy farm." She smiled at him. "It seemed the safest and most appropriate place. Everyone that saw me thought I was praying."

"You minx! And you so proper! I never would have thought that of you!" he exclaimed in delight. And then the dance ended.

She had three very agreeable partners until the end of the hour, which were the doctor, Mrs. Brisley's husband (a big man, but all muscle; it looked to Amelia as if he was still in the habit of seeing personally to his dairy and herds), and the mayor's son, who blushed and stammered, but managed to keep his feet under him.

During that time, the poor lone bowl of punch on the side table was joined by a tower of crisp biscuits, a heaping plate of wafer-thin slices of unfrosted fruitcake, and several platters of brown-bread-and-butter sandwiches. Perhaps the person responsible for refreshments had waited to see how many were in attendance, rather than wasting food. After the first hour of dancing was complete, the band took a recess and so did the dancers. The punch proved to be negus, and not to be despised after an hour of exertion that certainly heated the room. Amelia quite lost track of Serena, but that was of no matter; there was nowhere else she could be except this single room, and it was highly unlikely she would have left it. So when the band took their well-earned short rest, she secured a slice of cake, a couple of sandwiches, and a cup of punch. The refreshments were certainly equal to the ones at Payne's, and the cake was better.

She had finished the last crumb, and put her cup aside with the rest, when she saw Nightsmith approaching with a sinking heart. *Oh, well. He is a very good dancer.* She put on a brave face and an indifferent smile and greeted him.

"Come to claim your dance?" she asked.

"I should have thought that was obvious," he replied. "I would like at least four respites from insipid simpering tonight. I know I am safe with you. And your cousin is highly intelligent and doesn't simper."

"Hmm," she replied, allowing him to lead her to a forming set. "I should think she does the very opposite of *simper*. Why did you come here if you dislike being pursued so much?"

"Harold insisted we come," came the unexpected reply. "I agreed. He said—well, he said a great many things, but the most pertinent was that we could establish our previous acquaintance with you here in public, and avoid any unpleasant gossip later when we take you out to our estates to work."

Trust him to be focused on getting me out to fortify his property. Still, she *had* promised. And it wasn't just his odious self she would be helping, it was an entire estate full of perfectly innocent and probably very nice people who were also mages or mage-adjacent. And all his animals. Perfectly innocent animals that would do poorly if she did not go out to do that work.

"Well, as I told the captain, I have fortified the town and land for about a mile in diameter, centered on the minster. When would you like us to come? Our At Home days are Tuesday and Saturday, and we are *supposed* to expect one of Lord Alderscroft's agents on Monday morning." She wanted it very clear to him that she had other things to do than hang about waiting on his pleasure.

The dance began, cutting short his answer, and it was a little while before they could converse again. "Would it be agreeable if I sent the carriage some Wednesday morning?" he asked, apparently having remembered his manners. "And my housekeeper can arrange an early nuncheon before you return to Axminster. Channeling probably is fatiguing."

"It is," she replied, all business. "I would like you to find the center of your estate, and I can work there. We can be ready at eight. Seven, if you prefer. We are used to farm hours."

He blinked at her. "Really? I—thought—"

"Since you already know you are *safe* with me, and I believe I can trust you to keep this confidential, back home Serena and I are accustomed to doing the same work as our tenant farmers and servants," she said bluntly. "Our plantation could not survive as it has without slaves otherwise, and slaves we will not have." The last was said with an emphasis she felt was warranted. "Both of us could manage a house without the servants Alderscroft so kindly provided, but if we are to keep up the proper appearances and be treated as gentry, we must have servants."

Once again the dance parted them, and when it brought them back together again, he seemed a little subdued.

"Does Alderscroft know all this?" he asked diffidently.

"Probably. Our families have no secrets from the Anglefords, and I must assume they told his lordship all about us, when we proposed to set up an enterprise here." She shrugged, not really interested in discussing what Alderscroft did or did not know.

"But you seem . . . very natural, very comfortable in the part you are playing." It was as if he didn't quite believe what he had heard.

"We're very adaptable," she said shortly. "I have, within the space of the month of December, helped hunt and butcher wild game—and I do mean *personally* butcher—then participated in a magic Hunt for a spearfinger—successfully, if I do say so myself—then danced at the governor's New Year Ball. And that is in and amongst ordinary duties like cheese-making, household chores, dressmaking, mending—oh, many things you don't even think about because your servants do them all for you."

"Both of you?" he asked, looking as if all this came as a great surprise to him.

"Both of us," she said firmly.

"But . . ."

"I told you. We are very adaptable. Everyone on the Stonecroft plantation is. We can be working in the kitchen together, then turn around in the next hour and entertain like gentry and no one would ever know where we'd been before we donned our pretty muslins."

That kept him silent for the rest of the dance. Once or twice it looked as if he was going to say something, but he didn't. When the dance was over, he bowed a little more deeply than custom required. She wasn't sure if he was being ironic, or acknowledging that she was far more than he had taken her for.

Her next dance was swiftly claimed by the doctor. "I hope you'll forgive me for concentrating on my footwork and not on conversation," he said ruefully. "I'm not *terrible* anymore, but I'm not the dancer that Nightsmith is."

"Nightsmith has very little to do and a great deal of time to do it in," she said, just a little waspishly. "You, on the other hand, have a great deal to do and very little time to do it in."

He blinked at her. He probably had not expected a woman to criticize a man, or at least not to another man. "That . . . seems just a trifle . . . harsh?"

There were a number of things she could have said, but she settled for, "I fear it is the nature of those of us with 'the scent of the shop' on us to be impatient of those who do not have to work for a living."

At that point the dance began, and since it was a very lively one, he did not have the concentration to speak except for a pleasant compliment or two, and she was inclined to let the whole thing drop.

Next was a very old gentleman, who did his best, and was so cheerful about it that she vastly preferred him to Nightsmith. After that, an affable farmer, *not* a mage, who spoke in tones of happy wonder and in detail about how much better his crops were suddenly doing. "I cannot account for it, but I pray it continues," he said in fervent tones. "We were looking at a thin harvest and hunger until now. We should have a normal harvest so long as there is not an unnatural frost." That brought her unalloyed joy; what she had *hoped* would make a difference actually was.

And the next dance brought the captain to her side again. "I'm having an uncommonly good time," he said, with amusement. "I confess I did not expect much. But the musicians are competent, and since everyone knows I'm a poor marriage prospect, I'm getting some very entertaining partners."

"I hope you are charitably dancing with some wallflowers," she told him with mock-severity. "It seems unfair that they cannot have some innocent pleasure and must watch while others dance."

"That is who I am dancing with!" he replied. And the figures parted them for a while.

"I am concentrating on the spinsters, who know I am not able to support a wife, and so have no delusions about me. I had no idea how clever some of these ladies are! The *best* of gossips! I have heard astonishing things about the goings-on of this town that I never would have guessed from its sleepy aspect!" he said with great glee when it was their turn to "rest and wait."

"Pray tell, do!" she urged him. "I have been harboring delusions of writing a novel, and this could give me grist for my mill."

"Some of these lovely ladies have a secret passion for a Mr. Collier, who is a teacher at the Methodist Sunday school where children are taught to read and write along with their religious instruction. So much so that at least two of the dear ladies told me that some of the marriageable girls were known to have abandoned the church at one point to 'try their luck' with him." He seemed in sympathy with them rather than mocking them. "He must be an extraordinary man to have caused that!"

"How on earth did you manage to pry *that* information out of them?" she asked in astonishment.

"Apparently I have the kind of face that people trust."

And on that note, the dance became too involved for further conversation.

For the last hour, Mr. Nightsmith turned up as arranged, and the dance called by the master of ceremonies was *precisely* what she wanted, given her partner. It was an extremely lively Scottish reel, with very intricate footwork and absolutely no time for conversation. This allowed her to enjoy having an excellent partner without having to deal with the vexation of actually talking to him.

When the last dance was over, despite the fact that everyone was going to need to go to services at church or chapel in the morning, most people seemed inclined to gather in small groups and talk. She and Serena found each other easily enough, and without either of them feeling the need to stand about and gossip as many of the locals did, they said their goodnights to those partners who had been notable, and slipped out the door. Although the only light came from a torch set in a holder just outside the guildhall door, there was more than enough to see two things: the welcome sight of Ethan with the shay, and the equally welcome sight of Nightsmith and Roughtower vanishing into the darkness in what was presumably Nightsmith's curricle, moving away at a spanking pace.

Amelia had gotten in first, and watched the lantern on the curricle until it was gone around a curve in the road. "Now, that is how I like to see that man," Amelia said, as Serena got into the shay next to her. "Receding from me."

Serena laughed. "He definitely got on your wrong side. Amelia, you do not hold a grudge, you positively *cherish* one!"

She had to laugh—because it was true. "Well, it does not matter. I only need be civil to him. I can manage that."

At least, she thought, as Ethan drove the pony carefully along the main street back to Honeyrose Cottage, *I hope I can manage that.*

The next day was Sunday, and they turned up for services at the minster—although she was heavily tempted to call in at the Methodist chapel instead, to get a glimpse of this Mr. Collier who was so tempting for the spinsters of Axminster that they forsook their faith for the chance to catch his eye. Methodist preaching, however, was known to be long, ponderous, and full of brimstone, and in her limited experience, while Methodists were enthusiastic hymn singers, "enthusiastic" did not necessarily translate into *good*. But as it happened, Vicar Podding was a decent, if not brilliant, preacher, and one who was inclined (at least judging by the sermon, which was on the theme of "judge not, lest ye be judged," but told in the gentlest way possible) to take the foibles of his congregation in stride. He clearly favored *leading* his flock rather than bellowing at it. He was also a *brief* speaker, and to Amelia's pleasure, the gentleman who had been serving at the pianoforte last night was doing his duty at the organ this morning. He was obviously not a performer of great note, but he was good, and he was clever at choosing pieces that were well within his competence that were not so common as to elicit a yawn.

They returned to the cottage on foot, as they had arrived—walking shoes being perfectly acceptable at church—to find Mrs. Sawyer waiting for them in a state of what could only be described as "great anticipation" right at the door. The reason for this was obvious as she handed each of them an envelope.

"These came by messenger, special, from Averly Hall," she said, almost breathlessly. And when Amelia looked at her blankly, she added, "Mr. Nightsmith's establishment."

"Oh." She could not put any particular enthusiasm into the response, but opened the envelope. Surely it wasn't a letter. What on earth would he have to write to her about?

Unless he has a property we can lease . . . or better still, purchase. If that proved to be the case, and the property really was suitable, it would put her in his debt, but for James's sake she would bear it with a smile, as long as they weren't supposed to be such near neighbors that she would be expected to entertain him regularly . . .

But it was no such thing. It was an invitation on heavy linen paper. A wreath of printed flowers surmounted by an elaborate printed bow enclosed the writing. And it was *all* handwritten, with only the decorative touches being printed.

A Welcoming Ball, it began, followed by a double-ended wand. A nice touch that only an Elemental mage would recognize, which meant that only Elemental mages would be invited. Then, *Miss Amelia Stonecroft is invited to attend, at Averly Hall, on Saturday evening, at 8 o'clock, a ball to welcome her and Miss Serena Meleva to the environs of Axminster. RSVPBS.* Which meant "RSVP By Scrying." And with the invitation was a little token that would allow her to connect to his scrying instrument. Presumably a scrying ball or bowl such as she had, since he was an Earth Master himself.

"Good lud," she said aloud, more than a little shocked.

But Serena already had hers out and was uttering a suppressed squeal. "Another ball! A real ball and not an assembly! Oh! We will be able to meet *all* of the other mages hereabouts, including the ones that could not come to Alderscroft's ball! And we *won't* have to hold our tongues, and we'll be able to be ourselves!"

"That," Amelia replied dryly, "depends entirely on Nightsmith's attitude toward those mages that are not . . . sufficiently *exalted* enough for him."

"Oh, don't be silly, Amelia, I saw him dancing most amiably with Mrs. Brisley tonight, *and* with that dear little girl who was just old enough to come to an assembly, the shy one. Miss Sarah Jane Pennington. Why, her mother is the cook at the coaching inn! He seems just as egalitarian as Lord Alderscroft."

At least where fellow mages are concerned. Amelia softened just the tiniest little bit. "Well, in that case . . . I don't see how we can refuse such an invitation, since this ball is in our honor. I shall go get my scrying bowl."

Soon they were both seated at the dining room table. With the token placed under the bowl, she gently teased power from the little source she had created beneath the cottage, and filled the bowl with it, where it appeared to her eyes as a glowing golden mist. So it remained, as she waited patiently, until someone would respond. She fully expected it would be one of Nightsmith's servants rather than Nightsmith himself, and she was not surprised, when the mist cleared and sank into the bowl, to see an unfamiliar, bespectacled face peering up at her from the depths. "Miss Stonecroft, I presume?"

the young man said, the warmth of his tone echoing the warming of his eyes. "I am Mr. Nightsmith's secretary. Allow me to have the pleasure of welcoming you here, and informing you that Mr. Nightsmith has the option of two arrangements for your attendance at the ball. He will send a carriage for you to arrive at six, and you may return the same way, or if you prefer, he would be pleased to host you overnight, along with Miss Meleva and several other of his guests, to return to Honeyrose Cottage the next day."

Before Serena could urge staying overnight, she replied, "We are very grateful for the conveyance, and we certainly would not want to impose any more than that on Mr. Nightsmith's hospitality. He has our deepest thanks for such an unexpected courtesy and the delight that this ball presents."

The secretary nodded. "Then it is settled. You can expect the carriage at your door at six p.m. Saturday night." He waved his hand, ending the conversation.

"Amelia! We are going to be fatigued and flagging, and—" Serena began.

Amelia cut her short. "No more fatigued than after Alderscroft's ball, and although the distance to Averly Hall is likely greater, the traffic will be much lighter than in London, and there will be a full moon. We can rest in the carriage, which we surely will *not* be able to do if we stay overnight—you *know* that all those who have not yet met us and are also staying will want to engage us in endless conversation when the ball has come to an end. And we really *must* attend Sunday services if we are to remain in the good books of the people of Axminster."

Serena pouted a little, then sighed. "Yes, I am sure you are right. But I *would* have liked to see what a truly great estate looks like."

"You will have every opportunity when I am—" she stopped, and then laughed. "I am a fool. He is sending the carriage for us at *six* so that I can channel for his estate before the ball itself! That cunning wretch! He makes me pay for my pleasure!"

Both Serena's hands flew to her mouth, and she gasped a little. "Oh! I do think you must be right! But—as he is an Earth Master himself, he will certainly invoke the power source *for* you, ahead of time, to save you most of the fatigue."

"If he doesn't already have one established, which he probably does." She found herself laughing. "Well played, Phillip Nightsmith! Well, I know you now. You shall not trick me a second time!"

15

IT would have been an uneventful week, had they not had the ball to look forward to at the end of it.

Lord Alderscroft's agent did indeed turn up, after first sending a note from the coaching inn to ask if they would be available. This appearance of his lordship's agent staying overnight at the coaching inn, of course, was as good as hiring the town crier to announce to the entire town that she and Serena really knew and were being patronized by his lordship. So things were likely to become much more interesting in regards to those in Axminster who were *not* mages.

This would probably be a "good" thing rather than a bad one. Since anyone known to Alderscroft was unlikely to be a sharpster or get into dun territory, lines of credit would magically open up at the butcher, the baker, the greengrocer, the grocer, and anyone else with the inclination to send bills rather than insist on ready money. The seamstress would, sadly, be disappointed to find they had already kitted themselves out in London, but perhaps her disappointment could be assuaged with the purchase of bonnets, stockings, and gloves. They certainly *did* want to stay on the right side of the

local seamstress. There were always emergencies, after all, and repairs that they did not have the skills to execute themselves.

Everyone would, of course, want to know *how* a couple of colo-
nists (as, aggravatingly, they were being called) came to know his
lordship, but they had a story for that. "His lordship is an abolitionist,
as are we, and my father has written to him frequently on the subject."

That had been Amelia's solution, and Serena embraced it whole-
heartedly, even though it was possible this would undermine their
charade that Serena was Italian. *One should never tell a lie when a
shading of the truth is far better.* They already knew Alderscroft's
thoughts on the matter, for he had been instrumental in finding
places for some of the escaped slaves the Stonecrofts had harbored,
and their father had, indeed, written to him frequently over the
years, not caring to impose on him by speaking by scrying bowl.
Such letters were, of course, ostensibly about shipments of nonexis-
tent luxury goods, sable furs and narwhal tusks, and only another
mage could clear off the obfuscating text to reveal the magically
scribed words beneath. When dealing in human lives, it was unwise
to speak openly. Letters could be intercepted and read at any point
on their journey, and there were many who would be very happy to
dismantle the Stonecrofts' tiny kingdom out of pure greed.

And of course, their business here, which would require the help
of the agent, was perfectly above board and yawningly ordinary.
And it was anything but a secret. They'd already spoken about it over
many a cup of tea, either in their own parlor or in the parlors of those
they were paying calls to.

The agent turned up, was treated to tea and some excellent cake,
and regretfully stated that he did not know of any properties available that would suit. "That, however," he interjected, before they
could show their disappointment, "does not mean that one will not
become available. It is quite remarkable how once a requirement for
such-and-such a property becomes widely known, people who had
not before this had any notion of selling or leasing suddenly think
about that hundred acres or so that is inconveniently situated or too
woody or rocky to farm. When that property is not producing any

income, they begin to consider whether it might profitably be leased or altogether disposed of. Especially to someone in the good graces of a peer." As they brightened, he smiled. "I will let it be known in the inn before I depart, and from there the word will fly. I will make it known that if anyone is curious, and is disinclined to treat with ladies, they can reach me at my residence."

Aside from that slight souring note of "disinclined to treat with ladies," they were happy with what he had to say.

More, many more, ladies of Axminster came to call on them after the assembly, and still more came when their business became widely known. Amelia found most of them tedious beyond measure, since they had very little to say beyond the doings of their children and husbands. Their education was limited, their interests few, and all rooted in the domestic scene. But Serena was perfectly happy to chatter with them, and Amelia could at least speak with them about receipts for American dishes and herbal remedies, and about their gardens. And at least if they were tedious, she could pay them only half her attention and work on needlework. Those winter gowns were not going to sew themselves.

They went in turn to call on their callers, but took care not to stay overlong. The one place they *did* spend an entire two hours at was Mrs. Brightman's cottage; they came bearing gifts and returned with gifts of their own. They brought a bottle of truly excellent sherry, and returned with a bottle of mead and the receipt for making it, a gift which Mrs. Sawyer pounced upon with great glee. Without the restraining presence of Dr. Partridge, the old witch unfolded her personal budget of information on many of the town's persons that was quite enlightening, and gave them a very good idea of how to avoid any future misunderstandings or unpleasantness. And it was very entertaining. The people of Axminster had no idea how observant their "wise woman" was. She wasn't judgmental; just very observant and quite witty.

It was hard for Amelia not to keep going up to her room several times a day, checking her gown and accessories over and over for defects it always turned out were imaginary. This ball loomed very large in her mind, despite her dislike of Phillip Nightsmith. Amelia had to admit, at least to herself, that she was more nervous about *this* ball than Lord Alderscroft's.

She couldn't think why this should be; she'd gotten over—she thought—Nightsmith's cold and cruel comments. Captain Rough-tower would be there, and the captain was an amusing scoundrel. And just because she did not care for their host at all, there was no reason to expect any unpleasantness whatsoever. Nightsmith would *never* say in public the snide things he had to Roughtower. She and Serena would not be part of a concert this time, so there was no chance they would incur any more such comments. In fact, the invitation to stay overnight really signaled a genuine attempt to be hospitable. But her anxieties were almost keeping her awake at night, all the more because there did not seem to be any logical reason for them.

Still, Saturday arrived at last, and a beautifully turned-out chaise pulled by two high-stepping matching duns arrived at their doorstep. Jackie was allowed to hold the horses and nearly burst with pride as the groom helped Amelia and Serena into the conveyance. As the day had turned chilly, and the evening was likely to be more so, both had their autumn cloaks over their ball gowns. Amelia had considered arriving in an ordinary gown and changing once her work was done, but she thought better of the idea after due consideration of the plan. She already had discarded the notion of bringing her scrying bowl as very inconvenient, and had only the small amber globe with her in her reticule; she had repurposed it and made it her own to avoid endangering Alderscroft in any way, and had done the same for Serena with the one she had found on the mantelpiece. A gown and accessories would be impossible to carry about at a ball, and too easy to misplace if she left them in the care of a maid.

As the chaise moved away, however, she could not repress the continued unease she was feeling. "I wish we could have gone in our own coach," she said fretfully to Serena. "If something happens that is distressing, we will be at Nightsmith's whims as to whether he will have another conveyance brought up to take us home early."

"But we don't *have* a coach," Serena said, pointing out the obvious.

"We could have hired one. I wish I had thought of that." She could not help but twist her hands in her lap to relieve some of her tension. But it didn't help.

"Well, you didn't. And anyway, unless we also hired a coachman, we'd be taking Ethan away and Mrs. Sawyer would probably discover she needed him for something important," Serena countered. "And if we were realistically able to *support* another conveyance, a pair of horses, and an actual coachman, where would we put them? Why *are* you in such a state?"

"I don't know," she admitted. "I am not given to premonitions. Or megrims. Perhaps . . . perhaps it is just that for the next six hours, we will be entirely at Mr. Nightsmith's mercy—"

That observation sent Serena into a peal of laughter. "Oh, do stop making a Cheltenham tragedy out of a perfectly *lovely* invitation, you goose! Phillip Nightsmith is quite a decent fellow, and if he hadn't gotten in your bad books, you would have found that out already. He has *slightly* outdated ideas about women, but that is because he has no notion of what life in America is like for a woman. At the assembly when I partnered him, I had the mother-wit to compare us to those brave ladies of old, who handled *all* the affairs of their men when those silly beasts were off tilting at Moors in the Crusades, or each other in all of those interminable wars. He looked very thoughtful when I had done so, and said I had *quite* given him an entirely new outlook on the subject."

Somehow that did not make Amelia's anxiety any less. But she pretended that it had, and at least they had very pretty countryside to look at. There was something entrancing about country that had been under cultivation for hundreds of years. Even the parts that were left wild looked planned. *Serena probably hates this.* But something about it appealed to the part of her that loved order.

Mind, I also love Mrs. Brightman's chaotic garden . . .

Her anxiety ramped up as soon as they reached a lane along a high stone wall that *surely* enclosed their destination. Once in that lane, they joined a loose cavalcade of various sorts of conveyances, all evidently on the way to Averly Hall as well.

Her worries ebbed somewhat when she realized that they were following a common single-horse shay, and being followed by a plain farm cart loaded with the farmer and his family, all dressed in their very best. Then they bloomed again when they turned in to a drive that ended in a vast expanse of raked gravel and a magnificent stone edifice that could not have had fewer than eighteen or twenty guest rooms. She was no judge of architecture, but it looked to her as if it must also be Tudor, or at least Jacobean.

At least it's not a castle.

It might just as well have been, though, given the size and magnificence of it. Three stories tall, with immense grounds and a second wing that was just as tall as the original building. And a vast, manicured lawn that was at least twenty acres, dotted with actually sculpted bushes. It was easily a match for Alderscroft's town house.

But the driver of the little shay was greeted with great care by the butler and footmen at the entrance, as were they, as they were handed down out of the chaise. And the occupants of the farm cart were not directed to the kitchen entrance, but greeted just as she and Serena had been. Nor did the farmer and his family show any of the awe that she would have expected.

The entrance hall was small by modern standards, but was two stories tall, and boasted beautiful oak wainscoting right up to the second floor, and a handsome wooden stair going up to a balcony across the back wall. To the right was a fine fireplace with a cheerful fire in it, just enough to take the chill out of the air. Phillip Nightsmith himself was there, greeting his guests, but he handed that task off to an older woman with a strong physical resemblance to him as soon as Amelia and Serena entered the room.

"Thank you for coming, ladies," he said, with a touch more warmth than necessary. "Miss Amelia—"

"I have already come prepared to fortify your lands, Mr. Nightsmith," she said, interrupting him. "Although—" she softened her tone a little "—the fact that you invited *others* here at an earlier hour than strictly necessary for the ball makes me think I may have misjudged your intentions."

He had the grace to color a little, and the honesty to answer, "Well . . . I did invite you and Miss Serena early in the hopes that you *might* be willing to at least look at my preparations and tell me if I needed to do anything else. And I invited these others early because they were traveling the farthest, and I wanted them to be rested for the ball proper."

"Do you often hold such balls?" Serena asked, tilting her head to the side, in a manner that would have charmed even the coldest heart. "If we are to remain in this neighborhood, I certainly hope you do!"

"I am accustomed to giving a ball or two when I am at home. I do not spend all of the Season in London, though I do travel there for part of it. I usually arrive late and leave early; I am accustomed to traveling light and by horseback, since I have my own small establishment and stable there." He bestowed a smile on Serena. "So inclement weather need not inconvenience me beyond staying a night or two longer at an inn than I intended."

His "small" establishment is probably as large as the Anglefords' home, Amelia thought to herself.

"But allow me to introduce you to my mother, and if you are prepared to bestow on me the favors of your gifts, I shall take you to a room where you can refresh yourself."

Amelia chuckled. "I should be delighted to meet your lady mother, and I am in no more need of refreshment than you are yourself. Please make the introductions, and let us be about the business at hand. I shall be in *much* more need of rest after the fact than before it."

He led her over to the dusky-haired lady, who was wearing a velvet gown the color of claret, with gold-bead embroidery in a pattern Amelia recognized from one of her magazines, called "Flames of Arabia." It was, without a doubt, the product of an expert *modiste*, and one far above the talents of the most excellent Madame

Alexander. "Mother, may I present to you Miss Amelia Stonecroft and Miss Serena Meleva? Ladies, may I present my mother, Lady Nightsmith?"

Since the lady held out her hand in a most friendly fashion, Amelia took it that curtsies would not be required. She had a very firm handshake. Lady Nightsmith also had a pleasant, resonant alto voice. "Miss Amelia, my son has told me what you are doing, not only for Axminster and our estate, but indeed, for as much of the county as you can reach, and I am speechless with gratitude. Little birds tell me that the farmers around Axminster are already seeing improvements in their crops."

Amelia was impressed. She had not expected a titled lady to take any interest in the welfare of those outside her walls, not even one who was an Elemental mage. "My father has always driven home to us that those of us who are sufficiently gifted are obligated by virtue of our fortune to pledge those gifts to the service of others," she replied.

"Then your father is a wise man, and your country is the better for having him in it," came the reply. Then she turned to Serena. "Miss Serena, you are as welcome to our home as your cousin is."

"And with far less reason!" Serena laughed, which made the lady laugh herself. "Is there anything I can assist with while my cousin is improving the landscape?"

"I should take it as a compliment if you would care to tour the house and grounds," came the reply, and Lady Nightsmith gestured to an elderly footman, who was instantly at her side. "This is Carstairs, who is Earth, and knows more about the history of this place and our family than I do. Would you care to be guided by him?"

"I should, above all things!" Serena said enthusiastically. "Grounds first; that way we have the best light, and I need not remove my cloak only to don it again."

"Very good, mum," said Carstairs, looking pleased. "If you will come this way?"

With Serena getting her wish and amused, Amelia turned to Nightsmith. "Shall we? You are Earth; you know what I need."

"Indeed I do; if you would come with me?" He offered her his arm; it would have been churlish not to accept, so she did.

He brought them under the balcony and to a short passage on the right that led into a comfortable parlor, rather than the passage on the left that the others had taken. "This is the private part of the house," he said. "As opposed to the guest quarters. Country houses are often divided like this, so that the guests may move about as they choose without disturbing those in residence. I am taking you down into the cellars."

"What, do you plan to have me conjuring amidst the wine?" she responded.

"You'll see," was the enigmatic reply.

The rooms were all furnished in mingled, yet harmonious fashion, with pieces that were surely Tudor or Jacobean comfortably cheek by jowl with a modern settee, or Chesterfield chair. Very fine carpets muffled their footsteps, and there were small fires in most of the fireplaces.

From the parlor he led her into what was clearly his study. Placing his hand on the wood paneling beside the fireplace, he pressed, and she saw the glow of magic about his hand for a moment before the panel moved inward, then slid into the wall.

Well, that is cunning. A hidden passage, like in a novel! It must have been useful during times when others were hunting "witches."

"The stair is narrow; would you rather follow or lead?"

"Follow," she said. "So if I lose my balance, I shall have you to break my fall, and I will land softer than you do."

He actually laughed dryly at that. "As you will," he said, and led the way down a tiny spiral stair, which surely could never have been big enough to admit women of the previous eras in hoops and panniers and farthingales.

Perhaps they stripped to their shifts!

"Captain Roughtower warns me I must never get fat, or I shall never fit into my working room," he remarked over his shoulder.

"I think you stand very little chance of getting fat," she said. "Just how do you know the captain, anyway? You seem very unlikely friends."

"I have known him since childhood, although not very well until he became an adult. We are very distant cousins, very much removed, but we share something rather odd. Since both our estates are entailed, we are each other's heirs until we wed and have sons."

"How on earth did *that* come about?" she asked, astonished.

"Before this estate was tied up, my great-great-great-great-grandfather bequeathed part of this estate to Roughtower's equally great-grandfather, his younger brother, and both of them put their property into entail at the same time, so it could never go out of the bloodline." He reached the floor of the lower level, and turned to assist her the last few steps. "At the time, Harold's property was worth a very great deal, as it was a supplier of the very best yew for longbows and crossbows, the best ash for spear shafts, and the best oak for quarterstaffs and furnishings, and sometimes the beams for houses. The trees on the plantation are extensively pollarded for that purpose." He shrugged. "Now, because they were pollarded rather than allowed to grow into single trees, the trunks are not thick enough for the masts of our sailing ships, and only a few every year are good enough for yards and spars. With upholstered furniture being the mode, fine wood is no longer needed for the frames, and can be anything. Stone and brick are more fancied than wood and wattle-and-daub or beautiful wainscoting for houses. So what was bringing in good, reliable money for quality wood has been greatly reduced as he competes with lesser products. He has even been forced to clear-cut some sections to sell for firewood, barn rafters, and bean and hop poles." He paused. "While I consider him to be my friend, I am not blind to his faults. He is a fellow mage, and I owe him something for that. I do what is feasible with someone like Roughtower. I let him use my home as his, but not my money. I fear that if I did, he would emulate his father and live far beyond both our means."

On the one hand, she was tempted to give him a sharp set-down for being so uncharitable. On the other hand—she'd had just enough acquaintance of the captain to know that he was a charming rogue, whose charm was calculated, and whose personality was such that he probably would like, very much, to become addicted to vice. Amusing to be around. Not so amusing to be married to.

"Well, he must find himself a wife who will indulge enough of his whims to make him feel satisfied without loosening her hold on the purse strings," was all she said. "Fortunately I think my paltry thousand a year is not enough to tempt him."

Meanwhile she looked around.

She found herself, not in a dank, rock-walled cellar, but in a very pleasant room, which she could already tell was oriented to true north. It was paneled in oak (some of the oak from Roughtower's estate?) and had a tiny fireplace to warm it, and an example of Axminster's finest carpet covering the entire floor. Fine copper candelabra on all the walls gave a good, clear light, and in the middle of the room was a round table with four comfortably padded chairs around it. The surface of the table looked—odd.

She moved to stand above it, invoked mage sight, and exclaimed with surprise.

"Yes," he said with a smile in his voice. "This is a topographical map of most of the county. The ley lines have been laid in beneath the surface in copper and infused with the magic of each proper line. Populations down to the village have been noted with gemstones, and the map is centered on Averly Hall."

"This is *beyond* useful!" she exclaimed.

"And I have prepared the source beneath the Hall to accept your use. You have only to place your focus on the map where the Hall is."

"Soonest begun is soonest done," she said, shrugged out of her cloak, and took her amber ball out of her reticule, placing it in the center of the map. Feeling the source he spoke of already humming beneath her, she took her seat in the northernmost chair; he took south, opposite her.

"If you will trust my protections, I shall ward you while you channel and fortify," he said. "That will save your power and double your concentration."

"I accept," she said immediately. She might not *like* him, but she did trust him. Alderscroft trusted him, and she did not think that he was easily fooled. And besides, he had given her access to his power reservoir; if she wanted to, she could drain it dry or place traps in it. That was showing a degree of trust higher than hers.

She closed her eyes and used her mage sight and her focus to delicately probe his reservoir. Solidly and competently built, it would definitely need a bigger "pipe" to the ley line if she was going to pull as much out of it as she intended to.

Rather than actually make the "pipe" bigger, she just added a second. He could always pinch it off later if he decided he didn't need a reservoir of that size anymore. That was a matter of moments, and then the real work could begin.

Without thinking, she spread her hands to the furthest extent of the map on the table. There were two ways to do this; the first was to create a boundary as far as she thought she could go, and work within that. But the second, which she preferred, was to establish a "seed" under this house, create everything she wanted to do—fortify, warm, and nurture—then "grow" the seed. Like inflating a pig bladder; push it out as far as she could until she couldn't push it any farther. The "nurturing" part included something that she had been doing instinctively, but now realized, after reading the grand duke's book on Earth magic, that she needed to do deliberately.

Soil was either living or dead. Dead soil included things like soil that had been heated so much nothing would grow properly in it anymore, had been poisoned with salt or chemicals, or had been killed magically. But soil could be almost dead if it was drowned or chilled badly enough. She needed to make sure that she cultured that living aspect so that it could grow healthy crops even in the midst of constant chill and an early and harsh winter.

So (and she was very aware of Nightsmith's magical "eyes" on her, observing closely), she began. First to channel power inside the boundary, then to harness that power to nurture the soil and the plants in it, then to channel power to push the boundary out further, then channel more power to fill the new boundary . . . and so on.

It was soothingly like knitting; once she established her rhythm—push, channel, nurture, push—it was just a matter of concentration and pushing her own personal boundaries. Between every push, she paused a moment to replenish her own personal magic; the nearest ley line was too powerful to take from directly, but sipping from Nightsmith's expertly constructed reservoir was not unlike sipping crisp spring water from a honey-flavored pool.

He's truly an excellent mage. If only he wasn't so unpleasant and cold.

She was vaguely aware of a slight updraft around her; this whole chamber must have been built a little like a chimney, with unseen ventilation in the ceiling. That only made sense; otherwise with all the candles around her it would have been worse than stuffy in no time, and anyone in it would start overheating. As it was . . . she was perfectly comfortable, surrounded by gentle warmth and the honey scent of real beeswax candles. Without a doubt, this was the most perfect workspace for an Earth mage that she had ever encountered, and in the back of her mind she wondered if there were similarly perfect chambers in this place for Air, Water, and Fire mages.

And then . . . as she had known she would . . . she reached the limits of her strength, and not even replenishing her stores of magic could help with that. The "muscles" that moved magic were just like any others; when you pushed yourself far enough, they became exhausted, and not all the honeyed tea in the world would let you get one step farther.

She had plenty of warning; more than enough to tie everything up neatly, make sure there were no leakages and no loose ends to be exploited, just like finishing an invisible hem neatly and hiding the knot.

"Hide a knot as you would a secret." How many times had the older women of the plantation told her that when she was sewing—or working magic? Appropriate to both. An open knot could be picked apart or cut off, and all your hard work could be undone.

When it was all done, she leaned back against the supporting cushions of the chair, hands flat on the table and stretched right out to the rim, and sighed.

Only then did she open her eyes and look, and was somewhat astonished to see that she had, apparently, managed to cover *most of the county of Devon* with her magic.

She knew immediately *why,* of course. Nightsmith had taken care of so much that she usually would have needed to do that she was free to use every particle of her personal stores to concentrate on the important business.

Then she looked across the table at Nightsmith, and for once his expression was perfectly readable. He was dumbfounded. He was currently staring at the table—the table itself glowed with warm, dark golden energies, reflecting what she had done in the real world—and finally looked up at her.

"You covered the entire county," he said, his tone flat with astonishment. "The *whole county.* Devon—is exceptionally fertile. You will be preventing actual starvation far beyond its borders."

"There will still be hunger," she temporized.

"But not starvation." He, too, leaned back in his chair. "Are you too weary to move?"

She took stock of herself, and shook her head.

"Then I suggest you retire to the greenhouses for further recovery. I think you will find them conducive to that state. Just ask the servant stationed outside my study to guide you." He seemed to be breathing heavily.

"Thank you," she said politely, just a little irritated that he had neither praised her work nor thanked her for it. It would have been polite, at least.

So rather than sit there under his eyes, she wrapped herself in dignity, got to her feet, and ascended the staircase, determined not to show how tired she was. Once at the top, she sagged a little, took a moment to recover herself, and went to look for that servant.

A very short time later, she was in the orangery, ensconced in one of those high-backed wicker-like chairs from India. Most of the greenhouses were too utilitarian to "relax" in, and the one for flowers—well, the *wall* of scent that had struck her when she entered was very off-putting. But someone had decided to make the orangery a little, calm haven, and she was taking advantage of that fact. It smelled of damp, moss, and orange blossoms, but mostly oranges, with a little lime and lemon.

She had been tempted by the delicious aromas to purloin an orange for herself, but two things stopped her, and neither of them was the thought that Nightsmith would be annoyed if she did. The first was that she had no idea what a newly ripe orange looked or smelled like. All the fully ripe ones, of course, had already gone to the refreshment tables in a room next to the ballroom, probably taking the form of slices floating in a rum punch to make them go further. She had never actually seen an orange that was not fully ripe; oranges in her world were a once-a-year treat, at Christmas, and were saved, pondered over, and at last savored, with the peel carefully reserved for candying. *Men* saw them more often, in their cherished rum punches carefully mixed and set aflame in the meetings of various fraternal societies in homes and taverns. But then, in her experience, *men* got far more of the good things of the table than women, on the specious grounds that women had delicate constitutions that needed to be protected from rich foods and drink.

Delicate constitutions, indeed. No wonder widows get plump. They are no longer being "protected" from good things.

The second reason why she had not purloined an orange was because she didn't want to give Nightsmith another thing to tut about.

So she merely sat where she was and let the gentle warmth of the charcoal stoves placed throughout the hothouse lull her into relaxation. And thought, rather cynically, *There are people who will be crowded together, shivering, in a single bed once autumn arrives, and worse come winter, but Mr. Nightsmith, the most eligible bachelor in Axminster, will have his ripe oranges!*

The sound of Nightsmith clearing his throat at close hand woke her unpleasantly out of her reverie. She opened her eyes.

"In light of your undoubted expertise in Earth magic, and the great good you have done for this county, I have come to a decision," he said, stiffly.

Oh lud, now what? she thought with irritation. *Crown me Queen of the Ball? Give me a spaniel puppy? Gift us with two of his precious riding horses before Alderscroft can? Give me an orange?*

"I have a list," he continued.

Of course he has a list.

"We are both Masters," he continued. "You are reasonably intelligent. Your education is superior for a female. Your conversation is not vapid or flirtatious."

Her mouth nearly gaped open at his audacity; she found her stomach tightening, and her ears reddening. Surely he was not—was this his idea of a—

"I can put up with that appalling accent; it is no worse than that of the people of Plymouth. Under the instruction of my mother, you will come to understand appropriate behavior in this country, such as not taking encores when you perform in public. The country hereabouts will require both of us as winter deepens, and I would rather you were not an inconvenient distance away. So." He straightened his cuffs and cravat. "We might as well be wedded as soon as possible, before real hardships descend."

He did it. He really did it.

Anger rose from her stomach and suffused her entire being. If she had been a Valkyrie, he would have been dead. If she had had a knife in her hands, he would have been missing his scalp. She was so furious that she was torn between laughing and crying. She settled for laughing.

He stared at her as if he suspected she had gone mad.

She, herself, was not entirely certain that she hadn't.

"I don't see—" he began, obviously irritated.

"Of *course* you *don't see,* Mr. Nightsmith," she drawled, tuning her speech to the sort of thing one would hear out in a South Carolina cotton field. "Of *course* you *don't see.* You will never *see* anything that does not pertain to *your* ideas and *your* comfort, and that's the God-blessed truth! Why, look at that little speech of yours. Not one word about what *I* might want, but every single word from you was '*me, me, me.*' *You* can 'put up' with my accent. *You* want me to 'behave by your standards' in public. *You* want *me to work for you. You* want me more *convenient* to you. How . . . *big* of you."

He straightened, shocked to be spoken to like that.

"It just so happens that *I* have a list too," she continued, not quite snarling. "And it just happens that you do not have the fundamental qualities that I consider indispensable in a husband. You do not respect me. You expect me to be subservient. You consider me inferior to you in every way except my mastery of magic. But most of all—*you are not kind.*"

She had, all unconsciously, gotten to her feet, and with every accusation, she poked him in the cravat with her index finger. Except for the last, when it was, *"you"* (poke) *"are"* (poke) *"not"* (poke), *"kind"* (with such a hard poke that he actually fell back a pace).

Now she crossed her arms over her chest. "I will work with you, *Mister* Nightsmith, but I would not marry you if my father stood behind me with a cutlass, trying to force me! Not that he would, after that little speech. He'd probably take his musket and run you out of the state and onto a boat and get one of our Air Masters to blow you back to England!"

And while he stood there in shock, she gathered up her cloak and reticule and marched out of the greenhouse, uncertain of her direction, and not really caring what it was, as long as it was away from him.

16

AMELIA was stopped by a hedge.

It seemed to be part of what was undoubtedly a very lovely garden at the back of the house. Well, more than a lovely garden. It was a breathtaking garden.

If you like your gardens all tidy and manicured, without a soul or a sign of anything that is not utterly under control.

It would not be sunset until well after the dancing started, so she had quite the view of it, and not all the neatly laid-out beds, the graveled paths, the ornamental ponds, and the manicured shrubbery in the world could convince her that it was superior to Mrs. Brightman's ordered chaos.

But she stared at it with such anger that it was a wonder that parts of it did not spontaneously combust.

"That was quite a speech," said Captain Roughtower from behind her.

She whirled, both hands clenched into fists, quite prepared to box his ears. "Did that odious prig bring you with him to reinforce his courage?" she rasped, ears burning with mingled anger and embarrassment. "Or were you skulking around the orangery for some other purpose?"

He held up both white-gloved hands in a gesture of surrender. "Neither! I swear it!" he proclaimed. "Believe me, or do not, but I was looking for a lemon!"

That was so absurd that it *had* to be true. "A lemon! Pray, tell, for what reason?"

"To suck?" he said, weakly. "Too many sweets laid on inside. I was hungry, but I need something to take the sweetness out. 'Tis like to give an old soldier unused to such luxury dyspepsia."

"You have never suffered from dyspepsia a day in your life," she replied acidly. "And you are not an old soldier."

"There you are wrong on both counts. But don't fly at me! I was not mocking you! I found your behavior altogether admirable, and it's a set-down that Phillip has long needed." He lowered his hands at last. "He is quite too used to being the most important person in the room, and you are very right, no one could ever accuse him of being *kind*."

Her hands relaxed, and her face and ears cooled. She tossed her cloak over her shoulders, now very glad that she had instinctively brought it with her, since she certainly did not want to go back into that hothouse again, and the air was very cool. "Thank you," she said dryly.

"Oh, do not mistake me," Roughtower said. "I am not an angel myself. I literally cannot *afford* to be kind. If I am kind to my men, they will slack off and do as little as possible. If I am kind to the sort of servants I can afford, they will rob me of what little I have. If I am kind to strangers, given the company I keep outside of mages, I am likely to be robbed or otherwise taken advantage of. I am so out of the habit of being kind that it takes a tremendous effort of will and thought to do so. And in my turn, if I am done a kindness, or even given an opening, I will take every possible advantage of it." He shrugged. "I know the sort of man I am, and I acknowledge that fact, which is more than can be said for Phillip."

"So what possible advantage do you propose to get from me?" she asked, just as frank as he was. "I have already fortified and warmed your land. And I sent you seeds and instructions on how to plant them once the land was prepared for them. What else could you want from me?"

He laughed. "More than you know. I can take you home now, if you would rather not stay after so insulting the host. My estate is on the way back, and if you can run your eye over the house and tell me what your dwarves and gnomes and kobolds could realistically do with it, and what I would realistically have to exchange with them for that work, I would appreciate it. Perhaps even open a line of communication with some representatives?"

"Can you see them?" she asked frankly.

"If I put my mind to it. It's a strain, and I need to use actual magic, but I can see them if I know they are there." He didn't look at her with a pleading look; in fact, his expression was unreadable, but it seemed like an honest offer of an exchange.

She raised her hand to rub her temple and realized she had taken her gloves off to work and not put them back on. She looked in her reticule. Not there. Nor was there anything she could write with, or on. "Oh, lud. I'll never find Serena, wherever that guide has taken her, and anyway I do *not* want to set foot in that house again for at least a month, if then—"

"Do not concern yourself. If this is a bargain that you are happy with, then come with me to the stable. You'll be safe enough. Phillip will never think to look for you there, and while the groom is putting my horse to my gig, I can run in and leave a note with Lady Nightsmith for her. Phillip has no quarrel with Serena, and won't play the churl in front of his mother. He'll see her home in a coach, same as she arrived, if she wants to leave early and follow after us. And if she doesn't, there are plenty there who will see she has a fine evening and she can return home when she expected to. But it is, of course, up to you what course of action you wish to take." And instead of assuming he had a superior notion to anything she could think of, he stayed, and waited, to see if his plan had her approval.

"Then I will agree to the bargain," she said. And laughed, sardonically. "If only I had waited to quarrel with him until after I ate! I am starving."

"Of course you are! I felt your Working all the time you were doing it! How far did you extend your influence? Past my estate?" He paused, and his eyebrow raised. "Past Axminster?" Both eyebrows came up. "To the edge of the *county*?"

She nodded.

"Good lud, woman! No wonder you are starving! I shall be like a naughty child and steal from the kitchen for you before I return. Come along; from back here the stables are easy to reach." He did not presume to reach for her hand, but she gave it to him anyway. He tucked it into the crook of his arm, and they walked swiftly down paths he seemed very familiar with until they reached the stables, out of sight from the drive, behind the house.

Once there, he put his fingers to his mouth and gave a rude whistle, which made all the horses' heads pop up, and summoned a stableboy like a jinni from a bottle. "Adam! Just who I want. This lady is feeling ill and I pledged to see her home. Put Pepper to my gig and bring it around while I run and tell her cousin."

He ran off before the boy could say anything. The boy sighed dramatically—probably well aware that he could expect no largesse from Harold Roughtower. Fortunately, Amelia was always in the habit of keeping a little ready money with her at all times. She gestured to the lad and wordlessly pressed a tuppence into his hand. Since he had been expecting nothing, that put wings to his heels, and by the time Roughtower returned, carrying with him a little crude, rush basket of the sort one gave to children for a picnic, an aged dapple-gray gelding had been hitched to a gig that had clearly seen better days and had been repaired without any regard for how it looked afterward.

The captain handed her up onto the seat, the springs creaking alarmingly, handed her the reins and the basket to hold, then climbed up into the driver's position and took the reins from her. He slapped them vigorously on the poor beast's back; the gelding gave a visible sigh and shambled off.

"See if there's enough in there to keep body and soul together until you get home," he urged. "I need every bit of my attention to keep this fierce stallion from bolting with both of us."

She laughed, as she was supposed to, but it cooled her temper somewhat. Enough to consider what it was going to look like if she was up in a gig at this time of the evening, alone with a man, without a groom in attendance.

She decided that she did not care. *So what if it spoils my marriage prospects in Axminster? It won't spoil my marriage prospects among the mages.* After that demonstration of her channeling and nurturing powers, which every mage in the entire county of Devon was surely aware of now, there was very little that would stand in the way of a male mage offering for her.

Then again, this was the country. Women probably drove out with men who were not relatives and not grooms all the time. When there was work to be done on a farm, it tended to get done by who was fittest for the job without worrying much about appearances.

So as the old beast made the best he could of the mile-long driveway, she removed the butcher's paper tucked in over the top of what was in the basket. There was a stoneware bottle, firmly corked, a pear, a hard-boiled egg, and something that looked like a small pie, except that it was a crescent.

"The little thing that was raiding the provisions for me apologized that 'It ain't a lady's nuncheon' and she'd purloined from the coachmen and grooms' meals because the cook was guarding the superior provisions like a hawk." He glanced over at her. "Since you are a fierce Amazon of America, I assumed you'd eat anything that wasn't raw."

"And some things that are," she admitted. "And I don't mean vegetables and fruit. What is this?" She held up the crescent of crust.

"Pasty. Typical working-man's dinner in the fields or the mines here and in Cornwall. Quite tasty, and the one thing my cook *can* make reliably, besides bread and sausages." He glanced down at the basket, then back to the horse, because the old nag seemed to have the distressing habit of wandering over to the side of the road. "You won't need an explanation for the pear, nor the egg. The bottle is either beer or scrumpy. Be careful with the scrumpy. One bottle and—"

"—you start to glow, two and you start to *go*. I'm aware, though I have not tasted it myself. My cook won't let me." She uncorked the bottle and took a cautious whiff. It smelled like hard cider from home, with an unfamiliar sweet, woody, earthy aroma mixed in with the usual apple and apple-alcohol. She tasted it. Same flavor as hard cider, with the same taste as the extra scent. It wasn't bad, just different. "Seems fine, but I will be careful."

She wrapped the crescent in the butcher paper to save her fingers, still lamenting the loss of her gloves, and cautiously took a bite as he turned the horse onto the road. Now the beast seemed to understand he was going back to his own stable; he resisted a moment—obviously because the provender was much better at Nightsmith's establishment—then sighed again, and trudged onward.

The pastry was good, basic pie pastry. Inside was a mix of chopped beef, potatoes, turnips, and onions, with what tasted like a mix of the same herbs she would use in a stew. Delicious! Before she knew it, she had eaten the whole thing, and wished she dared lick the crumbs off the paper.

The egg went the way of the pasty. She took a sip of the scrumpy, decided that she liked it very much, and took a series of mouthfuls as large as the jouncing of the gig would allow.

"Likkun, dooee?" he said. She shook her head, wondering if she had imbibed a little too much—then she realized he was speaking in broad Devonian, and she had not been expecting that.

"It is very good," she replied honestly. "Better than a lot of our hard cider."

"The Devonian that cannot brew a decent lot of scrumpy is a poor thing, and much pitied," he replied. "If you are not having that pear, I will."

She handed it to him. He stripped off one glove with his teeth, the other not leaving the reins, and ate it that way, wolfing it down too fast for the juice to run down onto his fingers. "My thanks. That will hold my body and soul together until we reach my estate, where there should be some bread and bacon about, at least."

"Is it far?" she asked, eyeing the sun. *It must be past eight. The sun goes down at half past nine. It will be at least eleven before I am home safe.*

"Not much farther, or this old screw would never get me there and back before tomorrow." He slapped the horse's back with his reins, and the old nag shuffled a little faster. The well-tended wall finally gave way to the kind of dry-laid stone wall that was very common around this country. The scrumpy was giving her a very warm feeling, but she was used to holding her alcohol, so she was not at all concerned. She knew very well the dangers of hard cider, but her father's apple brandy was even more perilous. Some people had accused it of sneaking up behind them and hitting them on the head.

She tucked the empty basket under the seat for safe-keeping and held the bottle carefully to avoid spilling anything on her gown and cloak. Whatever that "different" taste was, it still remained odd, but not unpleasant. Certainly not mold!

"Did you fight in America?" she asked, idly. "Or on the Continent?" She wasn't sure if she expected an affirmative, but she simply wanted to make certain he had not trampled her country in the 1812 war. She rather thought he was too young to have fought in the Revolutionary War.

He laughed. "Not I. My father took pride in being able to purchase a commission for me with the Guards, but *certain parties* keep all mages in the military at home, lest such a valuable resource fall into enemy hands. So I have never actually *fought* anywhere, and the only shooting I have done is pheasants, partridge, ducks, and geese. My fellows have been known to chide me or curse my good or bad luck that sees me unaccountably transferred time and time again, and put in charge of a lot of green 'uns instead of properly going off to war."

Well, good. She wouldn't have dueling emotions over bargaining with him. "Did you ever—" How to put delicately the question if he regretted never having been on a battlefield?

"Never," he said decisively. "I took that commission knowing very well I would never see a shot fired in anger." He glanced at her again. "I should think a Quaker would sympathize."

"Well," she temporized. "At least you are not someone I can directly hate for trampling all over my nation as if you owned it. And yes, Quakers are pacifists. So I suppose I do sympathize."

He nodded. "I will accept that. I am quite used to settling for whatever crumbs I can get. At least they are crumbs of accord instead of apples of discord."

"Does Phillip hold that against you?" she asked, curious.

He laughed. "Phillip knows what happens to mages in the military quite well. Every mage in England knows, although I've heard rumors of a couple of mages in the Scots Guards who are allegedly with Wellington." He shrugged. "If such a thing is true, it was arranged by Alderscroft, and they are his men, and probably safe, attached to Wellington's personal guards."

"It would be prudent," she suggested, and took another sip.

He changed the subject, and began asking her about her home, her parents, her siblings and "cousins." She carefully steered clear of giving him exact information, but recounted anecdotes instead, funny ones about the plantation, and darker ones about the Hunts. She carefully did not say that she had participated in the Hunts herself, although she also did not say that she had *not*. She was certain she could hold her own against such a non-warrior, given how unequal their powers were, especially if she could call forth her Elemental allies, but she did not entirely trust him, still.

We're using each other. I know it, and he knows it, and we both know the other knows.

Long before she began to worry about the time, the stone wall gave way to unkempt hedges that reached well above their heads, and she spotted a break in the hedges ahead, and a pair of decrepit iron gates, rusted open, half buried in the green branches.

"And so you behold the glory that is Heathcombe," he said sardonically, as the horse picked up its pace and rattled them through the gap.

There was a long, overgrown drive with a large house at the end, probably about half the size of Averly Hall and built of the same stone as much of Axminster. From here, the gaps in the slate roof of the west wing were obvious; some feeble effort had been made to patch them with boards and such, but it was obvious even to her that such efforts were fruitless. She suspected that if the house had been of wood, it would be sagging in places, and if of beam and wattle-and-daub, it would have been disintegrating. But from where she was, there was no telling how bad it was inside.

He pulled up in front of the house, in an area as overgrown as the drive. Half a dozen large and rough-looking men came out to see who had arrived. That was when alarms rang through her.

"I thought you said you only had two servants," she said thickly. *What is wrong with—*

She felt a sudden dizziness, and knew immediately what was wrong with her.

"You—drugged me!" she slurred. "The scrumpy?"

"Clever girl. Of course I did. I thought you might not recognize the taste of hashish, and I was right." His expression was unreadable as she felt the drug take over her senses, and reeled, and fell from her seat.

The last thing she remembered with horror was that he caught her as she fell.

She woke to candlelight, and the smell of hot tallow. Cheap rush-lights had been stuck on every available surface within a sort of room that had the scent of "underground," but was too regular to be a cave. She was lying, bound, on her side, skirts tucked decently around her ankles, across the broad base of a statue, a slab almost like a table—or an altar. Her head swam, but that did not prevent her feeling both rage and horror. She turned her head to look up at the statue.

It was a white marble statue of an enormous snake, easily twice the height of a man, its head and part of its body raised high above its own coils.

At least—she *thought* it was a statue. Until it moved its head, and looked down at her out of milky, blind eyes.

She couldn't help it. She screamed hysterically.

The snake paid her very little heed. Instead, it flickered its tongue and began to move toward her. She thrashed, trying desperately to roll off the base, but she could not get purchase on the marble before it had cast one of its coils over her, holding her in place. Then it stopped moving again, as if the effort had fatigued it.

She screamed herself hoarse, called for help, wept—all the while her mind a blank. What was this thing? Where had Roughtower found it? What did he want with it? What did he want with *her*?

Finally she ran out of energy, voice, and every emotion but fear. And that was when Roughtower stepped out of the shadows at the end of the room.

"I see Glykon accepts you," he said, in tones of dry amusement, as he paused before the altar (was it really an altar?) with his hands behind his back.

"Are you going to sacrifice me to it?" she rasped, trying to sound defiant, although to her own ears the words just sounded pathetic.

He chuckled. "And waste such a valuable resource as an Earth Master and a Channel? Goodness, no! Look how far your power has already awakened him! Glykon is a Roman god of the earth; I found him down here when I stumbled on the entrance to his old temple as a boy. I found the spell to awaken him in old scrolls stored carefully away in tarred chests down here. I broke into the chests expecting treasure, and found it, but not what I was anticipating! I was very good at Latin and had no trouble reading the scrolls, but I was too weak to awaken him myself. I bided my time, knowing sooner or later I would find an Earth Master I could use or trick into doing it.

Then along came *you*, everything I needed! So I managed things so that half of the power you sent this way would go straight into rousing him partway from his long sleep, and the rest into spells that keep him barely half awake, and cooperative. It was my great good luck that these spells were made for Roman priests to use, not mages. Even someone with no inherent magic in themselves can use them, so long as a true mage gives the spells power."

Her mind buzzed with thoughts going in many directions. If he wasn't going to kill her, what *did* he want? How did he expect to get away with this when Serena would almost certainly raise the alarm when she did not come home? Why would Roman priests want their god to be under their control?

The answer to that last dawned on her as she struggled with a drug-hazed mind and the heavy coils of the snake thrown over her.

What good is a god to his priests if the god can't be controlled to do what the priests want?

Glykon wasn't a *god*, of course; he was some sort of extremely powerful Earth Elemental, like the Horned Hunter or the Spirit Bear. A god obviously could not be controlled by a mere human, still less by a human with no power, or as little power as the captain had.

Or me, really, compared with a god.

The captain sat idly on the corner of the altar. "I am not going to kill you, and I am not going to allow Glykon to kill you. You are a great source of power; why would I do something that witless? No, my dear Miss Amelia. I am going to turn you. I am going to use a combination of drugs and love spells on you until your world centers on me and my desires. Then I will wed you—I already have the special license—and anyone who wants your magic to ensure that they don't starve this winter will have to come to me, and pay dearly for the privilege."

She laughed at that, although the laugh was mostly hysteria. "Love spells don't work."

"On the contrary, the ones I am going to use certainly do. I have tried them extensively, and I had planned to use them on some heiress—until you came along." He smiled at her. "Not everything in the grand duke's library is benign, my dear, and he lacks anything on that library that might be thought of as 'security.' I have spent many nights copying specific spells meant for the ungifted into my research, being careful to avoid those that required blood sacrifice. *Nothing* gets the attention of the Masters of the White Lodges like blood sacrifice. I fancy I have evaded their attention altogether, operating right under Alderscroft's nose."

The drug haze cleared slowly—too slowly—from her mind. "This will get his attention," she warned.

"I think not. Access to you will only come through me, and I will make certain of that." He rocked back on his heels a little. "You will *refuse* to do anything I don't want you to, you'll weep and fall into hysterics if I am parted from you. Alderscroft will grit his teeth and comply, and by the time the weather turns again, you and I and all that lovely money I will have collected will be happily living together. You're not unattractive, you will be eager to be pleased, and I will do as *I* please."

She shuddered. There had been stories among the slaves about magicians who could render someone into a pliant submissive condition, willing to do anything, including kill themselves, to please their master. She'd thought them nonsense, but what if they weren't?

"Furthermore, thanks to you, I will be able to send Glykon to crush Phillip, and I will inherit his property. No one will connect me with his death. No one is going to rescue you, because that note I left for your cousin says that you and I are eloping to Gretna Green. If anything, "rescuers" will spread themselves up and down the North Road to Scotland and won't be looking for you here at all." He chuckled softly. "Needless to say, I won't be home if they come here. By the time they realize their mistake, you will be firmly in my power and Phillip will be dead. Then I will be free to wield either death in the form of Glykon or life in the form of your magic to get everything I want. And even if I am wrong about the Huntmaster, and he *does* defy me and attempt to take you, Alderscroft can call all the Hunts on me that he cares to; they won't be able to stand against a god. Now do you understand?"

He reached out and patted her hair like a child. She snaked her head around and sank her teeth into it. He howled in pain and slapped her face so hard it nearly dislocated her neck, forcing her to open her mouth and let go. "Bitch," he snarled, nursing his wounded hand.

"How do you plan on explaining a human bite mark through your hand?" she taunted him. She was hoping he would slap her again; marks on her would show anyone that saw her that no matter how she was acting, she was *not* going along with this willingly.

And also . . . the pain of the slap was doing a lot to clear off the fog of the drug he had given her.

"I'd say you're going to regret this," he told her sullenly, as Glykon swayed above her, "but you're not going to have enough mind left that isn't mine to regret anything once my potions finish brewing and I cast my spells."

He made a sudden gesture, and her words died on her tongue. That was when a chill enveloped her. Until that moment she had not believed he could do what he had boasted he would.

He grinned at her stunned expression. "I was very disappointed to discover no gold or silver in this temple, but the treasure here was much more valuable. The priests here had no magic of their own, but they had an entire library of spells to use by taking someone else's. Having some minor power of my own, I am already far outpacing what they could do. I have everything I need to make you into my obedient slave. But ideally, by this time tomorrow, you'll be begging me to allow you to serve me, and this will leave your friends and family convinced that this marriage is all your idea."

"Serena is not that stupid," she replied, trying desperately to think of something she could do. "She will never believe I have been concealing affection for you all this time."

"Serena will be dismissed because she is a mere female, and as such is a poor judge of other people's minds," he said with a laugh.

"Oh, my dear, never underestimate the capacity of a male to believe the stupidity of females. Yes, even the precious Elemental Masters, *who won't even allow women into their London club.*"

With a sinking feeling, she knew he was right. Not Alderscroft— but if the captain was right, that wouldn't matter. Alderscroft could not call a Hunt against a fellow of the White Lodge unless it could be proved he was using forbidden magic, and the Huntmaster could get the majority of his Lodge to vote for the Hunt. Roughtower had been exquisitely careful—like her, no one believed love spells worked— and he hadn't killed or even harmed someone yet.

"You'll be happy, Amelia. You will sincerely believe that I suit every particular of your little list. And to be sure, I will pay you enough attention that you will be satisfied and never doubt me." He laughed again. "Why, I shall even find your brother James that property he wants, and trust me, he will be so grateful to me that your sudden infatuation will seem perfectly natural in his mind. In fact, while I cannot *sell* him Heathcombe, I could certainly lease it to him at very agreeable rates, and it might just suit his needs. Then he will be doubly grateful to me. Now, you will have to excuse me. I have preparations to make and—"

The muffled, but unmistakable sounds of combat interrupted him, and he frowned. "Don't go away, my dear. It seems someone has got the attention of my lads. I'll have to go see to it."

Despite his languid tone, the way he sprinted out of the (underground?) room made her think he was more concerned than he pretended to be.

A warm spot between her breasts reminded her suddenly of the grand duke's gift, which she had not taken off since he gave it to her—what had he said?

Something about reminding spirits and the like of their fundamental nature. Roman spirits!

If only she could get *at* the thing and somehow make physical contact with Glykon! But the creature's coils lay over her from just below her breast to her knees, trapping her hands behind her back.

She writhed—or tried to—and kicked, and twisted, but she wasn't able to move even the smallest amount—

"Hssst!" said a tiny voice in her ear.

She turned her head. It was a brownie. In fact, it was the brownie from Honeyrose Cottage, Sarah Small!

"Master! I ken somethin' wrong in thy magic, and came t'help." She gazed up in terror, but with resolution, at the snake looming over them both. *"I be but small, but what can I do?"*

"There's a silver coin on a necklace around my neck," she whispered back. "Can you get it out?"

The brownie reached cautiously across her chest and tugged at the heavy chain. Slowly, she felt the coin inching its way up, until it popped into sight on her skin.

"Now pick it up if you can," Amelia continued, hoping that there was nothing about the coin that would harm or frighten the brownie.

But Sarah reached for it and picked it up without hurt. *"Now?"* she whispered.

"Get it off and touch the snake with it," she said, as the noise from outside grew louder—and *definitely* included the canvas-tearing sounds of Serena's battle snarls! *Please, dear God, do not let her have come alone!*

But try as little Sarah might, she could not get the clasp to undo. It was as if the clasp had fused the moment Amelia put on the necklace. *"I be tryin', Master!"* the little brownie wept. *"I be tryin', but I canna!"*

Amelia gulped . . . because if this didn't work, she was putting the brownie right in harm's way, and *she* would be unable to help Serena.

"Sarah, if you don't want to do this, you don't have to," she said, unable to stop shaking in fear. "But we need to get the snake to touch the coin. If we can't bring the coin to the snake, we have to bring the snake to the coin—"

But Sarah stood up straight, and tugged on her bodice. *"Say no more, Master,"* she said, though her voice shook. *"Sarah Small will do get yon task a-done."*

And to Amelia's horror, the brownie climbed up on her chest, picked up the coin in one tiny hand, and frantically waved the other. *"Hark ye! Ye gurt feckless barstard! Come ye a-down here!"*

The snake stirred. It had been looking toward the entrance to the room, but now it bent its head and gazed down at them. *Oh dear God, protect and preserve Sarah!* she prayed. The thing's head was more than large enough to swallow both of them. Sarah would go down its gullet like a currant down a goose's throat.

The tongue flickered out, and it bent its head down further, inch by inch. Flicker. A little further. Flicker. A little further. The mouth started to gape, but Sarah held fast, keeping the coin over her head between herself and the snake. Flicker. The mouth closed. Flicker. The head descended.

Flicker.

The tongue touched the coin.

The snake froze; it could have been the stone that Amelia had taken it for. And for a minute, there was no movement, no sound in the room, and she and Sarah held their breaths.

The snake's eyes blazed like a pair of clear emeralds with lightning behind them.

The snake heaved itself bolt upright; in a ripple, emerald green and topaz and pure gold raced across its scales, driving the pallid, frosty white before it. The entire beast shuddered—which was not at *all* comfortable, since Amelia was underneath part of it! A scent of new-mown hay, fresh earth under the rain, and roses and honey filled the air of the chamber, and there was a cracking sound as the altar underneath her split in half.

She screamed as she and Sarah started to fall—

But they were caught and cradled in the coils of the now fully awakened god, Glykon.

Glykon carefully arranged himself so that none of his length weighted her down and lowered his head toward hers.

But he spoke first to Sarah. *"Little Earth-child, there is a knife in the belongings of the traitor. Please bring it here and cut the Master loose. There is little time."*

He hadn't gotten any further than "knife" when Sarah had shot across the room and came back, pulling a hunting knife in its sheath by the handle. In no time, Amelia sat up, pulling her arms back around to her front and taking the knife from Sarah to free her own ankles.

She didn't need any directions from Glykon—she dashed for the dim rectangle of the door and up a set of carved stone stairs, knife still in her hand, into a scene of pure chaos.

A brazier of coals beside the hole that led down into the former temple had been overset, and fire blazed in the weeds and dried brush the captain must have used to conceal it. She could barely make out the figure of a man wrestling with another man; the light from the fire flared up and revealed a flash of scarlet coat.

Roughtower!

Neither of them appeared to be armed, but there could have been weapons on the ground. Beside him, Serena in leopard form snarled and held off four of the enormous thugs that had appeared when Amelia and the captain had first driven up to the house. There were two more on the ground, and they were not moving.

She hesitated a moment, but only to gather power. With a curse that had nothing to do with her magic, she turned the earth beneath the four thugs into a soupy quagmire. Shouting curses, they sank up to their knees, and instantly she hardened the earth again.

This was soft loam, natively, and wouldn't hold them for long— but it would long enough. As Serena leapt for the one nearest her, Amelia threw the knife, and it landed with a satisfying *thud* in a second one's back.

Serena tore the throat out of hers; Amelia's screamed— Roughtower let go of his assailant, and whirled—

And Amelia was knocked off her feet by Glykon as the great serpent shot out of the opening in the ground and slithered impossibly fast for Roughtower, knocking his assailant to one side.

The third and fourth thug decided they'd had enough; they somehow dragged themselves out of the earth, and took to their heels. Before Roughtower could react, Glykon had flung three coils around him, imprisoning him.

Then the snake's muscles rippled in the firelight as he squeezed. And squeezed.

Serena, naked as Aphrodite, came running at Amelia and flung her arms around her. "Are you all right? I *knew* that note was all gammon! Are you all right? What is that? It feels like a god!"

"It is a god," Amelia managed, as Glykon stopped squeezing for the moment. Roughtower could not do more than gasp, tiny, tiny sips of air. He could not speak, much less utter a spell, but Glykon hadn't killed him.

Yet. The Greek and Roman gods were not much known for mercy. And granted, Glykon *was* a deity of Earth and Nature . . . but Nature was not particularly kind, either.

The final, mystery man pulled himself up off the ground with a groan, and limped to join them.

It was Phillip Nightsmith.

There was a gash on his head, bleeding freely, one of his eyes had been blackened, and he was favoring his left leg, but he didn't seem to have any fatal wounds. "Amelia," he rasped. "Are you all right? Serena didn't believe your note, and neither did I—" he coughed a harsh laugh "—particularly not after that set-down you gave me in the orangery. What in God's name—"

Emerald light flared about them, so that they could see. Three bodies, definitely dead, lay on the ground; the fourth sagged lifelessly, held up only by the earth around his legs. Glykon reared above his prey, glowing emerald eyes fixed on them.

"*I am Glykon, Lord of the Earth. This is my imprisoner and torturer—and now, my lawful prey. This woman and the Earthchild freed me.*"

Nightsmith bowed, as low as he could with a damaged leg. "Hail Glykon, Lord of the Earth. I am Phillip, Master of Earth magic, and your servant. How may we serve you?"

"*It is I who shall serve this woman to repay my debt.*" Glykon turned his eyes on Amelia. "*What is your wish, Master of Earth magic and channel for the Earth?*"

She thought of many things she could say, and settled on one. "Justice," she said. "Your prey intended to murder this Master and make me his love-slave. Weigh him against that and his sins against you, and deliver justice."

The snake shook with what sounded like chuckles. *"Never has Justice tasted so sweet,"* Glykon said, and gave one last squeeze.

Then he reared up again, releasing the body, and slithered his way back into his temple.

Epilogue

"WELL, *now* what do we do?" Amelia asked.

They had left the bodies where they lay—Phillip intended to send a note to the Axminster chief magistrate in the morning, saying something about how Roughtower had left the ball in great agitation and a great hurry and had not been heard from since. Let the Magistrate make what he could of the two dead men with their throats torn out, the one with Roughtower's regimental knife in his back, buried up to his knees in dirt, and Roughtower himself crushed to death. There was, of course, no sign that any of them had ever been there, and Serena had destroyed Roughtower's note after she showed it to Phillip.

They had only brought two horses, so Serena had stayed in leopard form all the way back to Averly Hall, where she retrieved her gown from the stables where she had left it. Amelia had pulled her own gown up to her waist and ridden astride, and Nightsmith had not said a single word.

They had debated telling the others all the way back to Averly Hall. Finally Amelia had said something that Phillip nodded over just as they trotted into the driveway.

"It's midnight," she pointed out. "Or nearly. You and we have been absent from the ball that was meant to welcome us for the entire night, or nearly. Do you want them to make something up, or do you prefer to tell the truth? They are all Elemental mages; they are used to keeping secrets. And I don't think any one of them is going to mourn Harold Roughtower."

So in the end, they gathered everyone into the cream-and-gold ballroom before they could leave, sent the musicians home, and did just that: told the truth, and what Phillip intended to do about Roughtower in the morning.

Mr. Brisley was the first to speak up, stroking his chin gravely. "He got his comeuppance. I don't doubt he's been wicked amongst the bits of muslin, and broke hearts, a-practicin' of his love spells. So say we all, I think."

He looked about, and there were no dissenters.

"Anyroad, punishment weren't by *your* hand. Miss Amelia asked for justice, an' justice was served, jest like a Hunt. *My* question be, what does we do about a bloody great snake under his ground?"

A chorus of murmured "ayes" met that. It seemed that Roughtower had been dismissed out of hand, and any real anxiety was about Glykon.

"He's a Greater Elemental," Amelia pointed out, only now feeling very shaken and a bit weak inside, and sipping on a restorative sherry. "He's no different than any other Greater Elemental, he's just in snake form. He isn't going to be eating your flocks or herds; if he was going to do that, he'd have eaten Roughtower. Live and let live, I say."

"I'll answer for his behavior. He's on my land—or at least, land that will be mine once the magistrate sorts everything out." Phillip smiled thinly. "In fact, I fancy I like the idea of having a justice-minded Greater Elemental where I know where to find him."

"Better you nor me, Master Nightsmith," said Mr. Brisley, but he appeared satisfied.

There was a great deal more chit-chat, but the main topic seemed to have been disposed of fairly easily so far as the mages of Devon were concerned. They all headed homeward only a little later than their original intentions, leaving Amelia, who was now feeling entirely exhausted and ravenous, Serena, who was still so excited her hair practically stood on end, Phillip, whose wounds were being tended by Dr. Partridge, and Lady Nightsmith, all bestowed bonelessly in upholstered Chesterfield chairs and padded sofas in the exceedingly comfortable red-and-leather library. Lady Nightsmith insisted that she and Serena (and the doctor) spend the night, and would not take any answer other than "yes."

Now I am regretting I didn't accept his proposal. Well, not really . . . but she coveted this library.

Those handful who were staying overnight had taken to their rooms, probably to stay up and gossip about the most exciting thing to happen in Axminster since King James's witch hunts.

"Anyone hungry?" Lady Nightsmith said, calmly. "Oh, and Phillip, I am well aware that Miss Amelia was severely understating the case when she merely said you two had quarreled. I know the cause, and I suggest that you apologize immediately."

"But how—" Phillip gaped.

"Salamanders in the charcoal stoves, you goose. Apologize, if you please." One toe tapped impatiently on the fine rug. "And say nothing of this, doctor."

Phillip's head would have drooped, if the doctor hadn't been bandaging it. He sighed—but it was with the resignation of someone who understood that he really had deserved everything Amelia had said to him. "Miss Amelia, I was absolutely wrong about you, I was absolutely wrong to say the things I did, and I absolutely apologize from the bottom of my heart."

Serena looked from one to the other of them and back again. "What *did* you say?" she demanded.

"An ill-conceived proposal of marriage, and that is enough on the matter," Amelia said firmly. "I accept your apology, I am very, *very* grateful that you believed Serena, and I offer my humble thanks for riding to my rescue." Then she turned to Lady Nightsmith. "I am *starving*, thank you, Lady Nightsmith."

"Jane, please, dear," the lady said calmly. She rang for a servant, and issued some orders Amelia could not hear. "We need not be so formal among ourselves."

"Thank you. I think between you and the brownie, you'd have rescued yourself," said Phillip ruefully. "I was redundant."

"If you had not turned up, Sarah and I would have had no opportunity to release Glykon from his spells," she pointed out charitably, and looked down at Sarah, who had appeared at her side as soon as they crossed the threshold of the manor. "Sarah would probably have become a snack for Glykon if she was discovered, and my coin from the grand duke would have been taken."

Servants appeared just then with what looked like remains of the supper she had missed: bread rolls, sliced ham, beef, mutton and chicken, chunks of cheese, and pastries. Without waiting to hear what anyone wanted, they simply piled plates high and brought them around, including a plate of bread, pastries, and cheese for Sarah Small, and poured out champagne for everyone.

That kept them all silent while Lady Nightsmith nibbled on fruit and champagne.

"Roughtower did have one, singular good idea," Phillip said at last, applying champagne (internally) to his wounds. "About Heathcombe. I *think* it would serve every purpose you have for your brother James's undertakings, Miss Amelia. There are several fast-flowing streams with good rock foundations for mills. You could clear-cut some of those acres of pollarded trees, use the wood to repair the manor, and plant white mulberries. And the rest is admirable pasturage."

Amelia and Serena sat straight up—because if anyone would know the suitability of the land for James's projects, it would be Nightsmith. "Really?" Serena squealed. "Do you *mean* it?"

Nightsmith nodded, and his mother smiled approvingly. "Of course I mean it. The entail *might* end with Harold, and I can sell it directly. If it does not, I can offer, say, a two-hundred-year lease." His smile turned sardonic. "I suspect that in the light of the fact that the magistrate will rule that Harold quarreled with his thugs and they murdered each other, the inquest and probate will be settled quickly."

It was Amelia's turn to sit up quickly. "Oh! And having Glykon on the property would be *just* the thing! James has treated with Greater Elementals before! He knows *just* what to say to them!"

"All the better," Phillip said. And visibly steeled himself. "And that just leaves me one more thing, which I wish to do before I lose my courage."

Amelia blanched. *Oh, no. Oh, lud, no. He is about to propose properly to me—*

But he stood and went to Serena. "Miss Serena, I have never seen a lady before with your courage, wit, good sense, will, and mental strength, all of which match your beauty. Would you permit me to begin courting you?" He held up a hand to forestall anything she might say. "I say 'begin.' This shall be private between us. If after a year, you find that you do not wish to continue the courtship, or that you cannot come to love me, we will part as friends and colleagues. But—" he licked his lips, and looked *very* anxious, in a way he had not with Amelia, "—I hope, I pray, that you will agree. I . . . I hold you in great esteem. I . . . would like to hold you in truth."

Serena turned pale, and looked as if she would like to cry. "Phillip—I am not Italian. Half of my family—"

"Are former slaves, of course. I guessed," he said, so gently it sounded like a caress. "Amelia's vehemence about slavery gave me my first clue."

Serena's answer was to squeal and throw herself into his surprised embrace. "Yes!" she said breathlessly. "Yes! Yes! Yes!"

"Good," Lady Nightsmith said serenely. "Now I have a chance of seeing grandchildren before I grow too old to spoil them."

Amelia decided that this was a perfectly satisfactory answer to two of her lists, the two most important ones. Phillip clearly accepted Serena as she was, and had learned his lesson about being high-handed and superior—at least with the two of them. And James would have his property and could send for his damned goats, and *she* would be near at hand to make sure none of them died or ailed.

"In that case," she said, noting with amusement that Phillip showed no signs of wanting Serena to resume being "ladylike," and Serena showed no signs of wanting to leave his arms, "if you are willing to play host to us for another day and night, I can scry to her parents and you can speak with them yourself tomorrow evening."

"I think that would be most satisfactory," said her ladyship. "I shall send Robert over on a horse in the morning to avoid alarming your servants when they hear the news about the captain. In the meantime, I believe we can all seek our well-earned slumber."

"*I be drinkin' to that!*" crowed Sarah Small, holding up her doll's-teacup of champagne.

"And so shall we all," said Amelia, with deep satisfaction. "And so shall we all."